A Heart's Return

— Casey McKenzie —

Cover Photo Credit: Amber Wimberley/Working W
Special thanks to Carl and Josie & Steve and Colleen

To M-
You help me discover
a better version of myself by loving me.

Chapter One

Mel Snow turned onto the gravel drive stopping short of the shadows that spread below the arching branches. She couldn't go further, not yet. The rusty mailbox hung crooked on the square post just off the pavement. An S inside the faded outline of a snowflake was scrawled on the side in white paint in her handwriting.

It had been a foggy Sunday morning riding the tractor down the drive with her dad and Jessica to put up the new mailbox he had won in the Lebanon Springs Pioneer Festival. Both girls sat on either fender of a faded red International tractor that had belonged to her grandfather. Dad whistled a tune she could still remember, driving slowly with one hand on top of the skinny, cracked steering wheel. His other hand rested on Jessica's knee.

She was the oldest child of Thomas and Miriam Snow. Mel wasn't short for anything. She was just Mel. Her dad had picked the name and wore her mother down in the end. He used to tell her the story with a boyish twinkle in his eye. Over time, she had learned to love the novelty of her name.

The shadows continued up the winding drive that followed the contour of the hills and crevices of the land then disappeared behind a scattered patch of elms and cedars. Her grandfather had planted the largest walnuts and oaks along the drive, and her dad had added sycamores and cedars among them years ago, some too close together. Dad loved the greenish-gray and brown flakes of the sycamore bark. Nature's camouflage, he called it.

Thomas Snow: Deceased.

It was mid-September, but no sign of autumn foliage. The muggy Kentucky summers were known to drag on. She rolled down her window sticking her arm out into the hot, thick air that soaked into her pores like honey.

The drive curved right and then left. The farmhouse built by her great-grandfather sat behind the last patch of trees. What had had its beginnings long before her grandfather's birth as a simple one-bedroom shack had transformed into a two-story farmhouse as the farm and family grew. White paint chips littered the grass along the foundation's edge. A rusty gutter hung away from the eaves like a broken arm. It was not grand by any standard, but it stood tall and proud having sheltered four generations of Snows within its walls.

The same International tractor, now a muted red, sat beside the barn with a round hay bale stabbed on a metal fork sticking out the back like a growth. Mel had learned to drive on that old thing before she could barely reach the pedals. Her first wreck had happened when she was eleven, backing it into the Methodist preacher's front fender. His visits had been frequent after her mom's death, taking it upon himself to bring salvation to the family.

The awkward Saturday afternoon visits were an attempt to get the girls to Sunday School, but everyone knew Thomas Snow was not a church-going man. That afternoon Mel backed the tractor around the corner of the house forgetting that the preacher was inside evangelizing her dad. At the eerie sound of crunching metal, her dad and the preacher sprung out the front door like the house was on fire. The preacher's face turned red like the tractor. He ran back and forth in front of the car flapping his arms like a banty rooster.

Her Dad had thrown his head back in wicked laughter after the preacher had gone down the drive with his dander up. Dad had paid for the repairs, and the preacher's visits had dropped off after that incident. Saturday afternoons returned to woodcutting to keep winter's cold at bay or horseback riding over the almost six hundred acres of Snow land. Nature had been her father's true religion.

Mel pulled her Fiat beside the house. From here, the gravel faded away and dirt paths that filled with ruts and puddles led off to the barn and house. Dad had refused to gravel this part railing against the cost of gravel as the government's aim to break the little man. In his mind, Wall Street was directly responsible for this cost, and he was determined to beat them at their own game. Of course, he cursed the loudest when the rains came, and they walked back and forth from house to barn knee-deep in mud for days.

Thomas Snow. Deceased.

The weathered barn seemed closer now than it had as a kid. When it had been her turn to switch off the lights at night, she would run as fast as her legs would carry her back to the house for fear of being eaten alive by a pack of coyotes, every step scanning the field with her flashlight. It had seemed like miles to her then.

The whole place had shrunk. Her first kiss had been under the eaves of the dilapidated saltbox shed behind the house at a fall party her parents had thrown. She would have been eight or maybe nine, and Tony Irby had bet her fifty cents she wouldn't kiss him. He was older by a year. Mel proved him wrong, kissing him square and hard on the lips and had threatened to blacken his eye after he tried to run off without paying.

Her mom had loved those fall parties. Miriam Snow died when Mel was ten giving birth to a little brother who died soon after. The parties ceased, and her dad's face had weathered overnight.

Mel opened the car door but hesitated to get out. She reached over and grabbed a ponytail holder out of the glove box. Running her hands through her dark brown hair, she tried to smooth out the frizzy nest that had always had a mind of its own. In a desperate attempt to contain it, she'd cut it short last summer, but it had only made matters worse. It was finally long enough to put in a ponytail again at least keeping it out of her face.

It was still early in the day, but beads of sweat appeared on her forehead. Her pink short-sleeve oxford clung to her back. Mel circled her lips with lip balm in the visor mirror and traced the small squiggly lines across her forehead that had appeared out of nowhere last winter. The creases had deepened these past three months since splitting up with Patricia. Pain had replaced the forced numbness of the last twelve years, and she hated Patricia for making her feel again.

Mel stood by her closed car door and shoved her hands in her pockets looking to the house, to the barn, and then back to the house. No one was in sight.

A manila envelope glared at her from the passenger's seat. Part of her wanted to sit right back down in her car and return to Boston, but to what? One lonely place was as good as another these days.

Mel pushed herself away from the car and walked toward the back porch. The door would be unlocked—this was the country. It stood open behind the wood-framed screen door, but she knocked instead of letting herself in. This was her childhood home, but she was a stranger here now. After a knock and no answer, Mel stuck her head a safe way in for a visitor and spoke.

"Hello?" the question echoed off the walls in the kitchen. She stepped inside and scanned the room with her heart beating in her ears. A clock that Dad had bought at an auction, still crooked, hung above the microwave, stacks of mail piled high on either side of the table. A grey Formica table with red chairs stood in the middle of the kitchen dragging Mel back into a world she had done her best to forget.

A cabinet door above the stove stood open about an inch, the latch broken for as long as she could remember. The room smelled the same, old leather, wood, and coffee. Coffee cups rested in the dish drainer. Dad had always said it was a waste of energy to put coffee cups back in the cupboard if

10

you were just going to use them again the next day. Her mom had countered this theory: "Thomas Snow, we will not raise our girls in a pigsty!" Mom had had a determined way about her, but when it came to Thomas Snow's boyish grin and charm she had given in often.

Stepping out onto the back porch, Mel shielded her eyes from the sun surveying the land that spread out before her. Five hundred and eighty-three acres were stitched together by her great-grandfather, grandfather, and father. Her grandfather had bought up the bulk of the land having a keen mind for business. The land was more precious than gold to the Snow family. Standing here now, her silenced longing to return pressed heavily upon her chest.

Every field and paddock had a name. Weak clouds drifted along casting faint shadows upon the grassy fields. A dozen young quarter horses chomped on a round bale of hay by a run-in shed. The horses in the field looked like yearlings, but she couldn't be sure. Twelve years had weakened her horse sense.

A handful of black cows grazed under the trees by the pond in the next field over. Her dad had always played around with being a cattleman, but Snow Farms was known for its quarter horse breeding and training. This reputation ran generations deep, son learning from father. The cows had been her dad's hobby and usually more trouble than they were worth, breaking fences or eating a neighbor's crop. Most horse farms in these parts were Thoroughbred or Saddlebred farms. "Good for nothings," her dad had called them. A rich man's hobby.

The fall and rise of the lands were frozen in time and memory but felt foreign. The old gum tree at the corner of the house still had three makeshift ladder rungs nailed in place that had once led to a treehouse. The branches held no remnants of the hideaway.

Mel heard bumping and rattling coming from the barn. *Jessica.* She wiped the sweat off her palms on her jeans and walked toward the sounds.

The barn doors were ajar, and Mel tilted her head to peek inside. A slender woman, skin darkened by the sun, with muscular arms separated flakes of hay as she whistled. She wore jeans that bunch up around her boots, and a white tank top. A dark brown, wavy ponytail stuck out through the back of a John Deere hat. Dad had hated John Deere. Her hair had always been like their mother's, not quite straight but just shy of curly.

Mel watched her sister. In her mind, she had been coming home to a twelve-year-old scrawny tagalong with stringy hair and awkward limbs. A new urge to run gripped her.

As if Jessica sensed Mel's presence, she glanced at the doors for a second before going back to her chore. Mel's breath caught in her throat. She pushed the doors open to make herself visible before she lost her nerve, standing silent in the doorway.

"Morning. Can I help you?" Jessica's tone was business-like without looking up. She tossed a flake of hay over the chestnut head sticking out of the stall window by her shoulder and began pulling the leather glove off her hand one finger at a time.

"Hi, Jessica," Mel stammered.

Jessica dropped her hands to her side and squared her shoulders, her brows crinkled like she was trying to remember a forgotten story. Her ungloved hand formed a fist, recognition seeping in.

"It's been a long time." Mel mustered her courage and took two steps into the aisle of the barn. Shadows made it hard to see Jessica's face now. Mel stopped and rested her hand on a saddle draped over a portable rack to hold herself steady, not comfortable going any closer without an invitation.

Jessica stepped toward her and into the sunlight spilling in from the side door. "You."

"Yeah." Mel's voice cracked. "It's me."

"You show up after all these years."

12

"I'm sorry it's been so long."

The aromas of the barn swirled through Mel's senses as she watched the blood in her little sister's face drain. Mel breathed in deeply. Horses, shavings, manure, and hay. The rich smells of her childhood brought comfort and pain.

Jessica's face hardened. "There's nothing for you here."

"Jess," Mel pleaded.

"What do you want me to do? Thank you for coming home? Tell you I'm happy to see you?" Jessica kicked a grain bucket by her feet making the horse in the stall next to her jump. A yellow cat darted across the barn aisle and disappeared up a corner post into the loft.

"I didn't know about Dad. I'm sorry."

"Dad's dead. And you weren't here. You left us. Remember?" Jessica spun on her heels and walked down the aisle between the two rows of stalls with her ponytail swinging back and forth with each step. A motorbike started up from behind the barn and took off across the field.

Chapter Two

Mel took in her surroundings. This was the playground of her childhood. Her life and her plans had all revolved around this spot on earth.

Minutes passed and the fog in her head began to clear. Life trickled back into her legs, and she walked farther into the barn. The sharp sounds of horses chewing their morning grain and hay filled the dusty air with an occasional snort or stomp.

Walking along the aisle, her mind stretched for words: withers, mane, poll, blaze. Such a different life than the one she had built in Boston. Concrete, crowds, and cold, grey buildings that blocked the sun. Dust rose and drifted onto her green, cloth Toms from the dirt aisle hardened from years of hoof and boot.

Her native tongue came flooding back to her. Paint, Buckskin, Chestnut, Appaloosa, she examined each horse staring up at her through open windows, chewing, not bothered by her presence. This was the sacred world she had never wanted to leave. Never a natural in training like her father, her skills had run more toward management. Her dad used to tell her she was like her grandfather in that way. The day she had received her acceptance letter from the University of Kentucky farm management program, he had beamed with pride and driven her and Jessica to Lexington for a celebration supper. But that was before.

A family bragging wall stood at the end of the barn aisle. A wooden case with a glass front in the center, covered in a thick layer of dust. Wiping the dust off the glass she peered in at her family's story told through trophies, silver and gold belt buckles, and colorful sashes lining each shelf. The wall to the right held blue, red, white, and pink ribbons. Jessica's ribbons far outnumbered anyone else in the family. Well before she could walk, Jessica was hoisted into a saddle for lead line competitions; Dad holding on to her leg while he walked beside the horse. Jessica atop, waving at the crowd with squeals of delight like she was the grand marshal of a Fifth Avenue parade.

Mel leaned against the frame of the side barn door by the office. The rolling hills of grasses spread out before her moved like a green ocean in the hot breeze. Her office walls at The Center where she had worked and the crowded streets of Boston, felt stifling against the openness here. The winds that pushed the field grass rustled the trees above. A blue jay called out from a branch stretched over the barn. Mel closed her eyes. She had forgotten the sounds of stillness.

Two hours later, she checked into the Comfort Suites on the south side of Lexington. The room was hot and muggy and smelled of cheap air freshener. She ordered a bottle of wine and a large mushroom pizza from the hotel restaurant. Mel was in no mood to be around people.

Still saved in her favorites, Mel stared at Patricia's number on her phone. After four years of being together, Patricia had called it quits when her last attempt to convince Mel to see a couples' therapist had failed. "I'm exhausted, Mel. You're never going to let me in," were her last tearful words before the apartment door slammed, leaving Mel alone at the dining room table. Mel had moved out that night. Patricia was seeing a mutual friend from the gym now.

Patricia had been Mel's first serious relationship. Before her, stood a long, painful line of dates that never lasted over a few months. This was by design, although she had not been willing to admit it then. After a few dinners, movies, and nights spent together, the causal air of newness wore off. When casualness gave way to any resemblance of seriousness, the hours between texts grew longer, the dates farther apart, until Mel's hints worked their magic.

Patricia was the first woman not to take Mel's hints seriously, and her persistence brought Mel around. "I see what you're trying to do, but it won't work with me. I'm not afraid of you," Patricia had told her in a voicemail when Mel hadn't returned any of her calls after their third date. They moved in together three months later. Mel never lost the habit of retreating into her shell, and she never shook the feeling that she was a project for Patricia to complete.

Mel tried to sleep but couldn't stop seeing Jessica's face the moment she had realized who she was. It had been foolish to show up without calling first, but when the letter had come from the lawyer about her father's death and the inheritance, she had seen it as a way out of her bewilderment in Boston. It had been a rash decision to quit her job at The Center and run back to a life that only existed in smoky memories, but the fresh pain brought on by Patricia's absence caused her to look for a new place to exist.

Sometime after midnight, Mel threw back the stiff bedspread and climbed out of bed not bothering to turn on a light. The moonlight squeezed through sagging drapes casting an eerie light upon the room. She poured the last glass of wine from the bottle.

She held a grainy photo close to her face in one of the slivers of light. The corner of the photo was marked by the clip that kept it attached to the visor of her car. As much as Mel had tried to distance herself from the life she had left, she had not found the strength to forget.

In the photo, her dad sat on a chestnut gelding named Tumbleweed grinning wildly under the brim of a sweat-stained cowboy hat. A one-year-old Jessica sat in front of him with a small handful of Tumbleweed's mane between her chubby fingers. Mel was smooshed up against her father's back with a pink cowboy hat crooked atop her head. Three faces stared back at her, grins prominent on each face under similar noses. Her mom had said they were squished together like a ham sandwich. It was Mel's seventh birthday and her dad had promised them a ride to the creek. Mom came along on the tractor with the cake, and they churned homemade ice cream by hand.

The girls had splashed and shrieked in the creek while their parents danced on the bank under a weeping willow tree. Willie Nelson filled the air with "You Were Always on my Mind" between bouts of static on the tractor radio, but they didn't seem to notice.

Dad was gone.

Jessica hated her.

Chapter Three

Mel checked out the next morning determined not to need a hotel room for another night. Turning into the gas station adjoining the hotel parking lot, she slammed on her brakes to avoid a dented Dodge Ram pulling a livestock trailer full of pigs.

The pumps didn't have credit card readers, so Mel stood in a line after she pumped the gas with a cup of coffee in hand struck by how much denim was in one small building. It was a sea of blue. The woman and child in front of her wore long denim skirts with sneakers and she could tell by the pouf of hair atop the woman's head they were some type of Pentecostal. A young girl and an older gentleman behind the counter both wore denim jackets, one dark, one faded. The old man who had been in the Dodge Ram stood behind her in crisp dark denim overalls with silver snaps, the store crease evident on each side of the legs.

The cigarettes behind the uncombed head of hair on the older station attendant called to her when it was her turn to pay. She'd stopped smoking when she had started dating Patricia. There was no one around to be perturbed by her nasty habits now. Before handing him her credit card she asked for a pack of Camels and reached for a lighter beside the beef jerky. With a coffee and a full tank of gas, she jumped on Highway 68.

The gas station coffee was thick and bitter with a thin layer of oily substance floating on top. Mel rolled down the window and lit a cigarette holding the steering wheel steady with her knee. One drag. Then another. Her limbs tingled and the muscles in her shoulders softened. Today's encounter would be as harsh as the first, probably worse, but Mel wasn't planning on leaving until Jessica heard her out. If she was lucky, she'd catch her in the house. Something about this gave Mel hope.

Mel rehearsed her part of the drama about to unfold. She'd never been good with words—she could lose grasp of the entire English language when she needed it most. She feared it would turn out like the eighth-grade production of Romeo and Juliet.

In the play, Mel had been given a minor role, only three lines, but her brain froze when she walked on stage and the only words that came to her, as the gymnasium full of parents and teachers looked on, were the lyrics of Mary Had a Little Lamb. The horror lasted for what seemed like hours. That night, her dad had sat beside her bed until she had cried herself to sleep.

There was much more on the line today. Mel wondered if there was any real hope of breaking through the anger evident in Jessica's voice yesterday. She dropped the cigarette butt into the cup of coffee. It was a better use of the coffee anyway.

Waiting at the only stoplight in Lebanon Springs, she looked around the cozy town square. Mel shivered and reached for another cigarette. The McDonalds on the corner opposite the hardware store had outdoor seating instead of the old Playland. Uncle Jerry had taken her there for dinner the day Jessica was born, and she had played until her Dad returned from the hospital. The parking lot was full of trucks in every shape and condition.

Three old men in overalls sat on the bench in front of the courthouse. Were they the same old men from twelve years ago or had younger old men taken up the torch?

The sun reflected off the gold dome of the courthouse. She had gotten a speeding ticket her senior year out on Highway 42. Her dad had made her pay the ticket out of her savings and attend traffic school in the creepy courthouse basement. She was certain the building was haunted.

A tractor pulling a four-wheel wagon full of cut tobacco crawled through the light in front of Mel just as it turned green. The next half mile was taken at a top speed of 15 mph. The Old Goat Bar where her dad used to play pool was still standing. The building was the same shade of green that had always made her stomach queasy. The owner had purchased the paint at a scratch and dent auction to save a dime. Mel still couldn't describe the color exactly except to say it was somewhere between Johnson grass green and pond scum. They had added a window to the side with a neon light above it. "Drive-Thru Spirits" flashed in red making the building look like a Christmas village gone bad.

Fifteen minutes later, Mel crept up the winding driveway avoiding the potholes. The sunlight streaking through the trees heated the morning air. The spots of shade gave no relief, the air hot as it entered her nostrils. It was like a sauna most years. Her mom had grown up in Wisconsin and had never liked the summers here. Even winters were miserable often getting more ice than snow. Most folks said Kentucky had two seasons, hell and hell freezing over. For what she was about to face with Jessica, *hell* was fitting.

The field to the right was used as a hayfield. They would get one more cutting off of it, but by the looks of it, the summer heat had taken its toll. Half of this was hers now, the land over which she had cried herself to sleep for months after leaving. She had called the lawyer after receiving the manila envelope in shock. "I promised your daddy I'd find you if anything ever happened to him. He was a damn good man." The lawyer, a long-time friend of the family, had gone on to explain her father's wishes; Thomas Snow wanted his daughters to continue the Snow legacy together.

She parked the car in the same spot as yesterday. A black and brown mutt with long legs and a short body crawled out from under the porch barking. They had always had farm dogs around, and she wondered where he had been yesterday. Mel hesitated with her hand on the door handle for a second before noticing the long tail wagging wildly. It was staring up at her now from outside the car window. She pushed open the car door and two filthy brown paws landed on her lap. The rank smell of dog breath, a farm dog at that, filled the car. A fleshy tongue hung to one side.

"Was that necessary?" Mel wrinkled her nose and pulled her head to the side. Mel had wanted a dog in Boston, but Patricia said they smelled. The dog in her lap looked up at her, its right canine tooth was broken off at the tip. She scratched the beast behind the ears before pushing its front half out of the car. Two lines of fresh dirt smeared across her jeans. Satisfied with its welcome, the dog strolled back to the edge of the porch, looking back at Mel one more time before ducking out of sight.

Jessica stood in the half-opened screen door. She glared at Mel for a few seconds and then disappeared into the house letting the door slam behind her. Mel stepped out of the car, wiping off the streaks of dirt with one hand as she walked. She paused at the top of the steps. She wouldn't knock this time.

Jessica was seated at the table. As a kid, she would sit in the same chair and pout staring at the treehouse out the kitchen window after their dad had demanded she come down and eat at the table like a human being. Jessica raised her coffee cup to her lips, but her hand shook slightly.

Just like yesterday, Mel felt the urge to slink back to the car, but she willed her legs not to run. Pulling out the chair opposite Jessica, she sat down.

"What happened to the treehouse?" Mel asked.

"Boards rotted out," was all Jessica said.

They both sat in silence, eyes diverted. Just like in eighth grade, Mel couldn't remember a single word she'd rehearsed in the car on the way over. Jessica started fidgeting like a caged animal, and Mel feared she would spring free at any moment.

"It's good to see you."

Jessica didn't respond.

21

"I've missed this place."

Jessica's jaw clenched as tight as a new puppy on a rawhide bone.

"I'm sorry about Dad."

Anger flashed across Jessica's face. She stared at Mel yet stayed silent.

"I am sorry I wasn't here. I didn't know, I swear," Mel pleaded with her little sister.

"You wouldn't have known, would you?" Jessica said in a flat, cold tone.

"I am sorry."

"That's nice to hear. Really." Jessica squinted her eyes.

Mel searched her sister's face for any sign of hope. Green eyes like her own stared back at her, unblinking.

"That's all you're sorry for? How about the last twelve years? Or for Dad worrying about you every single day? Or for the hurt I saw in his face every time some nosey neighbor asked if we'd heard from you?"

"I didn't want to leave," Mel shot back.

"Funny that you'd come back now you think you've got something coming to you. I'll tell you straight. I don't give a damn what some piece of paper says or that lawyer. You won't get this place. Dad and me worked hard after you up and left us. You won't take this place from me." Jessica's voice shook. She clamped her mouth shut, staring deep into her coffee cup.

Guilt burned in the pit of Mel's stomach like cheap whiskey. "I didn't come back to take anything. I came back to—." There was no easy answer. "You don't know how it was—how confused I was. You don't know what it was like hearing Uncle Jerry tell me I had to leave—."

Jessica wrinkled her brow. "What the hell are you talking about? What's Uncle Jerry got to do with this?"

Mel's confused look mirrored Jessica's. "He's got everything to do with it."

The haunting storyline replayed in her mind scene by scene. That morning. The argument over chores. With her dad. He had said it was time to learn some responsibility and made her stay behind while he took Jessica to the horse sale with him. "That day. Dad was too ashamed to tell me himself. He had Uncle Jerry do it. I wanted to go with you, but Dad told me to stay home and finish my chores."

"You don't know what you're talking about. Uncle Jerry helped Dad search for you for weeks. He drove all over the state looking for you. Posted pictures in Louisville, Lexington, and even E-town. Talked to the sheriff's office, searched for you everywhere." Jessica's voice was raw and defensive.

Mel started to ramble aloud. "UNCLE JERRY took me to the bus station. Bought my ticket. He told me I had to leave. Told me Dad wanted me gone."

Jessica's face was frantic. "You're making no sense. What are you saying?"

"He caught me kissing." The wall behind Jessica's head began to shift. Mel tucked her hands underneath her thighs. Opening her eyes, she spoke in a low voice. "Uncle Jerry. He caught me kissing Emily Johnson at the football game the week before I left. He came unglued. He kept saying 'wait 'til your daddy hears about this.' He came—after you and Dad left for the horse sale. Said Dad didn't want me around—said I was going to hell. He kept going on and on."

Mel took a breath and stood up. "He drove me to Louisville to the bus station." Her cheeks burned. She leaned against the counter gripping the edge of the white iron sink. She would not take the blame for this. It was not her fault.

Jessica's brows creased. Silence.

"He bought me the ticket, Jess," Mel shouted. "Gave me a thousand bucks. Told me to go anywhere, but here. I panicked—chose Boston. It was just the first place that came to my head. New York or Chicago sounded too big, too scary."

Jessica finally spoke in a weak, skeptical voice. "You've been in Boston this whole time?"

Mel nodded but didn't look at her.

Jessica's voice grew louder. "But that makes no sense."

"Maybe they didn't tell you."

"I was sitting right here when Uncle Jerry said you'd probably run away with some secret boyfriend." Jessica pounded her index finger on the table. "And why would you just leave with him? Why didn't you wait for us to come home?"

"I don't know!" Mel yelled. The absurdity of that day sank in.

She had let Uncle Jerry browbeat her, and from that point on she had based the last twelve years on his lies.

"Dad was crushed when you left. I'd hear him crying in your room at night. Like after Mom died."

Mel wrung her hands together pacing in front of the sink. "I'm so stupid."

Silence stood between them like a thick fog, each sister grappling with her own confusion.

"So. You're—gay?" Jessica stumbled over the word.

Mel sat back down at the table. "Yeah."

"But why didn't you call or write or come back sooner? It's been twelve years, Mel."

Mel broke when she heard these words. The weight of the lies she had lived under made it hard to breathe. "I can't say for sure. I was confused—I thought something was wrong with me. Back then, I guess part of me thought he might be right about me."

Jessica leaned her chair back on its two legs and grabbed the box of Kleenex by the microwave. She scooted it across the table toward Mel.

"I used to have dreams about you being dead. Uncle Jerry kept telling Dad you'd run off and would be back when you were ready for forgiveness. I just thought you wanted out of here." Jessica's voice was almost a whisper. "I think it almost killed him, but Dad finally just stopped looking. Said if you wanted to leave we had to let you."

Mel looked across the table at Jessica. For a second, she saw the twelve-year-old sister she'd left behind. She saw abandonment.

"I didn't know, I swear." Mel reached across the table with an outstretched hand. "I can't undo the last twelve years, but I'd like to stay on for a while—if that's okay. See if we can figure things out—fix things." She stopped short of saying *between us*.

Jessica looked at Mel's hand and then back into her face. She started to move her hand toward Mel's but stopped. The ticking of the crooked clock filled the void in the kitchen.

With their hands in the middle of the table, inches apart, Mel saw it. Jessica's hand was brown and calloused with deep lines of farm life etched into them. Mel's was soft and pale. Jessica stood up but kept her hands on the edge of the table and her eyes planted on Mel's outstretched hand.

"I'd like to believe we can fix this, but some things can't be mended. I don't understand why Uncle Jerry did what he did, but you stayed gone. We're not kids anymore." Jessica took a deep breath and stepped back away from the table. "The place is part yours, Dad wanted it that way. I can't keep you from staying."

Mel didn't move. Out of the corner of her eye, she watched Jessica walk to the door and grab the green hat off the hook pulling her ponytail through the back. She hesitated with her hand on the screen door. "I'll try, Mel. That's all I can promise you." She didn't look up before shoving the door open and walking out.

Chapter Four

Mel sat at the kitchen table. Her red, swollen eyes focused on the empty chair across from her. Yes, she had stayed gone. It had been easier that way. Patricia had encouraged her to call or visit, but Mel had resisted out of bitterness.

"But what about your sister? I know she must miss you." Patricia had tried many angles of persuasion.

"She's better off without me there. Besides, they wouldn't understand." Mel had shut down the suggestions every time. Uncle Jerry's lies had created this path of bitterness, but she had lost herself along the way.

She would never see her dad again. Ache sank in like a stone. Mel had come home for more reasons than she could put into words.

Mel reached for Jessica's cup and plate and placed them in the sink. The chasm between sisters was vast. They had been close, especially after their mother had passed away. Her dad used to tell her she babied Jessica; Mel had always felt protective of her. Although six years older, they rode together, did chores together, and even slept in the same bed when it stormed.

Mel reached up and touched the faded white curtains hanging above the sink. Her first 4-H project. Small yellow daisies with green stems spotted the material. Dad had rushed out to the store for the material after Mel remembered the project was due the following day. Her mom stayed up late helping her sew them. She had won a third-place ribbon although the edge sat crooked.

Mel hadn't had much patience for cooking or sewing when she was younger, still didn't. She excelled in schoolwork, preferring to read or do homework. Her opposite, Jessica had announced in kindergarten she thought she could get by without it. It had been a struggle every morning just to get her to go. Arguing, complaining, even faking sick when it was time to wait for the bus. One morning she made herself throw up on the living room rug, but Dad had called her bluff, made her go, and grounded her for a week.

Mel hung the dishtowel over the oven handle and peered around the fridge into the hallway like it was a forbidden tunnel to a hidden kingdom. Jessica said she could stay, but she felt like an intruder in hostile territory.

The hallway opened up into the living room. The hardwood floor was bare now, but a leather recliner, her dad's favorite spot in the house, sat in the corner alongside an unfamiliar leather couch. A fireplace and mantle took up most of the front wall by the door, but they had only used it for holidays, special occasions, or during the turning of the seasons when the stove was not yet needed. A woodstove, draped with a checkered tablecloth during summers, sat against the far wall and a philodendron's green and yellow vines ran across the top and down the side. The smell of the woodstove on winter nights came back to her. Many nights, Mel and Jessica fell asleep in front of the stove, barely waking when their dad carried them up and tucked them into bed.

Everything in sight was covered with a thin layer of dust. Her grandmother's threadbare quilt draped over the back of the couch. Years of washing and line drying in the sun had caused the colored fabric to fade, but nothing was as cozy on a rainy day.

Having died when Mel was only four, she didn't remember much about her grandmother except that she and Grandpop had slept in the room off from the living room beside the kitchen, and that she made the best chocolate chip cookies and would let Mel blow bubbles in her milk when they were alone. Her grandfather passed away the same year Jessica was born. He had been a tall, quiet man that whittled in the evenings on the front porch. When she had asked her mom why Grandpop didn't talk to her, her mother had said he was more at home with the horses than little girls.

Beside the front door—used only by preachers, lawyers, or visitors who didn't know any better—was her dad's office. The heavy oak door creaked open scraping the floor. Mel stuck her head in. Pictures of tractors, cows, and horses long in the grave covered the walls. The faint smell of pipe tobacco, musty wood, and dust stung her eyes. The smells of her father. She closed the door sharply.

Mel braced herself on the dark, wood-stained banister. Lining the wall diagonally were school pictures from every year and family Christmas portraits strewn in between. She examined each photograph as if she were walking through the majestic halls of a museum. Stopping in front of her senior picture, she stared harshly at her own face as if to ask *what were you thinking?*

The first bedroom at the top of the landing was Jessica's. A pair of polished show boots and a dusty pair of Ariats sat outside the door. The bathroom to the right frozen in time with a claw foot tub taking up one side of the narrow room, the walls covered with pink and green tiles.

Standing in front of her old bedroom door, her heart pounded. The last time she had been inside, Uncle Jerry had been yelling at her from the hall while she shoved her clothes in a duffle bag. She had snatched the photo she carried with her off her nightstand at the last minute.

Like every other door in the house, it creaked open and scraped the hardwood floor below. Flipping on the switch, Mel was shocked to see familiar pieces of furniture inside the room. Old boards and cans of paint stacked up in the corner, an ironing board next to the window, and boxes scattered around the edges, but her bed, nightstand, and desk still sat in the place she'd left them. The bed held a pile of winter horse blankets. A signed Reba McEntire poster hung between the bed and window.

Mel turned off the light and closed the door behind her. At the end of the hall, the only door left upstairs. Her dad's room. She walked toward it, her footsteps echoing off the walls. One hand on the doorknob, the other on the door. She could almost see her dad sitting in the chair by the window behind the closed door. Mel closed her eyes and rested her forehead on the warm wood frame but couldn't make herself turn the knob.

Unlike twelve years ago, Mel made this choice to leave Boston, but the same searing fear ran through her veins now. She tucked the heavy bags behind the sofa until she could figure out what to do with them. The situation with Jessica was fragile at best. It was best to stay away from the barn for now.

Jessica didn't come in for lunch. Her truck rumbled down the drive in a cloud of dust, and Mel bet she would rather eat anywhere than here right now. As she watched the truck disappear, Mel breathed a sigh of relief mixed with a rush of regret. Where there had once been hushed talks and giggles for hours after bedtime when Jessica would sneak into Mel's room and beg to sleep with her now stood muted animosity. Doubting the lunch choices had changed much, Mel imagined Jessica sitting in The Old Goat Bar by herself. It was a bar, technically speaking, but a family-friendly one. Their dad used to take them there for lunch when they were on summer vacations. The girls sat at the corner table with burgers, fries, sweet tea, and one of the board games they kept behind the counter, while their dad drank a beer and played pool with Uncle Jerry or any other local that had come in and could spare the time. A lot of business could be done over a decent game of pool.

Mel found a can of tomato soup in the cupboard and rummaged the drawers for a can opener. In the process, she found spaghetti and pasta sauce. She could make that for dinner without screwing it up too much. The kitchen was quiet except for the ticking clock and the soft crunch of her Saltines. Mel tried to read a two-day-old Lexington Herald but kept reading the same paragraph over and over.

The truck pulled back into the yard as she washed the soup bowl. The screen door opened and by the look on Jessica's face when she saw her in the kitchen, she had been hoping this morning had been nothing more than a bad dream.

"I hope you don't mind." Mel lifted the bowl covered with suds.

"No. Of course not." Jessica's eyes darted around the kitchen as if she were looking for a place to hide.

"Listen. Is it okay? That I'm here, I mean? I'll leave if you want." Mel hadn't meant to say that last part.

Jessica didn't respond right away giving Mel her truest answer.

"It's just a shock, that's all." Jessica wrinkled her brow and tried a smile that didn't quite come off right. "Look, Dad wanted this. I sort of knew it might be coming, even if I don't agree with his decision. I said I'll try and that's what I'll do."

"I can make dinner for us at least." Mel wondered if she remembered how poorly she cooked.

"Sure. That'll be fine. I'll be in for supper around seven."

Jessica turned and walked out of the kitchen. She disappeared across the yard, dog by her side.

By supper time, and despite Mel's best efforts, the noodles had grown large and soggy, and she'd managed to spill oregano in the pasta sauce. She spooned out what she could off the top. An unopened bottle of red wine was unearthed in the cupboard while searching for a colander. There had never been wine in the house before, but Mel had never been so happy to see a bottle of wine in her life. Their mother hadn't drank, and their dad had been a beer or bourbon kind of man.

Her nerves were shot by the time Jessica drifted into the kitchen a few minutes after seven. Strands of Jessica's hair were untucked from the hat and her face was smeared with dirt.

"I'll be a minute." Jessica faltered raising her dirty hands in the air.

Mel listened to the creaking stairs under Jessica's boots. The sound comforted her.

Jessica came back into the room with a clean face and a different shirt. "Sorry about that."

"No worries. Sorry in advance about the spaghetti. I was never great at cooking." Mel turned to grab the two pans off the stove.

"I remember."

"I found this in the cupboard. Do you mind if I have some?" Mel tilted the wine bottle toward Jessica.

"I didn't know we had that."

"Would you like a glass?"

"If it's all the same to you, I'll have a beer. I'm not big on wine." Jessica didn't wait for an answer but went to the fridge and grabbed a bottle out of the door. She used the iron bottle opener attached to the wall above the toaster to pop the top taking a long slow drink before turning back around.

Without a word, Jessica sat down and dished noodles onto her plate. Mel poured wine into a mason jar at the sink and followed. She wanted to ask questions about Jessica's life and the farm but held back. This was enough for now.

Jessica did not look up from her plate.

"It's a good wine." Mel tried to keep things light. "The spaghetti's not as bad as I imagined."

"It's fine. Thanks." Jessica took another drink of beer. It looked oddly refreshing. Mel couldn't remember the last time she'd had a good cold beer.

"How did your day go?" Mel's voice sounded ancient and forced.

31

"Good. I've got a good batch of horses for training and some good help right now."

"You kept up the training?" Mel hadn't thought about who did the training in Dad's absence.

"Of course."

"That's good. You were always good with the horses." Mel searched for another safe question as she spoke.

"I've got a couple of boys who just graduated helping around the place."

Mel nodded her head. "It was hot today. Even the breeze was hot."

"It's been a hell of a summer. The last batch of hay was half what it should have been. We'll have to buy if it's a long winter."

Jessica sounded just like their dad. It's the first time Mel noticed Jessica's thick drawl and wondered what she must sound like to Jessica.

"What?" Jessica asked.

Mel was caught.

"Nothing. It's just. I guess I had been expecting a kid when I returned." Mel answered softly.

"You were gone a long time."

After washing the dishes, Mel joined Jessica in the living room. Jessica sat on the couch with her legs stretched out across the coffee table, the dog from this morning lying under her legs. His name was Sam Houston—Mel had learned this at the supper table. Dad had bought him for Jessica's graduation.

A M*A*S*H rerun played on TV. Mel hesitated before deciding to take a seat in the recliner. The girls sat like two small children watching Saturday morning cartoons.

As soon as the credits rolled, Jessica started upstairs mumbling something about an early morning. It was nine o'clock. Mel looked at her bags and debated.

"Should I just crash down here or—?"

"Oh yeah, right. You can sleep in your old room, but it's probably a bit of a mess." Jessica motioned upstairs with her head. "I'll grab you some linens."

Jessica didn't wait for her to respond. Mel grabbed her duffle bag and slung the backpack over her shoulder. She reached the top of the stairs as Jessica came out of the hall closet with an arm full of sheets, a quilt, and two pillows. She opened the door to Mel's old room and switched on the light with her elbow.

"Jesus. It's a junk heap." Jessica moved boxes aside with her foot and placed the linens on the ironing board. "I can move some of this shit out tomorrow."

"Don't bother. I can do it. It's not so bad. It's almost as big as some apartments I've lived in." Mel laughed.

"Seriously?" Jessica moved the horse blankets off the bed and piled them in the corner under the window. "Don't worry, they're clean."

Mel tossed her bags on the bed. "Small living. That's the city for you."

"I'd go mad." Jessica threw her hands on her hips and looked over the room again. "Well, good night then."

"Good night, Jessica—thanks."

Jessica looked at Mel with a funny expression and gave a little sound that was a cross between "yeah" and "well." Mel had no idea what it meant. Jessica's footsteps faded and her bedroom door closed.

Mel rummaged through her backpack and found the pack of Camels she bought that morning in Lexington. It seemed like days ago. Walking around the bed, she pushed boxes against the wall to make a path. The double window overlooked the porch roof and the front yard. The first window did not budge. After a struggle, Mel tugged the second window open halfway with a painful screech.

Mel lit a cigarette bending to blow the smoke out the window screen. She had done this same thing as a teenager only her dad had been on the front porch and smelled it that night. Grounded for a month with extra chores had been the

33

penalty. The extra chores had been added after she sassed him by telling him it was no different from his pipe.

The hot breeze carried the smells of the country through the window mixing with the silver swirls of cigarette smoke.

"What am I doing here?" Mel watched the swirls disappear.

Chapter Five

For the first three days, Mel stayed away from the barn. She told herself this was for Jessica's sake. The first day she moved the clutter from her room to the storage shed out back. Reading, wandering through a house haunted with memories, making sandwiches for lunch, and cooking supper made the days long. Mel couldn't stay on as a vacationing houseguest, and no progress could be made in mending what was broken if neither sister was willing to acknowledge the other's existence. Besides, this would slowly drive her mad. She might as well have stayed in Boston if this was to be her life.

After dinner on the third night, Mel asked Jessica if she could come to the barn. As was Jessica's nature, she said more in the silence before her answers than she did with the simple "sure" that followed, but Mel took her at her word the next morning.

The first few days, she had asked each morning what Jessica needed help with not wanting to overstep, but soon enough Mel took on the chore of watering as her own. They worked in silence until the horses were grained, hayed, and watered, but at least she felt useful.

Mel had resigned herself to small, odd jobs: dusting the trophy case, cleaning the office, and straightening the tack room. The object of each day was to be relevant but stay out of Jessica's way as much as possible. She was determined to keep up with Jessica's pace, but twelve years of city life had made her soft. Weekends of rest and relaxation didn't exist in this world. Horses were hungry, and stalls were still dirty. Saturday and Sunday were filled with dumping wheelbarrows full of manure and any other task that hadn't been checked off during the week. Boston mornings at the gym and hefting hay bales were as different as daylight and dark. This was the life Mel had mourned the loss of in her dreams, but she feared too much time had passed.

The alarm clock clanged. Mel kicked the sheet to the end of the bed and swung her feet to the floor. Her chipped, uneven nails were discolored. A blackened thumb throbbed from a hammer mishap yesterday while trying to repair a stall board that had been kicked loose in the night by a bitchy mare. Mel stared at the cracks beginning to appear in her palms. Blisters had formed and popped and formed again making her hands resemble the dry cracked earth in the lots behind the barn. Even the soles of her feet were sore.

Jasper and Cody, the two guys Jessica had hired after Dad died, made their daily appearance around eight. Mel and Jessica took care of the feeding, morning and night. Like their dad, Jessica didn't trust the graining regimen to anyone else. The boys worked Monday through Thursday cleaning the stalls in the mornings and exercising horses in the afternoons. Friday through Sunday tasks fell to Jessica and Mel. The boys were goofy farm boys, and Mel liked them right off. They both harbored quite a crush on Jessica, and they spent their days trying to outdo one another in feats of strength and horsemanship.

Mel felt the vibes. Jessica was putting up with her presence. The truth stung, but she reminded herself she was still here. Where Jessica moved with ease and finesse in barn life, Mel was awkward and forced. Jessica moved behind Mel restacking square bales, switching the order of bridles hanging on the tack room wall, or unrolling the watering hose only to roll it back up again tighter, neater, better.

Mel was on unspoken review with Jessica, but Jasper and Cody's evaluation was not as restrained. A few days after their first meeting, and after she had dumped a wheelbarrow full of manure in the barn aisle by accident, she overheard them behind the barn.

"She ain't that tough for a lesbian, is she?" Cody asked.

Jasper shot back in a defensive tone. "Hell, I don't know how they are. I ain't ever met one except maybe old Mrs. Kiki out on Turner's Lane. Dad says she hates men."

"Mrs. Kiki ain't no lesbian." Cody shook his head. "She's had three husbands, but she does hate men, everybody knows that. But in the movies, lesbians sure don't look like Mel."

Jasper laughed. "You been watching lesbian movies?"

"No, I ain't watched no lesbian movies. You know what I mean. They're supposed to be mean and ugly and wear men's clothes. Mel ain't none of that as far as I can tell. She's even sort of pretty for an older woman—but not as pretty as Jessica."

After morning feedings, Jessica spent the day saddling, riding, and unsaddling horse after horse. She would call for the boys from the round pen when she needed their help with a particular part of the training. Jessica hadn't offered a horse to Mel yet, and Mel was relieved. She wasn't sure she remembered how to ride, no matter how many people claimed it was like riding a bike. The fact that this bike happened to be a thousand pounds with a mind of its own fed her hesitancy. She had taken her share of spills as a kid, but those falls would hurt worse at thirty. The ground seemed to have grown harder, and she was in no hurry to get back in the saddle.

Lunch was quick as a blink; afternoons were repeats of the mornings only hotter. The boys left around five unless they wanted to go on a later trail ride, and most days Jessica didn't go in until the last faint colors of sunset filled the sky.

After Mel had done every odd job she could find to occupy her hours, she would stand at the back door of the barn mesmerized by Jessica in the round pen. She was more than good. A natural. She moved like a dancer at times, smooth and calm, never taking her eyes off the animal in front of her.

The nights had begun to offer a slight reprieve from the heat, but the mid-day sun still cooked them in their skin. Last week Mel unearthed a hammock while dislodging boxes underneath the bed and had strung it between the two maples at the front corner of the house. She'd taken advantage of the cooler nights and the star-filled country sky she'd forgotten. Her evenings were spent stretched out in the hammock after supper. Days were filled with work and dirt and heat, but nights were filled with a peaceful silence.

Jessica didn't offer up much conversation beyond the necessary. As a kid, she had never stopped talking. Mel wondered if she had morphed into this quiet being with age or if she was just guarded toward her. Some nights Jessica left after dinner and came home after Mel had gone to bed, never mentioning where she had been.

The big barn, as it was called, had stalls down both sides, only half were filled. Horses in training stayed here, most belonged to clients. Young horses of their own that showed potential were kept here and put in the training rotation. They were sold in the spring sales at Bowling Green. Rooster Cogburn, Jessica's show horse also had a stall of prominence, his nameplate in gold on the stall door.

Worry had spread across Jessica's forehead when Mel asked about the empty stalls. Their father was an old-school trainer, like his father before him, and some in the area preferred this. These were the stereotypical cowboys that would throw on a saddle and "ride the buck" out of a horse. Jessica was a modern trainer, preferring to gain the horses' trust instead of breaking their will. Horse people were a funny breed of humans, leery of new trainers even if it was someone they'd known for years. People were slow to accept new ways. Mel knew this firsthand.

Seeing the transformation from little sister to a strong, capable woman made Mel proud of who Jessica had become, but she made sure not to show it just yet. Training came as naturally as eating and sleeping to Jessica. Their grandfather would have said it was in her blood. Mel felt sure that same blood had somehow skipped her veins.

Jessica had four grain buckets in hand when Mel walked into the barn. Sam Houston, Jessica's four-legged shadow, took every step she took back and forth between the feed room and stalls.

"Morning." Jessica offered without looking in Mel's direction.

"Good morning," Mel answered too quickly. This was the first time Jessica had greeted her upon arrival.

Mel was halfway through watering when Jasper and Cody came in laughing and slugging one another in jest. They lived on the other side of Lebanon Springs and usually drove to the farm together. Jasper said good morning to Jessica sheepishly, and Cody walked by her with his chest puffed out reminding Mel of a scrawny rooster. Jessica seemed unaware of their boyish advances. She spouted off a list of chores for them to start on after the stalls were cleaned.

Mel held the watering hose just outside the stall door letting the water arch over the edge and fill the bucket. As Cody passed by, he winked and put his finger up to his lips begging for Mel's participation. Before Mel could figure out what he was up to, Cody cupped his hands under the hose and tossed the cold water in Jasper's face.

"You ass." Jasper wiped his face off with his white t-shirt sleeve.

"You need a bath if I have to work with you all day," Cody said slapping his knee with his cap exposing a fresh haircut. Like many farm boys, he sported a classic farmers' tan, and a thin line of white skin outlined his hair's edge on the back of his neck.

Jasper kept walking, his shaggy blond hair curled up around the edges of his cap. He looked like he belonged on a surfboard more than on a horse farm, but he was a good worker; they both were. Cody was the instigator of the pair. Mel had seen this from day one. Both boys had graduated with no desire for college. They lived at home with their parents and talked and dreamed of horses picking up work wherever they could. These two added life to the barn. If it weren't for their constant banter, the hours in the barn would have been almost void of human interaction. Almost identical in stature and walk, with their white t-shirts, jeans, and boots, they laughed on their way to the supply room.

Jessica didn't take any shit from the boys but treated them like adults and expected a great deal out of them each day. In turn, they respected her and tended to give a good day's work. Both nineteen, Cody and Jasper usually asked for a beer before going home, declaring they drank at home anyway, but Jessica flat refused. They always hung their heads in feigned misery but never missed an opportunity to ask again. It was their ritual.

Mr. Nathaniel Tomlin also worked on the farm. He had worked on Snow Farms since before Jessica was born. Nowadays, he worked only two days a week. Thomas Snow had called him Big Nate, although there was nothing big about him besides his imagination when spinning a tale. He was Mr. Tomlin to everyone else. He walked with a limp from a nasty fall off a green horse years ago, a story he told to anyone who would listen. Mel figured Jessica kept him around out of loyalty; he was retired from the railroad and didn't need the money, but he had worked this farm beside their father for years. His face was narrow and drawn now. He still had a few tuffs of hair up under his cowboy hat and a scruffy beard that took on the likeness of an abandoned bird's nest. These days, he fiddled around with rotting fence posts and pieces of tin that needed replacing on the run-in sheds in the fields.

When he had first seen Mel again, he had held her in a tight hug, smelling of tobacco and peppermint. He peppered her with questions, asking if she was married or had any kids, his left eyebrow raised but he said nothing when she told him she had recently busted up with her wife and had no kids. It was easier to call Patricia her wife rather than partner even though they had never married. It was like ripping a Band-Aid off quickly. Sharp reactions, like pain, stung for a moment but it hurt less than ambiguity in the long run.

Jessica walked through the barn aisle talking to a potential client on the phone. Mel finished filling up the corner water bucket in the last stall and wrapped the hose as tightly as she could manage on the wall mount by the feed room. The stalls in the smaller barn and the outside troughs were still left to do.

The smaller barn was home to Agent, a retired show horse, and a handful of geldings and mares Jessica used for lessons and breeding. She had started giving lessons at the request of a friend last spring, and as things go in the country, she'd picked up a few more by word of mouth. The money had come in handy after their dad's death, filling in the gap left by hesitant horse owners.

Leading this motley crew was an ancient miniature named Major. Mel was surprised to see this creature still alive, although their dad had always said he would outlive them all. He was pushing twenty-five years old now and had always been meaner than a snake.

Major earned his keep with this mean streak. Bitchy mares that needed to be taken down a notch or two would spend a day in the paddock with ol' Major. He had a way of changing perspectives. It was all he was good for. Their dad had picked him up for twenty-five bucks at a sale because he had grown too tall to be shown as a miniature. This ornery beast thought he was king of the horse world. He had no qualms about putting other horses, or humans, in their place with a swift kick to the chest, belly, or shin. Mel knew this from experience. She reached over the door and rubbed his jaw. He laid his ears back but pushed his jaw into her hand demanding more attention. Her father said he had the heart of a Clydesdale, but the heart of Satan might have been closer to the truth.

Chapter Six

Jessica stood washing the breakfast dishes when they heard Sam Houston let out a deep bark and abandon his cool dirt under the back porch. She leaned her body over the sink to see out the window toward the side of the house near the driveway.

"Aw, shit." She threw the dishtowel on the kitchen table and stormed out the back door.

Mel opened the screen door wide enough to see out, stopping abruptly. Uncle Jerry climbed out of his truck all smiles.

Listening from the door, Mel heard the curt tone in her greeting. She ducked her head back in the mudroom as a first instinct. His booming voice brought back painful memories.

Mel squared her jaw and stepped out onto the back porch still unseen by Uncle Jerry. She leaned against the screen door.

Uncle Jerry began talking about the weather on the cruise he had returned from in the deep thundering voice Mel remembered, but Jessica cut him off. "Why did you lie about Mel?"

Mel watched Uncle Jerry's face contort as if he'd been shot in the gut. His mouth hung open, but no sounds came out. Jessica stood in front of his truck with her hands on her hips and her legs spread wide like she was bracing for a fight.

"I'm not sure what you're—" He took off his hat and scratched his head. The top of his head was bald and shiny brown, accented by a scraggly band of grey hair that circled around the back of his head from ear to ear. The buttons on his plaid dress shirt strained around his gut.

"Don't." Jessica turned to look at Mel standing on the porch. Uncle Jerry's eyes followed her gaze and now his eyes widened to match his gaping mouth.

Uncle Jerry looked at Mel and then stared blankly at Jessica. "Jess, I—," his booming voice cracked.

"How could you do this?" Jessica shouted.

The flash of anger in Uncle Jerry's eyes did not go unnoticed. "I did it for you." The words pushed out between gritted teeth.

"Bullshit."

That lit Uncle Jerry's fuse. "I did what needed to be done. What was right. What your daddy couldn't do." His stance widened, but he stayed by the fender of his red Ford truck.

"Sending Mel away? Lying to us? That seemed right to you?"

Mel moved off the porch and stood a few feet behind her sister. Uncle Jerry's eyes darted back and forth between the two.

Uncle Jerry's jaw clenched, and his breath was labored. His eyes were dull and uneasy. "What she did—it was—sinful."

"And lying to your own family's not?" Jessica's sharp tone cut through the warm morning air.

"I did it for your own good." Uncle Jerry leaned forward but his feet stayed planted. "You didn't need her kind around influencing you for evil."

"You saw Dad. You saw him after Mel left. How could you do that to your own brother?" Jessica slammed her fist onto the hood of his truck.

"She was evil." Uncle Jerry drew out the words in his thick country accent and pointed a fat finger across the hood of the truck at Mel. The veins in his neck and arms began to

44

bulge under the collar and short sleeve of his shirt. "It had to be done."

Mel stepped forward to stand beside Jessica. "I am not evil, Uncle Jerry." Mel kept her voice flat, unruffled. "I'm gay."

"See? She admits as much." Uncle Jerry shook his head taking a step backward. "She chose to live like the devil."

"You bastard." Jessica's voice was hard. Her jaw was tight, and her eyes never left his face.

"How dare you disrespect me. You'll wind up in hell right alongside her." His face reddened.

"Don't talk to me about respect." Jessica's fists were clenched at her sides. "Get off this farm."

The words cut him. "Goddamn you, Jessica, you got no right—after all I've done for you."

"I won't forget this. What you did to Dad." Jessica's voice held steady.

"You're just as weak as he ever was." They stared across the hood of the truck in a silence that hung like fog. Uncle Jerry broke the stare and yanked his truck door open. Throwing the truck in gear, he made a tight circle that slung gravel out into the yard.

Neither sister moved. The truck fishtailed down the gravel drive until it turned passed the trees out of sight. Mel stepped to the side watching Jessica who continued to throw a hard stare toward the sound of the engine's rumble.

Jessica shoved her hands in her jean pockets before turning around, slapping her leg for the dog, and walking to the barn. Mel stood at the side of the house alone.

"So, what happened after you left?" Jessica asked that night at supper.

Mel took a spoonful of chili before answering. She had begun to think they would live out their days in silence. "That Saturday afternoon I got on a bus. I knew a thousand bucks wouldn't get me too far. I got off in Boston and tried to

45

rent a hotel room. They said I had to be twenty-one. I bawled in the lobby of the hotel."

"Why didn't you just come home?" These words spewed out like they had been burning a hole in her.

"Uncle Jerry was so horrible that day. He lit into me when I argued. You know how he used to get." Images of that day floated through Mel's mind. She felt the sting of his slap across her face.

Jessica stirred the chili in front of her without looking up. "But if you wanted to come home, you would have."

"I tell myself that now. I don't know, Jess. I guess I believed him—about dad and maybe about me. I kept thinking something was wrong with me and maybe it was bad for you to be around me. I walked around for hours trying to figure out what to do. That first night I slept in the bus terminal. It smelled like fish and urine. I'll never forget that smell. That's as scared as I've ever been. The next morning, I went back to the same hotel and asked for a job. An older lady was at the front desk. She said they didn't have anything for me but told me to wait in the lobby. After a few minutes, she came out with a name and an address. It was a local shelter that took in homeless youth."

"Then what?"

"I met with this lady, Mrs. Rogers. She listened. I stayed at the shelter for a few nights until she found me a room and a part-time job at a pet store. That next spring, I enrolled in community college. A few years later, I got my degree in psychology."

Jessica asked nothing more.

Two nights later, the interrogation picked up where it had left off.

"Why Boston?" Jessica asked after supper that night as if they had been mid-conversation.

"People always asked me that. I don't know. I panicked."

"Why didn't you at least call?" Jessica crumbled cookies in a bowl of ice cream with both hands.

"Scared. I think a part of me didn't want to hear Dad say he didn't want me here."

"He never thought that." Jessica's voice was defensive. "I mean, he didn't know, about the gay thing, at least I don't think he did, but he never would have thought that. He never would have sent you away."

Mel fiddled with the drawstring of her hoodie. "Back then, I was really mixed up for a while. One minute I was dating Jason Wagner the next I was kissing Emily Johnson."

"How come you never told me about—that?"

"I didn't want you thinking I was a freak," Mel answered without hesitation.

Jessica stood by the refrigerator listening.

"I should have called." Mel wrapped leftover cornbread in foil and stuck it in the oven.

Jessica walked down the hall but returned. "I tried to find you on Facebook."

"I've never been on Facebook. Too afraid I guess."

"Even I'm on Facebook, and I'm stuck out here in the sticks." Jessica shoved a spoonful of ice cream into her mouth and walked out.

Mel listened to the creaking steps and the bedroom door close upstairs.

Jessica left early on Sunday to deliver a horse and pick up another from a client in Louisville. Mel spent the day updating her resume and eyeing perspective jobs in the paper. Maybe it was better for both of them if she moved on. Maybe too much time had passed. Jessica could buy out her half, and Mel could start over somewhere else knowing she had at least tried to return and mend things. Maybe in the future, she could come back for awkward holiday meals just like other families. Mel emailed the lawyer to ask what steps needed to be taken for a buyout.

She found a youth center just outside of Nashville, and a therapeutic riding center in Mobile, Alabama. Nothing in Kentucky caught her attention. The cost of living made the thought of Alabama appealing, but she couldn't imagine what being a queer woman in Alabama must be like. But people were people in every spot on this earth. Kindness or discrimination knew no boundaries except the choices of individual hearts. Mel had seen a fair share of disapproving looks in Boston when she kissed Patricia on a park bench or when they walked hand in hand.

"Being gay isn't a choice, but being kind always is." Mel had often told the kids at The Center this. It had taken years for her to believe it herself.

When the truck and trailer pulled passed and stopped in front of the barn, Mel wondered if this was a quiet or questioning kind of day.

Jessica had just attached the water hose when Mel walked in.

"I can water," Mel offered.

Jessica said nothing but turned and grabbed the hay cart. Mel's nerves were worn thin by Jessica's silence. Part of her wanted to get in her car and just drive away, but the dwindling figure in her bank account kept her in check.

"You said you would at least try," Mel blurted out.

Both sisters looked at each other across the barn aisle.

"And that's what I'm doing."

Mel yanked the water hose out of the first stall spilling water down her jeans. "And how long are you planning to punish me, just so I know?"

"Look, you're the one that left. Never gave a thought to me or what it felt like to be left here alone."

"I thought about you all the time—."

"I needed you." Jessica's voice shook with rage.

"I fucked everything up, okay? Is that what you want to hear?" Mel raised her voice.

"I don't know what I want to hear."

"I can't take much more of this, Jess."

48

"I'm sorry to inconvenience you." Jessica clenched her jaw. "But you can't just show up after all these years and expect things to be the way they were. I said I would try. If that's not good enough for you, you're free to leave."

Mel stayed in her room the rest of the evening. She had found and claimed a wooden folding chair in the office and perched on it now blowing smoke out the open window. Her new rule was one cigarette before bed, but lately, she had been too tired to smoke it.

Jessica's words replayed in her mind.

I needed you.

The words bored through the crumbling walls she had built around her.

I needed you.

Mel had laid Uncle Jerry on the altar of blame, but Jessica was right. She had stayed gone.

Chapter Seven

The orange glow of morning spread through the barn aisle. Jessica was bent over filing Rooster's hoof. Rooster was a big bay gelding out of Poco Bueno bloodline. He had thrown a shoe yesterday in the round pen, and the farrier wouldn't be out until this evening.

"How did the lawyer find you?"

Mel was taken off guard. They had not spoken since Mel's outburst yesterday. She leaned against the stall door and propped her foot on the broken board behind her.

"DMV records. When I called the office, he said it was standard. Said he had made a promise to Dad." Mel continued. "I had come home late from work the day I found out. I'd changed my address, so it took a few days longer. He sent me a copy of the will, dad's death certificate, and a letter explaining what had happened. It was like I was watching a movie or something, only it was Dad that was gone."

Jessica stood up and stretched her back. She walked around to the other side of Rooster and raised his right front leg. The conversation must be over. Mel listened to the barn swallows chirping in the eave of the barn above the door.

"I only got worried when he didn't come in for lunch," Jessica said. The file swooshed against the hoof. "He looked peaceful when I found him. He died out behind the creek in Squealer's paddock, just sort of slumped over across the tractor fender. He'd gone out early to bush hog that steep bank where the thistles grow. The tractor radio was still playing." Jessica's voice trailed off.

"He always liked that paddock. Said the sunset was prettiest there," Mel added, unsure of how much she was allowed to say.

"We buried him by mom, of course." Jessica stopped filing and rested her hands across Rooster's withers. "I don't know what happens after we die, but I'd like to think they were re-united somehow."

"It's a nice thought. I hope you're right," Mel answered. She could see the family grave spot in her mind. It was beyond Timber Creek to the west. Her great-grandparents and grandparents rested there too. A cold chill gripped her when she thought of visiting the graveyard.

After dinner that evening, Mel wondered if she should escape to the hammock to give Jessica some space. Jessica said she was going to have a beer on the front porch and asked if she wanted to join her, gesturing the top of a brown bottle toward her.

Mel didn't try to hide the surprise in her voice. "Sure."

Only a thumbnail of moon shown above the tree line. The night air smelled of grass and the cows that lingered by the fence. Jessica sat propped against the corner post with one knee pulled up to her chest and the other stretched out. Mel stretched out in the porch swing.

"So," Mel broke the silence, "are you seeing anybody?"

"Sort of."

"Anyone I'd know?"

"No, his family moved here from Texas when we were juniors." Jessica raised her pant leg to remove the boot knife out of its sheath. She scraped a chunk of mud off the bottom of her boot. "Are you?"

She looked down into the neck of the cold bottle in her hands. "Not now." Mel wasn't sure if she was ready to talk about her own disastrous love life.

Jessica waited.

Mel stood and leaned against the white porch railing picking at the chipped paint. "Patricia. We split up a few months ago. Before I came ho—back."

"Were you—married?" Jessica asked.

Mel shook her head. "Just together. Four years."

Sam Houston roll on his back and flopped side to side in the cool grass like a fish tossed on a pond bank.

"Did you like it there?"

Mel hesitated to answer. It was a complicated question. "I liked Boston, but I didn't like myself there."

Jessica scrunched her nose.

Mel sighed. "After Patricia and I broke up, I finally started seeing how shut off from the world I was. With a chip on my shoulder, you could say. I still had a death grip on what had happened here while trying to pretend none of it happened. I wasn't happy, but I got good at looking like I was. Or at least, I thought I was good at it. All that time I was kind of a mess inside only I wouldn't admit it."

Jessica nodded.

"Coming back has made me see how messed up I'd let myself become."

"Will you go back? To Boston?"

Mel didn't miss the wariness in Jessica's voice. She wanted to be truthful with her, but she wasn't sure of anything right now. "I don't think so."

Mel heard a small pack of coyotes let loose in the distance. Their high-pitched cries gave her goosebumps. Sam Houston flipped from his back to his stomach with ears perked, ready to pounce or run. The cows grazing by the fence stirred.

"They killed one of the calves last spring."

"Always gave me the creeps," Mel answered.

They sat and listened to the howling. The pack had some poor creature cornered. The yelps and cries grew louder and more frantic until all went quiet. They were the loudest right before the kill.

"I was angry when he told me you would get half the farm."

Mel didn't respond.

"I told him you didn't deserve one blade of grass on this place."

"Do you still feel that way?"

Jessica took a long drink of beer before responding. "I would never have stayed gone like that."

"But do you still feel like I don't deserve to be here?" Mel needed this answer.

"I'm not sure."

"I wish I could change the way things happened, Jess. I should have come home sooner."

"I guess there's no sense in talking about it now." Jessica stood up and walked inside. Mel sat listening to the wind move through the leaves.

Later that week, they worked together on replacing the bottom boards in the round pen after it cooled down and the boys had gone home. Muscles were less sore, but she was once again too tired to sit at the window for a smoke. That night Mel lay in bed with the window open as a cooler breeze blew in the nightly howls of distant coyotes and farm smells. The stillness of the night was tangible.

Chapter Eight

Jessica stood by the two large barrels of grain scooping morning rations into the buckets by her feet. Sam Houston chewed on a piece of horse hoof left over from the farrier's visit yesterday afternoon.

"Mr. Tomlin said a section of fence needs repairing back in Clancy's paddock next to the Taylors' property. Mr. Taylor gets grumpy over fencing now that he's older. Thought you might like to ride back there with me."

Mel halted abruptly causing Sam Houston to stop chewing and look up at her.

"I thought I might take a look today after breakfast." Jessica dug the scoop into the grain.

Mel chuckled. "I have to be honest, I haven't been on a horse since I left here. I'm not even sure I remember how to ride."

"People don't forget how to ride. Besides, that paddock used to be your favorite." Jessica stated matter-of-factly.

This was Jessica in a nutshell. She saw life in logical black and white.

Mel's mouth went dry. She filled the watering trough in the dry lots out behind the barn and scolded herself for being such a coward. A far-away memory of the rush she loved on horseback fought the panic within her. This moment of courage made her stand a little taller.

Jessica offered to saddle Agent for her, but Mel said she would do it. Jessica quickly slung the saddle on Rooster and led him out the side door.

"Take your time. I'm going to run some energy out of this guy before we ride. He's still a bit full of himself."

Agent stood patiently in his stall chewing the last bite of hay he had snatched up before she pulled his jaw up with her hand. It took her a couple of tries before she remembered how to tie the side of the rope halter. Mel felt the movement of his jaw as he chewed, the smell of horse flesh filling her nostrils. Being left-handed and tying the different knots used on certain pieces of tack had always been a challenge. Often the finished product ended up backward or upside down. She adjusted the halter knot several times before she was satisfied with the look of it. Agent followed her out of the stall.

Mel pulled the lead line through the metal ring anchored in the post outside the stall door. Her dad had taught both girls the importance of the quick-release knot when tying a horse, but each attempt she made at this knot failed. She remembered how it was supposed to look and work, but she couldn't make her hands remember the moves.

"Please don't make me chase you," Mel whispered in Agent's ear as she settled for letting him stand ground tied with the lead line dangling from his chin to the hard dirt aisle. The courage she had held a few moments ago waned.

Agent stood on his best behavior while Mel brushed him and placed the saddle pad on his back. Just before she threw the saddle on, she remembered the trick to it. Her dad had shown her many times. She reached over and pulled the far stirrup up and hooked it on the horn. As kids, Mel and Jessica used to laugh at riders who didn't know this as they struggled to swing the saddle in place, or worse yet, hit the horse in the hindquarters with the stirrup causing the poor beast to bolt forward.

Mel lifted the saddle into position. Agent turned his head to the side, observing but remaining still.

After a few minor adjustments, Mel was happy with the way it looked. She was relieved to find a new cinch with a buckle that didn't require the old elaborate cowboy knot her dad had preferred.

The hard part was over. Mel had just finished putting the snaffle bit in Agent's mouth and fastening the bridle by his ear when Jessica came back into the barn with a sweaty Rooster following close behind.

"Ready?"

"Just about." Mel checked the cinch one more time, tightening it one more notch, before leading Agent out the side door.

"Good thing I worked Rooster. I would have had to fight him all the way there and back." Jessica swung up with ease and waited.

Mel stood square with Agent's left shoulder and tried not to think about how hard her heart was pounding. She held the rope reins with her ring and pinky finger and grasped the saddle horn firmly with the rest of her left hand. *It's just like riding a bike*. She whispered under her breath "left foot, left foot" not wanting to look like an idiot and swing up into the saddle backward. *Just pull up and swing my leg over. That's all there is to it.*

Mel's hamstring stretched beyond what was comfortable when she placed the toe of her dusty Toms in the stirrup. With her foot firmly in the stirrup, she knew she couldn't waver any longer. She bounced on the ball of her right foot giving her the momentum she needed for the pull up. On the third bounce, as if innate, her arms, stomach muscles, and legs all worked together for a brief second like a well-oiled machine, and Mel landed in the cool leather seat.

Agent stood like a bronze statue. She patted his shoulder in gratitude. The ground beneath her looked distant. She sat up straight and took a deep breath looking out beyond two fuzzy ears standing alert.

Jessica grinned. "See? That was easy. Let's go."

Mel squeezed her legs into Agent's sides. She tensed again as the massive animal shifted beneath her. The thrill of the moment flooded her senses. She tried to relax in the rocking movement, following Jessica through the back gate.

The air was cooler this morning; the sky was clear, still blue. The morning sun cast long shadows behind the two horses and riders. Clancy's paddock was the farthest paddock in the northeast corner and had been one of the last sections added to the Snow property. It was named after her father's cow horse and companion, Clancy. He was put down the winter he turned thirty-two, buried on the south side of the creek by the blackberry bushes. Uncle Jerry had been there that day standing beside her dad with cap in hand and patted him on the shoulder. She had caught sight of a tear running down her dad's cheek just before it disappeared with one quick brush of his leather glove.

Mel rode along in silence reacquainting herself with the contours of the land. Everything looked different from atop a horse. On days like today being back here felt like a dream. In Boston, she had refused to allow her mind to wander among the hills and trees of this property, but here among them now, she knew she could never shut them out again.

They crossed through Field Two and Skinny Jim's. Jessica opened and closed the gates as they went. Mel watched her bend over from atop her horse and unfasten the gate latch. She eased Rooster into a cross step to push the gate open. After Mel had passed through the opening, Jessica eased Rooster around the end of the long gate, never taking her hand off, talking him through each step. She was almost always in training mode.

Once they reached Clancy's paddock, Jessica trotted ahead of her, kicking posts and tugging on strands of barbed wire along the property line. She took a pen from her pocket and made notes on the back of her hand. Mel stayed atop Agent following the fence line at a walk, and he seemed content with the arrangement. When they reached the creek, Jessica asked if she wanted to stretch her legs for a minute or two. Mel swung herself onto the ground. Her legs looked normal, but she felt bowlegged like the old cowboys on spaghetti westerns. She looped the reins around a low maple branch.

"I bet your ass'll be sore in the morning," Jessica said.

"It's sore now. I won't be able to move in the morning."

"It feels good, uh? To be riding again."

"I can't believe it." Mel arched her back and looked around. The brush along the creek bank was thicker and the trees fuller. Birds scratching in the leaves a few feet away flew to nearby branches as Sam Houston plunged into the water.

"I didn't see him follow us," Mel said.

Jessica scooped up a couple of stones and tossed them one by one into the creek. "Oh, he's always around somewhere, and he never misses a chance to play in the creek. He'll smell worse than he already does."

After several minutes of silence Jessica swung herself back up into the saddle, and Mel knew it was time to get going. A prospective client, looking for a new trainer for several young Arabians he'd raised insisted on observing Jessica in action.

Halfway across Field Two after they passed the small rain gully, Jessica turned in her saddle, "Ready for a trot?"

"I'm not sure about that."

"Come on." Jessica didn't wait for an answer, putting Rooster into a trot. Agent didn't wait for a signal from Mel but took his cue from Rooster. She resisted pulling him back to a walk. Mel was regretting her second cup of coffee now.

Pressing on the balls of her feet she raised her butt out of the saddle slightly to lessen the bounce. Her eyes watered in the wind. They trotted smoothly along the fence row. Just before the corner, Jessica slowed Rooster down to a walk. Agent followed allowing Mel to catch her breath.

The barn came into sight as they made the corner by the old pine grove in the field directly behind the house. A small covey of quails burst upward like fireworks from among the pines. Agent darted to the side. He took a couple of long, sporadic strides but then stopped dead in his tracks. Mel grabbed for the saddle horn but couldn't recover her balance. Her upper body hadn't kept up with the quick sweep to the left. She hit the ground and rolled like a tumbleweed slamming her head into a stump with a thud. The trees overhead spun. In seconds, Jessica, Rooster, and Agent were standing over her.

"Dammit, Mel, are you okay? Don't move. Where does it hurt?"

Mel tried to push herself up but winced in pain grabbing the arm that had hit the ground first.

"Is it broken?"

Mel sat herself up against the stump with Jessica's help. She held her wrist in front of her and moved it forward then backward. She sucked air in through her teeth as the throbbing in her wrist intensified. "I'll be okay."

Mel took stock. Her hip and shoulder burned with pain. Grass stains marred her shirt and jeans. She spit grass and grit from her mouth.

Jessica tied Agent and Rooster to the fence. She knelt down on one knee beside Mel taking her wrist in her hand. She rolled it over gently. "It might be fractured or something. We better get it looked at."

Mel tried protesting, but Jessica shut her down. "What the hell happened?"

"Birds spooked him. I wasn't paying attention."

"I'll go get the Gator."

Mel grabbed her sleeve as Jessica stood. "No, just give me a minute. I can walk."

Jessica knelt back down beside her with the worried look of a mother. As Mel sat there, more points of pain began to burn and throb. She brushed away dirt from her chest.

Slowly, Mel's head cleared. With Jessica holding onto her arm, she stood. The field around her began to shift and distort. She rubbed her eyes and leaned back hard on the stump that had stopped her.

Both horses walked slowly behind Jessica, and Mel hobbled along picking pine needles and dirt out of her hair.

"Well, your ass won't be the sorest thing on you tomorrow," Jessica said.

Jessica unsaddled both horses and threw hay in their stalls. The skin on Mel's wrist and hand had started to shine. She couldn't make a fist. Her fingers felt like fat sausages plump on the grill and the pain shot up through her elbow when she moved them.

"There's an Immediate Care Center in Frankfort. Probably our best bet."

Mel sat down on a bucket beside the tack room. "I'll go have it checked out. You just stay here."

"Have you seen yourself? You look like hell. Besides, you're not in any shape to drive. What if you pass out or something and have a wreck? No, I'll take you. I'll call the Arabian owner on the way."

Dizzy and stiff, Mel wondered how much this would cost her, but she didn't have too many options.

Jessica called the client before she pulled out of the driveway. She told him she had had a family emergency and wouldn't be able to meet him today. By the look of her clenched jaw, he wasn't all that happy about rescheduling.

"I understand that, sir, but I'm happy to meet with you tomorrow or any other day this week," Jessica said in a business tone.

Mel couldn't make out the client's muted words over the engine noise.

"I assure you this couldn't be helped. But like I said—" the voice cut her off.

His last comment lit her short fuse.

"Well then, respectfully, you can train your own damn horses, sir."

She tossed the phone into the cupholder between them. "Asshole."

Mel's guilt matched the pain in her wrist. They drove to Frankfort in silence. Jessica pulled into the parking lot and parked in front of the clinic.

"I'm sorry about all this," Mel said before opening her door.

"Just stay on the damn horse next time," Jessica shot back.

Mel went numb. Jessica's words knocked any courage out of her she'd felt before the ride. Today's mishap lengthened her list of mistakes that hurt others in her life. She walked ahead of Jessica into the clinic.

Jessica sat in the waiting area flipping through National Geographic magazines a little too hard while Mel filled out the paperwork the receptionist had given her. Luckily it was her right wrist that began to resemble a purple balloon. She didn't want to ask Jessica for help.

After x-rays and an exam by a kind but an ancient doctor with a noticeable drawl, Mel and Jessica climbed back in the truck. A severe sprain but nothing fractured. Mel was relieved but felt foolish about such a rookie mistake. She adjusted the Velcro strip on the soft, black brace.

"Sorry for such a dumb mistake." Mel rolled down her window and propped the braced wrist on the window ledge.

"Last spring, I'd just gotten Rooster, and I took him out for a ride. It was chilly, and I wanted to open him up a bit and see how he handled outside the arena. It had poured the night before. I knew better. I was coming up the far edge of that front hayfield at a full gallop, and a wild turkey stepped out of the bushes like he'd been sitting there waiting for us. Rooster thought it was a monster, bolted to the side, and started bucking like a bronc. He slipped in the mud. Fell flat. I tumbled off him before I could even figure out what had happened. I was lucky I didn't break my fool neck."

Mel listened in silence wondering where this was going.

"I shouldn't have said that earlier. Things happen. This is a farm for God's sake, things are going to happen." Jessica drummed her fingers on the steering wheel.

"I'm starving. You want to grab something to eat while we're out? My shout." Mel offered. *I just paid for x-rays, what's a couple of beers and steaks going to hurt?*

"Sure."

After ordering beers, Mel's conscience bore down on her. "Sorry about losing the client."

"You might have saved me a headache. I have a feeling he was going to be a pain in the ass anyway." Jessica shrugged.

"But still—I'm sure the farm could have used the money." Mel had meant that to sound subtler than it did when it came out of her mouth.

The waitress sat two beers on the table, and they ordered steak and fries.

"Two summers ago, we had this client that was a nightmare. He would call every day, and if he didn't call, he would stop by. And he had this wild handlebar mustache. When he would drop by unannounced, he expected Dad to drop everything and work his horse. A few times he did it just to avoid the hassle. But after a few months, we could tell this guy was crazy." Jessica took a sip of beer. "One night, he stopped by after coming home from a sale just as we were finishing feeding, nearly dark, and practically demanded that Dad work his horse. Dad told him he'd be happy to work it first thing in the morning, but the guy wouldn't leave. Well, Dad had had enough at this point. There was a pair of clippers laying on the barrel just inside the barn door. Dad picked up those clippers and pointed them at the man. He said real calm like, 'sir, we're tired and we're hungry. I want you to load your damn horse up in your trailer right now and get off this farm before I am obliged to trim your mustache with these clippers.'"

"Did he do it?" Mel asked.

"Damn straight."

"That sounds just like something he would do." Mel laughed and held her sore ribs. She missed her dad more than words could say.

Chapter Nine

After Mel's fall, Jessica insisted that she take the weekend off. Her boyfriend Tommy was coming over to ride, and she would make him help her feed and clean stalls.

Saturday morning Mel woke up with bruises down her side and leg. Muscles she didn't even know existed ached and burned. She eased her way down the stairs holding on to the railing.

Voices floated down the hall from the kitchen. Jessica chattered away like a parrot on her perch but stopped mid-sentence when Mel walked in.

"Tommy, this is Mel."

Tommy looked up from his plate of pancakes and wiped his hands on his jeans before sticking out a hand to Mel. "Nice to finally meet you." His drawl was thicker than she had expected.

His black hair was long and wavy, and he hadn't bothered to shave. Muscular arms stuck out of a sleeveless Mt. Dew shirt, and a tattered John Deere hat lay on the corner of the table. Mel hadn't given much thought to the kind of man Jessica would be attracted to, but now she realized she wouldn't have pictured someone like Tommy.

"Heard you took a spill," Tommy said before stabbing another bite of pancake.

"How are you feeling this morning?" Jessica piled several pieces of bacon on Tommy's plate.

"Like hell. You ought to see the bruises. I look like I've been used as a punching bag."

"Jess says you've been living up in Boston. I can't stand cities. You like it up there?"

Mel eyed him. "It's beautiful there in its own way. Lots of green. Winters get pretty cold, but the snow is magical."

"You want some pancakes?" Jessica asked.

"Just coffee for now. I think it might hurt to chew."

"Can't believe you fell off Agent. He's the calmest horse in the barn. Lucky you didn't break it." Tommy chuckled and used his fork to point at Mel's braced wrist.

"It's been a few years. Just rusty I guess."

"I broke this arm," again, Tommy used his fork to point at his left arm, "in two places trying to impress some city girl visiting our neighbor when I was ten."

Jessica rolled her eyes. "Men. Always trying to impress the ladies."

"I told her I was a trick rider and tried standing up on my mom's old mare. The damn horse stopped to take a bite of grass, but I kept going—right over her head."

"I'll be sure and remember that trick next time I'm looking to impress," Mel said.

"Good grief." Jessica slugged him in the arm. "Who did you think you were, Wild Bill Hickok?"

Tommy grinned. "Yeah, but I didn't feel so big after my mom got done chewing me out in front of the girl and the whole neighborhood. I thought I'd never hear the end of it."

"Well, it's nice to meet you, Wild Bill." Mel stood but winced with pain. "Jess, if you're sure you don't need me, I'm going to soak in a hot bath."

"You should rest. I'll put Wild Bill here to work if he ever stops eating."

Mel spent the day inside. No new jobs had been posted that interested her. She wasn't even sure she wanted to leave, but she wasn't sure she wanted to stay. They were making progress—some days.

Leftover chicken and rice was supper. After their trail ride, Jessica and Tommy had gone out to meet friends at The Goat. Mel sat with a beer on the front porch steps leaned up against the post. The night was crowded with sounds of life, but the sort of life that filled you, made you feel a part of something bigger than yourself, not like the lonesome sounds of sirens and street noise of Boston. She leaned her head back against the post and closed her eyes.

Jessica's truck came up the drive a little after nine. A few minutes later, the front door behind her. "Mind if I join you?"

"I thought you'd stay out with Tommy to paint the town."

"Not much to paint in Lebanon Springs. Besides," Jessica sat down against the opposite post with beer in hand. "He wanted to play pool after dinner with some of the guys. I wasn't up for it."

"How was the ride? Good day for it."

"Yeah, it was nice. We rode back in Sherwood Forest. There's a fallen cherry tree on the fence. I'll get Mr. Tomlin to cut it Monday. It's a big one. Might send the boys back there to help him."

Sherwood Forest was a swath of thick woods on the northwest boundary of Snow Farms. Her father had left this area untouched except for camping, trail rides, and the annual Christmas tree. It butted up against the county wildlife refuge, and her father had insisted on keeping this free from paddocks and fencing. It was his way of giving back, he said. It had been called "the woods" until Mel came along. She had started calling it Sherwood Forest after her dad had read Robin Hood to her at night. The name had stuck.

"You and Tommy, it's serious?"

"Why? Don't you like him?" Jessica's tone warned.

"Just curious."

"It's something to do. I mean, I guess it's more than that. We've broken up more times than I can count, but now we're on again. He can be too much sometimes, but he's mostly okay." Jessica stopped but then added shaking her head, "I'm not a kid."

"I was only wondering." Mel tried to sound innocent raising one hand to say *I come in peace.*

"Anyway, things aren't much different than when you left, I guess. There's always been a shortage of decent guys around here."

"And girls, if I remember," Mel said under her breath.

"Yeah, well." Jessica stood up and walked into the yard a few feet.

"Mind if I ask you how it happened? How you turned—gay?" Jessica didn't turn around.

"I didn't exactly turn gay. I think I always was. I had a crush on Emily since third grade."

"Emily Johnson? Really? Who Uncle Jerry caught you kissing? But she married some lawyer from Lexington and got herself a botched-up boob job I heard."

"Yeah?" Mel chuckled at Jessica's way with words. "Well, I don't know her story, but I was never into guys."

"But you dated Jason Wagner."

"My attempt at *normal*."

Jessica turned to her. "Did something bad happen to you when you were a kid?"

Mel was unfortunately used to this question. Even open-minded friends had asked it. "I wasn't molested or anything like that, if that's what you're asking."

"That's good." Jessica turned and stared out into the darkened field.

"Does it bother you? Me being gay?"

Jessica waited before answering. "It's none of my business who you sleep with, but it's a little weird. I don't know anybody that's gay."

Mel laughed. "You kind of do now."

Jessica raised her brows. "Besides you, I mean."

Mel went inside and grabbed two more beers. Tonight was as good a time as any to bring up uncomfortable subjects. She had checked her bank account earlier, and the dwindling number gave her a new burst of panicked boldness.

She handed Jessica a beer. "How are things? I mean here on the farm." Mel held her breath. She wasn't as concerned about the answer as she was about how Jessica might react to the question.

Jessica exhaled. "Could be better."

Mel sat in the swing unsure if Jessica would continue. She dreaded the thought of this conversation dragging out over days, but she didn't want to come right out and say she needed money.

"People were used to Dad. They have a hard time seeing me as a legit trainer and not just Thomas' little girl."

"Think they'll come around?"

"Some of the locals tried to be polite about it, said they didn't want to overwhelm me, wanted to give me time to grieve, but I knew what they were doing. They don't realize he'd been letting me do a lot of the training for the past couple of years." Jessica turned to Mel abruptly. "Do you need money? I never even thought to ask."

"I'm fine." Mel cursed herself. Her shrinking finances had been the whole reason for bringing up this touchy subject. "I have a little bit of savings." Mel tried to salvage the situation, but she was out of practice being honest with herself.

They finished their beers listening to the sounds of the night. Mel stood up to leave mad at herself for letting this opportunity slip away.

Jessica broke the silence. "I'm no good at the books."

Mel waited in the doorway.

"I tried but I can't make heads or tails out of Dad's records. They're a disaster."

"I can look over them if you want. I got pretty handy at that kind of thing," Mel offered.

"I can show you the ledgers this week if you're up to it."

"I'll take a look."

Mel's body ached as she climbed the stairs. Her wrist had turned new shades of blue and purple throughout the day.

After seeing the state of Mel on Monday, Mr. Tomlin brought in some sort of homemade ointment his mother used to make, and the bruising had dissipated surprisingly fast.

Jessica had hinted at her riding again all week. By Saturday morning, she was downright pushy. "Just a few turns around the round pen. You know what they say about getting back on a horse after it has bucked you off."

Mel frowned. "Agent didn't buck me off. I fell off."

"All the same." Jessica gave her a told-you-so look.

Mel reluctantly agreed, holding her breath and taking just enough turns around the pen to satisfy Jessica.

That evening, Jessica called her into their dad's office. Tan ledgers were spread out across the top of the dark oak desk with years of coffee stains and water rings.

The entire financial history of Snow Farms was still kept by hand. They spent the weekend buried beneath ledgers, bills, and account records. Their father's presence was strong in handwritten numbers and notes. Piles of papers pulled from drawers, shelves, and filing cabinets covered the floor. They even found faded notes written by their grandfather when he was running the farm.

"No wonder you couldn't make heads or tails of this." Mel swept her hand across the chaotic piles.

"I knew he wasn't meticulous, but this is insane."

Training and payment records were sporadic, but it looked like he had kept every single piece of paper, letter, or photograph he had ever received. Thomas Snow may have been a top-notch trainer, but the room suggested he was more packrat than accountant.

Sunday afternoon, while digging through papers in the bottom drawer of the ominous beast of a desk, Jessica found an envelope stuck to the back of a 1984 Farmers'

Almanac with a thousand dollars in it. The faded pencil scribble on the outside of the envelope looked like chicken scratch and wasn't their father's handwriting. Neither could make out more than a few letters.

"I wonder how long that's been hiding there?" Jessica asked.

"From the looks of it, since the Truman era." Mel held the envelope up to the light.

They also unearthed their father's pipe under a stack of papers, and his stash of Pappy Van Winkle Bourbon, aged twenty years, in the bottom drawer.

"We should have a drink—to Dad," Jessica suggested.

Mel grabbed two whiskey glasses out of the glass cupboard beside the bookcase. They sat down on the floor amongst the stacks of paper and leaned their backs against the old desk. Jessica poured bourbon into the glasses on the floor between them.

"To Dad." Jessica raised her glass.

"To Dad," Mel echoed. The smooth burn warmed her chest and head. She reached above her for the pipe. "Mind if I have this?"

"You going to smoke it?"

"I don't know, maybe."

Jessica shrugged and poured two more shots into the glasses between them.

"I miss him." Jessica swirled the dark amber in her glass.

"I do too."

"We used to go at it after you left, maybe even more than you two, but we sure had a lot of fun too. He used to tell me 'few people get to do what they really love to do. We're the lucky ones.'" Jessica tossed the bourbon down her throat and said nothing more.

Mel spent the evenings that week entering figures into her laptop. Jessica hadn't seen the need for this extra hassle but was impressed when Mel showed her the charts that broke down their monthly expenditures by the end of the week. The numbers weren't as impressive. Beyond disorganized and long-neglected, the farm was like a ship with a slow and steady leak—several of them.

They wouldn't be out on their ass anytime soon. This was the good news. But they would need to tighten their belts if they wanted this land to remain. In a stack of unopened mail on the floor by the desk, Mel found records of two small bank loans Jessica didn't know existed. This sent Mel digging into the stacks of mail collecting dust by the microwave. There she found overdue notices but stopped shy of jumping on Jessica for her lack of organization.

When Mel went into town on a feed run later that week, she stopped by the bank to chat with the bank manager about the two loans she had found. The manager had been one of her dad's old pool buddies at The Goat, so the first few minutes were spent maneuvering around questions about her disappearance and return. Mel stayed patient and friendly with a big southern smile pasted on her face while she spoke vaguely of her return.

Her patience was rewarded. The manager didn't even have to pull up the farm records when Mel asked him about the two loans. One had been for a new hay baler last fall, the second had been for some type of family emergency. Mel had seen the hay baler still shiny in the equipment barn, but when she pressed him about the family emergency, he told her that's all he knew.

"I gave the okay on that loan myself after your daddy came to see me."

"But he didn't say what it was for?" Mel pressed him.

"Didn't need to." The bank manager leaned back in his chair. "I've known your daddy a long time, and if he said he needed money for a family emergency that's exactly what it was for."

Mel thanked him for his time and left the bank puzzled. Rural life had a mysterious code about it. At dinner, she explained the odd exchange to Jessica.

"What sort of family emergency?" Jessica asked.

"He didn't know or at least wouldn't say."

"And how much is that one?"

"Almost nine thousand. It was taken out in May. I made a payment on both and told him we'd catch it up in the next few months."

"Dad, what the hell were you up to?" Jessica said under her breath.

Chapter Ten

Jessica was trying as she had promised. Saturday morning while they set new fence posts for a larger round pen out beyond the dry lots, Mel listened to Jessica share her plans for a larger breeding program.

"Of course, better studs cost more, but the babies sell better. And with a few months of training, the two-year-olds would definitely bring in more." Jessica jabbed the posthole diggers into the hard ground.

"More vet bills though and feed. Isn't it better just to stick to training other people's horses?"

"I don't want to be stuck training other people's horses for the rest of my life." Jessica shot back.

"Sorry. I thought that's what you wanted." Mel stopped tamping the fresh dirt around the new post and looked at her sister.

"It is. Sort of. I just get tired of it sometimes. I'm not even thirty yet and my bones creak in the morning." Jessica kicked more dirt into the hole. "I don't think I'd want to be breaking in two-year-olds when I'm sixty, and I don't see the place getting ahead unless I change some things around here."

"Ever think about leasing part of the land out for farming?"

Jessica stopped the posthole diggers mid-strike. "I'd take a job in town before I'd let that happen. This land isn't going to be used for some crapload of beans or corn."

This made Mel laugh. "You sound just like Dad and Grandpa. Remember Dad always saying he'd sell his left liver before he let any of this place go?"

Jessica laughed and dug the posthole diggers into the hard ground. "He had a way with words, didn't he?"

"So, upping the ante in the breeding program would be a long-term project. What about having our own stud?"

"I've thought of that, I just don't know if it's worth the hassle. They can be a headache to handle. For now, the babies will give us some breathing room. Maybe train up a couple of young guys who don't mind taking a beating with the rowdier ones." Jessica wiped the sweat from her forehead with her sleeve. "What are your long-term plans?"

Mel looked at Jessica quickly but then looked away. "I'm not sure."

Jessica walked to the next marked spot and started digging. "You're different than you used to be."

"How so?"

"I remember you being so sure of yourself when you graduated. You had it all planned out. Going to college and then helping Dad with the business. You used to want to buy sheep, remember? Dad always said that was a terrible idea." Jessica laughed.

Mel remembered her father saying that sheep stunk worse than horses or cows put together and there would never be sheep on Snow lands as long as he was alive. "Things change," was all Mel answered.

"You just seem like you're sort of waiting for something bad to happen to you. Like you're walking around scared of your own shadow."

"Do you blame me? Look at what happened." Mel heard her own bitter tone.

"I ain't going to say that wasn't a shitty deal you got. But maybe it's time to stop being stuck back there with what happened."

Jessica's phone rang. She leaned the posthole diggers against the wheelbarrow and walked to the barn office. Mel took over the digging and with each strike of the metal

73

against the hardened earth, she screamed inside. Her head was cloudy but the view of herself through Jessica's eyes was crystal clear. Her dad used to tell Mel she had more gumption than three grown men. This is what she had returned to find.

It was Halloween, but Mel and Jessica were still in short sleeves. The cracked land needed a slow, soaking rain, but nothing indicated there would be one anytime soon.

One fleece and one hoodie hung over the top board of the round pen. Mel stood outside the pen with her elbows poked through the opening between the top and second board, her chin resting on her hands and one foot propped on the bottom board. Jessica had surprised her with a farm credit card and a pair of Ariats last week. The dust that settled in the brown leather creases made Mel smile.

Jessica kissed to a young roan colt on a lunge line surrounded by a cloud of dust. She held the line in one hand and a long lunge whip in the other with both arms stretched out like a crucifix. She tapped his round hindquarters with the whip each time he slowed to a walk, his head held high and his eyes wild, watching her every move. Jessica called this their "what the fuck" look.

New clients in Frankfort had called this week wanting to hire Jessica as a sort of broker as well as a trainer for future horse sales. This was an option Jessica hadn't thought of, but it piqued her interest. The Jacksons had relocated from Portland and were professors at the University of Kentucky. They owned Lippitt Morgans, the classic bloodlines, they had explained, and raised foals from an impressive stud they called Gus. Horses had been a family business, one they kept going on the side even with full-time jobs.

A handful of their own two-year-olds were ready to be broken in. Jessica would train these through the winter and sell them in the spring sale. Many of Snows' babies were out of a Mr. San Peppy stud, so they would bring a pretty penny when it came time to sell. Although still young, they had big round hindquarters that quarter horse people looked for in a young horse. Spring sales held the best luck at prices when horse lovers shook off their cabin fever and went in search of a new horse for the warm, sunlit trails.

Jessica had asked Mel to work up an exercise rotation for the older mares and geldings. After feeding she'd ride through the list and by doing so, she had ridden away her nervousness and enjoyed being back in the saddle. Even more than this, Mel felt useful.

This weekend was Mel's real farm test. Jessica and Tommy were going to Bowling Green for a sale, and Mel had convinced Jessica to take the whole weekend off and leave the farm work to her. She had been more surprised than anyone when Jessica reluctantly agreed.

Tommy had stopped by more often these last few weeks, mostly on weekends, usually staying the night. Mel kept to herself when he came avoiding the third wheel feeling that crept in over dinner or a movie.

She still eyed him with skepticism, but she was pretty sure she wouldn't have minded him so much if he didn't make himself at home so easily while she continued to navigate her place here. He had a history with Jessica, this land, and even with their dad, that Mel envied. Tommy was lighthearted and joked often. Maybe he was good for Jessica who leaned toward the intense side of life.

Chapter Eleven

Saturday morning started early, earlier than normal. When Mel met Jessica in the kitchen, Jessica was already running on full steam.

"I was up early so I grained before hooking up the truck and trailer. All that's left is hay and water." She poured coffee into a travel mug without looking across the room. Mel glanced at the clock above the microwave. It wasn't even six.

"Are you going to come back from the hotel in the morning to grain too?" Mel asked.

"What? I was already up. No sense wasting time."

"You do think I can handle the farm for one weekend without you, right?"

"Of course, I do. Don't be silly."

"Whatever you need to tell yourself." Mel filled her cup with the remaining coffee and started a fresh pot.

"Listen, just do the minimum. It's the weekend. Take it easy."

"Yeah, because that's what you always do on the weekends, right?" Mel was enjoying this. "Everything will be fine, Jess. I'll follow every single direction you wrote out. I'll clean the stalls, maybe I'll take a ride to the creek, but don't spend your weekend away worrying about me."

"A ride?" Jessica stopped stirring her coffee. "I don't think that's such a good idea."

"Will you relax, *Mom*? I'll text you before and after I ride. That way you'll know I'm not unconscious in a ditch somewhere."

"Unconscious? Shit. I think we should just drive back tonight."

Mel laughed. "Will you listen to yourself? I'm not five. I'll be okay."

Jessica frowned and walked out the back door.

After listening to several bursts of repeated instructions shouted out the truck window, Mel saw the taillights fade around the bend in the driveway. "Can you believe she finally left?" Mel scratched Sam Houston's head as he stared down the drive like a forgotten child. "Come on. Let's get to work."

Mel finished her chores by ten. She even took the time to scrub off the algae in the watering trough in Tiny Pete's paddock. Lunch would be a sandwich and a thermos of ice-cold sweet tea in Clancy's field by the deep bend in Timber Creek where the geese landed. Mel rode daily now, but today was different, meaningful. She'd been looking forward to this ride all week, but this morning she realized she'd been looking forward to this ride for over twelve years in the deepest, most hidden places of her soul. Her stomach flipped in anticipation.

She saddled Agent, the leather familiar to her dry, calloused hands. The packed lunch was tucked into her dad's old saddlebags and tied behind the saddle. Her skin tingled as she grabbed the horn and swung up into the saddle, almost effortlessly now.

At the back of the barn, and with one leg wrapped around the horn for balance, Mel stopped and gazed out across the fields. Agent waited for her command. She texted Jessica as she had promised. *Going for a ride. Text you when I'm back.* Mel turned to look in the shadowy barn aisle, remembering the day she returned. Three months had changed things. Swinging her leg back over, she pressed her knees into Agent's side. "Let's go, old man."

Agent sauntered along as if he knew what was on Mel's mind. Even though her stomach growled, she decided to take the long way to Clancy's field. This was her ride, her time to take it all in. The land, the years, the memories.

One hand holding the reins and one hand placed just below the bend of her leg at the hip. She rode along listening to grass and trees rustle and the steady creaking of leather beneath her. Sam Houston darted in and out of sight as he wandered the tree line beside her. It was a cooler morning and the fresh smells of the countryside danced upon the light breeze. She was glad she'd kept her fleece. Maybe autumn had finally decided to stick around.

The tall meadow grasses rippled. Hills that rose and fell with an almost deliberate finesse were cut with the sharp contrast of tree lines and fence rows. Agent's ears twitched back and forth in front of her listening to all the sounds she heard and many she couldn't. They rode along the edge of the pond watching turtles sunbathe on logs that jutted out into the dense green water. Her Dad's old John boat rested upside down against a fallen tree.

This was the pond she had learned to swim in when she was six. Her screams had filled the hot, summer air when the cold, slimy mud squished between her toes. Her mom had protested from the bank, "but Thomas, there's no telling what's in that water." Her dad yelled back, "there's a Mel in this water, that's what," before grabbing Mel around her waist and tossing her up in the air. Mel squealed with delight before her head disappeared under the murky water.

Mel reached the back gate and hesitated before leaning over to unclasp the latch. She was still wobbly at opening gates on horseback, but in truth, she always had been. Most often she lost hold of the gate while concentrating on the horse, or lost control of a bewildered horse by chaotic, unclear commands.

Today would be different. No one was around to critique or suggest she do things another way. Agent and Mel moved as if they had merged into one larger beast and each command and step were perfectly aligned. After hooking the latch in place on the other side, she patted Agent's shoulder. "We did it." He snorted as if in agreement.

Six Canadian geese sat like kings and queens on thrones in the creek's bend. In this spot, the creek widened, and the water slowed until the banks narrowed again at the edge of the field, the water rushing down a series of rocks and logs. She swung off Agent and tied the reins a lower sycamore branch. The large flat rock that had her name etched in the side would be her picnic table.

Mel ran her fingers over the edge of each letter as the wind brushed across her cheek making her shiver. The E and S were larger than the rest of the letters. It had been difficult scribing on stone with her grandfather's old, brown-handled Case pocketknife. She dug the knife out of her pocket and held it in her open hand. Her dad had given it to her for her twelfth birthday saying, "Don't lose it. It's a part of the family." It had taken many visits going over the same crooked lines again and again.

The geese honked in protest of Mel's intrusion.

"Geese stick together; they're like a family," her father had said as they sat on this same rock after an argument about a sleepover.

Her mother would have understood how humiliating it would have been to be the only girl in class not allowed to go.

"If one's injured or tired, another one stays with him. Me and you and little Jess have to stick together now. I know you're angry with me, but I sure do love you and your little sister."

Mel remembered the look in his eyes. They were a lot alike, him and her, they didn't always know how to talk about the things that bothered them. Mel wished she could talk to him now.

She took a bite of cucumber sandwich and watched the geese dunk their heads underwater with their tail feathers pointed to the heavens. Mel thought about Patricia. Their conversations on the metro, by the river, in the kitchen, in their bed at night. Patricia had told Mel many times that it felt like she wasn't really living life, she was just existing behind crumbling walls. What would Patricia say if she saw her now?

After lunch, she untied Agent and twisted her way through the maze of trees by the creek. Mel ran her hand along the rough, flaky bark of the thin river birch as she passed each one. The wild cane and river grass on the water's edge swayed in the afternoon wind. Most of the ash trees by the creek had been killed off by the ash borer that had spread through these parts. It was hard to imagine that an insect smaller than a penny could cause so much destruction, but here they stood leafless, hollow, and frail. The winds would eventually knock them down before they returned again to the land.

Mel heard the dreaded noise before she entered the barn to turn the lights off that evening. Finding the young chestnut mare thrashing in her stall, Mel pleaded with herself to stay calm. She opened the stall door to observe. Maybe she just needed a good roll.

Mel waited. The mare stood up but kicked her back leg toward her stomach every few seconds and slung her head from side to side biting at her belly. Mel tossed a small handful of grain in the corner bin. This should have been like honey to a bear, but the mare smelled it and turned away, doing the same to the flake of hay Mel brought to the door. It was as Mel feared; the mare showed the beginning stages of colic.

Mel's hands shook as she found the veterinarian's emergency number in her contacts. A calm woman with a soft voice answered the call and took the information Mel provided.

"Dr. Neil's on call tonight. She'll call you in a few minutes. In the meantime, walk the mare and try your best not to let her lay down."

"Sure. Sure. How long will it take Dr. Neil to get here?" Mel tried to keep her voice steady.

"I'd say no longer than thirty minutes, but she'll call you. Just keep the mare walking if at all possible."

Mel grabbed a halter from the tack room on the way back to the stall. The mare was rolling again. Luckily, the mare's head was facing the stall door. In between a roll, Mel fastened the halter and lead line around her head.

"Come on, girl. You can do it." Mel clucked her tongue and pulled up on the lead line putting pressure on the mare's head. The mare stood and shook the sawdust from her back.

Dr. Neil called as Mel was leading the mare out of her stall. She was leaving her house in five minutes. Mel detected an accent in the steady voice. She was only twenty minutes away, but those twenty minutes would feel like hours with a colicky horse in tow.

Four large animal vets worked out of the clinic. It was Kentucky after all—the need was great. It was just Mel's luck that the one on call was the only one she hadn't met. She hoped to God she knew what she was doing.

This weekend of all weekends. She walked to the end of the hall by the trophy case, the mare following slowly. She had done this many times with her father and the routine came flooding back to her.

Colic was like the worst stomachache you could imagine. That's how her dad had described it when Mel was a kid. Only, with a horse, they just about go crazy with the pain. You had to keep the horse from thrashing around or it could end up with a twisted gut, and that meant an expensive surgery or a painful death.

It was almost midnight. Mel wrestled with whether to call Jessica. She would have to admit failure if she called her, but she might regret not calling if the mare turned for the worse.

She watched the mare as they made the turn at the end of the hall. The mare tried to bite her side as she turned the corner.

"I know it hurts, girl. The vet's on the way." Mel desperately wished the horse could understand.

Back and forth from one end of the barn to the other for as long as it took. When she was old enough, she and her father had taken turns walking, getting coffee, telling stories to pass the time, and eating egg sandwiches at daybreak. When Jessica was younger, she would insist on staying with them but would be asleep on a hay bale curled up with a cat within an hour. Tonight, Sam Houston took Jessica's place and curled up against the wall by the tack room. Mel listened to each step. She whistled an old George Strait song while she walked.

The headlights illuminated the saddle racks in the open tack room, and relief washed over Mel. The vet appeared in the doorway, a bucket in each hand. Mel quickened her step to meet her at that end of the barn.

"I'm Dr. Katherine Neil." She sat the buckets down to her side and stretched out her hand.

A firm grip took Mel's hand. "Thanks for coming. I'm Mel, Jessica's sister. She's at a sale in Bowling Green this weekend."

"This our patient?" Without waiting for an answer, the vet placed the stethoscope in her ears and leaned in toward the mare's belly. Her small, slender fingers moved the end of the stethoscope to different spots on the mare listening intently with her tongue stuck in her cheek.

Mel watched her quietly. She was short and petite, looking more like a jockey than a vet, and Mel wondered if she was even strong enough to be a vet. She took off her brown barn jacket, making her look even smaller, rolled up her sleeves, and put on a long, clear glove reaching to her shoulder.

An orange newsy cap added to the jockey image. Her hair was short and blonde with bangs that hung over one eyebrow. Her jeans were tucked in tall, green rubber boots.

Mel stood alert at the horse's head as the vet continued her examination. The mare laid her ears back in protest and stomped her front hoof but stood still.

"Not much movement going on in there. We'll give her some oil." Dr. Neil removed the glove and tossed it in one of the buckets. "When did you first notice her? Has she been off her feed?"

"Right before I called your office. She ate her grain and hay this evening like normal, but I'd just come out to lock up for the night."

"Probably the cooler weather. Always causes problems."

Dr. Neil attached the tube to the metal plunging device immersed in the bucket of mineral oil.

"Hold her head still for me." With precision, Dr. Neil ran the tube into the mare's nose navigating the path to her stomach like she was reading a map. The mare stood still with her ears pinned back. Mel was grateful for the mare's docile nature, not sure if she could have handled a more rambunctious one. She held off a tinge of panic in not calling Jessica.

"You just visiting? You're from Boston, right?"

Mel wondered how she knew but reminded herself that this was a small town and her return was no doubt big news in the small-town grapevine. "Yeah, I mean no. I'm from Boston, but I'm not visiting. I'm moving back, I think."

"Missed these nights walking colicky horses, eh? Boston's nice. I was there a few years back for a conference. Visited Paul Revere's house. You've been there?"

Mel instinctively imagined seeing this woman across a busy Boston street. "Believe it or not, I never went in twelve years. I always meant to."

Dr. Neil laughed reaching out for Mel's hand and placing it on the tube going into the mare's nose. "Here, hold this steady for me."

"I grew up in Scotland, south of Glasgow mostly." Dr. Neil pumped the mineral oil into the mare's stomach. "Americans always ask me if I've seen the Loch Ness Monster. They're disappointed when they learn I've never even been to Loch Ness. I guess they think the lake must be right next door to every home in Scotland."

Giving the mare a gentle rub between the eyes, Dr. Neil began to slowly pull the tube from the mare's nose. "There you go, little one. We'll let that work for a few minutes. Looks like you know what you're doing here."

"I used to have to do this with Dad. It all came back to me when I saw her thrashing around in her stall. It's so frustrating, knowing they're in pain but can't let you know. Seems helpless, you know?"

"It gave you a fright, I'm sure. It's a good thing you caught it when you did. I'm used to them being so much worse by the time I arrive."

"Thanks for coming, Dr. Neil. Would you like coffee or something? I finally talked Jessica into putting a coffee pot in the barn office." Mel wasn't ready for her to leave, and she wasn't ready to be alone with a sick horse.

"It's just Katherine, please. I'd love a cup. I'll hang around for a bit and see how she goes as long as I don't get another call. On nights like this, these calls usually come in threes. If one horse colics you can bet another one somewhere is thinking about it."

Mel and Katherine walked and talked with coffee in hand up and down the barn aisle. The mare ambled along behind them. If they stopped walking the mare tried to lay down.

Katherine had moved to Kentucky four years ago after finishing her degree at Ohio State. Kentucky had been her mecca, and so it was an easy job to accept.

"Do you miss Scotland?"

"Oh sure. I try and go back each year. My mum and dad are in Edinburgh now; mum has family there. I miss the hills and the green." Her eyes gleamed. "If the sunset here hits the bluegrass on the hills just right, I get a wee bit homesick."

They made another turn by the stack of alfalfa hay and the mare reached out her neck to grab a bite. "That's a good sign." Katherine gave another listen to the mare's stomach. "I think we're getting some movement now. We'll give her a few more turns about the aisle."

She was right. Two more times down and back and the mare stopped and produced a pile of manure in the middle of the aisle. After a scare like this, a reeking pile of manure was cause for a celebration in the horse world.

"Looks like we're in the clear. Mind if I wash up my equipment before I leave?"

"Of course." Mel pointed to the wash stall at the end of the aisle.

Mel walked the mare a few more turns and led her to the stall. She took a sip of water and snatched a bite from the small flake of hay in the corner of the stall.

Katherine's phone rang while she rinsed the equipment. "Hey. Yeah, I'm finishing up. Looks like I'll be home within the hour. No sense waiting up."

Mel shoveled the pile of manure into a wheelbarrow telling herself she shouldn't eavesdrop. Over an hour had passed since Katherine's arrival, and Mel had talked with this stranger without her guard up. She walked Katherine out to her Jeep sorry to see her leave.

"It was nice to meet you, and thanks again for coming. You really saved me—and the mare tonight. I didn't want to have to call Jessica."

"You handled it like a pro. There's nothing you could have done until she showed signs, and then you did the right thing. I'm glad you caught it in time. Made my job easier. I'll call and check up tomorrow." Katherine climbed in and started the engine, leaning out the window with a grin. "I guess I should say welcome home."

Mel stood in the cool night air and watched the Jeep go down the drive. *Home.* Is that really where she was?

There was no use trying to sleep in the house tonight, she would only worry and hear imagined noises coming from the barn. She went inside and grabbed a cot and sleeping bag. Like nights of her childhood, she lay in the quiet darkness of the office with the door cracked and fell asleep listening to the snorts and nickers that swept through the barn and wondering when she might next see Dr. Neil.

Chapter Twelve

If Mel had been expecting a pat on the back from Jessica for a job well done, she was mistaken.

"Why the hell didn't you call me?" Jessica raised her voice after Mel told her, throwing a duffle bag in the corner and storming out the back door.

Mel followed her with dread. "It was midnight, and I called the vet. You made me save the number."

"Goddamn it, Mel. We could have lost a horse—a client's horse—all because you were too stubborn to call me."

"I wasn't being stubborn. I was taking care of things. You couldn't have done anything from two hours away anyway. Besides, it worked out. Dr. Neil came out and stayed until she was in the clear."

"What if she'd gotten worse? What if she'd twisted her gut? What were you going to do then?" Jessica opened the stall door and went in. She ran her hand along the mare's stomach.

"If she would have gotten worse, I would have called you. You left me in charge, and I did exactly what you would have done. I didn't always live in Boston, remember."

"That's not the point, Mel. You had no right taking a chance like that. You had no right." Jessica slammed the stall door shut. The mare's head jerked up from a pile of hay.

Mel took a deep breath before she spoke. "I have no right? No right being here—making decisions. No right to this land, this farm. Is that what you really want to say?"

"I didn't mean that."

"I think you might."

"Mel, please. That's not what I meant. But things could have gone bad."

"You think I don't know that? You think I wasn't terrified?" Mel pointed inside the barn. "I slept in the fucking office last night because I was scared something else would happen before you got home."

Jessica stormed out to the trailer and started unloading tack. Mel followed her sister at a march.

"You want me to leave? I'll go," Mel shouted. *And go where?*

"No, I don't want you to leave." Jessica flung a saddle onto the ground. "You should have called me. This was serious."

Mel picked up the saddle and slung it over her shoulder. "I know it was serious, and I treated it seriously."

Jessica slammed the trailer door shut. "I would have been responsible if that horse would have died."

"No, I would have been," Mel shouted back. "You left me to see to things. I did. You're not the only one who can do things around here."

Mel threw the saddle to the ground and stormed back into the barn. She didn't have the patience to saddle a horse, so she cranked the dirt bike by the office door and tore off through the side pasture. Tears clouded her eyes as she drove.

She sat by the creek and cried. Minnows swam frantically in the shallow edge of the creek, dashing between rocks and debris. Yesterday, this spot had comforted her. Yesterday, she had felt like she had been right in returning. The sun lowered in the sky, but Mel remained. If Jessica didn't want her here, she wouldn't fight her for the farm. She didn't have that kind of fight left in her. She mulled over her options but admitted they were few. Mel picked up an oval rock from the edge of the bank and ran her thumb over the smooth, cool surface.

Sam Houston nuzzled up against Mel's leg. She turned to see Jessica coming up behind her on Rooster but returned her gaze to the creek without a word. Jessica tied Rooster to a branch and sat down beside her.

"I may have overreacted earlier," Jessica said.

Mel remained silent tossing the rock she had been holding into the creek. The minnows shifted course and darted in all directions. Jessica cleared her throat and continued. "What I mean to say is I overreacted earlier. I did leave you to look after things."

"I wasn't being stubborn by not calling you." Mel still didn't look up.

"Dr. Neil called. She said you handled the whole thing well. She said she was glad I finally put a coffee pot in the office."

"I didn't call because I wanted to prove to you that I could do this, because I wanted you to trust me."

"You're right. You did exactly what I would have done. I guess I'm just not that good at giving up control. Dad—after you—" Jessica paused. "As he got older, he didn't always keep up on things. I guess I'm just used to carrying the weight of this place."

"What do you mean?"

"He was a great trainer, none better, but he wasn't always on top of things around here and it had been getting worse."

"I'm still having nightmares about the mess in his office." Mel finally turned toward Jessica.

"That's not the half of it. He was starting to forget things—major things, you know? He never said anything, but I think that's why he started having me do more of the training."

"You think he had dementia or something?"

"I don't know. I never said anything. But there were times—I mean, he wasn't that old, but he sure acted older than he was sometimes."

Mel couldn't see her dad as an old man.

"I'm sorry I freaked. I do trust you, Mel. And I do want you here. If you left now—again—." Jessica stood without warning and swung up onto Rooster.

Mel turned and watched her sister ride back across the field, never looking back.

It was after dark when Mel returned to the barn. Four horses stood tied in the barn aisle. She had picked up three young geldings to train and sell and a nice little Hancock filly that was green broke.

Jessica pulled an envelope from her pocket.

"This came in the mail. It was addressed to the farm, but it's for you."

Inside the envelope was a yellow post-it attached to a sheet of paper. *Attached is the appraisal you requested. A buyout would be straightforward. Let me know how you wish to proceed.*

"You're leaving?" Jessica asked.

Mel stared at Jessica unsure of what to say. "I just wanted to know my options."

"And what are my options? You know I can't afford to buy you out. It would ruin me."

"I would never do that," Mel stated emphatically.

"I'm barely making ends meet as it is."

"This was from before. When I didn't know if we could work things out."

"And now?" Jessica asked.

Mel shrugged and looked down at the papers in her hand. She knew she wanted to stay more than anything, but maybe Jessica was right before. Maybe she had stayed gone too long.

Jessica patted the filly on the hindquarters. "She was a bargain. Good bloodline. A guy was selling off his stock and moving to Michigan. I figured we could throw a few months of training on her without much trouble. I had thought you'd want something with a bit more pep—in the future."

"Jess." Mel waited for her sister to look at her. "You were right before. I don't know what I want anymore. Hell, I don't even think I know who I am anymore. But I'd like to stay and figure things out."

Jessica cleared her throat and wiped her eyes quickly with the edge of her sleeve. "This mare will need a strong hand for a bit, but I think you can handle her. I was thinking she looks like a Bonnie, but you can call her whatever you want."

Mel moved closer and looked into the horse's eyes. "Bonnie sounds about right."

Chapter Thirteen

The Lebanon Springs Pioneer and Founder's Day Festival that was held annually on the first Saturday of November was a mouthful. Her dad used to say the name was bigger than the whole damn town.

Jessica and Mel arrived before noon and parked the truck in the open field beside the fairgrounds at the edge of town. It was prime parking for the fireworks at nightfall. Jessica had chosen a spot close to the exit to beat the exodus after the finale. They had stuffed blankets behind the seats for the evening cold.

It was chilly but sunny. People had complained over the years and tried to move the festival to summer, yet it had remained—the unofficial kick-off of the holiday season.

The shrieks and screams of children reached them before they ever left the field. Turning the corner by the liquor store, throngs of people crowded onto the streets, many more than the population of Lebanon Springs. A band played country classics on the main stage of the courthouse lawn.

Booths ran along the four streets surrounding the courthouse. Late fall vegetables, Christmas ornaments, fresh apple pies, local crafts, and coon skin caps. You could find it all here. Kids could bob for apples, have their faces painted, and ride ponies for a dollar. There was even a huge plastic cow with rubber udders that the kids could "milk" beside the petting zoo.

The first stop was hot chocolate with marshmallows just like when they were kids. The smell of roasted ears of corn and sickeningly sweet funnel cakes filled the air as they maneuvered through the crowd.

"I think I'll have to break down and buy a funnel cake later. Want to split one?" Mel smelled the air.

"No way. They're way too greasy." Jessica pointed to the tent on their right. "I want to look in there. I need new socks."

The tent was crowded so Mel waited outside. She searched the passing crowd for familiar faces, not at all sure she wanted to see one. A teenage couple passed eating a funnel cake together, smiling as only young love smiled. The fall before she had left, she had come to this festival with Jason Wagoner. They had had a good time, Jason was always a kind, funny sort of guy, but Mel was sure they'd never looked in love like this couple.

"Feel these. Aren't they soft?" Jessica stuck a pair of alpaca socks out of the tent right in Mel's face.

"Yeah, those are nice."

"I'm going to buy a couple pairs. I'll get you some too."

Before Mel had a chance to say anything else, Jessica disappeared into the crowded tent again. Looking up, Mel's breath caught in her throat. A man coming out of the leather goods tent on the opposite side of the street favored Uncle Jerry. She saw it wasn't him, but she was nonetheless angry with herself for the fear that still gripped her at the thought of this man.

When they had been digging postholes a few weeks back, Jessica had said Mel was scared of her own shadow. There was a lot of truth in that. In Boston, Mel had been afraid to let her guard down in case she got hurt again. Here, with seeing the Uncle Jerry look-alike, she was afraid too—of this second chance being too good to be true.

As was often the case, Jessica was hungry, so Mel followed as she made a beeline to the food tent after paying for the socks. Jessica stood in line for a pulled pork sandwich, and Mel opted for a corndog and fries. Corndogs were her weakness. Jessica's line was twice as long. The round tables in the middle of the tents were full, so Mel waved to her from a straw bale she'd found in the corner next to the raffle table. This year they were raffling a push mower and a set of iron skillets.

"Mel? I thought I saw you over here." Katherine Neil, the vet, stood in front of her with a smile.

"Hi there. It's lunchtime for you too?"

"Just finished. I went with the pulled pork, although now I might have to get a corndog before I leave." Katherine pointed at Mel's plate in her lap. "That looks delicious."

"Jessica went for the sandwich too. She's still in line. To me, nothing tastes better than a corndog at a county festival. Want to sit?"

"Thanks, but no. I'm supposed to judge the hat-making contest in a few minutes. Just came over to say hi."

"Listen, thanks again for your help the other night. Jessica said you called."

"Any time, although I hope for no colicky horses for a long while."

Jessica walked up behind Katherine. "Here you are. Oh, hi, Dr. Neil. Want to join us?"

"Sorry. Headed to judge the hats."

Jessica turned to Mel with a gleam. "Let's go watch."

Mel didn't see the draw of a hat contest, but she was happy to continue talking to Katherine.

"Did Nathan come?" Jessica asked.

"He's wandering around somewhere. I haven't seen him since we arrived."

Nathan. That must be who called her the other night.

"How did you get roped into judging a hat contest?" Mel asked.

"For some reason, it's the vets' thing. Not sure when it started. It was going on when I got here. Each year they get one of us to judge the hat competition."

Mel looked at Jessica. "I don't remember this from before. Is it new?"

"They added it seven or eight years ago. Can't remember. The mayor's wife." Jessica rolled her eyes. "Each year there's a theme, right?" Jessica looked to Katherine for confirmation.

Katherine nodded.

"I had to judge last year too," Katherine answered. "I think there's a bit of seniority being thrown around since I'm the newest vet, but I don't mind. I enjoyed it last year."

Mel liked the cheerful nature of this woman. She made her feel lighthearted like the first warm day of spring.

When they reached the tent, Mel and Jessica found seats and finished their food. Her corndog was lukewarm by now but dipped in mustard it was still heavenly. This year's hat theme was "movie night." The hats were bright and gaudy with every interpretation of movie night one could imagine. Mel watched Katherine walk up and down the stage in front of the twenty or so women wearing their hats, a requirement of the competition, talking and laughing with each one.

Nathan's a lucky guy. Mel blushed at the thought.

Just before twilight that evening, Mel and Jessica made their way back to the truck. Spreading the blankets in the back, they leaned against two hay bales Jessica had tossed in before leaving the barn that morning. They had coffee in a thermos and Jessica poured two cups. Mel balanced a funnel cake on her knee.

"Better than I even remembered," Mel said.

Jessica shuddered.

"You sure you don't want any?" Mel held out the white paper plate covered with the greasy food of the Gods.

"No way."

"I may be in a sugar coma by midnight, but it'll be worth it."

"They don't have funnel cakes in Boston?"

"I'm sure they do, but I don't remember seeing them anywhere." Mel licked powdered sugar off the tips of her fingers.

"Are you glad—" Jessica paused while two teenagers passed. "That you came back?"

"At first I wasn't sure. But, yeah, I am." Mel ripped off a piece of dough and ate it. The first burst of color lit up the sky with red sparks. "You know what you said about me waiting for something bad to happen?"

"Sorry about that. I shouldn't have said that." Jessica took a sip of coffee and watched the sky fill with green squiggles of light.

"No, you were right. When you were buying the socks, I saw a guy I thought was Uncle Jerry. My heart almost stopped. I don't know how to get my life back on track, but I'm going to try."

"What do you want to do?"

Mel shook her head. She had been asking herself the same question. "I'm not sure."

"Did you like what you did in Boston?"

"Yeah, I think so."

Jessica's face said she needed more of an explanation.

"I liked working with the kids, helping them, but I didn't really choose to do that. I started doing it because it was a job I was qualified to do. I didn't think about whether I wanted to do it or not." Mel waited until three more bursts exploded above them. "Now I think, what if I choose something and it's the wrong thing?"

"Remember that saying of Grandpa's that Dad would always say when stuff went wrong around the farm?"

Mel strained her mind but couldn't recall. "Which one?"

"If you can't outrun the devil, at least dance in the storm, and he'll think you've gone mad."

Mel burst into laughter. She remembered. "What the hell does that even mean?"

"I don't know." Jessica joined her in laughter. "But it's the first thing that came to mind, and it never fails to make me laugh."

95

Chapter Fourteen

Jessica shoved her cell into her back pocket and hung her jacket on the peg by the back door. "They've got some nerve. No way in hell I'm sitting down and pretending that man's family."

Mel stopped washing the dishes and waited for the explanation she knew was coming.

"That was Aunt Doris. Invited us over for Thanksgiving. Said Uncle Jerry never meant to hurt nobody."

Mel laughed and went back to washing. "Technically they are still family, Jess, whether we eat with them or not."

"You know what I mean. I'm not going to pretend he's not an ass over turkey and cranberry sauce. You go if you want to."

"I'm sure as hell not going," Mel answered flatly.

"Exactly."

"But you know how families are, pretending everything's perfect on holidays." Mel dried her hands on the dishtowel below the sink. "Did you and Dad go over there on holidays?"

When their mother had been alive, holidays had been here. Their mom had never been one to back down from Uncle Jerry's intimidating nature. Before that, when Mel was much younger, her grandpa had insisted holidays be here too. Grandpa and Uncle Jerry had never seen eye to eye.

"Most of the time. A couple of years Aunt Doris decided to visit her sister out in Denver. Uncle Jerry never liked going out there much, said they were socialists. Last year they came here, but Aunt Doris did most of the cooking. We deep-fried a turkey in the backyard."

Jessica took the mail from inside the jacket pocket and tossed it on the kitchen table. Mel had managed to dig her way through the towering stack of neglected mail that had once surrounded the microwave as she attempted to make heads or tails out of the farm's rickety finances.

"I hope you're going to cook us something good." Mel shuffled through the stack of mail. She opened one with a yellow change of address sticker on the front. It was a notice for her storage unit in Cambridge. It was paid up through February.

"It'll have to be me doing the cooking if we want something good."

Mel threw the dishcloth that was draped over her shoulder across the table at Jessica without looking. It missed and landed on a sleeping Sam Houston making him jump up and bark.

"I'll make you a deal. I'll feed the horses on Thanksgiving and Christmas if you'll cook," Mel said.

"Deal."

The November days cooled and shortened. Muted leaves fell like snow in an overnight thunderstorm. Jessica started building a fire in the woodstove to knock off the morning chill. The dry wood heat could warm a body like nothing else. Autumn's reign was short; winter was impatient. On Thanksgiving morning, Mel found a thin layer of ice on the water buckets.

Farm life was a constant challenge no matter the season, but it was certainly no picnic in the winter. Mud turned to frozen jagged earth, and cold grabbed hold of your bones and wouldn't let go. Chores and training continued despite it all. After a day in the cold, the night's slumber came hard and fast once in the warm.

Jessica made good on their cooking deal. Turkey, cranberry sauce, stuffing, green beans, mashed potatoes, even apple pie. Like their father, neither of them liked pumpkin.

"Where did you learn to cook like this. It certainly wasn't from me or dad." Mel took a spoonful of apple pie and vanilla ice cream.

Jessica smiled. "YouTube, mostly."

Their conversations were lighter now, comfortable.

"What were your holiday traditions in Boston?"

"I tried not to have many. I usually volunteered to work—it made it easier. We always had a meal for the kids at The Center. We tried to make it special for them. It helped them keep their minds off what they might be missing at home, and in a way, it helped me keep my mind off what I was missing out on too."

They were both sleepily watching *The Last of the Mohicans* after another round of turkey when Sam Houston announced a visitor.

Mel reached the back door first. Uncle Jerry froze and stared at her through the door window with his fist in the air preparing to knock. Jessica arrived and let out a not-so-quiet groan.

"Hello, Uncle Jerry." Mel opened the wooden door but left the screen door closed.

"Mel." Uncle Jerry nodded. "Jess."

No one spoke.

Uncle Jerry raised a paper bag he was holding. "Your aunt sent you girls over some leftovers."

Jessica's silence felt like a brick wall behind Mel.

Opening the screen door, Mel took the bag. "Tell her thanks."

"Jess, I was wondering if I might borrow one of the hay wagons like last year. We're setting up that nativity scene at the church this weekend." Uncle Jerry craned his neck to talk around Mel.

When no response came, Mel turned around but kept her hand on the door handle. Jessica shot daggers. She finally spoke. "Just bring it back when you're finished with it."

"Sure. Sure. Will do." Uncle Jerry turned as if to run but stopped before he reached the stairs. "I'll just hook up now if that's okay, no need for help. Y'all have a happy Thanksgiving."

Both sisters stood at the door watching him drive to the hay barn.

"Like I'd help him," Jessica said under her breath.

"If that wasn't strange, I don't know what is." Mel closed the door. She set the paper bag on the table and started pulling out plastic containers and a pie pan.

"I wouldn't eat that. He might have poisoned it." Jessica grabbed a roll from the stove.

Mel laughed. "He's a jerk, but I doubt he would try to kill us."

"You don't know. You could have died in Boston for all he knew."

"That's different. Besides, I think he just desperately needed a hay wagon. Either that or Aunt Doris made him come over." Mel stacked the containers on the table. They were all matching butter containers with the contents written on top with a black sharpie. Mel eyed the container marked corn pudding, but Jessica's skepticism got the better of her.

Jessica pulled back the foil on the pie and rolled her eyes. "Pumpkin. That figures."

"Hey, are the Christmas decorations still in the attic?" Mel asked.

"Yeah. We didn't use half of them in the last few years. Dad and me hated taking them down in January. One year they stayed up until Valentine's Day."

"Let's use them this year. We can cut a tree tomorrow."

"Only if you take them down after the first of the year," Jessica answered.

Mel had never been a shopper, but she had tagged along with Patricia and her friends on Black Friday for the past four years out of habit. They would arrive at the mall before dawn and Mel would spend the day taking bags and boxes to the car for her.

This Black Friday Mel awoke to the smell of the woodstove chasing away the morning chill. Memories had always been strongest around the holidays. How many times had she awakened imagining herself here only to shut her eyes tight and block out the painful thought seconds later?

Jessica was almost finished feeding by the time Mel stepped into the barn. They had agreed to take the long weekend off, but Jessica said she needed to work two of the new horses before they went in search of a Christmas tree. Working only two horses was about as close to a weekend off as Mel had seen since her return, so she decided not to push it. Out of habit, Mel cleaned a few stalls and brushed the mud from Bonnie's mane and tail before going inside to hunt down the decorations.

The stairs to the attic pulled down just outside her bedroom door. Mel climbed up the ladder carefully sticking her head above the attic floor like a groundhog on a sunny day. Dust filled her nostrils making her sneeze three times. Nothing happened when she pulled the cotton chord attached to the lightbulb overhead. Climbing back down, she went in search of a flashlight and a new lightbulb. By the time lunch rolled around, light had returned to the dingy attic, and Mel was covered in dust and cobwebs. Six Christmas boxes sat on the living room floor.

"You were serious, weren't you?" Jessica had a turkey sandwich in one hand and a glass of milk in the other.

"Yes." Mel dusted off the front of her shirt.

"I was serious about you cleaning up in January. You look like Pig Pen from Peanuts." Jessica shoved the last bite of sandwich into her mouth. "Let's go find a tree."

"Be honest. Aren't you the least bit excited?" Mel asked.

Jessica walked out of the room without answering.

100

They hooked the small trailer to the tractor and drove back to Sherwood Forest. Jessica drove, and Mel took her place on the fender like she had done so many times as a kid. A Lexington radio station had started around-the-clock Christmas music at midnight. Bing Crosby crooned "Silver Bells" over the thumping engine.

Jessica pulled the tractor along the clump of evergreens.

"Remember how much mom loved Christmas?" Mel asked.

"A little, but she loved any reason to celebrate, didn't she?" Jessica jumped off the tractor and grabbed the bow saw off the trailer. "I remember her Christmas apron. The one with the reindeer."

"Aunt Doris made herself and Mom matching aprons that year. Maybe before you were born."

"Remember when Dad and Uncle Jerry tried to cook Thanksgiving dinner and the color of that turkey?" Jessica laughed. "It was orange."

Mel turned up her nose but laughed. "And you called it a Halloweeny turkey. Mom and Aunt Doris knew it would be a disaster. They waited until the guys made a mess of things and then they warmed up the turkey they had cooked the day before."

By the time they agreed on a tree and returned, it was almost dark. They knocked out the evening feeding together and carried the tree inside through the front door leaving the tractor on the lawn until morning. Mel poured a glass of wine and Jessica grabbed a beer. Ornaments, lights, garland, and ceramic houses came pouring out of the boxes.

Mel arranged a few houses of the Christmas village on the mantle while Jessica added garland and white lights to the stair spindles. The lights on the trees were multi-colored, and ornaments from their childhood hung heavy on the branches. Mel hung the green and gold ball with the phrase *I luf you, Mommy* she had painted in first grade in front, amazed it had survived the years.

They dug out a ladder from the hall closet to place a wooden angel on top. The wings had been broken and glued back on many times. Even her head had had to be reattached after she mysteriously leaped from the top of the staircase one year. Neither girl had ever owned up to it.

Mel wrapped the two pillars of the front porch stairs with multi-colored lights and arched a garland over the front door.

"Not sure who's going to see all this. Can't even see the house from the road." Jessica's decorating spirit had waned.

"We'll see them," Mel answered.

It was almost midnight before they plugged in the lights and admired their handiwork.

"That was a day's work." Jessica plopped in the recliner.

"Don't sit down. Let's see it from outside." Mel grabbed Jessica's hand and pulled her to her feet.

Mel stopped in the middle of the yard and waited for Jessica who walked slowly with her arms crossed against her chest and shoulders hunched. Mel could see her breath in the night air. Jessica didn't turn around quick enough for Mel, so she grabbed her shoulders and turned her facing the house.

"Just look at it. Isn't that the prettiest sight you've ever seen?" Mel asked.

Christmas had a way of slowing down the most hurried of souls. Mel stood at the back door of the barn watching flurries dance across the field teasing with the possibility of a white Christmas. Temperatures would climb just enough to turn the winter wonderland into a muddy mess by noon but for now, the scene was tranquil. A cardinal sat on the fence post by the gate as if posing for a Christmas card.

Jessica took the challenge of Christmas food seriously. The kitchen smelled of fresh biscuits and bacon when Mel came down from the shower.

"Let's eat breakfast in the living room this morning. Dad would have disapproved," Jessica said with a grin.

Mel started a fire in the fireplace.

"Good job." Jessica sat the coffee pot on the table beside the recliner. "You remembered to open the damper this time."

Mel laughed. "Yeah, I'm a quick learner."

The lights on the tree and banister brightened the living room as only Christmas lights could. The atmosphere wrapped around Mel like a warm fleece blanket.

"I think Dad would be proud of how you've continued with this place." Mel spooned strawberry jam onto the steaming biscuit in front of her.

"You think? I hope so. I hear him in my head a lot, disagreeing with me on some decision I've made or some training technique I'm using."

"Yeah, but he would have been proud of you."

"I still can't believe he's not here, out fixing something in a back paddock."

Mel nodded. "I know it sounds bad, but sometimes I wonder why he's gone, and Uncle Jerry got to stay. I know it doesn't work that way, but it's harder when it's the nice person that dies too soon and the world is left with—the Uncle Jerrys."

Jessica was quiet for a minute. "I think Dad knew you would come back."

Mel wanted to think her sister was right. "He always seemed to be one step ahead of us, didn't he?"

Mel slathered butter on another biscuit. Carbs did not exist on Christmas, and they barely existed in her mind anymore on any other day.

Jessica smiled. "Let's open our gifts while we eat."

Jessica handed her two gifts, and Mel jumped up to grab the gifts from under the tree she'd wrapped for Jessica. She hadn't been sure what to buy her, but Jessica had liked a wool sweater in a catalog a few weeks back. Mel ordered it and watched the mail like a hawk until it arrived. She had copied the photo she carried of the two of them with their dad and had it framed in a recycled barn wood frame.

"I remember this photo." Jessica ran her thumb across the edge of the frame. "I love it."

"Mom called us a ham sandwich. The horse was Tumbleweed."

"Dad always talked about that horse. Thanks, Mel."

Mel opened her two gifts. The first was a grooming kit with her initials engraved on the side. Mel laughed when she opened the second. It was a packet of pipe tobacco.

"I figured you had the pipe, so you might as well try to smoke it. Pretty good, huh?"

"I'll be like some old mountain woman on the front porch in a rocking chair snapping green beans with a pipe hanging out the corner of my mouth."

Even with the void they both shared, Mel couldn't have imagined a more perfect day.

Chapter Fifteen

The week between Christmas and New Year's Day it poured with rain. Jessica only exercised the horses that couldn't afford a week off. They drove into Lexington twice. Once to catch a movie and once to check out a new pub owned by a client.

It was Jessica's idea to stay up on New Year's Eve and watch the ball drop in Time Square as they had done as kids. Around eleven, Mel went to replenish the snacks only to find Jessica snoring on the couch when she returned.

Last New Year's Eve, Mel and Patricia had gone to Cape Cod with friends and were still awake when the sun came up the next morning. They had fought on the drive home. How different life was here. Mel stayed up long enough to watch the ball drop, finished off both glasses of cheap champagne from Walgreens, and sat watching the fire dance in the fireplace. The possibilities of the new year held promise and for the first time in a long time, she didn't dread the future. Covering Jessica with her grandmother's quilt, she made her way upstairs.

Jessica insisted on the southern tradition of black-eyed peas and ham for New Year's Day. This was said to bring prosperity and good luck; Mel ate two helpings knowing she needed all the luck she could muster.

The first week of January turned bitter cold and it gave Boston a run for its money. The wind cut into her skin, and Mel's toes numbed as she rode. Water in the stalls had to be busted morning and night. Leather was stiff and cold, and it was impossible to maneuver in gloves. In between rides, Mel and Jessica would warm up inside the barn office in front of the space heater. It gave relief in the moment, but it made going back out into the cold even more brutal.

The co-worker Mel had stayed with after her breakup called to say she was moving at the end of the month. Mel had a closet full of clothes and books stored at her place plus the storage unit in Cambridge that didn't come cheap. After talking it over with Jessica, they agreed the sensible thing to do was to go and take care of things. It was a vicious time of year to return to Boston, but Mel knew it was time to put that part of her life to rest—even with the uncertainty that prowled in her soul, she needed the closure of her Boston life.

Jessica drove her to the airport in Louisville.

"You are coming back, right?" Jessica asked pulling up to the curb.

Mel smiled. "I guess you're stuck with me for now."

Jessica laughed nervously.

It's just one week. I can do this. Mel watched the truck pull away.

Mel's coworker, Anna, picked her up from the airport. Boston had a heatwave of temperatures in the twenties that week. Mel was ready to go home before her first full day. Sidewalks piled high with snow made her feel claustrophobic, and the white tunnels full of hurried people unnerved her. No matter how late she stayed out with friends she woke up every morning before six.

Mel's friends flooded her with questions about Kentucky and farm life as if it were a third-world country.

"Don't you get bored?"

"There's no time to get bored. We're too busy. Most nights I crash and sleep like I'm dead."

"Could you teach me to milk a cow if I came to visit?"

"It's not that kind of farm." Mel smiled.

106

"There's more than one kind?" The table erupted in disingenuous laughter.

The jokes went on throughout the dinner.

Sharing a car back to the apartment, Anna asked Mel if she was happy.

"Not yet, but I'm getting closer."

"You seem different."

"In what way?" Mel asked.

"You always seemed to be trying too hard when you lived here."

"I think I was just trying not to feel." Mel stared out the window at the shops she walked by a hundred times.

"Feel what?"

"Rejection, fear. Life."

"Mmm." As if she knew.

That night, Mel lay in bed thinking about what Anna had said. A siren screamed on the street below and flashing red lights bounced off the wall above the bed. She was exhausted at day's end on the farm, but it was a different kind of exhaustion than she had experienced in Boston. Here, her life had been a constant churning inside, trying to convince herself and everyone around her that she was fine, and life was as it should be. The noises rising from the street below made her long for the distant cries of coyotes.

Saturday afternoon Mel's plane to Kentucky was delayed several hours because of icy runways at Boston Logan Airport. Drained, she arrived in Louisville just before midnight.

The pressure eased in Mel's chest when she saw Jessica standing in the baggage claim area. She wore her barn jacket and mud-covered Ariats. Mel hugged her awkwardly. They had never been a hugging kind of family.

"Thanks for coming." Mel slung her duffle bag over her shoulder and followed Jessica to the truck.

They stopped at a Waffle House off I-64 on the way home.

"So, how was it?"

"It was weird. I didn't fit in anymore."

"Because you smelled like a horse?"

Mel laughed. "Yeah, I'm sure that was it."

"Did you fit in before?" Jessica asked.

"I thought I did, but maybe not."

"I was afraid you might decide to stay," Jessica said.

"I did wonder what would happen if I got there and it felt like home."

"But it didn't?"

"No. I don't think it ever did," Mel answered.

"Does here feel like home?"

"Truth is, nowhere feels like home, or at least not how home used to feel. Not yet." Mel shrugged.

The waitress brought two plates of waffles and home fries. Jessica asked for another syrup emptying the first bottle on the golden brown waffles in front of her.

"Why don't you just get it in a to-go cup and drink it on the way home?"

"The syrup's the best part." Jessica grinned.

For the next few minutes, the girls ate in silence. Mel watched two older men seated at the counter argue over the name of the actor in a vaguely familiar eighties film on a grainy TV hung on the wall above the coffee pot. One swore it was Kevin Bacon and the other bet him twenty bucks it was Kevin Costner. Mel watched the gravelly screen long enough to see that it was Kurt Russell the two men were arguing over and that made the scene funnier than it would have been otherwise.

Mel had burrowed under her quilt around 4 am but woke up just before seven. This was now considered sleeping in. The creaky old house welcomed her home. By the time Mel showered and changed, Jessica was already back from the barn making coffee. Neither of them felt like cooking this morning so they settled for muffins and microwave bacon.

"I think I want to sell the Fiat," Mel said.

"Aw, but it's cute." Jessica tossed a piece of bacon to Sam Houston. "But it's not too practical around here, is it?"

"And I could fit it in one of the potholes between here and Frankfort."

"Our tax dollars hard at work," Jessica smirked. "What are you going to get?"

"I always wanted a Jeep when I was younger."

"Now we're talking." Jessica's eyes widened.

"Not that kind. A Cherokee or something useful."

"That's boring."

"I can use it for supply runs, feed—you could use it too, when you don't need your trailer. It'd save on gas."

"Still boring but I guess it makes more sense. I can ask Tommy to keep an eye out. He's always poking around the car lots around here." Jessica walked to the sink with her dishes. "Listen, I was doing some thinking while you were in Boston."

"Should I be scared?"

"The farm's getting by—barely, but we could do better. We've got to bring in more training. If I start showing again, I know I can bring in more business. I could even take some of the horses currently in training to the local shows, so folks can see what I can do. You know, just sell myself a bit more. Remind folks we're still here. Everyone around here knew Dad, but I need them to know I can stand on my own." Jessica hesitated. "With you here helping with feed runs, exercising, the books, you know—."

Here it was. The real question.

Mel had been asking herself this same question while in Boston, no, since she first pulled into this winding drive last summer. Wasn't this all she had ever wanted? Mel sensed Jessica's uneasiness with her silence.

"I'm in," Mel blurted out before she lost her nerve.

Jessica looked like she was breathing again.

"That's a lot to take on. You sure that's what you want to do?" Mel asked. "I know I have two left feet when it comes to training, but I'll pick up the slack in anything else."

"I have the boys here. I can have them do more of the lunging and warming up. I can focus on the technical part and let them do the extras. As long as I keep an eye on them."

"Can you afford the time to train you and Rooster for the shows? It's not worth killing yourself."

"Can't afford not to. I'll start with some of the local shows and see how it goes. Besides, I kind of miss it."

Mel didn't miss the excitement in Jessica's eye.

"Let's do it," Mel repeated her commitment more for herself than for Jessica.

Chapter Sixteen

The golden-edged wedding invitation was addressed to Jessica. A high school friend of hers was marrying their high school principal's son. The invitation was a plus-one, and Mel asked if Tommy would go with her.

"God, no. He hates weddings. He wears the same face at weddings that he does at funerals. It's depressing to be seen with him," Jessica tossed the invitation on the table. "You can go with me."

"Me? No thanks."

"You can't hide out here forever."

"I'm not hiding," her voice was too defensive to be convincing.

Jessica rolled her eyes.

"I'm not. I went to town for feed just yesterday."

"You have friends who still live here, you know. You should see them."

"I'm fine. I haven't talked to those people in years. Besides I've seen a few of them around town."

"Yeah, but did you talk to them?" Jessica's smirk told Mel she'd been caught.

What do you want me to do? Go hang out at the Goodwill on Friday night?"

Jessica wasn't amused. "Hey. Don't knock it. There are a lot of good deals in there. I got this shirt for two bucks." She pulled up the fabric by the collar. "Anyway, no one wants to go to a wedding alone."

It was settled whether Mel liked it or not.

For the next two weeks, Mel dreaded the first Friday of March. One night after feeding, Mel held up a teal dress over the stair railing. She had worn this dress to a wedding a few years back with Patricia. Jessica raised her head enough to peer over the back of the couch.

"You do remember this is a Southern wedding, right? Not the guv'nor's ball."

"Too much?"

Jessica cocked her head but said nothing.

Mel returned in a few minutes with a simple burgundy three-quarter sleeve dress with flowers around the bottom edge. "How about this?"

"Better." Jessica raised up on her elbows. "Don't get offended, but I'm kind of surprised you're wearing a dress. I'm not even wearing a dress. I hate the damn things."

"So, I shouldn't wear a dress?" Mel asked confused.

Jess raised her eyebrows at the obviousness.

Mel wrinkled her brow still not getting it.

"Well, you're—gay."

Mel cracked a smile.

"What?" Jessica shot back.

"You think just because I'm gay I can't wear a dress?" Mel laughed.

"Cut it out. It was stupid, I admit it." Jessica shrugged and threw her attention back to the TV. "How was I supposed to know?"

"I like dressing up. You know, we're all about as different as you straight ones. Of course, we're funnier in my opinion." It's the first time Mel had dared to joke with Jessica about being gay.

"You're not a bit funny." Jessica crossed her arms like a petulant child, but the words held no sting.

The pews inside the small brick church were filled despite their early arrival. An usher with a blue tie that was tied too short opened a row of metal folding chairs behind the last pew motioning to Jessica and Mel.

112

"We ain't seen this many people since last summer's revival meeting." He looked around the room like a kid at Christmas.

Jessica elbowed Mel and pointed to the front corner of the room behind the piano. Uncle Jerry stood like a palace guard outside the preacher's office door. If he had had dark sunglasses and an earpiece, he would have looked like an unusually plump secret service agent.

The wedding march began. Mel saw Katherine on the opposite side of the church next to a man she guessed was Nathan. You never knew who would show up at weddings or funerals in the South. He was tall with unruly, reddish hair and scrawny shoulders whispering in Katherine's ear. Katherine smiled and shook her head at whatever he had said. Mel wondered how long they had been together.

The church was stuffy and smelled of damp carpet. The older woman in front of them wore enough perfume to choke a horse. The minister welcomed everyone and began with a prayer. Mel took advantage of closed eyes to scan the crowd. Hairlines had receded and hairstyles, at least some of them, had changed, but she recognized several bowed faces.

After the prayer, the minister began a mini-sermon. The man seated in front of her sneezed to which several people whispered, "bless you." Feeling nauseous, Mel tugged at the neckline of her dress. She wasn't sure if it was the perfume hanging in the air or the preacher's archaic words about a woman's place.

Patricia had grown up in a fanatical household. She had even been forced through reparative therapy as a teenager. Mel's mood crossed over from comical to suffocating as the preacher droned on. Beads of sweat lined her hairline by the time the groom finally kissed the bride.

After the ceremony, Jessica was cornered by a couple asking about a horse they were interested in training. Mel excused herself from the conversation and wandered around the edge of the crowd into the fellowship hall where refreshments had been served. The air was not quite as thick

113

in this part of the hall. She wished for a glass of wine, but she knew better. *Tonight*, she promised herself.

A punch bowl surrounded by small glass cups sat in the middle of the long, narrow table. It reminded her of her high school prom. They had distracted Coach Edison long enough for David Kendal to pour a fifth of whiskey in the punch bowl. Where was David Kendal when you needed him?

Mel scanned the room as she ladled out a cup of translucent pink punch. She grabbed a flimsy paper plate and placed two pimento cheese triangles on it with a handful of Fritos and a pickle wedge. The window by the punch table was open. She breathed in the air from outside and took a bite of sandwich. Pimento cheese was something she had missed while in Boston. It was a genuine southern delicacy and northerners struggled to comprehend its simple splendor.

Through the accordion wall that had been folded back between the sanctuary and fellowship hall, Mel could see Jessica deep in conversation with a group on the far side of the sanctuary. The more engrossed she became in a topic the more she used her hands. She waived them now like a New York traffic cop. Mel smiled remembering the conversation earlier about the dress. Jessica looked every bit like a horse trainer. If stereotypes were accurate, Jess was a shoo-in for the gay sister with her navy dress pants, a printed oxford, and cowboy boots.

Mel placed a few more familiar faces throughout the crowd, some she could put a name to, and others were nameless faces from her past. Several, named and otherwise, welcomed her back cordially but with a coolness she had expected. Southern guidelines of hospitality were tricky to navigate. In such, Mel knew to pay close attention to the said and the unsaid. When a sweet little old church lady stated, "bless her heart" about some naïve, younger woman, any true southerner knew the unsaid in this situation is "she's as dumb as a doorknob, but at least she's pretty." These and other unspoken rules deemed it necessary for the wedding attendees to speak to Mel, but the underlying essence of their welcomes screamed of her status as an outsider, or worse yet, a traitor. Standing on the edge of the bustling room she was surprised to admit that her place here mattered to her.

Some of the familiar faces were high school classmates. Smiles and nods were given to those whose eyes Mel caught across the stuffy room. Small humans hung on their hips or clung to their legs. Patricia had talked about adopting children someday, but as usual, Mel had remained non-committal. Watching these couples juggle children in their arms made her thankful they had never gone through with it. Patricia had been the one with her heart set on three children, two girls and a boy. What a mess that would have been.

"It was a lovely wedding, wasn't it?"

Mel jumped at the sound of a voice from behind her. She turned to see Aunt Doris.

"Yes, it was." Mel's voice shook. She hated that it did.

"It's good to finally see you, Mel. You're looking good."

"Thanks." Mel felt like a trapped fox.

Aunt Doris leaned in and whispered, "I just wanted to tell you, your uncle never meant to hurt you, honey. He was just doing what he thought was right."

Aunt Doris' plastic smile never wavered.

Mel tilted her head and didn't blink. She could feel the blood rising in her cheeks. "Destroying our family because I was gay seemed right to him?"

"Destroyed? That's a harsh word, sweetie. Don't be so dramatic." Aunt Doris continued in her sugar-sweet southern accent with a polite little laugh. She sipped her punch and laid a wrinkled hand on Mel's forearm. "He just wanted to make you think about your life choices—maybe shake you up a little. I'm sure he never dreamed you'd stay gone forever."

Mel glared at this shriveled grey-haired woman and found her courage. "I'm gay, Aunt Doris. I've always been this way. This wasn't some phase of teenage rebellion I needed to be shaken out of."

"Your uncle is old school—so was your daddy. He doesn't understand such things. You know how it is."

Mel tightened her jaw. Aunt Doris continued sipping her punch and scanning the crowded room with an innocent air. Mel tried to gather her thoughts, but before she could speak, she heard a calculated voice from behind her.

"I'll tell you how it is." Jessica stepped between Mel and Aunt Doris like a guard dog. "Uncle Jerry tried to ruin Mel's life with this stunt. That's how it is, Aunt Doris." Her voice echoed through the fellowship hall. The buzz of the room diminished.

"Let's not make a scene, dear." Aunt Doris kept her smile fastened tight and didn't look Jessica in the eye.

"Jess, leave it. Let's just go." Mel placed her hand on Jessica's tightened bicep.

"Of course. We wouldn't want people to talk, would we?" Jessica ignored Mel.

A familiar fear ran up Mel's spine as eyes in the room stared their way, but then a thought occurred to her. Appearances be damned. She turned to her aunt. "You knew, didn't you?"

Aunt Doris' smile faded slightly. She still held the last sip of punch in her mouth as if she had forgotten to swallow it.

Mel was aware, by the tingling on the back of her neck, of the awkward glances of people in the room close enough to overhear. "You knew but said nothing."

"What's going on here?" Uncle Jerry bellowed in his gruffness.

Jessica glared at him for a hard second before grabbing Mel's arm. "Let's just go."

Mel brushed Jessica's arm away and said calmly. "I want both of you to know. No matter what you think, I am not ashamed of who I am. And I'm not going anywhere anytime soon."

Mel held Aunt Doris' gaze before turning to follow Jessica to the side door. Aunt Doris stood by the pink punch bowl, holding her glass of punch up to her lips. The syrupy smile had returned, and she stood frozen like a character in some low-budget science fiction film. Uncle Jerry stood by Aunt Doris with a dark scowl across his face.

Before stepping through the door, Mel turned to scan the room once more. Katherine stood with the bride's parents and their eyes met briefly. Mel caught the slightest nod of Katherine's head before she stepped out into the sun. Jessica was waiting in the truck with the engine running.

A few weeks after the wedding spectacle, Mel traded her red Fiat for a forest green Jeep Cherokee Tommy had found in Frankfort. She even got cash out of the deal, so she took Tommy and Jessica to dinner to say thanks. She drove away from the restaurant with the windows down and music playing a little louder than normal. The March air held a slight warmness marking the survival of winter. With the Jeep, and Jessica practicing for the show, farm errands were now her territory.

One afternoon while picking up fencing supplies to repair the creek paddock, the man loading the supplies spoke up.

"You're Mel Snow, ain't ya?"

Mel nodded at the lanky man.

"Homeroom. Mrs. Dillion. You probably don't remember me, James Wade."

She nodded again to buy time. He was almost bald and wore a short, crooked goatee. She tried to imagine him twelve years younger and with hair. It wasn't coming to her.

"I didn't say much back then. Don't say much now." James laughed at himself. "Me and Trisha Peters got married after graduation."

She remembered Trisha. Talkative slender girl that used to cry in biology class when they dissected frogs. Mrs. Dillion would have been tenth grade. She stared at the man's face as he loaded the wire. Nothing.

"It's been a while, hasn't it? How's Trisha doing?" Mel hoped to play it off.

"Sure has. Remember old Mrs. Dillion would write her name on the board every morning like we'd forgotten it overnight? Trisha's fine. We got two boys now. They're growing like weeds. Ornery as a pair of polecats."

Mel remembered Mrs. Dillion's oddities. "I remember Mrs. Dillion. Guess she thought we weren't all that bright."

"I heard you'd moved back. Trisha works down at the bank. She told me."

"Yep. Moved back to help Jessica."

"I was sorry to hear about your daddy. He was one of the good ones. Always took the time to see how things were going. Heard you was in Boston. Everybody's talking about it. Always wanted to visit Boston. Did you see where they poured out the tea?" James rested his hand on the fender.

"Yeah, once. They have a replica of the boat you can go on in the harbor."

"That's what I heard." He closed the hatch of the Jeep and smiled.

"Good to see you, Mel."

"Good to see you too, James. Tell Trisha hello."

The identity of this curious, soft-spoken man bugged Mel all the way home. She stopped at the house before going to unload at the barn. Dad kept every yearbook. Pulling it off the shelf, she thumbed through the pages. Finding Mrs. Dillion's tenth-grade class, she followed the rows of pictures and bad hair until she found James Wade Jr.

"Well of course!" Mel exclaimed slamming the yearbook closed.

"Junior" Wade. He had always sat in the back and had never talked much. Seeing the picture had jogged her memory. She knew why she hadn't recognized him. The

118

lanky man that had loaded the fencing today had been quite heavy with a greased back mullet in tenth grade. She saw the faint resemblance in his eyes now.

Chapter Seventeen

Jessica shouted from the round pen when Mel stepped out of the Jeep, "Let's plan a campout."

"Got the wire you wanted. What kind of campout?"

"What do you mean what kind? A campout. Back in Sherwood Forest. You used to like camping."

"What brought this on?" Mel asked.

"It's getting warm. Don't tell me you don't think it sounds fun. When was the last time you went camping?"

Patricia was not the outdoorsy type, and her friends in Boston spent their spare time going to New York to shops and shows. "The summer before I left. When Squealer nudged Dad in the creek."

"You see? We need a campout."

Mel could see that Jessica was determined. "Who's going to come to a campout?"

"Tommy and a couple of his friends, the boys, and—well, you leave that part to me."

Mel groaned.

"Trust me. This weekend is the show, so the second weekend in April. Two weeks away. It'll be fun." Jessica grinned like a little kid begging to play in the mud. She wasn't asking Mel for permission, so it was pointless to resist.

Mel was halfway up the stairs looking forward to her head hitting the pillow when she heard Jessica call her from the kitchen. Jessica was rummaging through the cabinet when Mel walked in in time to see her tuck a package of cookies under her arm.

"Looks like one of the young mares may foal soon."

"When?" Mel's anticipation had been building for foaling season.

"Tonight, I bet. Dad always said it was good luck to see the first foal of the season, I thought I'd keep an eye on her if you want to come."

The anticipation of foaling gave Mel a second wind. "Let me get dressed. I'll meet you out there."

"I'll start some coffee."

Jessica had just poured two cups of coffee when Mel walked into the office startling Sam Houston who had been sleeping by the door. He jumped up from his rug and growled.

"Remember me? I live here now?" Mel sat down in the chair by the door. The dog sniffed her leg and laid back down, resting his head on her boot. "Which mare?"

"The little roan. I put her in that first stall and gave her some hay. It's still kind of chilly out, but we can watch her from the office and turn the heater on if we need it."

"Dad always loved foaling season. He'd wake us up to see. Even if it was a school night."

"Remember when those three mares foaled the same night? He let us bring our sleeping bags out and sleep in here."

"Yeah, and you wouldn't stop talking and let me sleep," Mel said.

"I don't remember that." Jessica smiled coyly. "What did you miss most about here when you were in Boston?"

Mel looked around the wood-paneled office and thought.

"The sounds."

"Really?"

"I didn't notice until I came back. The horses pawing, snorting, even chewing their hay in the stalls, the sounds of the night as I'm falling asleep with the window open. The creaks in that old house, hell, even the sound of the water running through the pipes in the wall, I missed it all."

Jessica stuck her head out of the office and checked the mare. "Were you happy there with—Patricia?"

It was the first time Jessica had said Patricia's name.

"Not as happy as I could have been." A cat they called Tobias jumped up into Mel's lap.

"What do you mean?"

"I didn't see how guarded I was with everyone around me. The last thing she said to me when she left was 'you're never going to let me in.'"

"Did you know her family?"

"Part of them. She was raised in a crazy religious family. Like really kooky. Her older brother's a minister up in Vermont. He would say the craziest shit you've ever heard. My first, and only, Christmas with them he said the government should reopen Alcatraz and round up all the gays. He knew we were together, but it's like we were invisible."

"Hell, Uncle Jerry should friend him on Facebook." Jessica frowned.

"The thought of Uncle Jerry on Facebook scares me." Mel shook her head. "Anyway, Patricia was furious. They had a huge argument, he threw a bowl of mashed potatoes across the room, and we ended up leaving halfway through the meal. But about two years ago her mom up and left her dad. She even came down to Boston to visit. It was awkward, but she tried to be nice."

Jessica heard something out in the stall and Mel followed. The little mare was walking around the double stall in between bites of hay.

"I can't imagine how uncomfortable she must be." Mel leaned her head against the corner post.

"Have you ever wanted to do it?" Jessica asked.

"What? Have a foal?"

122

"Funny. Have a baby."

"I go back and forth. We'd talked about adopting, but now I think what a mess that would be. You?"

Jessica looked at the mare. "And experience that? Hell no. I've seen too many mares having foals to ever want to push something like a baby out of my body."

"Well, that's putting it plainly," Mel said.

Jessica went into the stall and checked the mare. "It'll be here tonight for sure. Promise not to get mad if I tell you something?"

"Depends."

"I was pissed when you told me you were gay."

"What pissed you off about it?"

"It's like I felt betrayed or something. I used to have this dream that you came home with a husband and a few kids."

Mel didn't say anything.

"I mean I've always sort of been grossed out by the thought of it. That probably makes me a horrible person." Jessica grabbed the manure fork and picked the stall clean.

"You're not a horrible person. It takes time for people to understand things that are different. It even took me time. When I dated Jason Wagner kissing him was one of the most disgusting things ever, but I still did it." Mel picked up Tobias who had been circling her feet. He purred and rubbed his head against her chin.

"I guess, if it's not your cup of tea, there's no sense ordering it." Jessica shrugged.

Mel loved Jessica's thought process when it came to life.

"Everybody's different. I mean, Patricia was married for about a year to a guy before she figured out it wasn't right for her. And I have a friend who didn't figure it out until he was in his fifties. He's got five or six kids and a bunch of grandkids."

"I bet that got messy."

"It depends. I had a colleague at The Center who came out as transgender, went through gender-affirming

123

surgery and her wife stayed with her. They have a pretty cool relationship. Her wife told her she loved her in whatever body she chose."

"I might have to think about that one for a bit." Jessica rested her chin on the pitchfork handle and watched the young mare in silence.

The moments in the chilly barn passed slowly. Jessica pulled a dusty Scrabble game out of the desk drawer while Mel went inside for snacks. In the middle of the second game, and right after Mel played the word *dozen* for triple points, the mare went into labor.

Just before dawn, a roan colt entered the world looking just like his momma except for a wide blaze down the middle of his nose. The mare nuzzled her nose into the foal bonding and coaxing him to stand.

The little colt was a determined one. He began the wobbly dance of walking faster than most. The young mare munched on hay but never took her attention off her baby. The colt would take a couple of steps on shaky legs and tumble over. Each time he tried his legs strengthened. Soon the little one gained enough control over his gangly limbs to instinctively nurse. This process had always fascinated Mel.

Jessica left a message at the vet's office. One of the vets would stop by in a couple of hours to check on momma and baby. As long as the foal was nursing, there was no hurry.

Jessica and Mel grained and watered the other horses before going to shower and eat breakfast. The day's chores didn't lessen just because you had pulled an all-nighter, but it did make the next night's sleep that much sweeter. Mel volunteered to cook while Jessica took a shower. She had put the eggs and toast on the table when Sam Houston let out a bark.

Katherine's Jeep appeared at the side of the house. Mel stepped out onto the back porch and motioned for her to come inside.

"Good morning. Sorry, my boots are muddy."
Katherine stood just inside the screen door.

"You could already plant a corn crop on this floor. A little more dirt won't matter." Mel almost laughed at her *country slang* creeping back in. "You have time for coffee?" Mel motioned to the chair closest to the door.

"Aye, sounds good. I'm moving slow this morning. Had a bull get himself tangled up in barbed wire last night. Had his heart set on a cow a few fields over. Gave his owners quite a fright."

"That sounds horrid. Hungry?"

Katherine's eyes lit up. "Starving."

Mel grabbed another plate from the cupboard and poured a cup of coffee. She was plating the bacon as Jessica came barreling down the stairs.

"Morning. You got here quick." Jessica grabbed a piece of bacon off the stove.

"Figured I'd stop by on the way to the office. I would have come sooner if I had known breakfast was involved."

The three women ate quickly and walked out to see the new colt. Jasper and Cody pulled up at the same time. Jessica left to get them started on a project she had for them while Katherine examined the mare and foal.

"Do you get tired of the late nights?" Mel stood in the stall door watching.

Katherine smiled with a stethoscope on the mare's stomach. She rubbed the curious foal's nose.

"Those times when we've had three or four bad nights in a row, I start asking myself why I didn't become a small animal vet with office hours. But I wouldn't be happy doing anything else."

"Your husband doesn't mind the strange hours?"

Katherine stood up straight and stared at her blankly. "He might if I had one."

"Oh, sorry, I assumed you and Nathan were married." The words tumbled out and Mel's cheeks reddened.

Katherine laughed loud. "Nathan's my little brother. God, I would kill him if he were my husband. He's a pain in the ass. Like most little brothers, I guess."

"Little brother?" It was Mel's turn for confusion.

"Two years younger. After I moved here, he took a position at the University of Kentucky teaching American History of all things. He's always been fascinated with it. He's writing a book on Civil War Weaponry now and finishing his Ph.D."

"I'm so confused." Mel laughed nervously. "All this time, I thought he was your husband."

"Nope. Just my foolish baby brother." Katherine closed the stall door. "Momma and foal are fine. That's a nice little colt. Nice coloring."

Mel tried to recover from her confusion. "You have horses?"

"I bought two last spring. One needs to come visit Jessica for a month or two. He's too green for me. The other one's spoiled but broke in good. I don't ride her near enough."

Jessica had walked in just in time to hear Katherine's last sentence. "Well, maybe you'd consider a swap."

"I think we could arrange something."

"Hey, we're having a campout weekend after next. You and Nathan should come."

"That sounds fun. I'm not on call that weekend."

"That's what I told Mel. Who doesn't have fun at campouts?"

Mel laughed. "You're like a kid about this, you know."

Jessica grinned.

"Younger siblings." Katherine winked. "I'm sure Nathan will be up for it. You'll learn soon enough that he loves a captive audience."

She turned to Jessica. "Let me know what you need us to bring."

"Oh, this is going to be the best," Jessica said.

After Katherine's Jeep pulled out of sight, Mel turned to Jessica.

"Nathan's her brother."

"Yeah?" Jessica shrugged her shoulders.

"I thought he was her husband."

Jessica howled with laughter. "Where did you ever get an idea like that?"

"I don't know. I just thought it," Mel answered.

"Don't tell Tommy I said this, but Nathan's cute. That messy red hair and all. He's like a nerdy version of that guy from *Outlander*. Funny as hell too. You'll like him."

Chapter Eighteen

It rained overnight making Saturday's show a muddy mess. The rain had stopped around dawn, but the air was thick with moisture. A surprising number of horse trailers lined the edge of the graveled driveway at the Fairgrounds in the next county. Up ahead, Tommy waved them in behind his rig.

"Damn it. We'll be covered in mud by the time we get home. Why didn't he grab a spot up there?" Jessica motioned up a slight incline behind the rental stalls.

Mel chuckled. "Did you hear how much it rained last night? We'll be covered in mud no matter where we park."

Mel waved at Tommy as she got out of the truck but went directly to the horse trailer. She heard Jessica chew him out for his choice of parking spots. Sam Houston jumped out of the truck and followed Mel.

"Yeah, you and me both ol' boy." Mel scratched his head.

They brought three horses for the show, Rooster, one of their three-year-olds, and a gelding belonging to a client who had promised to be here today. He had been more than happy to give his consent for showing. He had called earlier to say he was bringing his two grandkids. He was from Minnesota originally but had bought a place north of Lexington after retiring. Even with his flannel shirt and boots, he stood out in Kentucky like a sore thumb with that rich Minnesota accent, but he was likable enough once you got to know him.

It was important for business that the client be in the crowd to talk to people, and if this guy did one thing well, it was talk. Jessica would show his horse in a handful of the earlier classes, so she could be sure and present him with a ribbon or two. She might not be that handy with the books, but she had a sharp mind when it came to horses and humans.

Mel pulled the horses out of the trailer one by one and tied them to the side eye hooks while Jessica went to the show arena to get her number and sign up for classes. Kids of all ages, many on horses or ponies, weaved in and out of trailers, buildings, and people. Shiny aluminum trailers parked right alongside old rusty second-hands with men and women huddled in groups between them. Lighthearted banter rang out in bursts, and the flavors of meat on the grill filled the air.

Rooster stood tied to the horse trailer chomping on hay, unbothered by the banshee shrieks of children. His back leg cocked in a resting position.

The other two horses were different stories. This was their first show and heads were high and eyes wide, muscles jerking with each new noise. Mel tied the lead lines tight. She did not intend to spend her day chasing spooked horses all over the county.

Jessica untied the gelding and led him to a smaller practice arena to lunge him trying to avoid the large puddles in the low spots. Locals and out-of-towners stood watching, pointing, commenting on her every move. Mel had talked Jessica into putting the farm logo on the side of the trailer before the show. For better or worse, the microscope of a small town was shrewd, but it helped keep their name out there in plain sight. The more exposure the better.

Outside the show arena gate, Mel brushed the mud off the gelding's legs while Jessica did the same to her own legs. The gelding's head was lower and calm, but his eyes were still wide as they rounded the corner by the bleachers. The dust in the covered arena circled his ankles and legs before drifting toward the bleachers and burned Mel's eyes.

Only five horses showed in the conformation class and it was much easier to control the young horse from the ground than riding. This gelding was put together well; he just needed to behave and maneuver around the arena under Jessica's commands. The odds were in their favor for a ribbon. The client couldn't have been happier with the second place ribbon from the first show. He posed for a picture in front of the horse with his grandchildren like they had just won the Kentucky Derby. Mel took pictures with her phone and promised to email a copy when they finished.

Cody and Jasper pulled their rig up beside them after the first class.

"Are you boys ever going to learn to be on time?" Jessica barked at them.

They both just grinned and offered sausage biscuits and coffee as a peace offering. They saddled quickly and took off toward the arena.

The sun popped out after the lunch break and more trailers showed up for the afternoon classes. Mel, on her haunches to keep from touching the soggy ground, wrapped Rooster's ankles in bright blue wraps in preparation for the next class.

Mel's smile wouldn't go away. She was here, knelt in the mud and the muck putting wraps on a show horse. This was an odd place to feel the first hint of being exactly where you were meant to be, but in this precise moment, life felt as if it had aligned.

"If it ain't Mel Snow again."

Mel stood to see James, from the hardware store, and Trisha walking toward her. "Hello, James. Hi Trisha. Good to see you again. Are you showing?"

James took a draw on his cigarette. "No, ma'am. I'm about half scared of horses, I don't mind saying. Trisha's old man bought the boys a pony that's meaner than a junkyard dog. The boys can't catch him half the time. How about you? You showing?"

"Showing's not my thing, but I've missed coming to these shows. I'm just barn help today and, of course, moral

130

support. Jessica's showing though. You should talk to her about the boys' pony. She's good with ponies."

"We been meaning to do that. I told Trisha just the other day what that pony needs is some manners," James said.

"You like being back here? Must be a lot different from Boston," Trisha said.

"It is, but it's been good to be back."

"Not married then?"

Mel tried to determine if this was a loaded question. Trisha's face gave no indication. "Nope," was all she said.

"The boys are with their grandparents today. We're on a date." James wrapped his arm playfully around Trisha. "We're going to go get us a couple of hotdogs and sit and enjoy the show."

"Well, it's good to see you again. Enjoy your date and talk to Jessica about that pony." Mel knelt to wrap Rooster's other front leg.

"Will do."

The day ended with two firsts, three seconds, and a third-place ribbon. It was dark by the time the last class finished. Mel's back ached from sitting on the cold, aluminum bleachers.

A fight had broken out mid-afternoon over a minor infraction in the Team-Penning class, but the sheriff, who had been selling hotdogs in the food tent, broke it up after only a few blows. One of the boys turned out to be his grandson. Mel later saw the boy flipping burgers on the grill with a frown. She watched the same boy scrubbing the grill by the side of the concession stand.

The client had stayed until the end and cheered just as loud for Rooster as he had for his horse. His grandchildren were covered in mud after playing behind the stalls all afternoon. His granddaughter had fallen asleep in Mel's lap by the end of the show. Mel helped him to his truck with the kids.

"Their grandmother will kill me when she sees all this mud, but I always tell her a muddy child is a happy child."

Jessica appeared and thanked him for coming. He smiled like a kid and waved out the window as he drove away.

They loaded the horses in silence.

"That wasn't too impressive." Jessica latched the trailer door.

"You beat Tommy and Jasper out of first place in the Ranch Trail class."

"That wasn't hard to do. They had both had one too many by then." Jessica whistled to Sam Houston.

"It was your first show in a while. It'll just take a few shows to get back in the swing of things. I bet it felt good to be showing again." Mel had learned Jessica had gotten too busy with things around the farm the past few years and had stopped showing altogether.

"It felt really good," Jessica said.

Chapter Nineteen

The next Saturday morning was overcast. Mel checked her phone to see the odds of a downpour during the campout that evening. It was fifty/fifty. Jessica left for the store early convinced that the weather would cooperate. It was a bring you own beer, beef, and bullshit kind of gathering. The campout had grown into a production since Jessica had suggested it.

Mr. Tomlin had collected fallen limbs for the bonfire all week and stacked a pile of split wood for the smaller cooking fire. The bonfire was for show; the smaller fire was for cooking hotdogs and marshmallows without singeing eyebrows and arm hair. Jasper and Cody were coming over early to help transport things to the campsite.

Mel took her time walking to the barn breathing in the crisp, spring air. The air smelled green. She knew it didn't make sense, but the morning air filled her with a tangible energy she could only describe as green. Drops of dew covered each blade of grass along the path to the barn. A whippoorwill whistled its unmistakable tune from somewhere along the fence line beyond the stack of round bales.

Mel threw flakes of hay into the mare and baby's stall, the curious colt nuzzling her elbow as she stood watching. The little ones grew right before your eyes during the first few months. The office phone rang. Katherine Neil was on the other end asking if they needed another grill.

Climbing the ladder into the loft and swinging over the edge with ease now, Mel thought about the boys' critique of her lesbian toughness months earlier. She had never considered herself a tough person, but daily farm work had left its mark on her dry, rough hands and defined forearms. It was funny that being back in the south had made her gayer, at least by stereotypical standards.

Jasper and Cody arrived before noon, excitement plastered on their faces. They had talked of little else this week. Mel put them to work loading camping gear, lawn chairs, and straw bales onto the hay wagon. Cody had set up an old Army tent on the edge of the woods earlier in the week. They would take a load to Sherwood Forest and come back for more. The boys decided who would drive with a game of rock, paper, scissors, and Cody reluctantly handed over the keys he'd taken from the ignition after Jasper won best out of three.

Mel was in the kitchen when Jessica returned.

"I lost control," Jessica said with plastic bags dripping from her wrists to her elbows.

"I had a feeling you would." Mel followed her back outside to the truck.

"How many people are coming to this thing?" Mel grabbed the last four bags and shut the door with her foot. The kitchen table was covered with bags of chips, cookies, beer, meats, and soft drinks. "The boys are making their first trip."

Jessica opened a bag of cookies and poured a glass of milk. "I need energy."

Jessica's cell rang. Tommy was on his way over. "Bring more ice. I forgot." She tucked her phone into her pocket and grabbed another cookie.

"The boys should be back soon." Mel put cheese and hotdogs in the cooler. "You didn't answer me. People. How many?"

"I don't know for sure. I saw James and Trisha at the store and invited them. Tommy's brother is on leave for the weekend from Ft. Campbell, so him and an Army buddy are coming over."

Mel turned to look at Jessica. "How many?"

Jessica shifted in her chair. "Well, I lost count. Does it matter? Everyone's bringing their own food and booze. We're just providing the atmosphere."

Mel stared at her in silence.

"Probably twenty. Maybe fifty."

"Why didn't you just run an ad in the paper?" Mel asked.

After two trips with the tractor and hay wagon, the boys tied balloons and signs to the fence posts. The north side of Field One would be the parking lot. From there it was a short walk to the clearing in Sherwood Forest. If the weather did not cooperate, there would be a passel of stuck vehicles to contend with on Sunday morning.

Jessica and the boys had moved the cattle to Skinny Jim's paddock. Mel took the mare, Bonnie, out this morning to double-check the paddocks and gate locks. Nothing could ruin a party quicker than loose livestock.

Mel pitched the tent she had picked up on clearance at the sporting goods store in Lexington. She positioned it just beyond the picnic tables at the edge of the clearing.

Familiar faces began to trickle into the wooded area. Tommy introduced his brother Michael, who looked like he could be his twin, and Randall, his Army buddy. Randall had family in Western Massachusetts and had gone to Boston University for a semester, so he and Mel talked about the city and their favorite restaurants in Cambridge. Randall, who had a shy way about him when he talked, brought a hammock out of his backpack and hung it between two trees by the creek's edge.

As the group grew, Mel busied herself with organizing the food on long brown folding tables borrowed from the Rotary club. Jessica's high school friends came by the tables to say hi and grab beers. Just as it had been with

135

Jessica, it was strange to see them as adults with beers in hand.

The Jacksons arrived with their two teenage sons. Jessica's arrangement with them had worked out well, and they had become the type of clients you didn't mind seeing outside of the working relationship. The boys stood by their parents whispering to each other and examining the small clusters of locals that were forming. Jasper and Cody had finished setting up the Corn Hole game on a flat grassy area that Mr. Tomlin had mowed down last week. The Jackson boys veer toward this area. It took no time for their countenance to change as the competitiveness swelled.

Mel had her head stuck under a grill wiggling the propane hose when she saw the familiar Jeep pull to the edge of the trees.

"Sorry, we're late. I blame him." Katherine walked ahead of Nathan with an arm full of food. Nathan pulled a large gas grill behind him.

"Don't believe a word she says. She forgot to tell me we were supposed to bring a grill until we were at the end of the drive." Nathan parked the grill beside the one Mel was trying to light. "We finally meet. I'm Nathan, the younger, charming brother of the notorious Dr. Neil. Can I help with that?"

Mel shook his hand and handed him the lighter. "Be my guest. I don't think it's been used in a while. The natives will be restless for food soon."

"Help me with the rest of the stuff?" Katherine asked Mel.

"Sure." Mel took a few steps but turned back to Nathan. "Nice to finally meet you."

Nathan grinned a wide, toothy grin before ducking his shaggy red hair under the grill.

"Jessica got carried away with the campout. Sounds like the whole town might show up."

"Good. Things like this don't happen often enough. It helps people get to know one another. I like it." Katherine handed Mel two duffle bags and took the last three bags in hand before closing the door with her hip.

"When Mom was alive, she threw a party each year in the fall. She used to say it was good for folks to stop working so hard and just play."

"Jessica comes by it naturally then," Katherine said.

Mel walked behind Katherine through the trees. Her build was slight but athletic. She walked with intention, her shoulders square, speaking to everyone she passed. In a small community like this, almost everyone had animals, even if only a few chickens in the backyard or an old farm dog. Twenty or so people were now mingling amongst the trees, swapping hellos.

"Anywhere in particular we should set up the tents?" Katherine placed the bags on the table and grabbed one of the duffle bags off Mel's shoulder.

"Mine is that orange one there," she added with an awkward gesture. "Anywhere over there's fine."

"We'll stick Nathan's in that patch of trees way over there. He snores like the devil himself," Katherine said.

"I heard that." Nathan's voice behind her made Mel jump.

"I'll set up the tents. Got the grill lit for you."

"I'll do my own, thank you," Katherine said, defiant but cheerful.

Nathan shrugged and snatched a duffle bag off the table. He walked away with his fist stuck in the air. "Have it your way, Rosie."

Three metal watering troughs filled with ice had been placed on concrete blocks by the grills. Long brown bottlenecks stuck up from the ice like snakes in a pond. Mel had hidden a smaller cooler under the edge of a picnic table with her own stash of beer. Jessica accused her of being a beer snob. Maybe she was a snob, but if she was going to drink beer, she wanted it to taste like someone cared how it turned out.

Mel grabbed a bottle of Kentucky Bourbon Barrel Ale out of her cooler as the Jacksons walked over. As outsiders, an air of camaraderie hung between them as they talked small talk. Being an outsider in the south was difficult to describe due to the sweeping gestures of southern hospitality that made everyone appear friendly and inviting. And they were to a degree. The signs were subtle but present if you knew where to look. You were a stranger until you passed the test of acceptance, magically shedding the outsider skin like a snake in spring. It was difficult to pinpoint the exact moment of transformation except to say you would know it when it happened. The Jacksons and Mel were still in the testing phase. Mel offered them a beer from her hidden stash.

It had warmed up for a few hours during the afternoon, but with the sun setting, the evening coolness had begun to creep in from the edges, and a hazy fog drifted above the wider parts of the creek. The small group of outsiders talked about the different pace of life between Boston, Portland, and Kentucky. The Jacksons had sold five acres in Oregon and bought eighteen acres in Kentucky for roughly the same price. Alexandria worried about the boys' adjustment, watching them across the clearing.

Katherine joined the group and gladly accepted one of Mel's snobby beers. She lifted the lid of her small cooler revealing a stash of Scottish ale, chilling. The group clinked brown bottles together in the dimming twilight.

Tommy lit the small campfire, and the groups came like moths to a flame. Hotdogs were impaled upon sharpened sticks and held over the small campfire. Those who craved burgers, chicken, or steaks huddled around the two grills.

Nathan appointed himself grill master of ceremonies. He even brought an apron with him and wore it with a great deal of pride. His animated face lit up as he waved a long metal spatula in the air. He held an audience of those waiting for their meats to cook.

Mel stood by the small campfire roasting a hotdog, smoke stinging her eyes. Like a flock of starlings, clusters of people would gather in one spot and dismantle only to gather with new people in another spot moments later. The darkening sky brightened the fire's flame, and bursts of laughter and talk filled the chilly evening air with warmth.

"You're a million miles away." Katherine appeared beside her with a hotdog and stick.

Mel smiled. "Actually, the opposite. I'm right here. I didn't think I'd ever be here again."

"I can tell you've missed it."

"More than I even knew." Mel examined her hotdog. It had to be the perfect level of charred.

"One of my favorite American weaknesses, hotdogs." Katherine raised the hotdog out of the growing flame.

The picnic tables were crowded. Katherine and Mel found a spot at the end.

Jessica walked up and grabbed a pickle off Mel's plate.

"Anything else I can get you?" Mel looked at her in feigned annoyance.

"Maybe one of your fancy beers?"

"No ma'am. You should have thought of that before you made fun of them."

Jessica laughed and snatched a chip before walking toward the Corn Hole.

"I bet she's glad to have you home." Katherine reached into her cooler and handed Mel a cold bottle of Scottish ale. "My turn."

"Thanks. I don't know. I hope so. It was tense around here for a bit, but we're doing okay now."

"Thinking of sticking around then?"

"I think so. We were close growing up. Especially after mom died." Mel squirted mustard onto her hotdog.

"Mind if I ask why you left?"

Mel stopped chewing and looked at her.

"I don't mean to pry," Katherine said.

"I figured you knew."

"I just heard there was some sort of family fallout, but I try not to give too much stock to the rumors I hear on calls. I'm kind of like a bartender out here. People are always telling me their woes and other peoples' business." Katherine smiled.

Before Mel could decide just how much to divulge of their family secrets, Jessica yelled for everyone to gather around. It was time to light the bonfire. They followed the crowd circling the towering pile of branches set in the middle of the large clearing of trees.

Katherine looked on with her eyes wide. "I love bonfires."

Jessica gave an impromptu speech and told the group about their mother's parties. She thanked everybody for coming and told them to stay as long as they wanted, but if they were still here at sunrise, she would have no trouble putting them to work. The group cheered.

Jessica lit the fire. Two guitars appeared from somewhere in the darkness and Tommy's brother took a fiddle out of a case. Songs, some old, some new, filled the night air, and dancing shadows stretched longer as the flames grew.

Jasper came through the crowd recruiting for the next Corn Hole and Katherine volunteered. Lanterns hung by each Corn Hole board spaced twenty-five feet apart and the whoops and laughter coming from that area of the woods indicated it was more interesting to play in the dark. Mel suspected the beers might have a hand in the growing difficulty as faceless shadows tossed bags into the air and patted each other on the back. A glow-in-the-dark Frisbee could be seen flying in the open field behind the cars.

Mel wandered back to the food area and busied herself with organizing the food. The tables looked like a tornado had hit. Jack Taylor, whose father owned the property adjoining Snow Farms to the north, had rekindled the smaller campfire, now dwarfed in size by the blazing bonfire. Two younger women sat roasting marshmallows listening to Jack who was deep into last winter's deer hunting tales. Mel didn't recognize the women, but she could see by their faces the all-American boy was leaving an impression.

One or two people at a time came to the table for more food occupying Mel's mind with small talk. James and Trisha came to the table for dessert and to say goodbye. Their babysitter had to be home by eleven, so they wouldn't be staying the night. They were bringing their boys' pony over next week to begin training and thanked Mel for the suggestion.

James patted Mel on the back and tossed his head toward the group of men standing around the bonfire. "Not too many prospects in this crowd, is there, Mel?"

"James, you talk too much." Trisha shushed him and turned to Mel. "Never you mind him, honey. He don't know his ass from his elbow sometimes."

"What'd I say now?"

"Honey, I told you." Trisha smiled politely in Mel's direction and spoke in a quiet voice. "Mel's not interested in—men."

"You were serious about that?" James looked at Trisha in shock. "Aw, Mel, I'm sorry. I've gone and stepped in it now for sure."

"It's okay." Mel attempted a little laugh.

"She might let you off the hook, but I won't." Trisha put on her mom voice. "You've got to quit talking before thinking."

Trisha placed her hand on Mel's arm before they turned to leave. "And you just go right on loving whoever it is you want to love, honey."

Mel grabbed another beer from the cooler and a hoodie out of her tent. The musicians were still going strong by the bonfire. The woods took on an eerie nature with the lanterns hung throughout. The largest of the groups encircled the musicians, some singing along. Mel melted into the edge of this group.

Two songs later and nearing midnight, Katherine appeared from the shadows the bonfire splashing her face with light as she neared.

141

"I lost miserably." Katherine picked up a lawn chair a few feet away and sat it next to Mel's chair. She stretched out her legs toward the fire and leaned her head back.

"I'm no good at that game in the daylight fully sober. I didn't even bother," Mel said.

"Those young guys are pretty good. A few of them are sloshed, but still better than me."

The fire popped.

"Tommy's brother is pretty good on the fiddle. It's one of those instruments you can feel if it's done right," Mel said.

They listened. One of the guitar players started playing "Country Road."

"My mum loves John Denver. She used to tell my Dad that John Denver was the only man she'd ever leave him for."

"Do you talk to your parents often?"

"Oh sure. She calls me and gives me all the local gossip. Who did what. Who's getting married, who's having babies."

"Have they visited you here?"

"Nathan brought them before he moved here. That trip made him want to move. They complained about how hot it was. My younger sister and her husband, who live near London, want to come over this year, but haven't set a date yet."

The music switched gears. Guitars changed hands and they began to play an upbeat song Mel didn't recognize. Off to the side, the once shy Randall had loosened up and started an awkward dance while others around him clapped and egged him on.

The crowd's participation, along with several beers, fueled his odd dance moves, which could only be described as an Irish jig mixed with some sort of hip hop. It was difficult to watch, but the sort of train wreck you couldn't easily turn away from. He motioned for others to join him, but no one budged. Undeterred, he singled out several women extending his hand, begging them to join him. Two women

142

on the other side of the fire took his hand and stood up but sat back down as soon as Randall turned his back. He made his way around the circle, his legs continued to twist about like a rubber chicken. He reached for Mel, but Mel gripped the arms of the camping chair and hung on tight, shaking her head.

Randall danced in front of Katherine who wiped away tears from laughter. She shook her head, but Randall dropped to his knees before her while still twisting his torso and arms. The rowdy group began to cheer. Katherine doubled over with laughter. She yelled "why not?" before clutching Randall's hand and lifting him off his knees.

Katherine danced a few circles around his goofy drunken moves. She took the hands of several others pulling them to their feet. The music picked up speed. Katherine circled and spun through the group dancing with ease.

As the music ended, Randall took a clumsy bow and lost his footing in the process. He fell into one of the guitar players before tumbling toward the bonfire missing it by inches hitting his head on one of the boundary rocks. The sleeve of his jacket caught fire.

Nathan was sitting closest. He sprang out of his seat and smothered the small flame with a shirt, but not before it burned Randall's hand and wrist. Silence and concern replaced the laughter.

Jessica took ice from the cooler and placed it in a plastic bag. The gash above his ear would need stitches. Nathan and Michael, Tommy's brother, helped him to the truck. Michael wasn't a drinker so he drove him to Frankfort to the Emergency Room. Randall sat in the passenger's seat with the ice pack on his head and waved.

After the incident, the music mellowed, and conversations took a quiet turn. Mel's eyes grew heavy. Twelve or so people had stayed on into the night. The rest opted to go home to children or at least to warm beds. The impromptu band abandoned the bonfire for the more intimate campfire. Mel added more wood and stoked the flame.

Jessica squeezed a plastic chair between Mel and Katherine. She sat on Tommy's lap discussing artificial insemination procedures with Katherine. Mel had an in-depth conversation with Nathan about Civil War weaponry before he fell asleep mid-sentence, his cheek resting against his fist. Mel sat and listened to bits of small conversations going on around the fire. She thought of Trisha's comment earlier. It was just like people to surprise you, good and bad.

A little after three, Katherine stood up and arched her back. "I'm done for. Jessica, Mel, this has been lovely. I can't remember when I've had this much fun. We should do it again."

A round of goodnights. Katherine walked into the darkness toward her tent.

Jessica sat in Katherine's chair and smacked Tommy on the arm seeing he'd dozed off. "How about fixing me another hotdog?"

Tommy frowned but got up slowly.

"Admit it. This was a good idea," Jessica said to Mel.

"It was much better than I expected. It was fun."

Jessica grew serious. "I'm glad you came home, Mel."

"So am I."

Tommy appeared with a stick and hotdog handing it to Jessica.

Not liking the third-wheel feeling that crept in, Mel said good night. Inside her tent, her once heavy eyes seemed permanently open. Last spring about this time, she was days away from her bust-up with Patricia. So much had gone wrong last year, but without those heartaches, she wouldn't have ended up here. Here. Home. *I am home.* Mel watched shadowy figures around the fire through the mesh window of her tent.

Sleep didn't last long. A shriek pierced through the woods, and Mel sat straight up in her tent, eyes wide. Her hands struggled to unzip the tent door. Tommy held a dead snake on a stick above Jessica's head. The shriek turned to shouting. Jessica punched at Tommy's chest. Those awake cheered her on.

Mel laid back down pulling her sleeping bag up to her chin. The air on her cheeks was cold. The sides of her tent sagged in heavy from the morning dew.

It was almost six. Every small stone and twig dug into Mel's back compelling her to face the morning chill. The ground was much harder than it had been when she was a kid. The smell of smoke, bacon, and coffee rushed in through the opening. She sat up and slipped her hoodie over her head.

Jessica handed her a coffee cup and a pop tart when she walked up to the fire.

"Thanks. Did you even sleep?"

"Nope. We played penny poker. I won seventeen cents."

"Hallelujah, we're rich."

Over the next hour, people began packing up their things and heading home. Most had livestock and pets at home waiting to be fed. Tommy had eggs and bacon cooking on a Coleman stove. Mel warmed her back to the rekindled fire.

Only Tommy, Nathan, Katherine, Cody, and Jasper remained. They cleared off one of the picnic tables and dished up from the iron skillets. Katherine sat down across from Mel.

"How did you sleep?" Mel asked.

"Like a baby. I hate for this to end."

"To tell you the truth I was kind of dreading it, but I have to hand it to her. It was a great idea."

"She'll be glad to hear you say that. I think she looks up to you, you know."

Mel moved the eggs around her plate with her fork. "I doubt that."

"I can see it," Katherine answered. "Hey, we should catch a movie sometime."

Mel opened her mouth to speak but closed it without saying a word. She stabbed a bite of scrambled egg. "Sure. That sounds fun."

"I'll text you."

The last of the hardy campers left after breakfast. Jasper and Cody made one trip to the barn with the hay wagon before going home. Jessica hitched a ride with the first load to start feeding. Mel stayed behind to clean up.

Chapter Twenty

Katherine texted Mel on Monday making plans for dinner and a movie on Friday night. Later that week, Katherine texted again suggesting they ride into Lexington together.

That night Mel lay awake telling herself this was nothing more than a friendly invitation and it was no big deal, but her self-talk was unconvincing. These things could be tricky. First, Mel did not know if Katherine knew she was gay. Second, and only in the cover of darkness, she thought about how attractive Katherine was.

New clients arrived before lunch on Friday dropping off two yearlings for what Jessica liked to call baby boot camp. Mel was grateful for the distraction. Yearlings couldn't be ridden yet, their bones weren't strong enough, but it was never too early to teach them barn manners. Over the next month, these young ones would be taught to lead without trampling their owners, stand still for the farrier, and load and unload without drama. It also made their training as a two-year-old a hell of a lot easier.

The clients' two young girls asked if there were any babies in the barn. Mel took them to see the foals while their parents signed contract papers. They were closer in age than her and Jessica, but they reminded Mel of them when they were young. The older one bit her bottom lip and held out her hand to pet the foal cautiously, but the younger one walked right up and threw her arms around its neck exclaiming in a high-pitched voice, "Oh, I love you." Mel held back laughter. This was Jessica to a T when she was younger.

The filly's short, wiry tail flipped back and forth like a windshield wiper while the girl hugged it. This foal wasn't shy around humans and came from a good-natured mare who stood close by munching hay. Mel's dad used to say that some horses were born loving humans and others didn't give a damn about them one way or another.

By four o'clock, Mel went inside to get ready. Katherine would pick her up around six. Mel poured a glass of wine before going upstairs to shower.

Mel was ready by five but changed her outfit two times after that. She settled on jeans and a pink oxford with a button-down collar. She cleaned the dust off her boots with a damp cloth. Looking in the mirror she laughed thinking about the odd looks she would receive if she had gone out in this getup while in Boston.

At six, Mel sat at the kitchen table with a book and an empty glass of wine. She had read the same paragraph three times. By six fifteen, she checked her phone for the tenth time to make sure she hadn't missed a text. Mel ran possible conversations in her mind, trying to sound friendly without flirting. It was a habit that drove her crazy but a difficult one to get rid of. She had told herself many times this week to simply enjoy this night for what it was. *For God's sake, keep it in perspective, and don't get all weird.*

Six thirty. Katherine had probably gotten caught up with work and was running late. Mel worded and reworded a text in her head before picking up her phone. She would send a casual text just to make sure she was all right.

At seven fifteen, Jessica stopped just inside the kitchen door and frowned.

"You're still here."

"You're right." Mel didn't smile but tried to sound humorous.

"What happened?"

"Not sure. I texted her, but she never responded."

"Probably a farm call or something. It's easy to lose track of time when things get crazy." Jessica kicked off her boots and sat down at the table with a glass of water. "I'm meeting Tommy for dinner. Want to tag along?"

"Thanks, but I'm fine. I think I'll just crash early if I don't hear from her. I would have probably fallen asleep in the movie anyway. I'm beat." Mel shrugged.

"Well, if you change your mind. I'm going to grab a quick shower and then head out." Jessica shouted as she walked down the hall.

Mel sat at the kitchen table listening to the water run upstairs. Her chest was heavy. She checked her phone one more time. Nothing. Pouring another glass of wine, she went out to the front porch and sat on the porch swing.

Mel awoke before Jessica the next morning. The house was still. She hadn't heard Jessica come in last night. Before going downstairs, she turned off her phone and tossed it on the bed. It was just the movies. Sam Houston was waiting by the backdoor and walked beside her to the barn. She scooped grain into buckets and told herself there was a perfectly reasonable explanation for why Katherine hadn't shown up.

Mornings in the barn alone were comforting. As soon as the horses heard the first grain scoop, they came alive with anticipation. Low snorts and swift kicks to the stall walls signaled their impatience. You'd think they hadn't eaten in days. Mel liked to feed the mommas first, figuring they had the hardest job these days. She took her time in each stall to play with the babies. Three mares had foaled this month with another two on the way. If Jessica's breeding plans worked out, the barns would be full of babies in a few years.

The morning chores calmed her troubled mind. She made coffee in the barn and leaned against the doorframe watching the sunrise alone with her thoughts. She was tired of hiding behind her walls. Jessica was right. She needed to get out more. In fact, it might not be so bad meeting some of her

149

old high school friends for lunch sometime. Look at how much fun the campout had been although she'd been dreading it. Sipping her coffee, she determined to stop avoiding them like the plague when she saw them in town.

The grass in the field shifted with small gusts of wind changing shades of green with each turn. It would be ready to cut in another two weeks if the rains cooperated. Haying was hard work. Aching muscles and itchy skin covered in dust and sweat, but it was enjoyable in its own way. No sleep was as sweet as the one that came after a day in the hayfield.

The fields called to her. She gulped the last swig of coffee and tacked a scribbled note to the feed board in case Jessica got worried. In a few minutes, the back gate opened, and horse and rider trotted toward the creek.

Mel sat by the creek for an hour until she spotted the dark clouds rolling in. She had been imagining sheep on the hillside behind the bend. Maybe she could buy up a few sheep as a side business, make some money of her own. When she thought about the future, Mel's head grew foggy. Although she felt more at home here every day, she still didn't know what she wanted to do. Jessica had her training. Mel had never had anything grab her in that way, but maybe it was time to find something that did.

Despite being full of determination and plans when she was younger, most of the last twelve years had just happened to her. She hadn't chosen. A professor had found her the job at The Center in Boston. She had stayed because it was comfortable. Patricia had left her alone and empty. Desperation had shoved her back to Kentucky in the first place.

Mel swung up in the saddle and pointed Bonnie toward the barn. What did she want out of life? Mel was afraid to answer, afraid it wouldn't happen, afraid this happy life she was on the edge of discovering would vanish like smoke.

The clouds burst when she was a couple of hundred yards from the barn. She eased Bonnie into a smooth lope. By the time she reached the barn, Mel was drenched.

"Didn't time that one well, did you?" Jessica stepped out of the office and tossed her a towel. "I'll unsaddle Bonnie. You dry off."

Mel toweled off her hair and wrung water from her shirt. Jessica shouldered the saddle and walked to the tack room. Mel followed.

"You okay?"

"Sure. Why wouldn't I be?"

"I don't know."

"I just felt like going for a ride. That's all." Mel avoided looking at her sister but sensed Jessica studying her.

"This tack room's a mess." Jessica picked up a broken halter and tossed it aside. "Want to tackle it today since it's raining?"

"Sure." Mel needed to be busy.

Jessica and Mel tore through the tack room until lunchtime. They arranged the halters by size and type, repaired or tossed broken pieces of tack, and oiled the saddles. Jessica's constant jabber kept Mel's mind off topics she'd rather not think about. The first few months of silence were long gone. By the time Mel's stomach started to growl the room looked sharp. The slow drips from the trees on the barn roof were all that remained of the rain.

"Let's take these to the Jeep." Mel grabbed a stack of winter blankets. "I'll take them in and wash them this week." They were ripe with horse sweat and dirt. Blankets didn't fit in a normal size washer, so they took them into the laundromat on Main Street and used the industrial-sized machines.

"I don't feel like cooking. Let's just go to The Goat. I'll beat you in a game of pool." Jessica put the blankets she'd been carrying into the back of the Jeep and closed the hatch. "But for God's sake let's take my truck so we don't have to smell those nasty things."

It was mid-afternoon when they returned, and Mel remembered her cell phone tossed on the bed.

One message.

151

She listened to the voicemail. Her smile faded. It was her dentist's office in Boston calling to schedule a cleaning. Mel exhaled slowly and lay back on her bed.

Monday morning, the first hay bale Mel tossed down from the loft busted in the middle of the aisle, and she kicked another one off the edge in anger. Jessica eyed the pile of hay with a curious look but said nothing. At breakfast, Jessica asked Mel if she wanted to go for supplies and wash the horse blankets. Mel knew they didn't need supplies, but she agreed.

Mel drove into Lebanon Springs with the windows down to keep the rank smell of the blankets at bay. She shifted her body with the sway of the Jeep maneuvering the long, slow curves of the country road a little faster than she should have.

Next door to the laundromat at the Country Crumbs Café, Emily Johnson, the girl she had kissed so long ago, sat by the window with two women Mel didn't know. Mel put the Jeep in park a little too hard and pulled the blankets out of the back without looking their way.

Being stood up had made her ornery. Straight people didn't own this town. Why should she be the one skulking around the outskirts of society because she was back in the south and someone might be offended by her gay agenda of washing horse blankets? Mel shoved quarters in the machine like she was playing the slots. She stepped onto the sidewalk, shoulders back, walking past the window and into the diner like the women were invisible.

Once inside, Emily called to her waving her over.

"It's been ages, Mel. Join us for coffee."

Mel had been outplayed. As quickly as her loud and proud resolve had come to her, it melted. Now she fought the urge to run back to her Jeep.

Don't be a chicken shit. Mel took a big breath and walked to the table with a strained smile.

Emily introduced the two women seated with her. The waitress brought another coffee cup out and asked if she wanted anything to eat. Mel shook her head and thanked her.

"You've been home for months now, and we haven't seen you. How was Boston? Are you going mad being back in this old boring city yet?"

Mel smiled. At just under two thousand people, Lebanon Springs could barely warrant being called a town much less a city.

"Boston was good. It was a good place to get a degree. And beautiful—especially autumn."

"Autumn." Emily laughed and touched Mel's arm. "Listen to you and your northern talk."

Mel quickly moved her arm to add a spoonful of sugar to her coffee even though she usually drank it black. Emily Johnson in the flesh. She wasn't even that pretty, and Jessica might be right about that boob job.

"What did you study?"

"Psychology."

"No farm management?" Emily sounded shocked. Turning to the women, she said, "Horses and farming. That's all Mel ever talked about in high school."

"Not many farms in Boston." Mel tried her hand at humor.

The small talk continued. Mel checked her watch. She had been there six minutes and the blankets washed for thirty-four. *Crap.*

"What did you do up there in Boston?" Came a thick drawl from the women wearing yellow. Mel hadn't paid enough attention and couldn't remember the names of the other two women.

"I worked with LGBTQ+ kids—most had been kicked out of their homes," Mel answered but did not look at their faces, staring out the window at an old man on a lawnmower with an American flag duct-taped to the seat. The small-town icon cruised up the sidewalk in front of the courthouse. She saw four reflections in the window under the gold lettering of *Café* backward but cast a hard look into her own face. In the reflection, Mel saw Emily shoot a warning glance at the women.

Mel squared her shoulders and turned back to the table. "It was a good job. A lot of these kids had nowhere else to go. It was tough to see them struggle with the rejection."

Emily spoke up. "My oldest son plays on a Little League team over at Shelton Park on Saturdays. My husband's the coach. You should come and watch sometime."

Mel had surely imagined Emily's emphasis on the word husband.

"We're pretty busy at the moment." Mel folded a napkin corner as she spoke. "How many kids do you have?" Children were safe conversation topics. Mel had asked the jackpot question.

Emily's eyes lit up. "Well, since you asked, we have three and I just found out I'm pregnant again. Joe wants his own team, I reckon."

The other two women, who had two each, squealed and clapped their hands. They talked the rest of the time about their kids. To hear these women tell it, their offspring were Einsteins and headed to the big leagues.

Mel's phone rang. Katherine's name appeared. She tucked it back in her pocket and stood to leave. "I better get back to it. Good to see you again, Emily, and nice to meet you." Mel nodded at the two nameless women.

Mel told herself to wait until she got home to listen to Katherine's voicemail. She told herself this same thing three times backing out of the parking spot and making a left at the court square. Two minutes later, she pulled into the Dairy Queen parking lot.

Mel? It's Katherine. I was hoping to catch you. Listen, I've been trying to get a chance to call. Dad was in a car accident Friday morning on his way to work. I'm in Scotland with Mum. He's had a couple of surgeries, but they think he's through the worst. I'll try to call again. Bye.

Mel hit replay.

Katherine called again Tuesday morning. Mel answered on the first ring.

"How's your dad?"

"Hi. Banged up. He's got a couple of broken bones and a lung that doesn't want to stay inflated, but the doctors think he'll bounce back. He's a mess, but he's handling it better than Mum."

"Anything we can do for you from here?"

"I hate to ask but do you think you could board my horses for a few days? Nathan's flying over in the morning, and we'll both stay on through the weekend at least."

"I'm sure Jessica won't mind. Will Nathan be home?"

"Should be. Thanks. That'd be a load off. I'll tell him to expect you. Hold on." Katherine talked with someone in the room with her.

"I've got to run. Listen. Sorry about the movie night. I'll make it up to you. Thanks again."

Chapter Twenty-One

Katherine returned on Sunday and made good on her promise. Jessica and Mel returned her horses on Monday morning; Jessica refused to accept any payment. Katherine came around to Mel's side of the truck and suggested Wednesday night dinner and a movie since she would be on call the next two weekends. They agreed to meet at the cinema after work and go to dinner afterward. Jessica invited herself until she remembered she had a late lesson that evening. Mel was secretly relieved.

Despite stopping for gas and driving slow, Mel arrived at the Lexington cinema thirty minutes early. She backed into a spot in the near empty parking lot and waited, leaning her seat back and twirling her key chain around her finger.

In the fading daylight, she couldn't bring herself to admit she was attracted to Katherine, but the butterflies in her stomach told a different tale. While she couldn't quite figure out, or at least be honest about, her feelings for Katherine, she had thought of little else the past few days.

Two vehicles pulled into the parking lot. The first truck was Tommy's dad's Ford. It was hard to miss, faded green except for the orange tailgate Tommy had replaced after backing into a pole one night at a horse show. He pulled into a spot on the other side of the lot. The car that had pulled into the lot behind Tommy pulled up beside the truck. A girl Mel had seen around town got out of the car and walked around to Tommy's door.

Tommy stepped out of the truck and leaned back into the open door while the girl ran her hands playfully through his hair. Her laughter drifted across the parking lot making Mel squeamish. Tommy held the girl in a rough embrace and kissed her, his hands clutching at her breasts. Mel tightened her grip on the steering wheel.

The girl placed her hands squarely on Tommy's chest and pushed away from him. Her high-pitched cackle made Mel's skin crawl. She ran around the front of the truck to climb into the passenger seat. Tommy crawled back in and pulled her to him. The back tires squealed as the engine roared and the two left the parking lot the same way they had come in.

Mel cranked the engine to follow them but caught herself. *What the hell are you doing?* She turned off the engine and leaned back in her seat wishing she hadn't seen what she had seen.

"Nap time?"

Mel's eyes opened quickly. "Hi. Sorry, I was thinking."

Katherine's Jeep had pulled into the next spot over without Mel even noticing.

"You were somewhere else all right. How are you?"

Mel tried to shake off the feeling of dread. "Glad to be off the farm for the evening." She wanted to tell Katherine what she'd seen, but Jessica would never forgive her if she told someone else first.

"I brought you something." She stuck a paper bag through the window. "Sorry, it's not wrapped." She leaned on the door and waited for Mel to open it.

Mel pulled a bottle of Scotch out of the bag. "You didn't have to do that."

"It's Da's favorite." Katherine smiled. "Sorry for standing you up."

157

"You did manage to come up with a pretty good reason." Mel placed the Scotch on the passenger floorboard under a box of horse supplements she had forgotten to take out yesterday. "I don't want anyone breaking a window for that."

Katherine bought the tickets and picked seats in the middle of the near empty theater. Just about the time Mel started to panic about whether to sit in the seat next to Katherine or leave a seat in between them, Katherine held the theater seat down beside her. There was just enough time for Mel to ask about her father's progress before the trailers started. He was home and on the mend but refusing to follow the doctors' orders. Her mom would have her hands full for the next few weeks. The theater lights dimmed, and Mel tried to relax in the darkness keenly aware of Katherine's closeness.

After the movie finished, Mel followed Katherine to the restaurant. The scene of Tommy and the cackling girl came back to her. She gripped the steering wheel tighter. Jessica would be asleep by the time she reached home. But tomorrow would surely come, and she would have to tell her.

Why did people have to cheat? If he wanted to move on then fine, break the heart, and get on with it. Anger burned through Mel as she drove. She had accused Patricia of cheating a few months before the split up without any evidence whatsoever. Mel realized too late she was desperate to keep her well-rehearsed world from going up in smoke although they were both long passed miserable by that point.

Katherine picked a Mexican restaurant because she loved their margaritas. She ordered them both one with extra lime. The hostess seated them in a window booth with a candle in the middle of the table next to a miniature ceramic donkey with baskets slung over its back. The baskets were filled with colorful fruits that were disproportionately larger than the donkey's head. The donkey's ears had been broken and glued back on several times reminding Mel of the little horse and jockey that stood in Uncle Jerry's front yard. She had broken its ear off when she was ten trying to lasso him and had had to rake leaves the next weekend as punishment.

"I'll blame you if I can't get out of bed tomorrow morning." Mel raised the frosty glass to the center of the table. "Cheers."

"Cheers."

Mel nodded as cool tequila warmed her throat. "Did you get to do anything fun while you were home?"

"I met a few friends one evening after Nathan arrived. It was good to catch up."

"Anyone special?"

"Not really. But one of the doctors at the hospital was an ex-boyfriend. Quite a shock for both of us, I think." Katherine ran her finger around the glass edge and licked the salt off her finger. "You know, I never quite got the hang of dating. I spent my time as a teen with the animals. Becoming a vet was destiny, I guess. They're better listeners anyway."

"You've got a point there. Agent always gives me the best advice."

"We only had cats and dogs growing up, but one summer I took a job down the road mucking stalls on a farm. Since then, I was hooked."

"Cleaning stalls certainly weeds out the less passionate." Mel laughed.

"How about you?" Katherine asked. "Anyone special bring you back to the thriving town of Lebanon Springs?"

Mel blushed. She was better at asking the questions than answering them.

"God, no. No one since Boston." Mel saw that perfect opportunity she looked for when coming out to someone new. "Patricia. My partner—ex-partner." This was easier than *oh-and-by-the-way-I'm-gay* which always seemed to stop conversations dead. It also helped that Patricia was a typical female name stating the obvious. The fact that she was expected to come out to everyone new had always irked Mel, so she had found her own style of doing it.

"Oh," was all Katherine said, but it was not the "oh" Mel had grown accustomed to.

Mel continued to fill the silence wishing she could stop. "We were together for about four years. I wasn't a good person to live with. Too many demons, I guess."

"That's too bad. I'm sorry."

"Now I'm here," Mel cleared her throat. "Packed up my demons and we came back to where it all began."

"Where what began?"

"I'm sure you've heard the rumors." Mel dipped a chip in the salsa.

Katherine smiled." I could go to ten farms in a day and get ten different versions of the same story."

"It started with a kiss at a football game." The story, her story, poured out. She told her about Uncle Jerry and that day he took her to the bus station, told her how frightened she had been, and how that fear had turned to anger, and the weight of the shame she carried with her.

The food came. Mel went right on talking with Katherine asking questions in between bites. A faucet had been turned on, and like the night of the campout, Mel ached to tell this woman her story. In between bites and questions and another round of margaritas, Mel couldn't help but compare this woman to Patricia. With Patricia, Mel had guarded her words and opinions striving for just enough authenticity to keep Patricia satisfied with her façade of openness, but not enough to expose her true self. When Mel failed to be convincing, the conversation turned toward counseling and ended with explosive arguments and tears.

This unfamiliar yearning to tell Katherine her life story frightened her. By the time Mel took the last bite of her burrito, she was spent.

"I've talked your ears off, sorry. I bet you wish you'd stayed home now."

Mel looked into Katherine's face and tried to read what was happening behind her eyes, feeling foolish for having exposed so much of herself to this woman she barely knew.

Katherine reached across the table and placed her hand on Mel's forearm, her eyes wide and sincere. "I'm sorry you had to go through that. No one should have to."

The waiter came and poured more water.

Mel tried to regain her composure. She was not at all sure of her voice when she spoke. "It's working out okay."

Katherine insisted on paying the check. They walked down Main Street stopping to peer into darkened shop windows along the sidewalk. Mel asked Katherine about her childhood, wishing the night and this walk would never end. It was after midnight when they returned to their parking spots. They lingered beside the parking meter in front of Mel's Jeep.

Mel rolled a small piece of concrete under her foot. "I hope I didn't overwhelm you with too much information tonight."

"Not at all. Thanks for telling me your story. I think it's important."

"Well, you were a good listener, almost as good as Agent," Mel added.

"I've surely arrived then, haven't I?"

"You're not sleepy, are you?" Mel unlocked the door and rested her arm on the doorframe.

"No, I'm used to late nights. At least this one ends up in my bed and not in a barn with a sick horse."

"Good point. Well," Mel wasn't sure what to do next, "thanks for the movie. Drive safe."

Katherine had been standing a few feet away but stepped forward and hugged Mel. Mel awkwardly returned the hug.

Katherine pulled away and smiled. "Sorry, I'm a hugger."

Mel's words stumbled out. "That's fine."

"This was fun. Guess I'll see you soon." Katherine walked backward toward her Jeep. She waved out the window as she pulled away.

Mel drove home with the windows down, the night air was fresh. Brandi Carlile's soothing voice sang out "The Eye," and Mel sang along. She didn't care that she couldn't carry a tune in a bucket as her father used to say. She didn't care that she only knew half the words. When it was finished, she played it again.

"You were out late," Jessica said a little too loud as Mel entered the kitchen. She had slept through her alarm and woke up in a panic.

"Overslept." Mel stretched the palm of her hand across her forehead and rubbed her temples with her middle finger and thumb.

Mel poured a cup of coffee and snatched a cold piece of bacon off the back of the stove. Her cheeks warmed remembering how much of her story she had exposed to Katherine over dinner last night.

Katherine.

The buzz of last night was sabotaged by a flash of Tommy and the girl in the parking lot. Mel had often held her tongue when it came to Tommy. Any mention usually made Jessica bristle, and she had made it clear she didn't need protecting.

Maybe she'd get lucky, and they had broken up without her knowing. Jessica seemed about half pissed off at him a good chunk of the time. Mel had overheard her on the phone more than once telling him not to bother coming over. He hadn't been around in a couple of weeks. Jessica said she was too busy training for the upcoming show. Maybe she had moved on and wouldn't care about last night.

The thought of reigniting tensions between them was unbearable enough, but she couldn't stand the thought of hurting Jessica with this news. Why had it been her that saw Tommy? Mel cursed her inner coward.

Mel went with Jessica to move the cattle to Skinny Jim's paddock. Moving cattle was normally relaxing, but Mel fidgeted in the saddle today. In between the "ch-chs" "move ons" and whistles, Mel dug for information.

"Is Tommy showing next weekend?" Mel waved her arm out beside her to keep the cattle moving. She tried to make her voice sound as nonchalant as possible.

"Nah, he's been working a lot of extra shifts. He's saving for a new truck. Hasn't had time to practice."

My ass. Mel's anger flared.

"How was the movie last night?"

"Good. She brought us a bottle of Scotch."

"Oh, that sounds good. Her dad on the mend then?"

"Seems so."

A young steer bolted away from the herd jogging back to the pond.

"Oh no you don't." Jessica and Rooster kicked into action circling to bring him back into the herd. Mel kept the rest of the herd heading in the direction of the gate at the far end of the field.

"The hay's looking good. Mr. Tomlin will get the last of it cut today." Jessica swung back on her horse from latching the gate behind the last steer.

Haying was one of Mel's favorite farm events. "I can't wait."

"Tommy said he'd try to get off and help us."

Mel didn't want to see his face again. She took a deep breath and started to tell Jessica about what she saw. Her mouth went dry, and she hesitated. Two cows veered right, and Jessica followed.

That evening after the boys had gone home for the day, Mel took her place on the top rail and Sam Houston took his in the cool evening grass behind her. The upcoming show was an extreme horse challenge, an obstacle course for horse and rider, and would be fun to watch. Plus, proceeds helped fund a summer camp for kids.

Obstacles scattered the grassy area beside the arena. Jessica guided Rooster to side-step over a series of logs laid out in a wide W shape. Slow and easy. These events were about trust between horse and rider. Jessica had the patience of Job when it came to horses, but with people, she sang a different tune. Rooster moved with confidence around and over the obstacles. He trusted Jessica. Mel wondered if she would ever love doing something the way Jessica loved riding and training horses. The scene of Tommy manhandling the other woman raced back into her mind. Mel dug her fingers into the rail she was sitting on.

Mel gave herself a pep talk while she tossed extra hay to the mares with foals. Jessica whistled outside the back of the barn hosing Rooster down. It would be a shame to wreck her good mood. Maybe she should wait until morning.

Just suck it up and do it. Mel knew the longer she waited the angrier Jessica would be at her for not telling her.

The last tints of orange colored the horizon. Mel walked a few steps behind Jessica toward the house. Lightning bugs appeared ahead of them.

Just before Jessica reached the back porch, Mel spoke. "Listen, I need to tell you something."

Jessica stopped on the bottom step and turned around.

"It's probably none of my business, but—um—I saw something you should probably know about—but you may already know it. I mean, it may mean nothing to you."

"What?"

"Last night at the movies—in the parking lot," Mel stopped cold.

"What?" Jessica's voice held an edge of irritation.

"I saw Tommy." Mel swallowed hard. "With someone."

"Someone?"

"A woman."

Silence.

"When you say with—" Jessica's voice trailed off.

"With."

Jessica looked out into the darkening field behind Mel.

"Who?" Jessica's voice sounded restrained.

164

"I don't know. Maybe I've seen her around town, but I don't know—I'm not sure."

"Why didn't you tell me sooner?" Jessica snapped.

"I didn't want you to think I was in your business. I don't—" Mel faltered.

Jessica glared passed Mel into the field. She tucked her fist under her chin and swiftly popped her neck to the right and left. She had a habit of doing this as a kid when she was trying to keep herself from crying.

"That bastard," Jessica kicked the post and took a deep breath.

"Jess, I'm sorry, I—."

"Just drop it." Jessica turned and walked toward the house, slapping her leg to Sam Houston. She let the screen door slam behind her. Mel stood alone in the darkness her eyes fixed on the back door. She could have pretended she hadn't seen him. Upstairs, Jessica's bedroom door slammed shut.

The next morning the boys had come by for a trail ride. Jessica was sullen and quiet, except for when she was biting someone's head off. The boys got it good when they started playing with the water hose while rinsing their horses. Mel got it too when she forgot to secure a cinch before putting it on the rack after putting Bonnie back in the stall. When the boys got in the truck to leave, Mel envied them.

Mr. Tomlin was the only one that escaped Jessica's bad mood. He stopped by to remind them about the Derby party on Saturday. As if anyone could forget. Before her exile to Boston, Mel had been going to the Tomlin's Derby party since before she could walk. It was a tradition, a ritual. Jessica's mood lightened after Mr. Tomlin's visit, and Mel silently thanked him for the reprieve.

Chapter Twenty-Two

Today was Kentucky's day. Derby parties were scattered from one end of the state to the other. From simple, down-home parties to fancy, elaborate ones, everyone gathered around the TVs on the first Saturday of May to watch the horses run. *The most excited two minutes in sports*, they called it. Whether your pick for the winner was made by name, color, superstition, or statistics, everyone cheered for their pick from gate to wire. Civilized cheers morphed into shrieks and shouts by the final furlong.

You could love it or hate it, but just about everyone in Kentucky had an opinion on the Derby. There was little tolerance for neutral ground. Mel had tried to watch the Derby in Boston her first year, but she had burst into tears when the crowd sang "My Old Kentucky Home" and cried herself to sleep that night. After the pain of that one, she couldn't bring herself to watch another.

Next to the horses, and even this was arguable, food was the most important element of any Derby party. Mrs. Tomlin's food was the envy of the county and seeing the spread laid out before them on three folding tables joined together, it was no wonder why. The tables were covered with hot dishes, cold dishes, old family recipes, potato salad, ham, breads of all kinds, and of course, Derby pies and bourbon balls. Fancy city parties had nothing on country folk. Mr. Tomlin greeted them and handed them beers. No mint juleps here. This was strictly a beer and bourbon party.

Family and close friends sprinkled the backyard. The Tomlin's three grown sons were there with their families making the party feel livelier than it actually was. Jessica took her plate and mingled with Mr. Tomlin's sons. She'd been close to two of them in school. Mel took her time filling her plate wondering where she should sit wishing Katherine was here. Trisha waved her over to an empty lawn chair beside her. Mel had forgotten that Trisha was Mrs. Tomlin's niece, but she hadn't forgotten what she'd said to her at the horse show.

"I thought I'd see you here," Trisha said.

"I'd forgotten that Mrs. Tomlin was your aunt."

"Yep. I should be grateful momma wasn't as good of a cook as her. I'd be in more trouble than I already am." Trisha patted her flabby waistline.

"No one can beat her, that's for sure." Mel sunk her teeth into a bourbon ball and held her hand in front of her mouth. "God, these are delicious."

"How are things being back?"

"It's better now that we've worked out a few kinks between us." Mel swung her head toward Jessica across the yard. "There are still times I wake up and can't believe I'm here."

"I heard why you went away. They were talking about it down at the bank one morning. People get all riled up about things that shouldn't be any of their concern. I kept wishing I would have known back then, you know? Maybe I could have helped you some way." Trisha dabbed the corner of her mouth with a napkin.

"Thanks, Trisha. That means a lot. And thanks for what you said to me at the horse show. I should have told you that sooner," Mel said. "I was confused back then. It took me a few years to figure myself out."

"I sit in the pew, and I hear them saying it's wrong, but I have a hard time telling someone else their life is wrong when you're not hurting anyone. Who am I to tell you or anyone else who to love?" Trisha placed her hand on her heart. "Then I think 'what do I know?' I'm just the piano

167

player. But I can't help feeling like God ain't pleased with hating on someone because of who they love. Lord knows I'm no theologian, but I know about people, and the more love we got going on in this world, the better."

"It sounds pretty simple when you put it that way," Mel said thoughtfully.

"Well, for what it's worth, you just stick to being you and all the rest will work out." Trisha nodded her head hard once as if to say this was law in her book.

Just before four, Mr. Tomlin called everyone together in the living room. The horses were introduced, and their stories told. Bets were made for fun, and the party continued around the TV. Kids stayed outside until the horses were saddled.

When the time came for the horses to load into the starting gate, Mel wanted to pinch herself to make sure all this around her was real. The gates flung open. Today's blue sky promised a fast track. Mel leaned in toward the TV. Her pick, the longshot, was stuck in the middle of a tight group as they rounded the first corner. She kept an eye on the green and white silks worn by the jockey.

The favorite crossed the finish line three lengths ahead of the rest. Mel's longshot came in fourth. The longshot had always been her dad's pick. He would smile and say, "boy, just think if you had a hundred dollars on that one at sixty-to-one when he crossed the finish line. I'd do me a little dance." He and Mr. Tomlin had held a longstanding tradition of betting one another ten dollars on which horse would come in dead last. Mr. Tomlin had won most years saying he had a knack for picking the loser but never the winner.

After graining that night, Mel stood out back of the barn watching the horses graze in Tiny Pete's paddock. She had tried to explain to Patricia the thrill of the Derby, but the conversation had ended in a fight about animal rights. Sure, some assholes abused animals, horses included, but it was impossible to explain the relationship most horse people had with their horses. They were like close friends and some more loyal than blood relatives.

Jessica came around the side of the barn from the house. She handed Mel a bottle of beer without a word.

"This isn't the first time you know," Jessica said.

"Really?"

Silence. Mel wondered if that was all she was going to say.

"A few months before dad died. I caught him with some young girl from his work."

Mel hated Tommy for hurting her little sister.

Jessica continued. "He kept calling. After dad's funeral, he stopped by. I was too lonely."

"I know I've said it before, but I'm sorry you had to face that alone."

"It wouldn't have changed him dying." Jessica's logical side kicked in.

"I know, but I should have been here."

"Tommy swore it would never happen again, but I figured it was just a matter of time."

"What did Dad think of him?"

Jessica laughed a little. "They didn't get along. Dad said he was shifty—said 'you're too good for the likes of him.'"

"I agree with Dad."

Jessica chuckled.

"I'm serious."

"Well, at any rate, I'll not be burned again. At least not by him."

"Have you talked to him?"

"Not yet. He texted me today, but I didn't respond."

Sunday morning the sun beat down on the two front fields and the grass that had been cut on Thursday. It had been a warm, dry week—a rarity for spring in Kentucky—providing the perfect window for cutting hay. Some folks wouldn't have worked in the hayfield on the Lord's day, but Thomas Snow had always said weather dictates the haying, and if God had not wanted you to work on a Sunday, he would have guaranteed it didn't rain on a Monday.

Jessica had turned the hay allowing it to dry another day in the hot sun. Mel knelt at the edge of the field and grabbed a handful of crisp, cut grass. It crunched in her hand. There was a good mixture of clover this year. The horses would love it.

Mr. Tomlin started baling as soon as the dew dried, and Mrs. Tomlin came with him to fix the lunch. Before Mel's mom had passed away, the two women would sit under the shade tree at the edge of the field, gossiping and watching. Today, Trisha Wade joined her under that same tree, the branches stretched wider. James had offered to help with the hay in exchange for riding lessons for his boys. Jasper and Cody were bringing two friends with them. Haying was a communal gathering. Folks knew who they could count on when it came time to pull in the hay. Long before they were big enough to be any real help, Mel and Jessica had joined their dad on countless occasions in hayfields all over the county.

Jessica and Jasper stacked the bales the rest of the crew tossed onto the back of the hay wagon. The crew had just made their second full swipe along the far edge of the field when a familiar truck pulled up along the fence. Tommy slipped his hands into leather gloves and climbed over the fence, smiling. He walked casually—arrogantly, across the field.

Jessica stacked the bale Cody had tossed up to her before jumping down off the wagon next to Mel. "Just keep everybody moving."

Jessica walked toward Tommy.

Cody jumped on the wagon and took her place stacking. The tractor engine roared behind Mel. She couldn't hear what Jessica had said when she met Tommy in the middle of the field, but she saw his smile disappear. Jessica leaned in toward him and shouted. Mel threw a bale on the wagon, but she kept a close eye on her sister.

On the baler, Mr. Tomlin continued up the middle of the field between the group and the ruckus. He shook his head but kept the baler chugging.

The tractor and wagon turned at the end of the field to make another row. Now Mel didn't have to crane her neck to see, and they were one swath closer to the escalating conflict.

Tommy grabbed Jessica's upper arm and yanked her to him.

Mel dropped the bale she was holding and took off. Cody and Jasper jumped from the wagon at a dead run, beating Mel to the scuffle. Jasper slammed Tommy's chest with his forearm knocking him to the ground. Cody jumped on him holding his neck to the ground.

"You son of a bitch," Cody shouted just inches from Tommy's stunned face.

"Stop! Cody, don't!" Jessica yelled.

Mel reached Jessica's side. Jessica was rubbing her arm with her other hand.

Jasper grabbed at Cody's arm. "Come on, man. Come on."

Cody stood and adjusted his shirt glaring. Tommy jumped up from the ground and grabbed his hat that had gone flying, his face red and sweaty.

"You'll wish to God you hadn't done that," Tommy smacked his hat against his leg, dust flying.

Jessica pushed passed Jasper and Cody. "Go home, Tommy. Don't come back."

"I'll go when I'm damn good and ready." Spit flew out of his mouth as he spoke. "I could have these assholes arrested."

"Leave. Now." Jessica's voice was shaky but strong. "Boys, get back to work."

Cody and Jasper didn't budge. Tommy laughed. "Don't you tell me what to do, bitch."

Jessica's fist came out of nowhere and slammed into his nose. He screamed and hit his knees. His hands flew up and cupped his nose, but the blood ran off his chin and wrists.

"I told you to leave," Jessica said through clenched teeth, "and I meant it."

"You crazy bitch! You broke my God-damned nose," Tommy cried out as he stood.

Cody and Jasper stiffened.

"Leave it, boys." Jessica turned and started walking back to the hay wagon.

Tommy turned and walked toward his truck.

Mel, Cody, and Jasper stood like statues—eyes wide.

"Thanks for looking out for me," Jessica said.

The truck engine revved and grass and dirt flew as he sped down the driveway.

"That was one hell of a punch." Jasper walked up to Jessica and put his arm around her shoulder. "I'll think twice about giving you any grief again."

Jessica smiled. "Well, it's about time."

"Are you okay?" Mel asked, still stunned.

"Yeah, I'm fine." She rubbed her knuckles.

It was close to midnight when Mel heard a quiet knock on her bedroom door.

"Yeah?"

Jessica stuck her head in.

"Everything all right?" Mel sat up in her bed, squinting. The hall light shined in from behind Jessica's head.

"It's stupid, but would you mind if I slept in here tonight?"

She had been crying.

Mel got up out of bed and walked to the door. She hugged Jessica. After a minute, Jessica pulled away and wiped her eyes on her nightshirt.

"Climb in that side." Mel reached out into the hall and switched off the light before closing the door. "I hope you don't kick in your sleep like you used to."

172

Mel could just make out Jessica's grin through the darkness. "I probably still do."

The dark morning sky filled with the songs of birds. Jessica slept soundly beside Mel, her breath heavy and methodical. Moving the covers gently, Mel crept out of the bed and down to the kitchen, needing coffee and time to wrap her brain around the events of yesterday. The horses could wait this morning. Her back and shoulders were sore and tense from the hayfield. The look in Tommy's eyes yesterday made her uneasy.

Mel had just poured her second cup and was looking through yesterday's Lexington Herald when Jessica walked into the kitchen and sat down across from her. Mel handed her the cup she'd just poured. "You want some breakfast?"

Jessica just shook her head. Mel poured herself another cup and pretended to go back to reading the front page.

"Thanks for last night." Jessica stared into her cup.

"No worries."

"I'm taking the day off." Jessica picked at the edge of the table.

Mel had seen Jessica ride horses with the flu and a 101 fever.

"I'll call the boys and let them know. I'll feed too." Mel didn't miss a beat. "Listen. Why don't we drive into Lexington for lunch or something? I need some new jeans anyway."

"Sure. Whatever is fine."

"Okay then. You get ready while I go to the barn."

She called the boys on her way to the barn. They would come over and clean stalls while Mel and Jessica were out. Jessica was ready and waiting at the kitchen table when Mel returned. She went upstairs and dressed quickly before Jessica changed her mind.

Jessica stared out the passenger window. Mel switched the radio on to fill the silence in the Jeep. She knew

173

the words to country songs again. Patricia had hated country music, so she had gotten out of the habit of listening to it. Now she hummed as they drove.

They pulled into Cattleman's parking lot a few minutes before it opened and were the first ones in. Overalls and Stetsons soon filled the tables around them.

After lunch, they made the short drive to the mall in silence. Any shopping mall was one of Mel's least favorite places in the world. They were in and out in a hurry. Jessica suggested a movie and Mel quickly agreed. She parked as far away from the spot she had seen Tommy and the woman as possible.

Jessica sat beside her eating popcorn one popped kernel at a time just like she had done as a kid. She had chosen an action film. As the movie started, Mel found it difficult to keep her mind off Katherine. Less than a week ago, they had sat side by side in this same theater. Mel tried to put the movie night with Katherine in perspective as just a friendly movie night, but try as she might, she couldn't stop the tremble of attraction that ran through each time Katherine appeared.

Stepping out into the parking lot, Mel shielded her eyes from the sun. "No matter what time I go into a movie, I expect it to be dark when I leave the building. Ready to head home?"

"I'm hungry," Jessica answered.

"After a steak and all that popcorn?" Mel laughed. "Okay, Name the place."

Jessica chose pizza, but they couldn't agree on toppings, so they bought two.

Out of the blue, sitting at a booth in the back of the restaurant, Jessica said, "I can't believe I punched him."

Mel chuckled. "I couldn't either, but good for you."

"You know what he said when he grabbed me?"

Mel listened.

"He told me it was my own fault. And that I should get used to men looking for it somewhere else."

"Has he ever done this before? Hurt you?" This question had been nagging Mel since yesterday.

"Never."

Mel searched her face skeptically.

"I swear, Mel. Never. I mean we're both hotheaded. We've broken up, yelled, and fought—I even threw a manure fork at him a couple of times—but this was different. I swear to you, I wouldn't stand for anyone treating me like that."

Her answer satisfied Mel's concern. "Dad was right, you know. You're too good for him."

Jessica frowned. "You don't think there's anything—wrong with me, do you?"

"Wrong with you?"

"I don't know—I mean—I didn't always like having sex every time the damn wind changed, you know, or every time he wanted it?" Jessica said more to herself than to Mel. Under all that toughness, Jessica had a tenderness about her that wasn't seen often.

"There is nothing wrong with you." Mel thought of just how to word her next sentence. "That kind of thing is nobody's business but yours and no one's decision but yours either."

Jessica smiled but said nothing.

They hadn't expected to stay out that late, and Mel wished she would have asked the boys to feed. Jessica walked into the darkened barn aisle with only the moonlight shining into the aisle. She was as at home in this barn as she was in the house. Mel reached in behind the stud to switch on the lights.

"Shit," Jessica yelled out.

Mel followed her gaze and saw the opened stall door. Rooster was gone.

Chapter Twenty-Three

Jessica shouted orders as she ran to the stall, "Go check the other barn."

Mel ran with a burning in her stomach. She switched on the lights and checked each stall.

Jessica was in the tack room when Mel returned out of breath from running. Saddles and bridles were strewn across the floor. The glass in the trophy cabinet at the end of the barn aisle was busted and trophies were scattered in front of the case.

"Everyone else is here."

"My show saddle's gone."

Next to Rooster, this saddle was among her most prized possessions. A twenty-first birthday present from their dad. Jessica had joked that if the barn ever caught fire, she promised to come back for Mel after she got Rooster and her saddle to safety.

After a quick look through the office and the house, Jessica called the sheriff's office. They would send someone out to take a report. Mel tossed grain to the horses, while Jessica called Cody. They had left around three that afternoon, but all had been normal.

Within the hour two trucks pulled up.

"What are you doing here?" Jessica stood broad shouldered in the barn aisle.

Mel was shocked to see Uncle Jerry march into the barn behind Sheriff Collins.

"I'm not here to cause trouble, Jess. We were shooting pool when the call came in. Any idea who took him?"

Jessica didn't answer but continued to stare a hole through Uncle Jerry who didn't move from where he'd been standing just inside the barn door.

A big burly man with a beer belly, Sheriff Collins waddled over to the open stall. "This where he was taken from?"

"Yeah. We were in Lexington most of the day."

As the sheriff ask questions, Mel felt Uncle Jerry staring at her. Mel was no longer the confused eighteen-year-old, and this man was no longer allowed to bully her.

"Thank you for coming, Uncle Jerry." Mel did not look away and hoped he couldn't tell how fast her heart was beating.

Uncle Jerry stumbled over his words. "No trouble— wanted to make sure y'all was okay."

They both shifted their attention to Jessica.

The sheriff pulled out a notepad from his shirt pocket. "Noticed any strangers around lately?"

Jessica leaned against the stall door and hesitated. "No, but I should probably tell you about Sunday."

"I'm listening." Sheriff Collins shewed a cat away with his hat and sat down on a bale of hay beside the stall. Jessica told him about Tommy and the exchange in the hayfield. The sheriff chuckled and tried to cover it with a cough when Jessica told them that she'd punched him in the face.

Uncle Jerry straight up approved. "Good for you."

Jessica shot him a look.

"I'm not saying it was him for certain, but it would make sense," Jessica said.

The sheriff wrote down a few more words. "You sure you didn't leave your saddle anywhere? The trailer maybe?"

177

"It was right here." Jessica was running out of patience pointing to the rack.

"I'm just covering all the bases, Jess," the sheriff answered defensively. "I'll send somebody over to Tommy's place to talk to him in the morning.'

Mel marveled at the small-town feel of this investigation. She wouldn't be surprised if that somebody would sit down for a quick cup of coffee and a slice of pie too. She didn't know if this made things better or worse for finding Rooster.

"In the meantime, you two girls check the property in the morning and make sure Rooster ain't running around out there somewhere."

"He wouldn't have saddled himself," Jessica said flatly.

"I'm just saying check is all. No harm in checking." Sheriff Collins sounded like a father scolding his daughter.

Mel loved and hated this about the south.

Uncle Jerry had remained silent. As the sheriff got in his truck, Uncle Jerry held back, looking around the barn and then at Jessica. "Anything I can do to help?"

"Nothing I can think of." Jessica's face said she had weighed those few words carefully.

Uncle Jerry seemed satisfied. "I'll keep an eye out," was all he said before walking out into the night.

Jessica and Mel had started riding the boundary fences after the sheriff left, but a downpour had driven them back to the barn. When the boys arrived the next morning, they saddled up along with Mel and Jessica. Cody brought his younger brother who seemed hell-bent on getting in on the action and had jumped at the chance to skip school for a day. The consensus was that this was pointless, but as the sheriff said, it didn't hurt to check. Maybe the culprit had taken the saddle for some quick cash and turned Rooster out for spite.

Mr. Tomlin went to the neighboring farms in case they had seen anything from the night before. Worry

178

stretched across Jessica's face as she doled out paddock names to each rider. Rooster was like a best friend to her and not knowing where he was or what was happening to him was almost more than she could bear.

Everyone trickled back to the barn later that morning with no sign of Rooster. Sheriff Collins had called to say he had sent a deputy over to talk with Tommy this morning, but no one was home. He would call again with any news. Jessica took Cody with her to pick up horses from the Jackson's that afternoon saying she needed to keep busy.

Later that night, the sheriff called again. Mel answered the phone. The deputy had talked with Tommy. His father had vouched for him saying he'd been mending fences on Monday. Sheriff Collins asked for a picture of Rooster along with a copy of his registration papers.

"No fool in his right mind's going to try and sell Rooster around here," he said.

Jessica said she would run them by the office in the morning.

Mel, Mr. Tomlin, and Jasper ate lunch on the picnic table, and Rooster was the only thing on their minds. Jessica had gone into town early to meet with the Sheriff and stop by the insurance office. Cody had called saying he was sick, but Jasper said he just had a hangover.

"It just ain't right, stealing a defenseless animal," Mr. Tomlin said with his mouth full of ham sandwich.

Jasper piped up. "I know good and well it was that damned Tommy that took him."

Mr. Tomlin nodded in agreement.

"We don't know it was him for sure." Even as Mel said this, she doubted her conviction.

"Who else would have done it?" Jasper asked. "Everybody loves Jess."

Mr. Tomlin shook his head again. "I never did hold much stock in those Camden boys. A bunch of good-for-nothings if you ask me. They was trouble since the day their daddy took over the old Vandyke place. Ran the whole place into the ground in a matter of years and them fences ain't been mended in a month of Sundays, I'll tell you that much."

A lightbulb went off in Mel's head. She finished the last bite of her sandwich and told the men she'd forgotten to pick up some supplements Jessica asked her to get.

Mel drove with her arm out the window, a crazy thought gnawing on her. Jessica would throw a fit when she returned home, and the horses hadn't been exercised. Mel almost turned around at the foolishness of her idea.

The Camden place used to be the old Vandyke place, like Mr. Tomlin had said, and Teddy Vandyke had been one of her best friends in middle school. They had spent hours roaming that farm, even built a fort in the woods and fought off tribes of hostile Apaches on the weekends they could talk their parents into letting them play together. On many of these wild adventures, they had been pinned down in a dilapidated barn on the back of the Vandyke farm until the Lone Ranger and Tonto had showed up to help them out. The farm stretched between two roads, and the back of the property could be accessed without having to go near the house. The barn could be flattened or gone for all she knew. This was probably a waste of time.

She had only meant to stop and have a look from the road, but the fresh tire tracks of pressed grass leading to the barn beckoned her over the fence. Before she knew what she was doing, she had climbed through the barbed wire fence and peered through the broken boards in the back of the barn.

The window glass to her left was busted out at the corner. Mel stood on a concrete block and cupped her hands around her eyes like blinders to see inside the darkened barn. She could have sworn she saw movement in the corner, but the darkness was too dense.

Mel looked to the Jeep and back to the broken glass window. She should leave. There could be an obvious explanation for the tire tracks. She took one more look at the Jeep before turning to walk around the barn.

The barn door drug against the tall grasses as she pulled it to her. The afternoon sunlight shown upon the dirt floor inside. As her eyes adjusted to the darkness around her pieces of machinery, stacks of boxes and old tools appeared. Dust particles that floated across the beam of light filled her lungs with each quick breath.

Mel walked between the piles and stacks to the corner behind the wall. *Rooster*. He was tied to the wall eating from the hay bag that hung in front of him looking content and calm.

"That bastard," Mel mumbled walking over to Rooster. He nuzzled his nose into her chest. She scratched his broad chest and he let out a little blow spraying Mel's arm with spit. He was fine, and Mel was relieved.

"Let's get you home, big guy." Mel rubbed the white blaze between his eyes. Rooster took another bite of hay.

Mel reached for her phone in her back pocket to call the sheriff and Jessica, but it wasn't there. It must have fallen out in the Jeep seat on the drive over.

She stepped back out into the light and stopped just before bumping into Tommy. Mel backed into the barn catching her leg on a piece of metal protruding out from under a table. Her jeans ripped, and pain shot up her leg. It had caught her just above the boot top, mid-calf. She knelt quickly and squeezed her leg, her hands filling with hot liquid. Tommy came and stood over her saying nothing. Mel looked up, but his face was darkened by the shadows.

"What the hell are you doing in here?" Tommy spoke.

"Looking for a horse." Mel stood and limped backward a few steps to put some distance between them. She bumped into a large metal piece of machinery bracing herself against it. She winced with pain.

Her mind raced through options. The blood oozed down her leg. *Play it cool or get mean.* Her leg throbbing, she was in no shape for the latter.

"Listen, we just want Rooster."

"Why couldn't you just stay out of this?" Tommy turned and slammed his fist into a 4x4 post. The light coming in from the open door shined upon his back making it difficult to see his face. He was agitated, this much Mel knew, and she wasn't sure what he was capable of.

He walked to the middle of the room and pulled the light on. Mel looked to the door wondering if she should try to run. Even in the dimly lit room, she could see blood soaking through the jeans.

"You just made things worse." Tommy didn't turn around.

"Me? You stole our horse," Mel shouted.

"You're trespassing."

"You stole Rooster."

"I was going to bring him back." A tinge of regret hung in his tone that emboldened her.

She pushed away from the machinery and limped toward him. "What the hell, Tommy? How did you think this would end?"

"I don't know what I thought, okay?" Tommy shouted and turned around.

"I'm going to call the sheriff." Mel limped toward the door.

"No." Tommy lunged and shoved Mel. She tried to catch herself but tumbled into a pile of old boards and plywood. Dust and debris flew up around her; a nail sticking out of one of the boards ripped through her forearm.

"Son of a bitch." Mel screamed out and grabbed her arm.

"Mel!" A familiar voice shouted from outside the barn. "Where are you, Mel!"

Tommy locked eyes with Mel.

"In here," Mel yelled out.

Mr. Tomlin stuck his head in the barn door. He squinted his eyes to see through the dust and into the dim-lit room. He saw Tommy first, but his eyes grew wide seeing Mel lying in the pile of rubbish. In three quick strides, he

182

took her hand and pulled her out of the pile. He held a rifle in the other hand.

Tommy stood like a stone statue, a look of terror on his face. "Mel, I—."

Mel assured Mr. Tomlin she was all right, but he kept a tight grip on her arm. She was not at all sure she would have stayed standing without his help.

"You're in a heap of trouble, son," Mr. Tomlin called out over his shoulder as he eased Mel toward the door.

Mel sat in the same examining room she had been in when she fell off Agent. The nurse practitioner had finished stitching up the gash in her leg and arm and told her to lie still until she returned. Twenty-three stitches in all.

Sheriff Collins and two of his deputies had shown up soon after Mr. Tomlin. They had taken Tommy into custody and loaded Rooster in the county horse trailer. One of the deputies would drive Mel's Jeep back to the farm while Mr. Tomlin drove Mel to the Emergency Center. Mel had tried to call Jessica on her way to Frankfort, but Jessica hadn't answered. Out here, cell service was still patchy. Mel left a message.

"Jess, we found Rooster. The sheriff's taking him to our place. They got Tommy too, the bastard. Mr. Tomlin's driving me over to Frankfort to the Emergency Center now, but it's nothing. I'm fine. We'll meet you at home."

On their way, Mel asked Mr. Tomlin how he had ended up there. She sat beside him in his pickup with a red flannel shirt tied around her leg to slow the bleeding.

"You and me had the same idea about that old barn." Mr. Tomlin gave a conniving grin that made him look like a wrinkled little kid.

"How did you know about the barn?"

Mr. Tomlin laughed. "Because I used to play in that old barn when me and old man Vandyke was kids."

183

The thought of Mr. Tomlin as a scrawny little boy running wild through the fields made Mel smile through her pain.

Mel sat up on the examining table when she heard voices coming toward the room. The nurse came in with Jessica close behind.

"Goddammit, Mel. Are you crazy?"

Mel laughed. "It's only a few stitches."

"Mr. Tomlin told me. It could have been more than stitches."

"It might not have been one of my brightest ideas ever, but we got Rooster back."

Jessica sat in a chair in the corner of the room and watched. The nurse examined the stitches and gave Mel a tetanus shot to be on the safe side. Jessica's face grew pale when she saw the size of the needle.

"I think you look worse than I do." Mel stepped down off the table.

"Oh, shut up."

On the drive home, Jessica made Mel tell her the whole story again.

"I knew he had a temper, but I never thought he'd do something like this." Jessica shook her head.

"I think he just got his pride hurt and wanted to take it out on you, but then he panicked. He didn't figure we knew about the barn."

After hearing of Mel's adventurous afternoon, Mrs. Tomlin cooked the girls a dinner that could have fed ten hungry men and sent it over with Mr. Tomlin. He was still there when Sheriff Collins stopped back by. Jessica offered the men pie and coffee. They sat out under the Elm tree on the picnic table.

"He admitted to selling that saddle of yours over in Lexington. Doubt we'll be able to recover it," Sheriff Collins said matter-of-factly. "How's Rooster?"

"He's okay. Tommy—" Jessica looked at Mel. "I was going to say Tommy wouldn't hurt an animal, but I guess I should rethink what Tommy would or wouldn't do."

"His daddy bailed him about an hour ago. Madder than a hornet, threatening to sue, but I reminded him it was his son that caused all this trouble in the first place. I warned Tommy to keep his distance."

"Good. I don't care to see him any time soon."

"There'll be a trial, of course. Since Rooster's worth a fair bit." Sheriff Collins scraped the last bit of cherry pie off his plate.

"Do you think they'll cause us trouble?" Mel asked watching Jessica's face.

The sheriff leaned back and wiped the corners of his mouth with a napkin. "That was the best cherry pie that's ever crossed my lips. Oh, his daddy was spouting off down at the jail, but I'm sure it won't amount to much. Men like him are always talking big when their family pride is at stake."

The incident with Tommy and Rooster did not go away quickly. Twice, as Cody and Jasper left for the day, his truck was parked on the side of the road opposite the driveway. Both times he drove off, but his lurking made everyone uneasy. After his first appearance, Jessica had installed a gate across the driveway the next morning. Sheriff Collins stopped by the farm after the second time.

"Not much I can do seeing he's not on your property." The sheriff told them. "It's not likely he'll do you harm. He told me he regrets the whole ordeal."

"Regrets getting caught is more like it," Mel said.

"He's either waiting for us to leave, so he can steal something else, or he's just tormenting us." Jessica threw the handle of the pitchfork against the corner. "I would have never guessed he'd act like this."

"I'll have a word with him." Sheriff Collins promised her.

185

"Tell him to stay away from this place, or so help me, I'll punch him again."

Jessica had been furious after finding out he'd sold the saddle for five hundred dollars. It was easily worth four times this amount.

"All right, all right. I'll see what I can do. In the meantime, it wouldn't hurt you none to dust off that old Remington of your daddy's and keep it handy."

Mel marveled at this advice from a law enforcement agent. It was like stepping into an old western.

Thomas Snow had insisted that both girls learn to shoot, but it had been years since Mel had even held a gun. Jessica took the sheriff at his word, and later that night, took Mel out behind the barn for target practice.

"I don't think this is necessary." Mel dropped the rifle from her shoulder before pulling the trigger. "I feel ridiculous doing this."

"You used to like to shoot, and you used to be pretty good." Jessica motioned with her head at the tin cans set in a row on the top fence plank.

"Yeah, but this feels like we're preparing for a range war or something."

Mel tucked the rifle into her shoulder and closed her left eye. Squeezing the trigger, the gun went off. A tin can flew into the air and disappeared in the tall grass.

"Good shot, John Wayne." Jessica winked. "This ain't Boston. We've got to take care of ourselves."

"I'm out of practice. I was aiming at the next one."

Jessica opened her mouth to say something then stopped, seeing Mel's smirk. "You ass. You were not."

They shot a few more rounds before going inside. Mel felt guilty for enjoying their shooting session as much as she had, but the sound of that gun going off in her ears was exhilarating. Guns were an easy thing to hate these days. She had gone to rallies against gun violence with Patricia. Was this any different? They were putting holes through tin cans now, but the intention went beyond that. Tin cans were fine, the ping they made when the bullet made contact was brilliant, but Mel doubted she could shoot another human if it came right down to it and hoped she never had to test that theory.

Chapter Twenty-Four

Mel cringed when she saw the baby shower invitation from Emily Johnson's mother recalling the conversation she had had with Emily in the café. "Why didn't you get one?"

Jessica laughed. "Because I'm not her high school friend, and I'm so happy about that fact right about now."

"You could be my plus one. Remember I went to that wedding with you."

"Baby Showers are not plus one things. Besides, there's no way in hell, I'm going to one of those things. I can't stand the games they play—nobody else can stand them either, but nobody has the guts to say it." Jessica shivered like she'd just swallowed cough medicine.

No amount of pleading helped. Jessica would not be budged.

"Don't go if you don't want to."

"I feel like I should." Mel tossed the invitation on the table and followed Jessica to the barn.

"That's the difference between you and me. I wouldn't go if I didn't want to." Jessica shook her head.

"Well, aren't you perfect in every way, Mary Poppins?" Mel grabbed her work gloves from her back pocket and threw them at Jessica as she sidestepped out the door.

Mel did go to the baby shower. Each time she had complained about it, Jessica had shrugged and told her nobody was forcing her to go. It was annoying, even though Jessica was right, but when Katherine texted her asking if she was going, the event suddenly didn't feel so cringe-worthy.

Mel arrived at the church and scanned the parking lot for Katherine's Jeep. What if she'd been called out on a call at the last minute? While debating whether to go inside or just turn around and go home, Trisha knocked on her window.

Mel almost jumped out of her skin.

Trisha laughed but covered her mouth. "Sorry."

Mel grabbed the gift bag from the seat beside her and opened the door. "I should have been paying attention."

The door to the fellowship hall opened to blue balloons and streamers with blue baseball gloves and bats hanging from the ceiling. "I could be wrong, but I'm guessing it's a boy," Mel said.

"Emily's always going on about her husband wanting his own baseball team. Maybe this one's the pitcher." Trisha wrote her name on a name tag and pressed it to her blouse.

Mel was in line for the finger foods when Katherine walked in. Mel couldn't stop the smile that spread across her face.

"I thought you'd chickened out," Mel said when Katherine walked up to the food table.

"Are you kidding? I love things like this."

"Seriously? Why?"

"Come on now, they're not that bad. There's something sort of tribal about them." Katherine poured a glass of sweet tea. "Think of it as community building."

"Community building is festivals, horse shows, ball games, beer. This?" Mel frowned and looked around the room. "This is just a civilized form of torture."

"Aren't we gloomy today?" Katherine said nudging Mel's shoulder with hers. "Look around. Everyone's laughing and having a good time."

The games were as bad as Mel remembered. Mel did a decent job on the "Baby Animal Names," game, mostly because she knew that a baby alpaca was called a cria and that beavers had kittens but failed miserably at the "What's in Your Purse?" game realizing she was the only woman in the room without a purse. She'd shoved her ID and credit card in the back pocket of her jeans along with the thirty-two dollars cash from the cup holder in her Jeep.

Mel wished they served beer at these things. The game drug on.

Even Katherine carried a small handbag and won bonus points for the screwdriver and rock that were buried inside.

After the small crowd cheered when Katherine unearthed the rock from the bag holding it up over her head like a found treasure, Mel looked at her for an explanation.

"What?" Katherine smiled at her triumphantly. "I'm into rocks."

Mel shook her head but had to laugh. This woman had a way about her. A few more atrocious games accompanied by funny whispers from Katherine, and Mel lightened up. She wouldn't go so far as to say she was enjoying herself, but Katherine certainly made the torment more bearable.

After opening more gifts than any one baby could ever use, Emily came around offering more sweet tea. Her hand rested on the protruding belly.

"So glad you could come today, Mel. And you too Katherine. My Joe just thinks the world of Nathan. Says he's one of the funniest people he's ever met."

Katherine held her glass for a refill. "Don't tell him that. It'll go to his head."

"We've got to get you two to some of our events here at church." Emily wagged her finger at Mel and Katherine. "Find you some husbands."

Mel blinked in surprise. "I appreciate the offer, but I'm not really in the market for a husband," purposefully putting on a sweet southern tone to thinly masked the *go to hell* that floated in her eyes.

Katherine cleared her throat muffling a giggle.

190

"Yes, well—" Emily shifted uneasily from one foot to another rubbing her belly. "I better go check on the finger foods."

Mel rolled her eyes as Emily shuffled away. Katherine smacked her arm in playful rebuke.

The parking lot had cleared except for a few cars by the building. Katherine stood by Mel's open window. "There's Emily. Want me to ask her about those husbands again?"

"She's got some nerve."

"Maybe she's just clueless."

"Not likely," Mel answered, but her reply left too much unsaid. "Remember when I told you I kissed a girl at a football game?"

"Yes," Katherine answered waiting for more.

Mel waited for the unspoken to sink in. She saw the moment it did.

"Her?" Katherine asked.

"Surprise."

"But she's married now."

"Yep."

"Have you ever talked about it?" Katherine whispered.

Mel shook her head in horror. "And I hope to hell we never do."

"Wow. I never imagined." Katherine watched Emily's car leave the parking lot like she was trying to do just that.

"Anyway, that was ages ago. People change, decide they want different things. You have time for a beer?"

"Sure, maybe we can look for those husbands while we're at it." Katherine winked and walked to her Jeep.

"You're not going to let that go, are you?" Mel yelled out after her.

Mel looked in her rearview mirror at the traffic light in town. Katherine's mouth moved like she was singing. She was sure of herself. Mel liked that about her. She also liked how she felt around Katherine. Since realizing she was different from the other girls, at least where it concerned the all-consuming topic of boys, Mel had learned to guard her emotions. Few people put her at ease like Katherine, and Mel couldn't remember the last time she'd talked to someone and not second-guessed the motive behind their words. The light had changed. Katherine honked her horn and feigned belligerence throwing her hand out the window like a New York taxi driver. Mel waved an apology out the window and drove through.

Except for a couple of regulars seated at the bar, The Goat was deserted.

"Do you play?" Katherine motioned to the two pool tables off to the side.

"Horribly," Mel answered.

"Great. You rack, and I'll grab beers. You trust me to choose?" Katherine asked with a gleam but didn't wait for an answer.

Mel pulled two quarters from her pocket and released the balls. Katherine stood by the bar with one foot propped up on the rail below. Grabbing the rack from the wall, Mel set up the table.

"Thanks. You can break." Mel took a beer from Katherine and handed her the cue ball.

Katherine sat her beer on the high table beside the table and lined up the shot. "I ordered fried pickles."

"Dipped in ranch dressing they're delicious." Mel chalked the tip of her stick.

Katherine broke. A red striped ball rolled into the corner pocket in front of Mel.

"Luck," Mel said smugly.

"We'll see. Stripes for me."

"Loser buys." Mel raised her glass before setting it down and lining up her shot.

The loser did buy so the next two rounds were on Mel. "Tell me about this rock collection of yours."

192

"I never said I had a collection. I just like them is all." Katherine leaned over the table and smacked the cue ball into the triangle of balls.

Mel raised her eyebrows and sipped her beer.

"I always said if I hadn't chosen to be a vet I'd have been a geologist."

"I did not see that one coming." Mel laughed. "Why rocks?"

Katherine eyed her as if weighing out how much information to divulge.

The front door opened, and a couple came in with a baby in tow. Mel thought about being shocked but figured it wasn't worth it. Turning her attention back to Katherine, Mel waited for an answer.

"Okay," her eyes widening like a kid at show and tell. "Every fossil, every layer—rocks, they carry captions of their interactions with the environment around them over millions of years. Reading them is like reading the history of the earth!"

Mel's eyes widened.

Katherine stopped and looked around the room seeming uncharacteristically shy. "What can I say? I'm a nerd at heart."

"I love that about you," Mel said. *Shit.* Her thoughts had betrayed her by escaping. Stumbling to recover she said, "I mean, it's good for you, for people, I love it when people have—hobbies."

"Okay. Your turn. Tell me something that would surprise me about you," Katherine said.

"I don't know." A familiar panic gripped Mel.

"Come on. What's something you love?"

Mel thought hard. It had been a long time since she had thought of it. Mel opened her mouth but stopped.

Katherine laughed. "Let me guess. Pole dancing."

"Do I strike you as the pole dancing type?"

"Okay then. Knitting?"

"I think I'd prefer the pole dancing." Mel rolled her eyes.

193

"I could see it." Katherine squinted.

"What?"

"Pole dancing."

Mel picked up the blue square and chalked her cue stick not looking up. "Don't be ridiculous."

Katherine smiled and set up her shot. The solid yellow dropped into the corner pocket beside Mel.

"Ready to lose again?" Katherine hit her playfully on the shoulder with a pool stick.

"Where did you learn to play pool?" Mel was grateful for the change of subject.

"One semester we had this horrible professor for Parasitology. She would drone on for hours in the highest-pitched voice you can imagine. It was like fingers on a chalkboard to me. I told two of my friends I was thinking of dropping the class—I just couldn't take it. They made a deal with me. If I'd stay in, we would go to the billiards and have a beer after every class. I ended up with a B+."

"Well, at least now I know who to thank for losing." Mel smiled. "Your break."

Chapter Twenty-Five

Jessica walked into the barn aisle with James and Trisha's sweaty pony dragging his feet behind in the dust. The pony's head hung low, and his sides moved in and out from heavy breathing. He was out of shape and mean-tempered when he came. It was no wonder the boys couldn't ride him. His name was Silver, but Jessica called him Lucifer when the Wades weren't around.

He'd bitten Jessica the first day she worked him, and Mel wore an ugly purple and yellow bruise on her calf muscle the perfect size of his back hoof. He was still ornery after two months of training but had a better understanding of what he could and couldn't get away with.

"The weatherman's calling for bad weather tonight," Jessica said.

"Like tornado bad?" Mel winced. Tornados were one of the few southern wonders she had not missed at all while in Boston.

"They said not to rule it out."

Jessica unsaddled the grey dapple pony and called for Jasper to hose him down. "We'll get everything ready after we feed just in case."

Time spent huddled in the storm shelter out back of the house with dogs and cats, her mom, dad, and Jessica rushed into Mel's mind. The radio droning on tracking the storm's path. A single exposed lightbulb glared from the corner making shadows long and spooky. Two lanterns hung by the door in case of a loss of power. Mom sang to them in a soft, out-of-tune voice while Dad stood leaning against the narrow doorframe with a leery eye toward the clouds above holding his pipe between his teeth. The smell of his pipe came back to Mel. When the girls tired of songs, or when Dad came inside and shut the heavy door, he would make up silly stories about family members to keep their minds off the howling winds that rattled the door of their fragile haven.

The wall of storms headed their way reached from southern Indiana down into Tennessee. The routine came back to her as if it were innate, and to a Kentuckian, it was. After graining, Jessica rode one side of the farm on Rooster, and Mel took Bonnie out to the other. The heart of the storm was still hours away, but Mel kept a nervous eye toward the darkening sky. A tornado watch would be in effect until tomorrow morning. Once a funnel was formed and on the ground, that watch became a warning and the eerie sirens would fill the green-tinted skies. Unless you were the poor soul that met the funnel where it touched the ground, this usually gave you a few minutes to take cover. Mel shuddered and pushed Bonnie into a trot.

Horse and rider worked quickly. Gates were securely opened between paddocks allowing the horses to move safely from one field to another if it came to that. Horses, and animals in general, carried a keener sense when it came to such dangers as long as they had the freedom to move. Barns, no matter how sturdy, were no match for even a weak tornado and it was a rookie mistake to think otherwise. Their own horses would be turned out now to save time, and if the weather grew worse, the clients' horses could be turned out in a matter of a few minutes.

Mel and Jessica ate dinner in the living room. As kids, severe weather was the only time they were allowed to eat anywhere other than the kitchen table. The channels agreed, the potential grew stronger as the storm inched closer. The governor of Missouri had been interviewed and had already declared a state of emergency in three counties. Thousands were without power, and several dozen homes had been reduced to soggy heaps of rubble. Four people were missing from a trailer park south of St. Louis.

"This isn't looking too good." Mel leaned forward on the couch resting her elbows on her knees.

"To be on the safe side, I think I'll go ahead and turn the rest of the horses out." Jessica turned the volume up and stood to take the dishes to the kitchen. The weatherman returned to say the storms would be moving into the area around midnight.

Jessica went to the barn while Mel took supplies to the storm shelter. The grass had grown up around the door making it difficult to open. The last hard tug brought the door back into her knee.

"Damn it." Blankets tumbled out of Mel's arms onto the grass.

She reached for the string to turn on the light. It was cold and damp and spider webs stretched across the corners. The grey concrete walls remained unpainted. Mel was surprised to find their old drawings and scribbles still visible although faded through in spots. Mel touched the squiggly lines of a purple rabbit, the coolness of the wall seeping into her fingertips.

"Mel, you in there?"

Jessica was standing on the back porch when Mel ducked and exited the storm shelter staring up at her. The uneasiness must have shown on her face.

Jessica leaned over the railing. "We'll be fine."

With the horses turned out and the storm shelter stocked, there was nothing else to do but wait. Both girls sat and watched the storms approaching on the TV. Every few minutes, Jessica would walk onto the front porch and comment on the dark clouds or the wind picking up.

The rain started about eleven. First large, slow drops pinged against the metal roof turning to heavy sheets in a

197

matter of minutes. The storm was a determined one, and it left havoc in its frenzied path. Mel looked around the living room at all the photos and memories hanging on the walls. The thought of losing all this again was unbearable.

"Todd and Logan Counties. You should find shelter now," The meteorologist said with a tone that sounded like a worried parent. A funnel cloud had been spotted. Watch turned to warning. These counties were west of Lebanon Springs but too close for comfort.

It was the unpredictability of tornados that was so damn nerve-wracking. They appeared without notice and bounced around from hill to crevice changing directions on a dime. The funnel could choose to rip apart your tobacco barn but leave the broken lawn chair you'd been meaning to throw away for months untouched.

Around 11:30 the sirens shrieked through the green-tinted sky. A tornado touched down on the west end of the county and Mel, Jessica, and Sam Houston headed for cover. They sat in the shelter listening to the winds howl. Sam Houston bristled and growled a warning at the rattling door. The rains came in downpours followed by an unnerving stillness. The radio blared the location of the cloud through bouts of crackle and static. The bulb flickered but stayed lit. Mel jumped at a clap of thunder.

Jessica stood by the door just like their dad used to do until the rains came sideways.

"Remember that one that scattered all those cigarettes across the front hayfield?" Jessica asked opening a granola bar.

A cigarette stand had been picked up in one of the twisters that year. Mel wished she had a cigarette right now even though she'd given up on the idea of smoking.

"We found cigarettes in the hay bales that entire next winter." Mel laughed.

"Didn't they find a cash register in someone's car?"

Yeah, it had blown it through the windshield."

"Admit it, you missed this." Jessica laughed.

"Not one bit." Mel hugged her knees to her chest.

Time in the storm shelter felt like forever. The underground walls offered safety, but not knowing what you would find upon emerging from this box buried in the ground was menacing. Mel was eating peanut M&Ms when the weatherman gave the all-clear.

Light rains remained for several hours after the warning was lifted, but the worst was behind them. From reports coming in, Snow farms had been lucky. The storm had flattened a section of horse stalls and snack shack at the county fairgrounds two miles up the road. Mobile homes were destroyed, roofs were blown off, and power outages across several counties. No deaths reported yet. Dad had always said any building can be rebuilt. Mel and Jessica walked to the barn stepping over bits of debris and branches. They would have to wait until daylight to assess the damage.

Two horses stood with their heads hanging over the side fence, their eyes wild and jumpy. Jessica led them into their stalls. "At least here's two we don't have to find in the morning."

Mel asked if they should try and find the rest.

"It'd be a good way to get our necks broke being out there tonight."

"Good that we still have power." Mel tossed hay into the stalls.

"Luckier than some, I'm sure."

The pellets of rain pinged out a melody against the metal roof and bedroom window bringing beauty to the dark night. Mel couldn't fall asleep. Lightning flashes appeared, and the old house moaned beneath the steady wind gusts. When sleep did come it was painted with dark dreams, and she awoke only minutes later clutching her pillow with both hands, her heart beating rapidly.

In the dream, Katherine had called out to her from across an unfamiliar field, but Mel couldn't understand the words she was saying. Winds were howling in her ears, and she turned her head left and right, but it was no use. She tried to walk toward Katherine. Her legs wouldn't move. Huge links of logging chain wrapped around her feet, and when she turned behind her Uncle Jerry held the chain in his hand with a revolting smile. She tugged and yanked at the chain, but Uncle Jerry held firm. Her ankles bled from the tight chains.

Mel turned back to Katherine who was now being picked off the ground by a funnel cloud. Her mouth still moved as she rose higher and higher into the sky. The twister moved toward the barn. She pawed the ground like a wild animal trying to free herself. She picked up rocks and began throwing them at Uncle Jerry. He only let out a deep laugh and leaned back against his truck pulling the chain tighter with one hand and picking his teeth with a toothpick with the other.

Horses were happy to be back in their comfy stalls. Only Major, the hellion of a miniature, played hard to get the next morning. These horses were used to a life of luxury and were ready for their grain and hay. Several had wild eyes like they'd had a night out on the town. But not Major. He bolted like a wild stallion every time they tried to get close to him. He nestled himself in the small herd of cattle and Jessica said to hell with him and turned Rooster toward the barn.

Katherine was standing at the back of the barn when they crossed the field. She gave a big wave, and Mel's heartbeat sped up a bit.

"Seems like you dodged the bullet," Katherine said as Mel and Jessica dismounted.

"We'll have a lot of clean up, but structures seem sound. Lost a few pieces of tin here and there," Jessica answered.

"How did you fair?" Mel asked.

"No power and it got most of the barn roof. I was wondering if you had a spot for my two. I've been meaning to send them over for training anyway. Now's as good a time as any if you have room."

"Sure. Bring them on over; we'll make room. Oh, that's right, you don't have a trailer. Do they load okay? Mel can run over this afternoon." She turned to Mel. "You take the truck and trailer over."

Mel jerked her head to look at Jessica. It hadn't been a joke. "Sure," was all she answered. Of course, Mel knew how to drive a truck and horse trailer, her Dad has insisted she learn before she went for her driving test, but Jessica hadn't asked her to drive since returning.

"I'll make plans to be around this afternoon. They may be spoiled, fat, and out of shape, but at least they load well." Katherine shrugged apologetically.

Jessica lifted the saddle off Rooster. "You and Nathan are welcome to stay here until your power's back on."

"Thanks for the offer, but Nathan's been dying to use the new generator he bought last fall. It's big enough to run a small city." Katherine rolled her eyes.

Chapter Twenty-Six

Jessica and the boys left around noon for the sale and would not return until Sunday afternoon. With Tommy still lurking about, Jessica didn't feel comfortable leaving the farm unattended, so Mel had offered to stay behind. She sank into the hot bath carefully so as not to spill the glass of red wine. Her muscles ached. She had spent the day burning branches and limbs left behind by the tornado. Mr. Tomlin and Jasper had cut fallen trees all week and the woodpile would suffice for next winter's fury.

She took a slow sip of wine and held it in her mouth before swallowing, leaned her head against the back of the tub, and closed her eyes. The leaves on the sycamore outside the bathroom window rustled in the wind. She stayed there with her thoughts until the water was tepid. Throwing on her striped pajama bottoms and a white tank top, Mel went downstairs in search of something on TV.

Nothing interesting. The quiet halls reminded her of those first few weeks here. Mel thought of her return often and after so many months still found it hard to believe she was back here. Sisters were friends again, most days, and worked side by side to make this farm amount to something. She couldn't imagine herself anywhere else.

The strong knock on the back door startled her. Sam Houston stiffened and growled a deep, cautious growl. Slapping her leg, Mel walked into the kitchen with Sam Houston right beside her.

Mel leaned over the sink but couldn't see a vehicle in the driveway. She grabbed the rifle from the corner. Holding it down to her side gave her a strange sense of security, although she still doubted her resolve to use it.

Another knock. Mel peered through the crack in the curtain, then swung it wide seeing Katherine standing in the yellow glow of the porchlight.

"You scared me half to death." Mel placed her hand over her heart. "Come in. Come in."

Katherine looked to the rifle by Mel's leg. "Sorry. Guess I should've called. I just put some feed in the barn for my babies and thought I'd say a quick hi."

"Glad you did." Mel leaned the gun in the corner. "Sorry, we're all a little jumpy with this Tommy thing."

"Anything new?"

Mel shook her head. "Jessica's taken a couple of the yearlings down to the sales this weekend, and I knocked off early. Want some wine, or I have some Scotch someone gave me recently?"

Katherine stepped inside. "You sure you don't mind me busting in on your night off?"

Mel took the bottle of Scotch from the cupboard. "Of course not. So—Scotch? We can go out on the front porch if you want."

Mel poured two glasses of Scotch. Katherine stood behind one of the kitchen chairs turning the white beaded seam over with her fingers. Mel handed one of the glasses to Katherine and their fingers touched.

The night air was cooler than the last few nights. Katherine sat on the edge of the porch with her legs dangling above the rose bushes. Mel stretched out her legs, her back resting against the corner post. Her bare feet only inches away from Katherine's hip. She hadn't intended to be this close and pulled one knee to her, resting her forearm there. Mel watched Katherine take a sip of Scotch.

"That's good Scotch," Katherine said.

"All the way from Scotland or so I was told."

"I dated this guy in college who hated Scotch," Katherine began. "Da says a man that hates Scotch can't be trusted."

"Sounds about right." Mel swirled her glass.

"Da couldn't stand any of the guys I dated." Katherine chuckled. "Not a one. But in their defense, he usually made his mind up before he met most of them."

"Yeah, dads are funny like that. How's he doing?" Mel wondered if her worry for him had brought her over to talk.

"Giving everyone grief at every turn but regaining his strength. He called me today to complain about the new diet Mum's put him on." Katherine turned to face Mel. "Did you ever date? Guys, I mean?"

Mel had not expected this turn of the conversation. "Well, I—" her voice trailed off.

"Sorry, didn't mean to just blurt that out. Just curious."

Mel took a sip of Scotch and held it in her mouth momentarily. "Yeah, I dated a few guys in high school. It was what I was supposed to do."

"So, you aren't attracted to both."

"Not that I know of." Mel laughed.

Katherine's blank stare made Mel continue.

"I've never met a guy that I was attracted to."

"Oh. So, you just knew you were attracted to— women?"

Mel wiped the sweat from her palm on her pajama bottoms. "Yeah, at some point it just sort of dawned on me."

Kathrine took another drink and smiled sheepishly. "Sorry, I'm being so nosey."

"You're not nosey. I figure it's better for people to ask than assume. And let me tell you, I've heard some wacky ones."

"Like what?" Katherine poured more Scotch into both glasses.

Mel scanned Katherine's face in the moonlight. "My favorite was this guy who came up to Patricia, my ex, and me eating lunch on a park bench in Boston Commons. He told us God could take away our desire to become men. I stopped mid-chew and asked him what he'd said thinking I'd misheard him. He repeated it. Patricia jumped in before I could and told him she didn't know what he was smoking but there was no way in hell she wanted to be a man. I couldn't help laughing. The poor guy looked so stunned—like his whole theory had been blown to bits."

"What on earth did you do?" Katherine's nose was scrunched up to one side.

"He tried to go on for a bit. He said lesbians are disgruntled because they weren't born men in a 'man's world.' He wasn't mean about it or anything, but it's like he had it all figured out in his head and wanted to help—in some seriously demented way, I guess. We finally took our lunch and just walked away." Mel laughed remembering the man's eager face as he spoke.

"That's horrid."

"It's sad, but you sort of get used to people trying to save your soul, even in Boston. What's sad is that people can't just let you live your happiness and be glad there's a little more love in this world." Mel searched Katherine's face. She didn't know her well enough yet to read between the lines.

"How's Jessica doing?"

Mel knew a pivot when she saw one. "She's getting there. She didn't show it much, but I think that deal with Tommy shook her. The sale should keep her mind occupied this weekend. Plus, Jasper and Cody's constant banter are enough to keep anyone distracted."

"I'm really glad you moved back here, Mel."

"Me too." Mel patted Sam Houston's head. He'd fallen asleep next to her. "Some days it almost feels like I never left."

"Do you ever wonder how things would have turned out if you hadn't left?" Kathrine pulled her legs up on the porch and stretched them in Mel's direction. Her jeans brushed against Mel's bare foot.

"I try not to go down that path—it could drive me crazy—but I have wondered. It doesn't change anything, but it makes me sad to think I could have been here for Jessica when Dad died. But maybe he wouldn't have been okay with me being gay. Maybe it would have been worse if I stayed. You know, somehow busted the family up anyway. I wish I could know for sure what he would have thought about me."

"Do you think maybe he knew? I mean, I've heard people say that their parents knew their kids were gay since they were little." Katherine crossed her legs. Mel was grateful for the darkness.

Mel cleared her throat. "It's hard for me to know how obvious I might have been back then. I was confused as hell. I felt all wrong and all right at the same time."

"So maybe you had to move away to sort all that out."

"Could be. I was lucky to have landed with some people who really cared about me and helped me accept myself. It could have gone a different way, a horrible way, so easily." Mel took her last sip of Scotch.

"Another?" Katherine raised the bottle that sat on the porch between them.

Three more glasses of Scotch and their conversation continued. No matter the topic they landed upon, it was easy talking with Katherine. The ease was aided along by the amount of Scotch now swirling in her head. It was well after midnight when drowsiness moved in alongside tipsy.

"I should go turn off the lights in the barn before I'm too far gone," Mel said.

Katherine stood first and offered her hand to Mel. The strength of this slender woman was deceiving, pulling Mel up effortlessly. They stood inches apart, and Mel fought the urge to lean in closer. *Don't.*

Mel stepped back, wondering if she looked as wobbly as she felt. Turning when she got to the front door, Katherine still stood frozen in the same spot.

"Coming with me?"

With her pajama bottoms tucked into her rubber boots, Mel gave a quick glance in each stall making sure all horses were upright and stall doors were latched properly. Katherine sat on a bale of hay beside the door holding the yellow cat they called Limpy, one front leg was shorter than the other. He had showed up a few weeks ago, looking like death and made himself at home. Barn cats came and went as they pleased, and as long as they kept the mice at bay, they were welcome.

"Of course, everyone's healthy the night I have the vet here with me," Mel said.

"Yeah, it's like the opposite of Murphy's Law or something."

Mel switched off the lights, and they walked unhurriedly to the front of the house to retrieve the Scotch and glasses from the porch.

"You should just crash here tonight. Don't drive home." Mel hadn't meant to suggest that so brazenly, and a panic rushed through her chest.

It was a logical proposal. She didn't know how Katherine's head was feeling, but Mel would certainly not be comfortable driving.

"Might not be a bad idea." Katherine touched her head. "If it wouldn't be a bother."

"Of course not." Mel shrugged trying to play off her panic. "We have a spare room."

Katherine followed Mel inside. Mel and Jessica had cleaned out their father's bedroom months ago for a guest bedroom after a friend from Boston mentioned visiting but canceled at the last minute. This is the first occasion they had had to use it. Mel turned off the lights downstairs and Katherine followed her upstairs. She gave a quick tour of the house as they walked and stepped inside her room to find a tank top and a pair of shorts for Katherine.

"There are extra towels in the cabinet there by the tub. There should be a couple of new toothbrushes on the middle shelf too." Mel switched on the bathroom light. "If you need anything else, just ask."

Mel stood in the bathroom doorway. Katherine took a step inside and stopped. She looked to the tub, to the sink, and then directly into Mel's eyes. Mel couldn't look away.

Katherine's smile widened, and she tilted her head to the side. She leaned up to Mel's lips and kissed them tenderly. Mel's hand instinctively went to Katherine's hip as she returned the kiss. Katherine's hand rested on Mel's forearm. Katherine pulled back but left her hand resting on Mel's arm, her eyes holding the look of both shock and pleasure.

The pull of this woman intensified mixing with the Scotch that burned through Mel's body. She blinked hard and stepped back into the hallway. "Good night, Katherine. Sleep well."

Mel's movement broke the spell. Katherine stepped inside the bathroom, smiling, and held her hand on the doorknob. "Good night, Mel, and thank you," she answered just above a whisper.

Mel stood like a stone in the hallway after the bathroom door had closed replaying the last few seconds several times over. She could hear Katherine's movement on the other side of the door.

Don't. You don't heal from that kind of heartache.

Mel's head was throbbing to the beat of her own heart, her arm still hot from where Katherine's hand had rested. Walking into her bedroom, she didn't bother turning on the light. The darkness felt safer with feelings like these.

Mel bolted upright in bed when the sunlight warmed her face. She'd slept through the alarm, or maybe she'd forgotten to set one. *Katherine.* She was here. Just down the hall.

The Scotch. Katherine's touch. The kiss. It all came flooding back.

She stepped into the hall and saw the door beside hers standing open. Peeking inside, the bed had been made and the tank top and shorts folded at the end of the bed. Inside the bathroom, a damp towel hung on the hook behind the door. Downstairs, Mel found a note on the kitchen table. *Got an early call. Had to run. Thanks for last night. K-.*

Mel stood by the table holding the note in her hand. Now what?

Mel's flurry of emotions deepened when Katherine texted her after lunch. *Sorry about last night.* Mel was not sorry. Or was she? She couldn't decide, but she could think of nothing else for the entire morning, forgetting the water hose in one of the stalls and having to strip it clean after flooding it.

She cleaned stalls and tried to figure out how she felt. Had it been cowardice or strength that pulled her away? The boundaries had been clear with other women. Most of them she had either met through friends who knew she was gay or in the local gay bars back in Boston. Dating became somewhat routine when you knew the other woman was "hitting for the same team," as one of the bartenders at the bar loved to say. But this, Mel leaned the manure fork against the wall, this was a game all its own and she did not know the rules.

Other friends had dated straight women. She pushed the wheelbarrow out to the manure pile. Was that what Katherine was? If not, she had had plenty of opportunities to set the record straight, as it were, if she was gay. Mel dumped new shavings into the stall and led the horse back inside. Moving the wheelbarrow in front of the next stall, she admitted she wasn't sorry they had kissed. But Katherine was, so she would have to deal with that on some level. What if she hadn't stepped away?

After dinner, tired from the what-if games that played like broken records in her mind, and in a moment of uncalculated frankness, she texted Katherine her response. *Hi. I'm not sorry about last night. I hope you're okay.*

After she pressed send, she thought she might be sick.

Sleep wouldn't come. Frustrated, Mel tried to read on the front porch, feeling the need for more air than her room could give her, but night bugs dive-bombed her book and mosquitos feasted on her ankles as a midnight snack. She settled for watching Captain America until she drifted into a fitful sleep on the couch.

Sunday morning, on her way to the barn, Katherine's Jeep pulled up. Mel's hand went to her stomach. Sam Houston ran to greet Katherine, but Mel walked slower than normal.

Act normal. Mel warned herself.

"Good morning." Mel smiled too big. *You're trying too hard.*

"Hey there." Katherine raised her hand to shield her eyes from the morning sun. "Got a minute?"

"Sure. Want some coffee?"

"Sure. That'd be nice."

Mel and Katherine went into the kitchen. Mel was used to making coffee for two, forgetting Jessica was gone, so there was still some in the pot.

Mel poured two cups and sat down in front of her. "What's up?" After sitting down, she wished she would have sat on the end of the table and not directly across from her.

Katherine laughed nervously. "I'm not sure where to begin."

Mel grasped her coffee cup tighter.

"I wanted to apologize for the other night. I don't know what came over me. I mean, I could blame it on the Scotch—probably should blame it on the Scotch—but I don't want you getting the wrong idea about me."

"And what idea is that?"

Katherine shifted in her seat. "Well, with me kissing you and all. I didn't plan that. I swear. I mean, I'm straight. I like spending time with you, and I didn't want that to ruin anything."

Mel's heart sank.

"It wouldn't be the first time a straight chic made a move on a lesbian." Her words came out colder than she had meant.

"I'm sorry." Katherine's eyes glistened. "I didn't mean to take advantage of you."

Mel cringed. She was hurt, and a little humiliated, but she hadn't meant to be cold.

"Listen, I'm sorry I said that. I didn't mean it. Can we just forget about it?" Mel spoke softer, but her chest tightened.

"I feel like such an idiot."

"Hey, let's just agree to blame the Scotch, okay?" Mel attempted a smile.

"You don't have to be nice." Katherine used her sleeve to wipe a tear that had spilled down her cheek.

"I'm not, I just—" *What if I just tell her?* Mel thrust that thought from her mind. "Listen, I have to feed first, but I was going to ride to the creek. Want to come along?"

"I should go." Katherine stood to leave but added, "I've been up most of the night."

Mel stood and placed the cups in the sink. "Go home and sleep. Thanks for stopping by."

"Thanks for understanding. A movie soon?"

"Sure, you let me know when you're free."

Mel watched her drive down the driveway before walking to the barn. After she fed and watered, she split some of the larger pieces of wood that had been gathered from the storm's aftermath. Mel threw herself into the task and was dripping with sweat within minutes. Solace accompanied the exhilaration of the splitting maul's blunt end ripping shreds of wood with each blow.

Chapter Twenty-Seven

In the week that followed, Mel tried to forget the kiss and conversation by throwing herself into routine farm tasks. Water troughs in the paddocks were free of algae, the barn office had never been so organized, and the stacks of papers that still lingered in her dad's office covered half of the kitchen table in neat piles. Jessica had asked several times after returning from the sale what was bugging her, but Mel shrugged it off as a simple burst of cleaning energy.

Mel wasn't sleeping. Jessica asked about her bloodshot eyes. Allergies were the obvious answer. It wasn't a complete lie. The moments were like quicksand. Fear gripped her, although it wasn't the same as before. Instead of fearing pain or rejection, she feared she would be sucked back behind the wall. There was a war going on inside her.

Alexandria Jackson stopped by one evening to invite them to Phillip's surprise birthday party. Mel welcomed the distraction until Alexandria mentioned Katherine and Nathan would be there. That excitement soured in her stomach, wrecking her plan of avoidance. She dreaded the awkwardness, but she also feared her stupid tendency to overcompensate for awkwardness, by being too talkative and overly friendly. She always ended up looking like a fool.

She tried to convince herself it wouldn't be awkward. After all, they were both adults, and they had agreed to blame the Scotch.

Sleepless nights continued. Mel sat at the kitchen table with stacks of her dad's papers they had found in the back of his bedroom closet. She unearthed a couple of old letters her mom had written her dad before they were married. The envelopes were worn. One was folded and tattered around the edge as if it had been carried in a pocket.

She unfolded the letter carefully. Her mom's handwriting began, *Darling, in three short weeks I'll be Mrs. Thomas Snow.*

She could still hear her mom's soft voice. Laying the letter down in front of her, Mel allowed herself to wonder what life would have been like had her mom not died in childbirth. There they would have been, Dad, Mom, two daughters, and a son. Would they have had more children? Dad had disliked being from a family with only two sons, insisting that the larger the family the better.

Mel didn't often think of her mother. She felt guilty about this, but it had been so long now. She used to have imaginary conversations with her at night after she first moved to Boston. Mel would tell her she was gay, and her mother would hug her and whisper "I know, honey."

She would pretend her mom rushed into the room when Uncle Jerry was trying to make her leave and stood in front of Mel, hiding her from Uncle Jerry's wrath. "Leave my daughter alone," she would shout. Mel gradually stopped the conversations and the pretend scenarios forcing her brain to think of other things when her mother came to mind. She hadn't wanted to be angry with her mom for leaving their family, she hadn't had a choice, but she sometimes couldn't help it.

"Do you ever think about Mom?" Mel asked the next morning at breakfast.

"Is that what's been bugging you?"

"What? Oh, no, I told you nothing's bothering me." Mel got up from the table and placed her dishes in the sink. "I just found a couple of mom's letters last night."

"Yeah, I mean I think of her. I think I don't even remember half the stories I think I remember. I sort of put myself in the stories like I was there."

"Like what?"

"Remember that story you used to tell about you and Mom on the trail ride when you stopped to build a Snowman in Skinny Pete's paddock? Mom used frozen manure for the eyeballs? In my mind, I pictured myself riding behind Mom and I helped build the snowman, even though I know she was pregnant with me at the time."

Mel laughed, first at the memory of that story and then at Jessica.

Jessica continued, "I guess I just have so many more memories with Dad. Those are the ones I think about often. I still miss him every day."

"I'm sorry." Mel sat back down across from Jessica.

"He would have been so happy knowing you came home. I wish he could have been here for that."

Mel wondered if he would have been as happy as Jessica imagined. A tinge of envy hit her. Jessica had gotten twelve years, part of them as an adult, with their dad.

"I hope he would be happy."

"Of course, he would be—is."

"Maybe he wouldn't have wanted me here being gay."

"Don't be ridiculous."

Jessica's phone rang. "Morning, James. What's up?" Jessica motioned to Mel that she would meet her at the barn and walked out the back door.

Mel guessed James was calling about the pony or the boys' lesson planned for this evening. The pony had learned manners and the boys had learned a few too. Mel walked into the barn as Jessica was finishing the call.

"James called to tell me Tommy's dad is making noise all over town. He heard him in the feed store this morning telling people he wouldn't trust me with a horse because I can't control my temper." Jessica placed a halter on Rooster and led him into the aisle.

214

"What?"

"Yeah. And apparently, he told some people at the diner that I don't have a clue how to train a horse, just living off Dad's reputation."

"People know how he is. Surely they won't believe that nonsense."

"Yeah, but he does run the other insurance office and some folks have their horses insured through him. Plus, he's on the school board. He could make real trouble for us if he wanted to." Jessica shook her head and brushed shavings off Rooster's legs. "I have to show more. At some of the bigger shows. I need people to know me for who I am as a trainer in my own right."

Jessica tossed the saddle on Rooster's back and cinched it tight.

"Should we do something about Tommy's dad?" Mel asked.

"I think it's better not to stir the pot, but I'll call the lawyer. He's supposed to get back with me on a trial date anyway." Jessica swung herself up in the saddle. "I'll start practicing Rooster every evening after I'm done with the others. I'd like to see what he says after I win at State."

The surprise element of Phillip's birthday party was ruined when a neighbor saw him in the bank and asked what she could bring to the party on Saturday. Secrets and surprises were hard things to keep in a small town. With everyone now in the know, Phillip waved from beside the grill when Mel and Jessica arrived. Alexandria had put him to work after her plans were foiled.

"Welcome to my surprise party," Phillip yelled out.

Alexandria rolled her eyes and took the dish of baked beans Jessica had made this morning. "He's been obnoxious ever since finding out. I should have taken his gift back."

Jessica had insisted on coming early to work their four-year-old stud, Gus. She had fallen in love with this little guy a few months ago during training and didn't pass up a

215

chance to work him. Phillip had even mentioned showing him in the upcoming months and had asked Jessica if she'd be interested.

The arrangement with the Jacksons had worked out well for the farm. There was family money backing their professors' salaries, and they simply loved the hobby of buying and selling horses which kept a steady string of business coming in.

James and Trisha showed up without their boys. Cute as they were, their boys were quite the handful, and the parents never missed an opportunity to leave them with the grandparents.

Mel sat on the deck bench drinking a beer and listening to Phillip when she saw Katherine's Jeep pull up and park on the other side of Jessica's truck.

Nathan came up to the group first. Hugs and handshakes all around. Mel looked beyond him to see if Katherine followed. She was walking in the opposite direction toward the round pen where Jessica and Gus were loping. Was she avoiding her?

Cars trickled into the drive and the party grew. Mel stayed by the grill, and Nathan was already in the middle of his second larger-than-life story when Jessica and Katherine joined the group. Katherine looked at Mel and mouthed hello. Mel smiled too big and made an offer of a beer from the cooler beside her leg. Her heart pounded when Katherine walked toward her.

"Hi there." Katherine's fingers touched Mel's as she took the bottle from her.

"How's your week been?"

"It's been a busy one. I'm giving an A-I lecture Thursday afternoon up in Louisville. I feel like a professor preparing to teach a class. It reminds me why I'm a vet and not a professor." Katherine took a sip. "Hey, you should come."

Mel looked at her shocked. "You want me to come to your lecture?"

"Only if you want. If you're not too busy."

"I'll double-check with Jessica and text you?" Mel hadn't meant to say that as a question. Maybe this wasn't going to be as awkward as she imagined. Maybe the Scotch really was to blame and all she had to do was figure out how to keep her growing attraction in check.

"Sure. Just text me."

Alexandria called the group together to sing to Phillip. Katherine mingled with others in the group, and Mel watched her carefully through the crowd.

Mel sat with James and Trisha after filling her plate at the least crowded table. Not wanting to appear insecure, she avoided sitting by Jessica. Mel had friends, although she feared she was trying to convince herself of this more than anyone else.

Katherine was in line for food. She had a raised hand now clutching the beer bottle demonstrating the height of whatever she was talking about. Mel loved the way she used her hands to talk.

The gravel crunched in the driveway and Mel turned to see another car pull up. It was not one she knew. She continued her conversation with Trisha and Jason. Two men walked across the lawn, hugged Phillip wishing him happy birthday, and apologized for being late. James brought Mel's mind back to the table by asking Mel if she remembered that time Mr. Phelps, the biology teacher, gave a classmate five dollars for eating a live goldfish.

"Were there goldfish on the grill?" Katherine pulled out the chair across from Mel.

James repeated the story and Mel grew quiet. She watched Katherine laugh and crinkle her nose at the thought of it. Mel was envious of Katherine's ability to let what happened between them go. She never shared a kiss with a man that was memorable, so maybe Katherine felt the same about the kiss they had shared.

"Okay if I snag this spot?" The voice came from behind Mel.

"Sure, sure," Mel said turning to speak to the new arrival.

217

"Mel? Mel Snow?"

It took her a second before the dots connected.

"Oh my God, Jason. How are you?" Mel stood to hug him. Here stood her last high school boyfriend. Actually, Jason was her last boyfriend ever. Jason Wagoner in the flesh, muscular and dressed to the nines.

"Mel Snow. I can't believe it. You moved away." Jason sat down beside her.

"I was in Boston. I had no idea you were still around. You remember James and Trisha?" Mel motioned beside her. "And this is our local vet, Katherine Neil."

"Of course." Jason stuck out his hand across the table to Katherine and nodded at James and Trisha. "I left and came back. I teach History at U of L now."

James put the pieces together. "Am I going senile or didn't you two date back in high school?"

Mel blushed and shoved a spoonful of baked beans in her mouth. Trisha gave James a look.

"Yep, but she kicked me to the curb." Jason laughed. His laugh had always been contagious. "What brings you back here, Mel?"

Mel's life suddenly sounded uninteresting to her. "I'm back here helping Jessica now, Dad passed away last summer." She stumbled over the words.

"I'm sorry to hear that. I didn't know. We don't come to Lebanon Springs much these days. We moved Mom up with us and sold the house after Dad died four years ago."

Another voice joined the conversation. "Here you are. I thought I'd lost you."

A shorter, dark-haired man wearing a tight blue dress shirt walked up behind Jason. His dark goatee was as perfect as Mel had ever seen. He wore small diamond studs that stood out against his dark olive skin. Mel detected an accent.

"You won't get that lucky, mister." Jason laughed and pulled out the chair beside him. "Mel this is my husband, Enrique Iglesias."

The man stretched his hand across Jason and shook Mel's hand. "It's Emanuel. I married a comedian. Nice to meet you."

Jason introduced Emanuel to James and Trisha while Mel tried to process what had just transpired. Her ex-boyfriend, her final boyfriend who she hadn't seen in over twelve years, had just introduced her to his husband.

"Emanuel's from Guatemala but studied urban planning in the states." Jason was as talkative as the seventeen-year-old boy Mel remembered. "Mel, what did you do up in Boston?"

"I got my degree in psychology and worked at a center that housed homeless LGBTQ+ youth."

Jason and Emanuel exchanged looks. "Oh, we're going to have to talk," Jason said before chomping down on a hamburger.

The birthday group mingled, talked, and laughed throughout the evening. Mel discovered that Jason met Phillip at a conference earlier this year and they hit it off after learning of their common connection to Lebanon Springs. Jason followed Mel to the Jeep after they said their goodbyes, giving her a business card and said they must get together soon. He winked when said he had an idea that might interest her. She had no idea what that meant.

"Jason Wagoner. I can't believe it." Jessica looked back at the small group that remained behind.

"Crazy right? I was shocked."

"Did you two know about each other back in high school?"

"Nope. At least I didn't know."

"What are the odds." Jessica laughed. "I thought maybe you made some sort of deal together back then."

"I wish we would have been clever enough to think of that."

Billowing clouds hung overhead, but the chance of rain was small. At least that's what the weatherman had said this morning, but not having the best track record, Mel tied her poncho on the back of the saddle just in case. The fields called to her as they had when she was young.

Mel had woken this morning with an unexpected calmness about her resting under the turbulent thoughts like the riverbed lies below the rapids. Mel introduced herself to new clients before leading Bonnie out the side door.

"Where should we ride today, my friend?" Mel patted the dark bay neck. They did not have the same bond as Jessica and Rooster, but they were good mates. Bonnie had turned out to be patient, or maybe a tad lazy, and this suited Mel fine. Mel squeezed her legs and aimed her toward the back gate.

Bonnie was not a natural at gates, and she didn't always keep her head in the game. Mel got off and led Bonnie through. They would wander through The Flat and the paddock just to the east called No Man's Land before heading up the creek for a while.

The Flat was its namesake and the flattest part of the farm save the small piece of earth that held the house and barns. It ran between Skinny Jim's and the Creek paddock. The other fields rolled and tumbled softly with small rises and dips throughout each one. The Flat was scattered with batches of trees here and there and large rocks that jutted out of the ground making it a better grazing field than a hayfield. Their small herd of cattle spent a considerable amount of time here. Her dad had always said it would make a good football field minus the rocks.

Mel was in no hurry this morning. She eased Bonnie around the fence and out to the farthest corner toward No Man's Land.

No Man's Land. It had been her grandmother's favorite field. Their grandmother had been a feisty woman and she never minced words when it came to Mel's grandfather. They would get into a heated argument about something, and she would tell him, "I'm going for a walk before I do something I regret. Don't you dare follow me. I'll come back when I'm good and ready." If Mel's dad or Uncle Jerry would ask their father where their mother was, he'd just shake his head and answer, "she's gone off to No Man's Land again."

Stepping through the gate, Bonnie grabbed a quick bite of the tall grass before following.

"You know you'd be in trouble if Jessica caught you doing that." Mel closed the gate and latched it. This time, she didn't swing back into the saddle but walked along with Bonnie's head close to her shoulder.

Without realizing it, she spoke aloud. "It was just a kiss." Hearing her own voice, Mel laughed softly and looked around.

It's not like Mel had never kissed a random woman. She had made out with women at parties from time to time, but never a straight woman, that she knew of, and never standing in the doorway of the bathroom of her childhood home.

It was just a kiss though. They were adults; there was no reason why this should cause an issue between them. Besides, if yesterday was any indication, Katherine seemed to have forgotten. Mel was going to have to do the same. The only problem was that this one kiss opened a box of possibilities in Mel's mind that she was having a hard time closing.

Mel leaned against an old walnut tree that had been struck by lightning years before. Half of it had died and the branches were scraggly and bare, dead bits of limbs scattered the ground below, but the other half had managed to survive the strike. The sun had punctured a hole in the thick clouds above and she stood in the shade of the half that had survived. Bonnie grazed in the tall grasses beside her.

Jason Wagoner was gay. It shouldn't surprise her, but Mel thought she had always had a decent *gaydar* as they say. Had Jason guessed she was gay back in high school? She had no idea how obvious she was back then. Tomboyish yes, but plenty of farm girls are labeled tomboys and go on to have a

221

husband and a house full of *ankle biters*, to use her grandfather's term for children. But gay? She would ask him when she saw him again.

Intrigued by the scheme or idea he had in his head, she would try and meet him when she attended Katherine's talk on Thursday. *Katherine.* Mel's heart beat faster. The plan of forgetting that kiss was not working.

Bonnie jerked her head up and her ears pointed forward. Following her gaze, Mel was startled by what looked like a tent on the edge of the field behind the first layer of trees. She grabbed the reins and swung into the saddle. No doubt it was friends of a neighboring farm, or more likely kids, who did not understand the boundaries. It happened more than people would imagine. Dad had always told the story about a group of hippies that had come through back in the sixties when he was young, and it had taken their grandfather three weeks to get them to leave.

As she eased closer, there was a small strand of smoke coming from a fire in front of the tent. She waited until she was about ten yards from the tree line to call out. "Hello."

No movement. Bonnie walked forward. Mel called out again, this time louder. Mel pulled Bonnie to a halt when she saw a head stick out of the tent. "Well, hello there," a kind, scratchy voice called back.

Mel swung down off Bonnie as the head became a body, a wrinkly, half-naked body. A grey-haired man with khakis rolled up over his knees and a bare boney chest stood before her.

"Are you here about the ponies?" The man smiled with a toothless grin.

"Ponies? What? Sorry, who are you?" Mel tried to speak kindly.

"Chief Standing Wolf. Are you here to buy my ponies? We'll discuss a price. Come sit with me. I'm making tea." The ancient man gestured toward the small fire burning in front of the tent.

Mel stood stunned. What was the man playing at? "Do you know where you are?"

The man threw his head back in childlike laughter. "This is where I keep my ponies. Come, have some tea with me."

Mel took a few steps closer, noticing there was nothing that resembled tea anywhere. "Sir, do you have family in the area?"

"Shhh, the babies are sleeping in the teepee with my wife." He looked into the woods at what Mel could only imagine were the teepees in his mind. She looked around her.

"Okay. So, you live here," Mel stated.

The man nodded his head and smiled, rubbing his hands together close to the fire. It was at least eighty degrees out today.

Just go with it. Mel stepped closer.

"These ponies that you're selling, can you tell me about them?"

"See for yourself." The old man pointed behind Mel to the open, empty field. "They're Indian ponies, small and strong. Quick as jackrabbits, they are. Are you with the Rangers? They said they wanted my ponies for chasing outlaws, but the Army will probably pay more."

He's thought this through.

The old man sat by the fire with his legs crossed, humming. Mel took out her phone and texted Jessica, briefly explaining their "visitor," and imagining Jessica's face when she read it. *She'll think I've been drinking.* She told her to call the sheriff and bring the truck to this spot.

The frail man tossed a few small sticks and branches onto the fire. He must have been close to ninety by the looks of him. His skin was pale and freckled, and his shoulders slumped forward. His sunken eyes were bright, almost like a child's. A faded tattoo shown on his upper arm. She tied Bonnie to the tree and sat down across from him.

"How long have you lived here, Chief Standing Wolf, right?" Mel stumbled over the name.

"I was born right here. I learned to swim in that creek there and I taught my children when they were old enough." Again, he pointed to the empty field. Mel could imagine the ponies tied beside the creek's edge.

The old man seemed content to tell stories of his childhood eventually resting back on his arms outstretched behind him.

"Where do you live?" He abruptly stopped his story and leaned in.

"I live—on a farm nearby."

"Don't you just love this land?" The old man squeezed his eyes tight and shook his head.

"Yes. Yes, I do love the land."

He cocked his head and looked at her for a moment. "I can see you do. It's in your eyes. You can always tell when someone loves the land by their eyes."

Mel was moved. She continued the conversation with the chief, which wasn't hard to do, until Jessica drove up. The old man sat up and watched her with caution.

"It's okay," Mel assured him. "This is my sister. Jessica, this is Chief Standing Wolf."

Jessica gave her a look that said, *you're joking right?*

Mel didn't think he looked harmful, but she also didn't want to rile him up having no idea what he was capable of. "He lives here and is selling some Indian ponies." She spoke matter-of-factly with eyebrows raised to clue Jessica in.

"Right. Okay." Jessica nodded her head, the corners of her lips bent downward slightly. Mel had seen this particular nod many times since returning.

The chief offered Jessica a place at his fire, but she politely refused.

"What do you do?" He looked at Jessica.

Jessica glanced at Mel and rolled her eyes. "I train horses."

"Ahhh, you will train my ponies."

Mel continued the delusional conversation until the sheriff's vehicle pulled through the field. A woman got out of

224

the passenger's side and walked up to the group ahead of the sheriff.

"Hi, Mr. Peters. This is a nice campsite you've made for yourself." The woman smiled. "You gave us a run for our money this time. Didn't you?"

Mel stood and looked to the sheriff for answers. He shrugged with his arms crossed resting on top of his belly.

"It's about time you come home now. Paul and Charlie are missing you." The woman took him gently by the arm and lifted him upright. "You'll have to tell them about your adventures at dinner."

The man didn't resist. "What's for dinner?"

"I think it's roast beef tonight. You like that, don't you?" The woman guided the man to the sheriff's SUV.

As he walked past Mel, he took her arm. "You'll look after my ponies?"

Mel smiled. "Sure, I will."

The woman helped the man into the back seat.

"They've been looking for him for three days. He broke out of that retirement center between here and Frankfort. Not the first time either. Spends his days watching old westerns and thinks he's some Chief or something. He's a retired railroad conductor, they say." The sheriff scratched his head and climbed into his vehicle.

Mel and Jessica stood at the edge of the trees and watched the vehicle drive slowly through the field and out of sight.

"If that don't beat all." Jessica kicked dirt onto the fire with the side of her boot.

"I guess it's not every day I get to have tea with a Chief, eh?"

"Let's clean up his site and hope we don't run into any more chiefs anytime soon. Don't forget to feed those ponies." Jessica shook her head but laughed.

Chapter Twenty-Eight

Mel tried to sound casual that night after dinner. "If it doesn't mess up anything, I thought I'd take Thursday off."

Jessica's eyebrows shot up. "Got another date with Chief what's-his-name?"

"Standing Wolf. And not funny. Jason said he wanted to talk to me about something. Plus, Katherine asked me to go to a lecture she's giving in Louisville. Figured I could kill two birds." Mel wasn't sure she'd pulled off nonchalant.

"Yeah, sure. The boys will be here. I've got lessons that afternoon anyway."

Jason was thrilled when Mel called after dinner. He suggested brunch at a coffee shop near the campus.

Mel arrived early to make sure she found parking. She grabbed a table by the window, ordered coffee, and people watched until Jason arrived.

"Earth to Mel." Jason broke into her thoughts.

She stood to hug him. "Sorry, I spaced."

"Who has you so deep in thought." Jason laughed and sat across from her.

"Nothing like that. I just need more coffee, I guess."

Jason gave her a skeptical look but let the matter drop.

They began catching up on twelve years. She explained why she left. He'd heard rumors. Jason was full of questions and humorous comments. He had always been funny, and Mel had enjoyed his company all those years ago. They had both been struggling with their sexuality back then trying desperately to be normal.

"I only asked you out because you weren't like the other girls always wanting to make out in the stairwell," Jason told her.

Mel laughed. "Jessica asked if we planned it. I wish we'd been that brilliant. I was so relieved you didn't pressure me."

"But Mel, kissing Emily Johnson under the bleachers, seriously? You could have done better."

"Don't be mean. Besides, I didn't have many choices back then."

Jason nodded in agreement. "I was never so relieved as when I left this place behind. I could finally breathe when I went away to college."

"It took me a while to breathe again."

"That's it. I have to ask you something. Promise you won't say no until you've thought about it."

Mel eyed him with lighthearted suspicion. "You look like you're up to something. Like that time you talked me into skipping class to come to the rodeo in Louisville?"

Jason roared with laughter. "It's nothing like that. I'm a responsible adult now, Mel."

The waitress came and refilled their coffee.

"You and I both have our own stories of growing up gay in a small town—so do a lot of people. I have a group of folks, preachers, professors, and even some investors, who want to do something about this. Many kids, just like us, are running off to the cities or college as soon as they get the chance, but a lot of them would rather live in the country, stay home—they just don't feel safe doing so. We want to change that. We want to give them a chance at life here if they want it."

Mel was intrigued. "Like what?"

"Well, that's where you come in. We want to offer internships—apprenticeships—at supportive farms—with families—across the area for queer kids who are either kicked out, or worse, from their homes and communities. Some of these kids would stay if they had the choice."

"And how do I fit into your grand gay agenda?"

Jason laughed. "Good one and damn right, it's grand. Before we get more funding, we need a sort of pilot program. Show people it can work. I almost lost my shit at the party when you told me you worked with queer youth up in Boston. Mel, you're the opportunity—the missing piece to the puzzle—we've been waiting for."

Mel's mind reeled.

"Just think of it. We give these kids a nurturing environment right here in their own backyard and teach them skills that will help them. We can get them scholarship programs for colleges, but to local colleges, so they can stay in the area if that's what they want. If everyone who is different leaves, the change in communities like ours is much slower." Jason said this last line with so much conviction it gave Mel chills.

"I have to admit, it sounds interesting, but I don't know. It's not my farm, not really, and I doubt I could ever get Jessica into something like this."

"Just give it some thought. I know we can do this, Mel. I'm not much on signs, but I think it was no accident I bumped into you again."

Mel promised Jason she would give it some thought. The whole scenario was funny when she thought about it. Two exes, now gay, working on a project to save queer kids in the country. You couldn't make this stuff up if you tried.

The Convention Center was a few minutes away. She circled the block twice, missing the parking garage entrance the first time around. Louisville's one-way maze of streets had always confused the hell out of her. It was almost as bad as Boston.

228

How would she ever find a way to bring up Jason's idea to Jessica? It was not a conversation she looked forward to, but she had to admit she was intrigued by the idea. Jessica didn't take to change too well, and this undertaking would surely be classified as a complete life shift if she decided to go through with it. They had worked out their differences over the past months, but Jessica was never not in charge of what went on concerning the farm. To be honest, Mel hadn't minded it, and she was pretty sure Jessica intended to keep it that way.

Mel found the conference room number in Katherine's text and set out in search of it. She crammed into a crowded elevator going up.

She could do this. Plenty of people did it. Just friends. Yes, they were friends. Katherine got her the way most people didn't. Plus, Mel had never felt the need to prove or guard herself around her. This was the greatest relief of all. The elevator doors opened, and she oozed out into the hall.

Six or seven people stood at the edge of the stage on the opposite end of the room. Mel tucked her head inside and scanned the group. Katherine saw her and waved her in.

"I saved you a seat." Katherine hugged her.

"Front row?"

"Don't tell me you were one of those back row students." Katherine laughed. "I'm the second speaker. We each have forty-five minutes with a break in between."

The first speaker was monotone and reminded her of her high school gym teacher. Mel had been up early this morning and now found herself with heavy eyelids. During the break, she grabbed a cup of coffee, but she wouldn't have needed it. Katherine was on stage next, and Mel found it hard to concentrate on what she was saying. The way her body, hands, and mouth moved as she spoke was like artwork. Just watching her confident strides across the stage was brilliant. As trains of thought link one to another unchecked, Mel's cheeks burned when she realized she had been imagining herself introducing Katherine as her girlfriend. She took a sip of coffee, crossed her legs, and willed herself back to

Katherine's lecture topic. *Just friends, Mel Snow. Pull yourself together.*

The forty-five minutes were over in a flash, and Mel waited to the side while people surrounded the two speakers and asked more questions. After the room cleared, Katherine asked if she minded attending another talk with her. Of course, Mel was happy sitting beside her even if the topic of large animal arthritis was less than inspiring.

It was rush hour when they exited the convention center, and the streets were crawling with cars. Several restaurants were within walking distance, so they opted to leave their vehicles inside the parking garage. An Italian restaurant was closest. After looking at the menu on the outside of the window they agreed to go in. By now, they were both hungry enough to eat a horse.

They were seated at a corner table, and Mel made small talk about the Italian restaurant close to her old apartment in Cambridge.

"I need to talk to you about something," Katherine blurted out.

"Okay," Mel said cocking her head to the side. Whatever it was it didn't sound good, and by the look on Katherine's face, Mel braced for the worst.

"Listen, I'm not sure about any of this," Katherine bunched her napkin in her hand and then flattened it out in her lap, glancing around the room before looking back at Mel, "but I can't stop thinking about kissing you."

Mel's mouth went dry.

"What?" Mel's voice was louder than she had expected, and harsher.

"The kiss in the doorway."

"I remember the kiss." Mel looked around the crowded room and tried to soften her voice. "What are you thinking about it?"

Preparing mentally all week to act like the kiss didn't mean anything or even exist, Mel had not prepared for this kind of conversation.

"I shouldn't have said anything. I'm sorry." Katherine rearranged the silverware on either side of the plate.

Be careful. Mel breathed in deeply. *Let her off the hook.* "We had a bit to drink. It's okay, I didn't take it personally."

"We did. I tried to convince myself that's all it was for several days. But I'm Scottish for Christ's sake—I can hold my liquor." Katherine smiled nervously.

Mel melted. Each time Katherine smiled it touched her deeper.

"What I mean is," Katherine traced the lines of the red and white tablecloth with her index finger, "I wanted it to happen."

"Katherine, you don't have to—"

"I wanted to kiss you." Katherine looked directly into Mel's eyes, sitting up straight, before turning to look out the window. "It wasn't the Scotch."

The waiter appeared at the edge of the table.

Katherine spoke to him softly. "Can we get two merlots and a bit more time, please?"

The walls of the room went wonky in Mel's head. Like when she took much cold medicine, she sensed she was watching herself from a few feet above her body. She was glad she was sitting down.

"Are you okay?" Katherine asked.

"Yeah." Mel took a sip of water and cleared her throat. "I'm not sure what to say."

"By the look on your face, I'm not sure I should have told you."

Mel weighed her options. Close down again or speak. *Just tell her.* "I've been trying to forget."

Katherine winced.

Damnit. Mel reached across the table without thinking and grabbed Katherine's wrist just before she pulled

231

it off the edge of the table. Katherine's gaze went to their hands.

Mel spoke just above a whisper. "I was trying to forget—so I could stay friends with you."

Katherine looked up into Mel's face.

Mel continued. "I'm glad. I mean, I'm glad it wasn't the Scotch—that you wanted the kiss."

"Did you?"

Mel snapped back into her body like a whip and answered without hesitation. "Very much."

The waiter returned with two glasses and poured the wine. It seemed it took him hours to finish the pour and walk away. Only after he left did she see she was still holding Katherine's wrist. Releasing it, she smiled. "Sorry."

"Mel, I don't know what to do about this. I've never felt anything like this for a—for a woman. I've never felt anything this intense for anyone." Katherine's voice was cracked on the last word. "I keep telling myself it's the twenty-first century for goodness' sake, it's okay, but I didn't expect this from me. It's like I'm in school again, a bundle of emotions and not sure what to do with any of them."

"I'm not sure I can be an objective ear in this." Mel tried to lighten the mood seeing the distress on Katherine's face.

"Am I off-base?"

Mel searched Katherine's face but said nothing. Her mind was trying to catch up with the moment. She loved Katherine's bluntness.

Katherine hung her head. "I probably sound so foolish to you right now."

"You're not foolish." Mel paused and pressed her lips together. "And you're not off-base. I haven't been able to stop thinking about you since the first time I met you." Mel spoke the words she could barely imagine saying. She felt them turn inward and expand exposing corners that had only known darkness for so long.

Relief spread across Katherine's face. "The night with the colicky horse," nodding her head. "I couldn't sleep

232

that night. I kept trying to tell myself it was because I'd found a friend here in the community to do things with—which you are. I don't mean to say you aren't a friend."

"I know."

The waiter walked across the room toward them. Mel grabbed a menu. "We better order something."

As soon as the waiter walked away, Katherine said, "I wanted to kiss you that night after the movies."

Mel smiled. "I drove all the way home thinking about my bad luck in being attracted to a straight girl."

"Well, I am. I mean I was. I don't know what I mean. I long since grew out of all that rubbish teaching they told us in Catholic school, but I never imagined a scenario like this with me in it." Katherine was blushing.

"Catholic school?" Mel laughed.

"I know, I know, the stories, but I had boyfriends, I swear."

"What do you want to do about our scenario?" Mel felt bolder than she had felt in years.

The redness in Katherine's cheeks deepened. "All I can think about is kissing you again. Beyond that, I don't have much figured out."

The waiter's timing was starting to get on Mel's nerves. He brought their plates and filled their glasses. Unspoken words hung in the air threatening to engulf them. Mel felt as if she was holding dynamite in her hands—one wrong move and this could all blow up in her face.

"Listen." Mel saw the worried look spread across Katherine's face. "Maybe you should take some time and sort through your feelings. Maybe talk to someone."

Katherine looked beyond Mel to the world passing them by on the crowded sidewalk.

"Trust me, I like this," Mel waited for Katherine's eyes to return before pointing to herself and Katherine, "but I want you to be sure."

"My therapist has had her hands full since I met you."

Mel was shocked which made Katherine smile.

"She encouraged me to talk with you, but the last thing I wanted to do is screw up and hurt you. I couldn't bear that."

Mel was touched by the kindness in her voice. Katherine had never mentioned having a therapist; in these parts, therapists were reserved for the seriously disturbed. Sadly, something so healthy still held a great deal of shame.

Sure, Mel was confused about her feelings as a teenager, but as a teenager everything about life was confusing. This must be such a difficult process as an adult. Having your life turned on its head at thirty-something, especially in this way, must be scary as hell.

"Don't worry about me. I can be tough if I need to be." Mel smiled, but she didn't feel tough at all. "Make this about you. What do you want? We'll figure out the rest— together if you decide that's what you want." Mel stopped but then continued without thinking. "You are beautiful, Katherine."

"Th—thank you. See, I don't even know what to say right now."

"Well, what would you say if a guy said it?"

"Depends, but I would guess he's trying to sleep with me."

Mel laughed. "Stereotype, much?"

"Hey, you don't know the half of it."

After dinner and more conversation, they walked the three blocks back to the parking garage. Mel hesitated to say goodnight, not looking forward to the long drive back to Lebanon Springs alone but at the same time anxious to be alone with her thoughts. The parking garage security light buzzed overhead.

"Would—Would it be okay if I kissed you goodnight?" Katherine stood with her hands behind her back.

"Are you sure?"

"I'm not sure about anything." Katherine let out a breath and took a step toward Mel.

234

Mel pulled her gently to her. Their lips met. There were questions to be answered and feelings to sort out, but nothing had felt this right in a long time, if ever.

Chapter Twenty-Nine

A hammer pounded from behind the barn.

"Cody's leaving," Jessica said through clamped lips that held three nails. She took one from her lips and hammered the fence insulator into the new corner post.

"What? Why?"

"His Dad got him on over at the plant. I'm thinking that new girlfriend of his had something to do with it. Going out's not cheap."

Mel handed Jessica another handful of nails. "He does a lot around here."

"I can't much see him settling down and working in the plant, but maybe it'll be good for him."

"It'll be strange here without him. He's a hard worker. Jasper staying on?" Mel asked. A plan was forming in the back of her mind.

"He hasn't mentioned leaving. If both of them left, we'd be in a pickle. Cody will work until the end of the month. Said he'll still come over in the evenings and ride when he can."

Deep in thought, still feeling Katherine's lips upon hers, Mel let out a small shriek before her throat closed tight upon exiting the stall by the office. Tommy stood in front of the stall door she had been cleaning his hands in shoved in his pocket chewing on a piece of gum.

"Jessica around?" He didn't smile. He didn't look at her directly.

"She's—you shouldn't be here." Mel mentally reassured herself that her phone was in her back pocket.

"I just need to talk to her."

Mel examined his face and body language. He didn't appear riled up, but the alarm in her chest wouldn't turn off. "Wait here."

She walked down the aisle, turning to look at him. He sat down on a hay bale by the front stall. Jessica was in the next field over with Jasper and Cody working cows. Mel could see them from the back of the barn. She took out her phone.

"What's up?" Jessica answered.

"Tommy's in the barn—wants to talk to you."

"What the hell? I'll be right there."

Across the field, Jessica placed her phone in her back pocket and trotted the horse she was training toward the barn. Sam Houston who had been laying in the tall grasses out of sight, suddenly appeared by her side. Jasper and Cody turned their horses to follow.

Mel walked back inside the barn. "She'll be right up."

"Thanks." Tommy scratched the ears of the tabby cat that had made herself at home on his boot. The cat purred and leaned its head into his hand.

Watching him, she instinctively touched the scar on her arm that had resulted from his shove.

Jessica came in the side door with Cody on her heels. Her face was hard.

"What are you doing here, Tommy?" Jessica stopped a few feet in front of him.

Tommy stood slowly. "I'm not here for no trouble." He looked at Cody who stood by Mel with his arms by his side fists clenched.

Tommy continued. "Things got out of hand."

"Is that what you call it?"

"Jess, look. I'm sorry. I was angry, and I acted like an ass. I shouldn't have taken Rooster." He handed her an envelope.

"What's this?" Jessica took it from him.

"It's for the saddle. I know I got no right asking, and I deserve every bit of what I get, but would you consider dropping the charges?"

"What about Mel?" Jessica's tone was sharp. "You could have done some real damage. What were you thinking, Tommy?"

"I wasn't. I don't blame you for being pissed, but I'm in a real mess here." Tommy looked over Jessica's shoulder to Mel. "I'm sorry, Mel."

Mel didn't budge.

Jessica stared at the envelope and back up at Tommy. "What about your dad? He's saying shit all over town about me. You know it's not true. You know I'm a good trainer."

"I'll take care of Dad. He got carried away too. Guess it runs in the family." Tommy gave a slight, apologetic smile. "Truth is I don't blame you for pressing charges against me. If that's not enough for the saddle, I'll give you more when I can. I'm sorry, Jess. I really am."

Tommy turned and walked out his shoulders bent.

After calling the sheriff and the lawyer that evening, Jessica told them she'd get back to them both on what she decided.

Jessica slathered butter on her cornbread. "So, the sheriff said he was let go from his job. Some higher-up got wind of what he'd done. I'm a good mind to let it go. Not for him, mind you, but being the talk of the town like this does us no good, right or wrong. Of course, it's up to you too. You're the one that had to get stitches."

Mel thought a moment. "Do you think he's just playing us?"

"Could be. I've lost count of how many times we've broken up, but I'd never seen him go crazy like that before. I

238

think his pride got injured this time—and his hotheaded Daddy didn't help matters."

Jessica was right about the small-town talk. Even though many seemed to thrive on drama and gossip, folks were leery of being too close to the drama preferring to comment on it from a distance. It was one of the many intricate dances of southern-small-town culture. In the end, Mel agreed with Jessica and hoped the decision wouldn't come back to haunt them.

"Nathan's away for the weekend," Katherine paused, "and I wondered if you wanted to come to dinner Saturday night."

Mel didn't answer right away. She adjusted the phone on her shoulder and dropped the board she'd been holding.

"I wanted to talk to you, you know, about us, maybe—"

"Okay. Sure. What time?" Mel couldn't remember her head spinning around anyone as much as it did around Katherine. Even over the phone, she was mesmerizing.

"Six or so. Does that work?"

"Should I bring anything?"

Mel thought she detected a slight laugh in Katherine's voice when she said, "No, no, just you."

"I'll see you Saturday." Mel walked on clouds the rest of the day. Later that night she reminded herself that this might not produce the outcome she hoped for, but she was too far gone to be logical. There wasn't a day she hadn't thought about Katherine since that second kiss, even as busy as they had been with the second hay cutting, a local show, and two sales. Mel had welcomed the busy and most nights she had fallen asleep quickly exhausted from the long, hot day. Her last thought had always been Katherine.

"To hell with caution," Mel whispered in the darkness.

Jason had planted a seed and called three times to check up on it. It started taking root in Mel from the moment he mentioned it. She was happy having her life in Kentucky brought back from the dead, but she had also been hesitant to admit that something was missing. Could this be it? Work at The Center had become monotonous before returning, but years of living shut down from life had been a factor in the feeling. She might as well have been a robot, at times, in Boston as emotionless as she had lived her life. But what if she could do that work now, now that she felt alive again? Was Jason right about this working in the South? Somedays, she still had her doubts.

Mel decided to bring up the idea on a transport trip. A client had purchased a new horse while in Nashville on business and asked Jessica to pick it up for her.

"I have an idea," Mel started.

"Oh no." Jessica laughed.

"I'm serious. I mean it's not my idea, but I think it's a good one, especially since we're shorthanded without Cody."

"Okay. Shoot."

"Well, you know what I used to do back in Boston with queer kids."

Jessica held up her hand. "Wait a minute. I have a stupid question."

Mel waited.

"Am I supposed to say gay, or queer, or use the letters?"

Mel chuckled. "The letters?"

"Don't laugh. I'm serious. I feel weird saying any of them, because I don't know which one I'm supposed to use."

"Okay, okay. It depends on the person, but I call myself gay. I don't really like the word lesbian. Don't know why—just never liked it. I wouldn't use the word queer if I were straight, especially here in the south. It could come off as offensive. LGBTQ is fine, LGBTQ+, but it's okay to ask if you're not sure. Most people are okay with you asking as long as you're not being an ass about it."

Jessica sighed. "So, I should just stick to the letters?"

Mel laughed loud. "You'll be pretty safe if you stick with the letters, but just use gay. It's easier and the letters are sort of evolving, you see. Even I lose track. I had a friend back in Boston that always used *LMNOP* or *Rainbow Alphabet*. Of course, he was gay so he could call himself whatever he wanted, I guess."

"I'm doomed," Jessica said. "Okay, sorry. What were you saying?"

"You know I worked with kids in Boston. Most of them had been kicked out of their homes or treated badly by their families."

"Yeah?"

"Well, Jason and a few of his colleagues have an idea of starting something like that here," Mel explained the idea of teaching them to work in different agricultural fields in detail without mentioning the main detail that would affect Jessica the most.

"Wow. That sounds like a big deal. What's he want you to do?"

"Well, they need a pilot program, probably six months—something they can point to for future funding, scholarships, and participants." Mel paused. "And he's asked me to consider running it on our place."

"What?" Jessica had a way of packing a lot into that word.

"He's asked me to consider directing the pilot program for them." Mel kept her voice calm but strong. "It would be just a couple of kids, probably two or three at the most, and girls to start with."

"You've got to be kidding."

"I think I want to do it."

"You can't just—decide to start something like this."

"Look, I love being back here, with you, but I also need to do something with my life—something meaningful."

"You're helping me. Isn't that enough?"

"And I'd still do that. I love doing that. But I also want to try to help these kids—like me—if I can. Besides, it

241

would be like having free help, sort of, and we could use that, and you could teach them what you know about running a farm, working with horses." Mel tried to appeal to Jessica's business sense.

"There's liability issues and other shit. We can't have a bunch of kids running around here doing God knows what. What if one of them gets hurt?"

Mel's voice tightened. "It's not a sex camp for horny teenagers, Jess. Of course, there are liability issues to take care of and age limits to consider, among other things. Jason's got a lawyer looking into all that now, but if there's a chance for me to help them—I want to do it."

Jessica stared straight ahead.

"Listen. I spent a hundred nights wondering what would have happened if I didn't leave, if I'd stayed here where I belonged, but I didn't get that chance. I was uprooted. And I've suffered for it. I just want someone else to have the chance I didn't have."

"I'm not saying it's a bad idea—it's a good idea— I'm just saying I don't want it done here." Jessica pulled in front of the barn her jaw set.

Mel opened the door before the truck stopped. "Well, you know what, Jessica? Half of this Goddamn farm is mine, so I don't figure you get the last word on what you do or don't want here." Mel jumped to the ground and slammed the door behind her.

Chapter Thirty

Mel stood outside the back door with her arm raised. She hesitated for a moment before knocking. She had been in Katherine's barn several times but never inside her home. Her stomach flipped over time and again like someone kneading bread. She knocked glancing around the patio. A garden trellis covered in vines sat opposite a fire pit and colorful bricks weaved a design through the creek rock. Potted plants lined the outside of the square. Mel had just raised her hand to knock again when she heard movement on the other side of the door.

"Hi." Katherine pushed open the screen door. "Come in."

"Should I have used the front door?" Mel had instinctively come to the back door.

Katherine smiled. "I've been here long enough to know that only preachers and folks who don't know any better use the front door."

Mel laughed and stepped inside. "Then you are certainly a member of the secret southern society."

The back door led to a large mudroom and laundry. Beyond was the kitchen. The Neil house was a more modern farmhouse than the Snows but cozy. New appliances, dark wood cabinets, and hardwood floors.

"Dinner's not quite ready yet. I'm making one of mum's recipes. We call it *stovies*, but it's sort of a shepherd's pie type of food—only better." Katherine winked. "Not fancy by any means, but I make it whenever I miss home."

"Well, it smells delicious. Can I help?"

"You can pour us some wine." Katherine motioned to the counter by the sink.

"Sure thing." Mel poured two glasses and handed Katherine one.

"Cheers." Katherine smiled.

Mel leaned against the counter by the stove with a wine glass in hand, a close but safe distance from Katherine. Katherine chopped vegetables for a salad and Mel asked questions about how they came to own this place.

"I had an apartment in Frankfort the first year, but I've never been good at being closed in. I have a garden out to the side. It's a pitiful little thing, I do better with house plants, but I like to feel my fingers and toes in the dirt. It's soothing." Katherine scooped up the chopped carrots and tossed them in the bowl. "One of the other vets told me about this place, belonged to a cousin, no, nephew, I think. It was too big for just me, but then Nathan ended up coming over, so it's worked out. We both have enough space to not kill each other."

Katherine opened the oven door and the rich aromas that drifted out made Mel's stomach growl.

"What's that?" Mel leaned in.

"A crumble. Apple and blackberry. My favorite when I was a kid." Looking as at ease in the kitchen as she did stitching up a gash in a horse's leg, Katherine poked a knife in the middle of the dish and frowned. "I'm usually a good cook, but I've been a bit distracted today, so we'll see how this turns out."

"Distracted?" Mel laughed. "I saddled a horse today without the saddle pad. Jessica asked what the hell was wrong with me."

"So, I'm in good company?" Katherine closed the oven door.

"I'd say so."

They chatted about small farm details until the food was finished. Katherine had set the dining room table and lit a candle after bringing the food into the room. "Is this too corny?" She blew out the match with a look of fluster.

Mel sat the bottle of wine on the edge of the table and touched Katherine's arm. "It looks perfect. Thanks for inviting me."

Katherine leaned in and kissed Mel. Warmth ran down Mel's neck. Katherine pulled back. The moment didn't last near long enough. "We should eat."

Mel let Katherine take the lead in the conversation. Trying desperately to be patient, she asked about the food in Scotland. She barely heard a word Katherine said.

"I told my therapist about my idea for dinner tonight." Katherine finally started to put her out of her misery, but Mel could tell tonight's conversation was going to be a slow, painful process, that might possibly end in her death.

Mel nodded but kept chewing. *Let it be good news.*

"More wine?" Katherine's voice shook. She poured more wine into both glasses before Mel could answer.

"I'm glad you have someone to hash through your thoughts with."

"She's been a life-saver. I'm still confused as hell though."

Mel tried to brace herself for disappointing news, but it was no use.

"The first time I was going to bring you up in conversation, I almost canceled the appointment. I parked outside her office and couldn't make myself get out of the Jeep. I finally told myself, 'for goodness' sake, Katherine, quit being such a chicken.'" Katherine laughed at herself. "After I finally got it out and she started asking me questions, it was like she'd turned on a faucet. She finally had to cut me off."

"And?" Mel had to ask. It was all she could do to keep her voice calm. Her palms were sweating.

"I've been all caught up in labeling myself or trying to figure out why I've never felt like this before. I kept asking her if she thought I was gay or just confused, or if I was gay when I was a kid and just denying it. I asked her if she thought I was suppressing some horror from my childhood. She kept bringing me to the present and told me not to worry so much about labeling things this or that. She asked me to start by describing what I felt for you." Katherine stood abruptly. "It's stuffy in here. Do you want to take our wine outside?"

Mel looked down at her plate. They both had half a plate left, but Katherine hadn't noticed. Tonight's jumpiness was a side of Katherine, Mel had not seen.

"Sure," Mel answered.

Picked up her wine glass, Mel followed Katherine who was already headed through the kitchen and out the back door. Katherine kept walking around to the side of the house. Her small garden was situated in front of a wooden swing. She sat on the swing and patted the spot next to her.

"What do you feel for me?" Mel sat down and placed her arm on the back of the swing her hand reaching just beyond Katherine's shoulder but not touching it. Turning slightly, she looked at Katherine waiting for an answer.

Katherine turned to face her and took a deep breath.

"I feel everything. I feel safe, alive. I feel scared. I feel like I've known you all my life, like I can tell you anything. Like I don't want you to ever leave, like I'm going to burn up from the inside out." Katherine drew an imaginary circle in the grass with her bare foot. "I'm a mess. Have I scared you away yet?"

Mel relaxed a little. "I was hoping that's how you felt."

"But I'm still mixed up, Mel. I might hurt you. What if I'm no good at this?"

"Every relationship's different. Hey, I've done this," Mel waved her hand between the two of them, "and I don't think I'm particularly good at it."

Katherine scooted over to the middle of the swing and rested her bent knee on Mel's thigh.

"Nothing has ever felt like that kiss, that night," Katherine said just above a whisper. "I may not know what I'm doing, but I know I want this."

Mel's heart beat in every part of her body. With her arm behind Katherine's back, she drew her closer. Mel paused letting her whole being experience this moment. Katherine raised herself up and straddled Mel's lap, her hands resting on both sides of her face. Mel was aware of the fibers of their skins brushing against each other.

Time was lost. Hours, minutes, meant nothing.

The sun had long set. Night sounds filled the air around them. Mel sat in the same spot. Katherine lay across the swing with her head resting in Mel's lap.

"Kissing you is like nothing I have ever even imagined." Katherine smiled. "How can it be this different?"

Mel brushed Katherine's bangs aside and tucked them behind her ear. Whatever hesitation or reserve she felt the previous weeks, months, had melted into small, insignificant drops. Holding her hand out in front of her it was shaking. "Look what you did to me." Mel laughed.

Katherine sat up with her knee on Mel's thigh and her hand resting on Mel's knee. "But how did I not know this about me?"

"Everyone has their own experience."

"But this? This is huge."

"I'd have to agree with you there."

"Really?" Katherine scrunched up her nose. "I just thought—well, I just figured it was only me—since I've never kissed another woman."

Mel leaned in. "I've been about to go crazy."

"Why didn't you say anything?"

"Imagine that." Mel chuckled. "Hey, new straight friend, I'm attracted to you. I just figured I could handle the

247

attraction—the torture at times—or at least I kept telling myself I could."

"What do we do now?" Katherine pulled at a small thread on Mel's jean pocket. "What's next?"

"Well—" Mel hesitated to put into words what she wanted to be next.

As if Katherine understood the unspoken, her eyes widened. "Oh, I mean—oh."

Mel placed her hand on Katherine's knee. "It's important we do whatever we do at your pace. I won't pressure you."

"I don't think I'm ready for that. I'm sorry. Is that okay? That has to be rotten of me to say that to you."

"Listen. We can take this slow. I love being with you. Sure, *that* is a kind of a big deal to me, and it's something that will be beautiful but only when you're ready."

Mel cleared the table while Katherine loaded the dishwasher. They had dessert in the kitchen. Katherine asked about Mel's coming out and her past relationships. She was a good listener and she asked questions that made Mel dig deep into her soul for the most truthful answer she had.

The clock on the wall chimed. It was late. The concept of time was lost this evening in the bubble that surrounded them. Both looked at the clock and then at each other.

"I know you said it's okay if we wait on things," Katherine bit her lip before continuing, "but would you want to stay—without *that*—I mean?"

"I'd like that very much." Mel didn't hesitate with her answer. *Are you crazy?*

"It won't be—I guess—hard on you?"

Mel took a deep breath. "Well, it won't be the easiest thing I've ever done, but I'll be good. I just love being with you. But are you sure?"

"I'm becoming more certain every moment I'm with you."

Mel texted Jessica and told her she'd had too much to drink and would crash at the Neils. Jessica didn't respond which meant she was probably asleep on the couch with a movie playing. At least she wouldn't worry in the morning.

Katherine gave Mel a tour of the house. Unlike Mel, she had a knack for decorating. The walls were richly colored, and there were sculptures and artwork from Scotland throughout the house. It was a ranch so no upstairs, but it did have an unfinished basement that was not nearly as ghostly as the storm shelter out back of the Snow's farmhouse.

Mel was taller and a little bigger than Katherine, so Katherine snagged one of Nathan's t-shirts and shorts out of the dryer. "Okay, so he does come in handy sometimes." Katherine laughed.

"Does he know?"

"Not yet."

They walked down the hall to Katherine's room. Katherine stopped midway. Turning, she placed her hands on Mel's chest. "If you'd rather sleep in the guest room I'll understand."

"Having second thoughts?" Mel took Katherine's hands in hers.

"No. Definitely not. I don't want to make things hard for you. I just want you to be here in the morning. Is that completely selfish of me?"

"I agreed to this, remember? I promise to tell you if it's too much."

Katherine searched her face.

"I should probably tell you something though." Mel pretended to get serious.

"Okay." Katherine braced herself.

"I hope you're cooking in the morning because I suck at it."

"Good grief, Mel. You scared me to death."

Mel changed in the bathroom and brushed her teeth with her finger like she used to do as a kid when she would forget her toothbrush.

She stepped back into the room and closed the door. Katherine was already in bed with the quilt tucked under her arms. Mel breathed in deeply before crawling into the far side of the queen size bed. She lay on her side watching Katherine in the glow of the bedside lamp behind her head.

"Now I feel silly about asking you to stay." Katherine turned her head to look at Mel keeping her body straight and stiff.

"Look. Give yourself a break, okay? Just think of it as a sleepover like when you were a kid—one where you cook breakfast."

"Yeah, but I'm not thirteen anymore."

"Tell me what you were like when you were thirteen."

Katherine scooted closer and started talking about her teen years, her parents, and her friends. Mel kept her hand across her body on top of the blanket. She sensed Katherine relax as she talked about growing up. In the middle of a story about a turtle name Benedict that she had rescued and kept hidden in her room from her parents, she drifted off to sleep.

Mel lay beside her studying her sleeping face. Her eyes flickered under her eyelids. Her body pressed to hers, she felt the rise and fall of each breath Katherine took. Her mind was wide awake asking questions she didn't have the answers to.

Morning light streamed into the window beside the bed and onto Mel's face. She opened her eyes to see this had not been some fantastical dream, but she was lying beside Katherine who at some point in the night had taken Mel's arm for a pillow. The fingertips on Mel's right hand were tingling and Katherine's head was buried in Mel's shoulder. Sunday morning had never felt so good.

A crow cawed outside the window. Not the most pleasant of morning bird calls, but Mel remembered her grandfather saying crows always got a bad rep just because they couldn't croon like ol' Bing Crosby. She couldn't carry a tune in a bucket, so she had always a sort of kindred spirit with them.

Katherine stirred and rubbed her still closed eyes with the back of her hand. When she opened her eyes and looked up, Mel thought for a moment she was going to scream.

Her eyes widened. "You're here."

Mel smiled. "Were you expecting someone else?"

"Of course not." Katherine touched Mel's cheek. "I like waking up to you."

Katherine scrambled eggs with peppers and cheese while Mel made the coffee. They ate breakfast out on the patio, the warm, morning air smelled crisp.

"Do you think we should tell anyone?" Katherine asked.

Mel tore off the corner of a biscuit. "Maybe we should both give ourselves some time to get our own head wrapped around it."

"You're not sure either?"

Mel laughed. "I'm quite sure. I meant for you. It's not a small thing and you need to think about that. Once you tell people, you can't undo this type of thing if you change your mind."

"Are you afraid I'll change my mind?"

"I hope you don't."

Katherine scooted her chair closer leaning to kiss Mel. "I don't think I could ever get tired of the way this feels."

Mel needed to get home but was reluctant to leave. Nathan was due back this afternoon, and they had decided not

251

to tell anyone for now. Katherine would be covering extra shifts for the next two weeks while one of the other vets went on vacation. She would continue to meet with her therapist, and they would take things slow.

Katherine leaned in the Jeep window and kissed Mel one more time before she pulled away. At the end of their short driveway, Mel's phone rang. She expected it to be Jessica wondering where she was, but she saw the number.

"Is this what you call taking it slow?" Mel laughed.

"I already miss you," Katherine answered.

Chapter Thirty-One

The next two weeks drug out painfully slow for Mel. Katherine was swamped covering shifts and sorting out her thoughts and feelings, and Jessica had decided to pack the two weeks with more horses, more lessons, and more evening training sessions. A horse in training had kicked a board off the stall wall and needed stitches. Mel was disappointed when one of the other vets answered the call.

Mel had not broached Jason's idea again, deciding to let a little time go by before bringing it up again. It was a battle she was convinced she wanted to fight but wasn't sure how to best go about it. Jason understood and had eased off for now.

Each evening, Mel lay in bed exhausted, waiting for Katherine's call. Twice she had drifted off to sleep and missed the call altogether waking up in the middle of the night mad at herself. Katherine had stopped by once to drop off supplements Jessica had ordered and managed a quick kiss in the tack room when Jessica took a phone call.

Friday night, Jessica had gone, reluctantly, to a wedding in Cincinnati for a high school friend. She had begged Mel to go with her, but Mel had flat out refused.

"Absolutely not. No more plus one for me."

"You would really make me go alone?"

"Yes, I most definitely would."

"That's no way to treat your little sister." Jessica snarled.

"You should have thought about that before you worked us all week like a crazy woman." Mel laughed at Jessica's frowning face.

After a bath and a movie, Mel lay in bed talking with Katherine as she drove home after stitching up the jaw of a quarter horse who had decided to change stalls without the help of his humans.

"He was a mess for sure, but at least he was sweet, so he wasn't a pain to deal with. What a way to end my last extra shift," Katherine said. "I'm beyond exhausted."

"I was so glad when Jessica left at noon. She's been on a working rampage these last two weeks. She's about to kill us all. I fed early and came inside, vegged out on a ridiculous Lifetime movie, but I didn't even care."

"You're still watching TV?"

"Nope. Came up to bed a few minutes ago." Mel tucked a second pillow under her head. "Are you doing anything tomorrow?" Mel had plans of talking her into a Saturday morning ride.

"I don't know about tomorrow yet, but I think you have a visitor waiting on your back porch."

"Not funny." Mel sat up straight in bed.

"Are you just going to make them wait out there forever?"

"You're not serious." But Mel had already swung open her bedroom door and started down the stairs. She ran through the living room, causing Sam Houston to jump up from in front of the couch in a barking panic, and down the hall, dashing across the kitchen hitting her hip on the corner of the table. "If this is some kind of a joke—"

Mel pulled open the door and smiled. There she was.

"You are absolutely crazy," Mel blurted out.

"I couldn't wait any longer." Katherine stepped inside. "Do you mind?"

"You *are* crazy if you think I would ever mind you showing up on my doorstep." Mel noticed a small duffle bag by Katherine's side. Her mouth went dry. There was no time to ask questions; Katherine's mouth was on hers. Mel tasted her and melted in the moment.

They parted after a few minutes, breathing heavily. Katherine looked up at Mel. "I had no idea what I've been missing."

"Neither did I," Mel admitted.

Katherine's forehead crinkled in a way that made Mel weak. "You don't have to say that."

"You don't have a clue what you do to me." Mel glanced at the duffle bag and raised her eyebrows. "Can I take that for you?"

Katherine blushed and clutched the bag in front of her with both hands. "I thought I might stay with you tonight."

"Sure." Mel braced herself.

"No, I mean can I *stay* with you tonight?"

Mel's heartbeat sped up. Had she heard her correctly? "Are you saying what I think you're saying?"

Katherine stood tall and nodded letting the duffle bag dangle back to her side. Mel reached out and took it from her, their hands resting together for a moment. She said nothing but closed the door behind them. Taking Katherine's hand, she led her upstairs.

Only the moonlight lit the room. Mel did not turn on the overhead light. Closing the bedroom door to the world, she placed the duffle bag in the corner chair she'd taken from her dad's office months ago.

The energy in the room was almost tangible. Mel and Katherine faced each other standing by the side of the bed. Mel begged herself to remember that this was Katherine's first time. She would take it slow.

Katherine placed her hands on Mel's hips. Mel wore only a tank top and the boxer briefs she slept in. She hadn't thought to put anything on when she went downstairs to open the door. Mel felt Katherine's hands trembling against her skin before realizing her own hands were shaking at her sides. Katherine leaned in but stopped.

255

"What's wrong?" Mel panicked thinking Katherine had come to her senses and would run from the room.

"I'm scared."

"We don't have to—" Mel placed her hands under Katherine's elbows.

"Not that." Katherine shook her head. "I'm scared I'll do things wrong. I don't know how to do this."

Mel tucked her hand underneath Katherine's chin and stared into her eyes. The tenderness staring back at her was precious. "There's no right or wrong. It's just us. Together."

Katherine's gaze never left Mel's face. She slowly raised Mel's tank top and pulled it over her head. Only then did she gaze upon Mel's bare chest, letting her hand brush across her breasts. Mel shivered.

Katherine smiled and stepped back. She pulled her polo over her head and let it drop to the floor. She reached for Mel and pulled her onto the bed.

Sometime in the middle of the night, Katherine awoke, and they made love again. In the early morning light, Mel watched Katherine sleep. Katherine shifted and pulled Mel to her tucking her head under Mel's chin. She let out a long, unconscious sigh.

"Hey, sleepyhead," Mel whispered in her ear. "Are you going to stay in this bed forever?"

Katherine smiled but didn't open her eyes. She reached her arms around Mel's rib cage and squeezed. "What's wrong with that?"

"Nothing except we might starve." Mel kissed her forehead.

"There's no room service?"

"Not in this house. And remember, I'm a horrible cook."

Katherine released Mel and stretched. "Last night was unbelievable. I had no idea it could be that—real."

It was Mel's turn to blush. "It was beautiful."

"You're not just saying that?"

"Let me rephrase that." Mel touched Katherine's cheek. "It was absolutely beautiful."

"I can do better next time," Katherine said.

"I don't know about better, but I look forward to next time."

As it turned out next time was this moment. They held each other until the sun shone brightly in the room.

"I should shower. Is that okay?" Katherine sat up in bed.

"Would you like help?"

Katherine laughed. "I don't know if we'd get much showering done."

Mel admired her athletic body as she rustled through her duffle bag. "Maybe not, but it could be fun."

Katherine came to the edge of the bed and kissed her, jumping back when Mel tried to grab her.

"Shower," Katherine said sternly.

Still laughing and naked, Mel jumped from the bed and lunged for Katherine. Katherine opened the bedroom door and let out a gasp. Standing in the hall with her hand in the air getting ready to knock was Jessica.

Jessica's mouth and eyes widened at the sight of Katherine, and she had turned abruptly and ran down the stairs. Katherine got dressed quickly. The back door had slammed with a particular vengeance. Assuring Katherine it would be okay, but doubting her own conviction, Mel walked with her to her Jeep.

"I'll talk to her." Mel took Katherine's hand. "You have every right to be here. And last night was one of the best nights of my life."

"Why did I have to swing that door open?"

Mel reached out and pulled Katherine to her. Her tense muscles relaxed into Mel's arms. "Listen. It wasn't the way I expected to tell my sister about us, but it'll be okay."

"Don't joke."

"Okay, okay. But last night—I don't want anything to spoil that." Mel stepped back from the door and Katherine got in.

"Call me later?" Katherine asked.

"Of course." Mel leaned in the window and kissed her. Katherine stiffened. Mel stood in the drive with her hands tucked in her back pockets. The Jeep turned the corner out of sight, and Mel walked to the barn. She was not at all sure what to expect.

Jessica was saddling Rooster. The jerking motions of her hands with the leather told Mel what she needed to know.

"Jess, I—" That's as far as she got.

"What the fuck, Mel?" Jessica shouted and faced her.

"I didn't know you were home."

"She's our vet, for God's sake."

"What difference does that make?"

"People will talk." Jessica turned and grabbed the bridle hanging by Rooster's head. "I didn't even know she was gay. And how long has this been going on?"

Jessica rapid fired her thoughts. Mel took a deep breath. "Do you have a problem with me seeing Katherine?"

Silence.

"Jess."

"Yes! Okay? Yes, I have a problem with it. It's one thing for you to be gay, but—"

"But what?"

"Damn it, Mel. You and her naked in our house?" Jessica fitted the metal bit in Rooster's mouth and slung the reins over his neck.

"So, Tommy was always fully clothed all those times he stayed over?"

"That's different."

"Be very careful what you say next, Jess." Mel's voice was tight.

258

Jessica turned to stare at her. Without saying a word, she swung up on Rooster and left Mel standing in the barn aisle shaking with anger.

Mel sat on the back porch and called Katherine. She didn't mince her words about Jessica's reaction. It was important that Katherine knew. Mel had grown used to navigating around others' views no matter how illogical or hurtful.

"I'm going to tell Nathan."

"Okay. But don't be too disappointed."

"I'll be okay. I know I'm confused about some whys and hows and whens, but I'm not confused about how much I feel for you. It's one of the most complete feelings I've ever had."

Mel leaned back against the bench. "I know everyone's come a long way and all, but just make sure you're ready for pushback."

"Don't think I can handle myself?" It was Katherine's turn to try and lighten the mood.

"You're a vet in a small town in the South."

"Have you changed your mind about us?" Katherine spoke boldly.

"Not at all, but I won't lie—people's reactions can be shattering. He's your brother, so his reaction is going to matter to you. Are you sure this is the life you want?"

"Don't worry. Call me tonight?"

"You know it." Mel was about to hang up.

"Mel?"

"Yes."

"Thank you for last night."

Jessica brought Rooster back to the barn and left in her truck. *Here we go again*. Mel sat at the kitchen table trying to concentrate on the bills, but when she came across

Katherine's name printed on the vet bill, her head went elsewhere.

Hours later, Mel heard the backdoor open.

"Hey," was all Jessica said.

Mel cleared her throat to talk, but Jessica cut her off. "I don't want to talk about this."

"Okay." Mel was angry but changed the subject. "How was the wedding then?"

"Painful actually," Jessica shot back. "I was the only one there solo, except for the groom's aunt who had to be close to two hundred years old. It was a ridiculously expensive wedding, her family flaunting their money around like they were Kentucky Kennedys or something. It was embarrassing."

Although blunt by nature, this harshness was unusual for Jessica. Yes, she leaned toward opinionated and sarcastic, but not mean.

"Did they at least have good food at the reception?" Mel asked trying to find safe ground.

"The reception was crap. I got put at the losers' table."

Mel understood. "Was it crap because it wasn't good or because you were alone?"

Jessica shouted at her, "You could have at least told me about her."

Mel picked up the remote and switched off the TV, giving herself time to steady her voice. "I was going to. It hasn't been that long, and, well, we just needed some time to sort things out."

"Couldn't you date a stranger?"

"What's that supposed to mean?" Mel raised her voice.

"Christ's sake, Mel. She's our vet."

"I didn't know certain people were off-limits. Do you have a list?"

"It looks bad, that's all."

Mel shook her head. "Looks bad on who?"

"People know you're my sister."

"People knew that before I went out with Katherine, and most people knew I was gay before that too, even though they don't say it, just so we're clear."

"Yeah, but now you're just flaunting it in all our faces."

A gasp escaped Mel's lips. Jessica opened her mouth to continue.

"Stop." Mel's body shook with anger. "I like Katherine, a lot. And we have just as much Goddamn right to be happy as you or anyone else in this town." Mel was standing now, her face red.

"I didn't mean it like that."

"I think that's exactly how you meant it, but what hurts the most is that you think you're okay having a gay sister, but you're only okay as long as you don't have to think about it."

Mel stormed up the stairs and stopped midway. "What the hell makes you any different than Uncle Jerry?" Running the rest of the way up, she slammed her door with Jessica calling after her.

Chapter Thirty-Two

Mel was as stubborn as her sister on many things, and in her view, Jessica needed to make the first move. Voices were short and cold to each other. Mr. Tomlin, no doubt thinking of his good friend Thomas, had not minced words when he told Mel and Jessica that they had too much to lose to let anything come between them like it did before. "I don't know what went on between you two, but you're both doing yourself more harm than good, no matter what's been done."

Mel and Jessica frowned and walked in separate directions.

Two weeks into the standoff, Mel began to think this one wasn't going to work out. She wasn't sleeping again. Dinners were solemn with hardly a word between them.

With life gone awry with Jessica, Mel thought about her father more often. Not knowing his opinion of her weighed heavy on her heart, and if things did get worse and she had to leave, Mel didn't want to carry the unfinished conversations with her.

Friday afternoon, Jessica informed Mel she was going to Lexington to pick up a horse. They had done many of these jobs together over the past year, but this time there was no invitation. Mel waited until Jessica was out of the drive to saddle Bonnie. She had put this off for too long. It was time to visit her dad.

She rode slow and rehearsed her words on the way. It was silly really—to fear talking to a dead person. She would be no closer to knowing what he thought of her after the visit, but something inside her spurred her on.

After opening the final gate, Mel walked next to Bonnie. The graveyard was small and unkept, a small iron fence marked off the boundary put there by her grandfather. Her father had planted trees around the area when she was young. It sat on a small knoll a hundred yards or so beyond Timber Creek to the west, and she had gone out of her way to avoid this spot since her return.

Mel tied Bonnie to the branch of a walnut tree and stepped over the leaning iron fence. Her grandparents, great-grandparents, and a handful of children who hadn't survived long on this earth made up one side of the small enclosure. She picked up fallen branches and tossed them outside the space.

I should keep this spot up. It was the least she could do.

The next two graves she remembered. She had stood next to her dad holding tightly to his hand when they placed her mother and baby brother in the ground. Mel remembered his shoulders and arms shaking as he wept.

Mel closed her eyes a moment. When she opened them again, her eyes fixed on the newest stone in the plot. *Thomas Spencer Snow.*

Something about seeing it etched in the stone made it feel more real than ever. She knelt down on one knee. That felt too formal. She sat down in the grass in front of the stone and crossed her legs. Mel ran her hands over the warm grass in front of her. She did not know what she believed about the afterlife, but seeing him next to her mom, Mel hoped Jessica was right about them being reunited.

"Hi, Dad." Mel looked around feeling foolish. "It's me."

Mel pulled her knees up to her chest clasping her hands together. "I came home."

263

This wasn't working. Mel cleared her throat. *Just talk like he was here.* "I'm trying to work things out with Jessica. We were doing pretty good until recently. The farm's doing good. You'd be proud of her, I bet. She's a good trainer."

Mel relaxed a little.

"Wherever you are, maybe you can see all that happened back then. If you can't, well, it was a mess, and I'm sorry I didn't come home sooner."

Mel stretched her legs out in front of her. "I need to tell you something."

Mel took a deep breath. *How can it be this hard to come out to a dead person?*

"Dad, if you don't already know, I'm gay."

Mel had not expected the flood of emotions that rushed through her when she said those words. Her eyes filled with tears. She lay back in the grass and continued talking. She told her dad of her years in Boston, Patricia, how hard the last few months had been, and how much she missed him. She told him about Katherine and her troubles with Jessica now. She even told him about Bonnie and how lazy she was.

"I don't know what you would think of me, but I hope you'd be proud. Things didn't work out as I planned, but I have a plan to help other kids like me. I'll try to teach them all you taught me and give them a safe place to be. Here. On Snow lands."

As Mel spoke of Jason's idea, a knowing determination sank into her. The idea of destiny had never sat well with her, but this was the opportunity she had been looking for. She couldn't do it without Jessica's help. She would find a way to make it happen.

At dinner, Mel told Jessica she'd visited their dad's grave.

"I told him I was gay. I still don't know what he would have thought of me, but I hope I can do something with my life that would make him proud."

Jessica nodded but said nothing.

"I'm serious about the project with Jason, Jess, but I'd be stupid to consider doing it without you. I won't say any more about it right now, but I'm asking you to think about it and consider helping me. I can't give up on the idea of helping kids like me, but I need *you* to make it work."

Jessica agreed to think about it but said little else before going upstairs to her room.

Mel had dinner at Katherine's the weekend after she told Nathan. Nathan had been thrilled at the news and insisted on cooking dinner for the both of them. The back door was open and the smell of burnt cheese floated through the air when she crossed the patio. Smoke burned her eyes.

"Is it safe to come in?" Mel stuck her head in the door and asked.

Nathan stood by the stove fanning a blackened dish. "Keeping with the Italian theme, I've decided to go get pizza. That's better than *lasagna a la charred*, right?"

Mel looked to Katherine who couldn't contain her laughter. "No offense, but I'd say anything will be better than that."

"Change of plans, you two have some wine and I'll be back in a jiffy." Nathan picked up the pan holding it away from his face, but before he took the smelly dish outside, he kissed Mel hard on the cheek. "Welcome to the family."

Katherine walked across the kitchen and kissed Mel. She was still laughing. "He forgot to set the timer and fell asleep. But at least the chocolate cake was saved."

Nathan came back with two large pizzas and an order of breadsticks. They ate on the patio.

"I'm happy for you two." Nathan placed another pizza wedge on his plate. "Of course, I had my suspicions all along."

"Get off it. You did not," Katherine answered.

"I did. Especially when all you could talk about for days was 'Jessica's sister Mel.'" Nathan put on an obnoxiously high voice. "Did I tell you she came from

Boston? Did I tell you we're going to a movie? Did I tell you she's coming to hear my lecture?"

Katherine reached across the table and slapped him, blushing.

Nathan continued, "If you ask me, it's great. You always did have horrible taste in men."

Seeing them together made Mel happy but also sad about Jessica's distance.

"I wish Jess could have been here tonight," Mel told Katherine later that night as they sat in the swing by her garden.

"I thought about that earlier." Katherine lay her head on Mel's shoulder. "She'll come around."

Many nights after making love, Mel and Katherine would talk until daybreak. Mel told Katherine things she had never dared tell another soul. Having kept so much of her life shut off, even from Patricia, this openness excited and terrified her. At times, she wondered if Katherine would decide she had too much baggage to be worth the effort of a relationship.

Katherine talked, with no real filter, about her confusions and questions and newfound feelings. Some of her ideas made Mel laugh. With each passing day, Mel became surer of Katherine's attraction. Katherine's head was on straight, so to speak. She wasn't someone who just looked on the surface of her life, but she dug down into microscopic areas to see what went on. She examined her life as if it were one of her four-legged patients.

Jessica continued to distance herself but was not as cold as she had been at first. Mel knew she was working through things and tried to give her the space she needed. Katherine encouraged her to be patient and wait. "She'll come around," Katherine would remind her.

Mel took Katherine at her word and told Jason she was in. She told him of the standoff between herself and Jessica, but this didn't deter him. Jason was as excited as a

266

kid at Christmas and began immediately sending her documents and articles to read to fill her in on the months of planning and research. Mel spent hours reading and studying in her room after work.

Jason invited Mel to their place in Louisville for dinner; he was thrilled when Mel asked if she could bring a date. Mel and Katherine had gone to the movies a couple of times and out to dinner, but this marked their first event with others as a couple. As the evening approached, Mel's stomach was all butterflies.

Jason and Emanuel had just recently moved into a three-bedroom house in the East Market District of Louisville to give Jason's mother a little more space. Emanuel was a superb cook and served chicken *pepián* from his home country of Guatemala. Their cat, Matilda, took a liking to Katherine and wouldn't leave her lap.

"He won me over with his skills in the kitchen." Jason tousled Emanuel's hair while he worked his magic at the stove.

"And here I was thinking it was my skills in the bedroom," Emanuel stated matter-of-factly. "Can you make yourself useful and pour our guests some wine?"

"Oh right. Right. I forgot that was my job." Jason winked at the girls who had taken a seat on barstools.

The guys had met in college and had married in New York City one Christmas Eve. They traveled to Guatemala every summer to see Emanuel's large family, and his mother had just been up for a visit. Jason told them many stories of miscommunications and his frequent Spanish screw-ups.

"I can tell when I use the wrong word or phrase. Her eyes get wide, and she looks to Emanuel for an interpretation." Jason laughed. "But hey, I'm trying."

Dinner was served, and the conversations continued. Jason inserted business here and there. Mel again reminded him that Jessica was not yet on board, but he waved off her concern. This was a minor detail. He asked Mel to describe a typical day in the horse training business and jotted down notes on his napkin. Emanuel rebuked him playfully.

After dinner, Jason shooed them to the living room while they prepared dessert and coffee. Emanuel had made *rellenitos*, a kind of homemade, deep-fried donut, and served it with coffee from his family's plantation near Lake Atitlan.

"It's a good thing you two don't live close." Katherine licked her fingers. "I'd be at your house for dinner every night and twice my size."

Emanuel smiled. "You're both welcome any time."

"I just thought of something while in the kitchen. It's a great idea if I do say so myself. Katherine, would you be willing to offer some classes or take a teen with you on your rounds? Maybe some hands-on stuff, nothing too detailed, but give them a taste of what it's like in the vet world?"

"I'd have to talk it over with the other vets, but I don't see why not."

Jason was beside himself. "It's all falling into place. I can't tell you how long I've wanted to start something like this. It took a while, though. After I left, I was convinced I never wanted to see this place again."

"What changed your mind?"

"It was history really. The key to change—the good kind of change—is exposure. Time after time, we see it." Jason shook his head. "Acceptance comes so slow in some places because people aren't exposed to as many ideas or different lives, different viewpoints. They're good people with good hearts; change just comes with exposure. That's where I got the idea."

"I know I'm sort of new to all this, but I like your ideas, and I'll do what I can to help you." Katherine placed her hand on Mel's knee and gave it a squeeze.

"This one," Jason raised his glass toward Katherine and winked at Mel, "is a keeper."

Driving home Mel and Katherine talked excitedly about their evening and plans for the future.

268

"The guys are lovely. They remind me of my grandparents bickering back and forth." Katherine scrunched her nose. "What do you think we look like to other people?"

Mel laughed "I never thought about it, but I feel like I'm in junior high or something with my first real crush. So maybe that's what we look like."

"Silly young kids in love—just with a few more wrinkles," Katherine added.

"You speak for yourself about wrinkles." Mel rubbed her forehead. "I've got to get Jessica on board. Not to mention, I'm tired of us being at odds."

"I know she'll come around, Mel."

"Yeah, but when? I could force the point and threaten to split up the farm, but what good would that do? What would I teach the kids? How to start a tractor and mend a fence?" Mel laughed at herself. "No. If this is going to work, I have to have Jessica with me, and it has to be her choice."

"Would it help if I talked to her?" Katherine asked.

"I don't know what would help, but I think the fewer people mixed up in my hostile territory the better for now." Mel smiled and reached for Katherine's hand.

Chapter Thirty-Three

The knock on the front door was so faint, that for a second Mel thought it was the creaking of the old house. She stopped and listened. The second knock was stronger. The tall brunette woman stood holding her handbag in front of her with both hands. Her face held a vague familiarity in it, but Mel could not place her.

"Hello. Can I help you?"

"I'm looking for Thomas Snow."

Hearing her father's name jarred her. "I'm sorry. He's—he passed away last year."

She twisted the purse handles between her fingers. "Are you Jessica?"

"No, I'm Mel." Mel pushed the screen door open. "Would you care to come in? Can I help you with anything?"

"Mel." The woman smiled and said the name as if it meant something to her. She walked inside but stopped just a few feet in.

"Am I interrupting anything?"

"No, no please, come in. I was cooking some dinner." Mel motioned the woman to follow her into the kitchen. "Sorry, but have we met?"

"No." sticking her hand out. "Sorry, I'm Abigail. Abigail Clark."

"Nice to meet you. You look familiar is all." Mel pulled out a kitchen chair. "Please, have a seat. Can I get you a cup of coffee or glass of tea?"

"Coffee would be great if it's no trouble." Abigail looked around the kitchen.

"We've always got coffee going around here." Curiosity was getting the better of Mel. She poured two cups and grabbed a tin of store-bought cookies out of the cabinet. "Did you know my dad?"

"Not really, but—" Abigail took a sip of the coffee. "He helped me out last spring."

The back door swung open. Jessica and Sam Houston came in like a whirlwind. "Oh, sorry, I didn't realize you had company."

Mel stood. "Jess, this is Abigail Clark. She was looking for Dad." Halfway expecting Jessica to recognize the stranger, Mel watched her closely.

"Oh, hello. Did Dad train for you?" Jessica hung her cap on the hook and kicked off her boots.

"Train? Oh, no. I don't have any horses. I'm sorry to hear about your father." Abigail cleared her throat. "I was just telling Mel that he helped me out last spring."

"Really? With what?" Jessica opened the fridge and poured a glass of sweet tea and leaned against the sink.

"Well," Abigail looked from Jessica to Mel. "I needed surgery, and your dad gave me the money for it."

Mel and Jessica waited for her to say more. Abigail took another sip of her coffee looking around the kitchen like she was contemplating leaving.

"I'm afraid I don't understand. You said you didn't know Dad." Mel sat her coffee cup down a little too hard.

Abigail closed her eyes and breathed in deeply. She opened them and sat up straight in her chair, placing her hands on her lap. "I only met him once. When he met me in town to give me the money. I'm your—cousin."

Mel and Jessica looked at one another and then back at Abigail.

"Cousin? But how—" Jessica started.

"Your Uncle Jerry. He's my father."

That's it. She's got his eyes. Mel's eyebrows shot up.

"What?" Jessica said in a tone half skeptical and half shocked.

The timer on the stove went off and all three women jumped.

"Sorry." Mel stood. "Would—would you like to stay for dinner?"

Mel had a million questions.

"I couldn't impose." Abigail's voice was apologetic.

"It's no trouble. And I'll confess it's more for selfish reasons. You've just opened quite a can of worms." Mel stuck a knife in the middle of the chicken pot pie and closed the oven door. "It'll be ready in about ten minutes."

Jessica sat staring at Abigail. "Uncle Jerry has a daughter? But when?"

"My mom and your uncle. I guess they had a thing a few years ago. Twenty-eight years ago, to be exact."

"Does he know about you?" Jessica asked while Mel was doing the math in her head.

"That's a different story—a long one, but your dad, he found out about me. Your uncle told him."

Mel was ready this time. "And the surgery?"

Abigail's face contorted slightly.

"I'm sorry. I don't mean to pry," Mel inserted.

Abigail shook her head. "No, it's okay. I came here to tell your dad that I was okay and that I would pay him back as soon as I could. I was—you see, I—the surgery, it was a gender affirmation surgery—in Mexico."

Mel nodded her head slowly, but Jessica looked at Abigail with confusion.

Seeing Jessica's face, Abigail clarified. "I'm transgender."

Jessica raised her eyebrows. "Oh."

An uncomfortable silence followed and the tension in the room hung like a southern summer's humidity. Abigail sat tall, not offering any more information.

"Dinner should be about ready. Jessica, would you see to the drinks?" Mel kicked into action. Jessica hesitated a moment before moving to the cupboard.

272

Dinner was served giving the three women an excuse for small talk. Mel had many questions and she suspected she was not alone in this. Jessica sat with her eyes fixed on the plate in front of her. Mel decided to go for a safe question in hopes of learning more about Abigail and lessening the tension.

"Did you grow up around here?"

Abigail swallowed the bite she was chewing. "Just south of Cincinnati, in Covington, so not far."

"I didn't know who my father was until a few years ago. I found some old photos and letters my mom had hidden. She had always told me it was a wild weekend in New York with her college roommates. I thought it sounded sort of romantic. I confronted her, and she told me the truth. She'd found out he was married after several months and cut off all ties. Only after he left did she find out I was on the way. She's a second-grade teacher, and she raised me on her own."

"Have you ever met Uncle—your father?" Jessica piped in.

"I tried, several times, but he refused."

"You're not missing much," Jessica said under her breath before saying, "Sorry, I probably shouldn't have said that."

Mel held back a chuckle. *You got to love her.*

Abigail said she had started contacting Uncle Jerry about two years ago. He refused to acknowledge her, and her mother refused to accept her as anything other than a son. Out of desperation, she had asked Uncle Jerry for money telling him she would never contact him again if he gave it to her.

"He called after the letter. He told me I was going to hell. He said that's the trouble with people like me—living like the devil and telling everyone they must accept this reality. He said he would never father a pervert, so my story couldn't possibly be true."

Mel's heart broke.

"Sounds like him," Jessica added coldly.

"And your mom?"

"She's why I came back. She's trying, I guess—no, not really. I've never been good enough for her, and this was just one more thing to be disappointed over. I live in Texas now." Abigail's face relaxed with the last statement.

"I hope she comes around," Mel added. Something about her smile made Mel think she'd found solace in Texas.

"I had sort of given up hope by the time your dad contacted me."

"Dad contacted you?" Mel asked.

"He called me and wanted to meet me. I met him for coffee, and he sat there and listened to my whole sad story." Abigail tore off a piece of bread. "He talked about both of you. He said he wanted to help me because he hoped someone had helped you, Mel. He apologized for my father. Jerry had gone to your dad and told him that I was trying to blackmail him. Thomas asked me how much money I needed for the surgery and two weeks later, I received a check in the mail."

The unexplained loan. Mel thought.

Jessica sat at the end of the table with a stunned look, a bite of potatoes resting on her fork. "What else did he say?"

"He bragged about how good you were with horses." Abigail smiled at Jessica. "He said you were better than him, but he tried not to show it—didn't want you getting a big head. I remember sitting there wishing I had a dad that lit up when he talked about me."

Mel sniffed and blinked back tears. "Dammit. I had no idea."

After dinner, Abigail took a quick tour of the barn before leaving.

"Please keep in touch." Mel hugged her. "And come back any time."

"I will." Abigail sat down in her car. "And I'm serious about the money. I promised myself I would pay it back. I'm not sure yet when that'll be, but it'll come."

"We're not worried about the money. We're just happy to meet you," Mel answered.

"I'm happy to meet you as well." Abigail cranked the engine. "And it will come."

As she drove down the drive Mel waved. "That was quite a surprise."

"You can say that again," Jessica answered.

The yelp of a puppy made Mel jerk her head up from the books sprawled out before her on the kitchen table. In Jessica's arms, a fluffy bundle of energy struggled to break free.

"Happy birthday!" Jessica smiled wildly.

"My birthday's not until the end of the month." Mel sat stunned.

"I can't help when they were born." Jessica frowned and handed the puppy to Mel.

The fuzzy face splotched with tan, black, and grey with a white triangle above the right eye licked Mel's cheek. "Australian shepherd, yeah?"

"Yep, and he's registered. From a great bloodline. You should see his daddy. Beautiful," Jessica beamed. "I remembered you used to have pictures hung up in your room. I hope you still like them. A little too late if you don't."

"Aw, Jess, I love him. You didn't have to."

"I know, but I wanted to. I've been a bit of an ass to you lately. More than a bit. This doesn't make up for that, but I'm sorry—and happy early birthday."

The puppy struggled against Mel's chest. She placed him on the kitchen floor, and he preceded to do a little dance before peeing under the table.

Mel laughed. "And so it begins."

"He's your dog now." Jessica scrunched up her nose.

"Thanks a lot." Mel stood and grabbed a wad of paper towels. "I'll have to stock up on these."

Jessica cleared her throat. "Hearing how Uncle Jerry treated his own flesh and blood made me ashamed of the way

I reacted to you and Katherine. I don't always know what I think about things, but I know I don't want to be anything like him. So that's at least a place to start."

"You aren't anything like him, Jess. I was angry when I said that. I'm sorry." Mel knelt to pry the dish towel that had been hanging on the oven handle out of the puppy's mouth.

"No, you were right. I can't say I'm okay with you being gay and then lose my shit when you start seeing someone. Besides, I like Katherine a lot. She is funny and nice. I guess you'd be crazy not to like her—I mean if that's what you go for—what you like." Flustered, Jessica went to the fridge and poured a glass of sweet tea. "Anyway, I remembered how dad always told us we've got to stick together like geese. Besides, it's none of my business who you sleep with. I know you weren't waiting around for my approval, but I just wanted to tell you."

"Thanks, Jess. It means a lot to hear you say that."

Jessica picked up the puppy. "Have a name in mind?"

"I'll have to give it some thought," Mel answered.

They walked out into the backyard. Sam Houston was lying under the tree, and the puppy made a beeline for him as soon as Jessica placed him on the ground. Sam Houston jumped up with a look of shock and disgust when the puppy dove onto his nose.

Mel laughed, "Sam's going to hate you for this."

"You know a few weeks ago when you told me in no uncertain terms that the farm is half yours?"

Mel winced. "Yeah?"

"Hearing you talk about why you want to help Jason with this project, and after you stormed out of the truck like a rabid bear, I sat there and thought, *now that's the Mel I remember.*"

Mel groaned. "I was pretty worked up."

Jessica smiled. "It's the first time I saw that fire, that determination, I remember from when we were young. I don't know if I'll be any help—I'll probably screw things up right and left—but if you want to give this a go, I'll help, or at least I'll try to stay out of your way."

Chapter Thirty-Four

Jessica sprayed off Rooster after a trail ride. "Let's have dinner this weekend."

"We normally do."

"No, I mean all of us."

Mel wasn't getting it.

"Us. You, Me, Katherine, Nathan."

Mel raised her eyebrows. "Oh."

"What's wrong with that?" Jessica seemed to take offense at Mel's hesitancy.

"Nothing. Are you sure?"

"Of course, I'm sure. Why wouldn't I be?"

Mel smiled. This little sister of hers was a wonder. She took her own sweet time in making up her mind about things, but once she did, she plunged full speed ahead.

So, dinner was planned. Jessica had coordinated with Nathan, even before she had mentioned it to Mel, and the two of them cooked the whole meal. Jessica even bought and drank red wine having often declared it was against her religion to drink wine over beer. Mel's stomach was in knots all afternoon, with disastrous scenarios playing out in her head.

Katherine walked outside with Mel when she took the new puppy, still nameless, out to the bathroom while Nathan and Jessica heated the apple pie. They stood under the old Elm tree behind the house.

"You doing okay?" Katherine kiss Mel on the cheek.

"Jessica's handling it better than I am." Mel laughed. "I'm a bucket of nerves tonight."

"You, Miss Gay Pride herself?" Katherine winked. "I can tell. Your laugh changes when you're nervous. It's normal, I guess. She did flip out at first."

The pup bit at Mel's boot.

Nathan yelled out the back door. "Hey, you two. Don't make me come out there and get you. The ice cream's going to melt."

Hand in hand, Mel and Katherine walked back into the kitchen.

"Mel, you've got to name that dog," Nathan declared.

"I can't decide. I need suggestions."

They took turns throwing out names for the new pup. Jessica grabbed a pen and paper out of the drawer by the stove and started writing down possibilities.

After dessert, the name search continued on the front porch with the half-empty bottle of Scotch Katherine had brought from Scotland. Nathan pulled cigars from his bag.

"I have a pipe," Mel announced like it was show and tell.

"You smoke a pipe?" Katherine looked stunned.

"Wait right here." Mel went into the office and grabbed the pipe and tobacco. Stepping back onto the porch Mel added, "smoking may be an overstatement. I smoke *at* it mainly."

Katherine and Nathan looked at each other.

Jessica explained, "It was Dad's pipe. Mel's tried several times to smoke it but ends up getting mad because it won't stay lit. Last week, she chucked it way out into the yard."

"I'm still trying to find my technique," Mel said sticking the pipe between her teeth. She lit a match and held it up to the pipe shielding it with her other hand.

"You are full of surprises." Katherine laughed.

Nathan lit his cigar. "Remember old Mr. McGee that lived on the corner by Gran? He smoked a pipe. How about McGee for the pup?"

"He would do smoke tricks for us," Katherine added. "Can you do a trick for us, Mel?"

"I can't even keep the damn thing lit yet." Mel struck another match.

After several more matches and no luck, Mel laid the pipe aside.

"Here. I've been looking for a cigar buddy." Nathan handed her a cigar and lighter. "Katherine will have none of it."

"Count me in." Mel smiled.

Nathan reeled off several Scottish band names as suggestions for the pup, and Jessica and Katherine mashed these names together in random orders. After the jumbled mess of hilarity, Mel decided on Finnegan McGee, Finn for short.

Mel walked into the small diner in Frankfort and scanned the tables looking for Trisha. She had called last night to ask her to lunch saying she had a huge favor. It had sounded even more mysterious when she asked if Mel minded driving into Frankfort instead of meeting in Lebanon Springs.

"Thanks for coming out, Mel. I know y'all are busy." Trisha stood and hugged her.

Mel returned the hug awkwardly. "I'm glad you called. It's good to see you. Jessica was working me too hard anyway. Nice to have a break."

The waitress, who Mel was sure she had seen at a local horse show, brought menus and waters. Trisha knew what she wanted, so Mel quickly scanned the menu and ordered the daily special: Roast beef, fried okra, and mashed potatoes with gravy.

"And a sweet tea, please," Mel added, grinning at Trisha. "I sure missed sweet tea when I was in Boston."

"I can't imagine living any other place than the South." Trisha shook her head. "We went to Chicago once before we had the boys. I was a nervous wreck the whole time—so crowded and noisy."

Mel smiled. If Uncle Jerry had not derailed her life and sent her away, this could have easily been her.

Trisha went on. "Are you glad to be back here?"

"I am. I missed this place a lot."

"I told you I had a favor to ask of you." Trisha sighed. "It's a biggie, so feel free to turn me down flat if you want to."

"I'll help if there's any way I can," Mel answered.

"It's my niece, James' niece, his older sister's kid. Rachel. She showed up at our door on Sunday." Trisha paused while the waitress sat the teas and cornbread in the middle of the table.

"Is she okay?" Mel asked.

Trisha leaned in and spoke quietly. "She's—like you, you see. She told her parents, and they went crazy. Called their preacher in, and he wanted to do an exorcism or something on her. She refused, and they told her she couldn't stay there if she wasn't open to being cured. That's when she left. She's no kid, mind you, but she's young—and scared, I think."

Mel's heart broke. "How old is she?"

Trisha thought. "Nineteen. Mel, it was the saddest thing I've ever seen. I opened the door, and she just burst into tears and fell into my arms."

"Have you spoken to her parents?"

"She begged us not to tell them she's here. James wanted to call his sister, but I convinced him not to." Trisha shook her head and leaned back in her chair. "He's none too happy about any of this."

"Do you want me to talk to her?"

The waitress brought their food, snatching the salt and pepper shakers from the next table over.

"That might help, but that's not the favor." Trisha looked at Mel. "James has agreed to let her stay, but only if she gets a job. He ain't too sure what he thinks about all this."

281

"Ok." Mel took a bite allowing her time to think. "What can I do to help?"

Trisha leaned in across the table. "Jessica was saying how y'all have been shorthanded since Cody left. Rachel was raised on a farm, cows, mostly, but a few horses along the way. I was thinking you might be able to use her over at your place."

Life was funny.

"Does she want to do that sort of work?"

"Honestly, she ain't sure what she wants to do, but she's a hard worker. She'll try her hand at anything. A good-natured kid. She was working at the bank up there part-time, but she didn't like being cooped up inside all day. I figured, even if it was only for a little while, it would do her some good to be around you, you know?"

"It might work, but I'd have to talk with Jessica." Mel wondered if this would be asking too much too soon. "We can't pay much, just so you know."

"It's not about the money, and if don't work out I won't blame you one bit. I just want her to be around people that understand her. I don't know what she's going through, but if we can just love on her a little bit, maybe things will be okay."

This woman's heart was golden.

With James unsure, Mel couldn't afford to wait to talk with Jessica. As was her custom, she rehearsed all the way home. Jessica was showing interest and patience in the upcoming project with Jason, and Mel hoped this new idea would be received the same.

Mel parked the Jeep in front of the tractor. Jasper loped a buckskin mare in the round pen.

"Where's Jessica?"

"She took that edgy gelding down to the creek to work him."

Jessica had a favorite spot for this. Mel saddled Bonnie quickly.

282

Bonnie held a slow trot while Mel thought of exorcisms and the fear they must conjure in a young girl trying hard to figure out an already confusing life. The hair on the back of her neck stood on end.

Up ahead, Mel spotted Jessica.

"You're soaking wet," Mel yelled to her from the creek bank.

"Damn horse. More stubborn than scared. You'd think I was asking him to cross piranha-infested waters." Jessica eased him to the creek's edge not letting up until his front feet touched the water. As long as he wasn't fighting her, she would ease up.

"What's up? How was lunch?"

"Good. I think I have a solution to us being shorthanded if you're interested." Mel rested her forearm on the saddle horn.

"Let's hear it."

"Right. Okay, first keep an open mind. James and Trisha have taken their niece in. She left home and came to them for help."

The gelding Jessica was on took two steps backward.

"Oh no you don't." Jessica urged him forward, but he side-stepped twice instead of going forward. "Damn you. We ain't going home until you decide to cross this creek."

Jessica kept working him until he walked forward and stepped into the water again. This time the water came up to his knees.

Mel waited, knowing the routine.

"What kind of trouble is she in?" Jessica eyed Mel skeptically.

"Not really any trouble, except with her parents' morals." Mel hesitated. "She's gay."

Jessica nodded. "And let me guess, they're the Uncle Jerry type."

Mel smiled at her wording. "Sounds like it."

Jessica started working with the horse again, urging him kindly but firmly. The look on her face told Mel she was thinking about more than getting the horse across the creek.

After another balk, the horse lunged forward into the creek and up the opposite bank.

"Now that wasn't so bad, was it?" Jessica patted him on the neck. "This time let's take it a little slower so you don't ram my vertebrae together."

Mel waited while Jessica urged the horse into the water again making him stop in the middle of the creek. He stood like a statue his eyes wild like there might really be piranhas in the water.

"Damn it, horse, just settle a bit. There aren't any monsters in this creek." Jessica smiled up at Mel. "What do you think?"

Mel wasn't sure if she meant the horse or Rachel. Either way, the question surprised her. "I think we should give her a chance," Mel answered determinedly.

Jessica urged the horse up the bank beside Mel. "Okay then. Let's give her a chance."

Trisha brought Rachel over the following morning. Mel introduced herself but hung back to talk with Trisha letting Jessica take the lead in showing her around.

"She was so nervous this morning," Trisha whispered.

"I'm sure she'll do fine. How's James handling it?"

Trisha knelt down to pet the cat that was winding around her legs. "We talked last night. He's never had to think about things like this much. He's awkward around her, but I reminded him she's still the same little girl that used to tag along behind him when he'd go up to help on their farm."

"Any word from his sister?"

"Rachel called her parents last night and told them where she was. They were none too happy about it. They called James and told him he was paving Rachel's path to hell. That didn't sit too well with him. He ended up telling his sister that hell might just be for parents who turn their back on their children." Trisha's eyes were wide. "He may be confused, but he's a good man deep down."

Jessica walked back through the barn with Rachel. "That's pretty much all there is to it. Sound all right to you?"

"Yes, ma'am," Rachel answered.

"There's no need for any ma'aming around here." Jessica laughed. "Let's find you a manure fork and some gloves."

Chapter Thirty-Five

Finn slept between Mel's and Katherine's feet on the cool concrete in the arena. They had spent the morning walking around the fairgrounds through barns full of cattle, sheep, goats, and even chickens on display. Finn had tuckered himself out with excitement. Along with sleepless nights and endless puddles sopped up with rolls and rolls of paper towels, Finn had provided hours of comic relief with his goofy personality.

After an unsuccessful protest on her part, Rachel had come along to the horse show with them. It had not taken long to recognize Rachel's tendency to give herself the short end of the stick.

"A day off will do you good. Besides you put the boys to shame by how hard you work." Jessica shot Jasper a feigned scold.

"You're just saying that." Rachel scooped a pile of manure from the barn aisle.

"I don't just say things unless I mean it. You deserve this day, and well—I'm the boss." Jessica smiled.

Jasper scoffed warranting a sincere scowl this time.

Jessica had shown last night and would show again this afternoon. Mel and Katherine sat eating pork sandwiches they had picked up from the food tent. Rachel had gone in search for a list of tack supplies Jessica had given her. The arena was scattered with only the most serious of horse people this Wednesday morning.

"Katherine? It is you! I told Cole it looked like you."
The voice over Mel's shoulder was boisterous.

"Well, hello there." Katherine placed her plate on the empty chair beside her and stood to greet the two men. "What are you two doing here?"

"I'm working. They needed vets and my old boss is on the committee." The taller man jabbed the shorter, husky one beside him. "He's just goofing off here. "Are you showing?"

"Oh, goodness no." Katherine laughed. "I'm here to watch a friend."

The shorter man leaned over and stuck his hand out to Mel. "I'm Edgar."

"Sorry, this is M—el." Katherine stumbled over her name. "Mel. My girlfriend—Mel."

Cole laughed and leaned around Katherine. "I'm guessing your name is Mel?"

Mel shook his hand smiling. "Lucky guess."

Katherine's face had turned red. Cole and Edgar were classmates from college and were now working in two small towns in Indiana. They sat next to Katherine and caught up on other classmates and life, telling Mel stories about Katherine during school. Jessica's name came over the loudspeaker. Katherine hushed both men.

Jessica and Rooster entered from the far end of the arena. The confidence showed in Jessica's straight back and relaxed grip of the reins. Rooster's ears were alert, one forward and one turned back attentive to both rider and task at hand. The class was Ranch Trail, and it was by far Jessica's favorite class out of the five she had signed up for. Mel wiped her sweating palms on her jeans.

"My nerves are shot already." Mel leaned over to Katherine.

"I'm a bit nervous myself. Good thing Jessica keeps calm, or we'd all be a mess."

"She's in her element," Mel said proudly.

287

Ranch Trail was just real life, Jessica said. A series of obstacles dispersed throughout the arena simulating everyday ranch life, Jessica loved it because of its practical aspects. "It's all well and good for a horse to learn to take the right lead and look fancy, but if he throws you every time he encounters something new the horse is no good to anyone."

In this class, judges looked for a horse's responsiveness and willingness to tackle each obstacle and the rider's effectiveness in communicating with their mount. Rooster walked through the first obstacle of branches and logs, as he did almost every day on the farm, without blinking an eye. Jessica was always diligent in making him face new situations when they arose on the farm, and his trust in her was evident on the course.

Each Ranch Trail class was set up differently and competitors were not allowed to practice on the course before competing. A map was provided to show the layout and expectations before the competition began. Jessica had studied it the night before until she had each post memorized.

Between the next two obstacles, Jessica put Rooster into a nice smooth trot. He jogged over the six logs with perfection only clipping the last one with his back hoof. Mel held her breath while they side-passed over the L-shaped logs. Rooster knew to move off the pressure of Jessica's legs in this maneuver, but sometimes at home, his stubbornness overrode his knowledge. Only once did he balk for a second, but Jessica kept him focused and finished without incident.

"Just be finished already," Mel whispered on their way to the final obstacle.

Katherine smiled and patted her knee. "Almost there."

Jessica sat back in the saddle, and Rooster stopped squarely beside the wooden "cowboy." On his arm hung a rope attached to a small sled. Jessica took the rope and secured it. Pausing for a moment, she eyed her path. They would pull the sled around three small trees in pots before returning to the spot and replacing the rope on the cowboy's arm.

Rooster took deliberate and determined steps, Jessica purposefully walking slowly around each tree. To knock a tree over with the sled would cost points, as would swinging out too wide. Precision was key in this final obstacle. What took less than a minute seemed like ten to Mel.

Jessica smiled and waved to the small clapping crowd after replacing the rope on the wooden arm.

"She did it." Mel beamed.

"That was an excellent ride."

Katherine's friends were impressed and asked for business cards. It had been a spectacular ride.

"Sorry I messed that up." Katherine frowned after her friends left.

"What?"

"Introducing you."

"I got upgraded to 'girlfriend.' What's messed up with that?"

"Should I have called you something else?" Katherine asked.

Mel laughed and put her arm around Katherine. "No, I'm very happy with my new title."

"Don't laugh," Katherine tugged on her ear lobe, "but I've been practicing it in my head. I can't believe I messed it up."

Mel couldn't hold in her laughter.

Katherine's voice grew serious. "I thought, what will they think? It was quick, but it was scary. It caught me off guard. It's strange, isn't it? It shouldn't be like that, being scared about something that makes me so happy."

"Have I ever told you that I have an amazing girlfriend?" Mel squeezed her shoulder and kissed her on the forehead.

Jessica's voice burst into their moment. "Did you see that?"

"You definitely kicked ass," Mel responded.

"Congratulations, Jess. It was a spectacular run," Katherine added.

Jessica took the plate out of Mel's lap and started eating the fries.

"Have some fries," Mel said.

Smiling, Jessica kept chewing. "Rooster was spot on. Four or five people have already asked for my information. This is it. I can feel it."

Choosing to compete at the larger shows had been a wise decision on Jessica's part. She'd come in second overall, and her impressive rides had inquiries pouring in. Being sure not to take on too much all at once, she would spread the new clients out into the first of the year, normally a slow time anyway. Spring held the promise of much-needed finances for repairs and a start for Jessica's breeding plans.

Plans with Jason progressed. A lawyer interested in the program had agreed to draw up contracts and guidelines, and Jason had donors willing to fund the pilot program. He was busy now trying to get a board of directors together for oversight. Mel had been working on schedules and courses, books, and learning guides. The idea was self-confidence, practical experience, and basic horse farm knowledge that could help them land jobs and give them a leg up in college. A mixing of both her worlds, the more Mel dove into possibilities, the more excited she became about the potential of this program.

Mel was in the middle of piles of mail, papers, and library books on the kitchen table when Katherine came in the back door.

"You better have that cleared off by Thanksgiving." Katherine leaned over and kissed the top of her head.

Mel showed her a holiday card they'd received from Abigail. With Thanksgiving two weeks away, Mel had been reluctant to make holiday plans, but Jessica had once again surprised Mel by inviting Nathan and Katherine over to celebrate.

Jessica's logic had kicked in. "They're family, aren't they?"

"Well, yeah, but you don't want it to be just us?"

"No offense, but it's more fun when they're here." Jessica had shrugged and walked out the back door.

"How was the call?" Mel asked hesitantly. Although planning to go home for Christmas, Katherine had decided to tell her parents about her relationship with Mel when she called them this afternoon. Waiting only made her feel like she was hiding a part of herself. She had told Mel she would call her afterward, and Mel wasn't sure if her showing up was a good sign or a bad sign.

"It's done." Katherine sat down with a heavy sigh.

Mel closed her computer and stacked the papers to the side. "Want to go for a walk?"

They passed through the side gate at the edge of the house and walked along the tree line following the dirt path the cows had created. It wasn't until they turned the corner by the pine grove that Katherine spoke.

"It wasn't as bad as part of me imagined. I had worst-case scenarios playing in my head."

Mel smiled. "Well, that's something. What happened?"

Katherine stopped and placed her hands on her hips. "It's not like they're religious or even conservative, for Christ's sake."

"What did they say?"

"Mum told me she supports the gays, but she didn't think I could possibly be one. And Da, well, he didn't say much, he never does, but he kept changing the subject."

"Listen, just give them some time. It sounds like it just shocked them is all. They'll come around."

"I told them about you. I told them how happy I was and how life just fit with you, you know?" Katherine started walking again, more like a military march.

Mel jogged to catch up. "And they'll see that for themselves. They will. Remember it took a while for you to come to grips with all this too. Cut them a little slack. It's a lot to take in."

291

"Great, you're already taking their side." Katherine pulled a brown leaf off a low branch.

Mel laughed, reaching for Katherine's arm to turn her around. "I'm not taking their side. I'm reminding you to be patient—we've switched roles. They'll come around."

"I guess you're right. It could have gone worse."

"Just out of curiosity, what was your worst-case scenario?" Mel asked.

"It began with mum fainting on the kitchen floor." Katherine chuckled.

"See? We're off to a really good start then."

On Wednesday before Thanksgiving, Trisha called Mel. "You're going to be sick of me asking you for favors."

"Your first favor has been working her butt off in our barn, so I doubt that." Mel laughed. "She puts the boys to shame."

"I'm awfully glad to hear that. She's loving it, and it's like she's a different person. Rachel's the reason I'm calling."

"What's up?"

"Thanksgiving is at her parents' house this year, and they are refusing to allow her to attend unless she agrees to meet with their pastor. Even James is torn about going, tried to talk sense into them, but he doesn't want to upset his mom, her health failing and all."

"That's horrible. How's Rachel taking it?"

"Honestly, she wasn't too keen on going anyway. I just hate the thought of her sitting here alone."

"Look—she can join us."

Trisha laughed. "You read my mind. Do you want to talk it over with Jessica and call me back?"

"No need." Mel hoped this was true. "Katherine and Nathan are coming over, and we'd be happy to have her join us."

"If you sure it's no trouble—it would sure help us out of a tight spot. To tell you the truth, I'll be glad when this day is over. Families."

"Tell Rachel to be here around noon. I can't promise Jessica won't put us all to work before the day is over, but it's a chance we'll just have to take."

"I'll make a pie and send it over with her." Trisha's voice sounded relieved. "I'm sure glad you came back here, Mel."

"Me too."

"Happy Thanksgiving!" Nathan shouted as he walked through the back door. Finn jumped up and barked. Nathan had a way about him that wound up kids and dogs like an out-of-control toy.

"Hey, Finny ol' boy. How's my boy?"

Finn went wild. Jessica rolled her eyes.

"If he wets on the floor you're cleaning it up." Mel hugged Nathan and took the box of food from his arms.

"It smells delicious in here," Nathan said. "I left Katie in the dust. She drives like our grandmother."

Mel punched him on the arm after setting the box down. Katherine was on call today, so she needed her Jeep just in case. Farm animals did not honor holiday hours. By the time she arrived, Nathan had grabbed a beer from the fridge and stole a deviled egg from the plate by the stove.

"I don't know how you live with him," Jessica chimed in.

"It's not for the faint of heart, I assure you." Katherine shook her head.

Nathan's boisterous laugh almost made them miss the faint knock at the back door.

Mel opened the screen door. "Come on in, Rachel."

With arms full, Rachel turned sideways and squeezed inside. "Aunt Trisha sent some things over."

"Oh, good lord. Looks like she cooked a whole meal." Mel relieved Rachel of the bags.

"Two pies and her special corn pudding. Oh, and a bag of rolls from the store. Thank you for having me over."

"Glad to have you," Jessica answered. "Want to help me set the table?"

"See, I told Trisha she'd put you to work," Mel said.

"You did, did you? Well for that, you can get drinks ready. And Nathan, take that dog outside before he pees on the floor."

Nathan stood at attention and mocked a salute.

Warmed by the voices and laughter that filled the kitchen, Mel couldn't help but compare this holiday to last year. So much had changed. Having a smooth relationship with her sister had been a distant hope, but now to have Katherine, and even Nathan, in her life, was more than she would have allowed herself to bet on. The house felt like home.

Chapter Thirty-Six

Winter's chill came swiftly, and before Mel knew it, she was breaking ice off the troughs again. Nathan and Katherine went to Scotland, but Katherine called every night. The Christmas traditions that began last year, the tree, the decorations, the Christmas movies by the fire, continued and grew. This year, Jessica hung stockings on the stalls in the barn and placed a wreath above the main door. The weekend before Christmas, she held an open house for clients new and old. Jason and Emanuel came out to see the operation firsthand. With any luck, they would begin the pilot program in the spring.

Jessica once again insisted on black-eyed peas for the new year. "They worked their magic last year. We best not tempt fate."

An unexpected fear struck Mel when her phone rang a few minutes after leaving Cincinnati where she had spent the weekend with Katherine at a seminar. She released Katherine's hand and dug her phone out of her pocket. Snow had been falling since just after dawn and was coming down hard now.

"Have you seen Jess?" A worried edge in Jasper's voice made Mel's mouth go dry.

"I'm in Cincinnati. What's wrong?" Mel's voice broke slightly on the last word.

"I don't want to scare you, but something's not right here. I was supposed to meet her to work that new gelding I bought at the sale, but the horses haven't even been fed. Rooster's not in his stall. I tried to call her, but she's not answering."

Don't panic. "Did you check the house? Is her truck there? Maybe she ran out for something."

"I stepped inside the kitchen and called out. The lights are off, but Sam and Finn were in there. Her truck's out by the barn. The trailer's hooked up."

"Can you go upstairs to her room?" Maybe she'd fallen sick in the night. A nasty flu had been going around for weeks. Of course, it would be just like Jessica not to let anyone know, but that didn't explain why Rooster was out. Mel felt Katherine's head swinging back and forth between watching the road and looking at her for answers. "Stay on the phone and go check."

Mel could tell Jasper was jogging to the house, but it still felt too long. She followed him in her mind's eye through the kitchen, the living room, and up the stairs. He knocked on the door and said Jess' name loud a few times before opening it. "Nope. Nothing. The bed's not made."

Her bed was never made so this was no surprise. Sweat appeared on Mel's forehead. *Don't panic. It's probably nothing.*

"Okay, listen. Is anything out of order in the barn?" Mel's mind went to the worst, Tommy, but they hadn't seen him again since he came and tried to smooth things over months ago. He seemed sincerely sorry for all the trouble he'd caused. What if it all had been for show?

Don't go there.

A more reasonable explanation was she'd gone to help a client with a horse or maybe the cows had pushed through the fence. Last month they'd spent an evening helping Mr. Thompson get his cows back in after they'd pushed through a fence onto the wildlife refuge that edged both their farms.

"She'll show up," Mel said this more to herself than to Jasper. "You know how things go."

"Let me look around and call you back. Should I feed?"

"Just give hay." Mel knew how picky Jessica was about graining. At least this way they wouldn't accidentally grain twice, and she would save Jasper an earful of Jessica's rebuke. "She'll be around shortly. Do you mind staying for a bit? We should be home in about an hour."

"Sure thing."

"Thanks, Jasper. Tell Jess to call me when you find her."

Mel reluctantly let him off the phone. She told Katherine the parts of the conversation she hadn't heard, and Katherine agreed she was probably just busy with something that had come up and would be back soon. Mel sent a quick text to Jessica trying not to sound like a frantic, overprotective mother.

Headed home now. Any plans today? Mel's hands shook as she typed.

The minutes crawled by. Mel was grateful for Katherine's attempt at distraction, but it wasn't working. She finally gave in to her fears and called Jessica's cell. It went to voicemail. She had just placed her phone back in her lap when it rang. She answered it without looking to see who the caller was. "Jess?"

"There aren't any tracks," Jasper said.

"What?"

"There aren't any tracks in the snow. I just noticed. It's been snowing here since before breakfast. Maybe a couple of inches already."

Mel's heart pounded.

Jess, where are you? Think, Mel.

"Did you check the other doors? When did you talk to her last?"

"She called me around lunchtime yesterday and asked if I wanted to bring this new gelding over and work

297

with him. But Mel, there aren't any tracks." Jasper's voice sounded young and scared.

"Okay, listen. I'm sure she's fine." Her mind was kicking into action now. "Just in case, can you call Cody or someone and see if they can come over? Look for the cows. If there's a break in the fence, she's probably there. Maybe you two can help her."

Cody had come over at least once a week since starting his job at the factory which he hated.

"I'll get Cody over here."

"Thank you, Jasper. I'll be there as soon as I can get there. She'll turn up."

There should be tracks. Mel called Jessica's phone again. It went to voicemail. She dialed the number again, but no answer.

Mel turned to Katherine. "There aren't any horse tracks leaving the barn."

Katherine reached over and squeezed Mel's hand but kept her eyes on the road. Her voice was steady. "That doesn't mean anything. You said yourself the cows could have gotten out. Maybe it was earlier before the snow started coming down good. She'll be fine. I'll call Nathan. He can go over and help."

Mel had thought of that but had talked herself out of the idea. "Not yet. If it turns out to be nothing, she'll be furious if I had the whole county looking for her. No, the boys will find her. She'll chew me out enough for that."

Katherine laughed. "You're probably right."

The next hour felt like six. In unusual Kentucky fashion, it seemed the salt trucks had rightly anticipated the snow, so the roads were slushy but not dangerous. Mel occupied her mind with preparing a defense when this all turned out to be a huge misunderstanding. It was almost working until Jasper called to say they had found the cows, but no downed fence or Jessica.

"We're almost there. Meet us back at the barn."

"If she's going to throw a fit, I might as well make it worth my time," Mel said with a less than convincing laugh after ending the call. "Is it still okay if I call Nathan to help?"

Nathan said he would meet them there. "I'm a little rusty on my riding skills, though."

"It's okay. We'll pull Agent out of retirement. He'll take it easy with you."

"Try not to worry, Mel. She'll turn up."

Of course, she would. All this worrying was in vain.

"Sorry you asked me to come along now?" Mel asked her.

"Never." Katherine took her hand and kissed it.

The closer they came to the farm, the more Mel wished her phone would ring and it would be Jessica on the other side chewing her out for overreacting.

But the phone stayed silent.

It was noon and about two hours since Jasper's first alarming call. Jessica should have been back by now from wherever she'd taken off to. It was too cold for her to have stayed out this long without an excuse. Mel threw on warmer clothes and dug out the extra coats from the hall closet. The heavy snow was beautiful but would soak them all to the skin in a matter of minutes. She searched the house quickly for anything that Jasper might have missed, desperate to find a note or a sign explaining why she shouldn't panic.

The boys saddle three more horses while Mel made a quick pot of coffee in the office. Katherine and Nathan could pair up with Cody and Jasper since they weren't as familiar with the layout of the farm. She divvied up the fields between them. Nathan and Cody would ride the fields west of the barn and head clockwise, Katherine would go with Jasper to the east. Because it was dense and tricky, Mel would start in Sherwood Forest and work her way east. It was the best place to ride when the snows came. The fields east were more wooded and hilly, plus the largest veins of the creek ran through these fields. The layout of the land with hills and crevices made it impossible to see far, so much of the land would have to be covered.

Mel had her leg in the stirrup ready to swing up when Katherine came up to her.

"It's pointless to say it but try not to worry."

"I keep telling myself that, but you're right, it is useless."

"You be careful." Katherine kissed her on the cheek.

"I will. You too. Tell Jasper to slow down if you need him to."

Katherine nodded and squeezed her hand. "We'll find her."

Under different circumstances, this ride would have been tranquil. The cedar branches hung heavy with snow. Mel weaved in and out looking for any signs, calling Jessica's name every few steps. The silence between her calls filled with the creaking leather of the saddle beneath her. Each fallen tree partially covered with snow made Mel's head jerk and her heart pound. Jessica could be anywhere. Should she call the sheriff for help? *Don't think the worst.* But the worst was all that seemed to flood her mind as she rode.

The call came just after 2 pm. Mel's hands were stiff reaching for her phone.

"We got her, Mel. We got her," Jasper yelled into the phone his breath short and choppy.

"Where?" Mel shouted.

"Just north of the creek fork in Skinny Jim's. Get an ambulance here. She took a spill."

"Stay with her. I'm coming."

Mel wanted to spur Bonnie into a run, but she knew she must first get help on their way. She dialed emergency services and quickly explained what had happened. An EMT unit would be on its way. She called Cody and asked them to return to the barn and guide them to the spot.

Mel refrained from letting Bonnie have her head. It would do no good for another accident to happen. Her mind rushed to bad endings as she rode. After entering the field, she scanned the tree along the creek for signs of the small group. Jasper waved his hat above his head.

In one fell swoop, Mel jumped from her horse and handed the reins to Jasper. He had covered Jessica's torso with his coat. Katherine knelt on the other side her hand resting on Jessica's shoulder. Mel could see one of Jessica's legs was turned out below the knee in an unnatural way. Her face was cold to the touch. Jessica's eyes fluttered and opened when she touched her cold face but closed again.

Jasper knelt on the other side and spoke in a whisper. "I found Rooster. He's at the bottom of the embankment. He's still breathing, but—"

Mel knew. People, snow, trees, memories, time blurred together. She kept her hand on Jessica's forehead saying her name. Jessica didn't open her eyes but moaned and turned her head to the side.

Jasper was on the phone with Cody. Mel heard a voice in the distance telling her the EMTs were on their way. Jessica's eyes fluttered every few minutes giving Mel hope.

Mel didn't know how long she stayed there before hearing other voices. Strong hands had her by the shoulder pulling her up. She stood a few feet away from Jessica's body watching the EMTs work. Katherine's arms held her steady.

One of the men said, "She's stable but she's broken both lower bones in her right leg."

Mel sucked in the cold winter air.

The paramedics eased Jessica onto a flat board and strapped her down. Their vehicle was parked on the flat area a hundred yards away. The hill and snow made it impossible to get closer; they carefully began their descent along the more gradual side of the embankment. Jasper came up the steep edge with a rifle in hand.

He cleared his throat. "Mel, What about Rooster? I can—take care of him—if you need me to."

"Show me." Mel followed Jasper down the slippery incline. Katherine followed close behind.

"I think his front leg's broken." Jasper's voice was low.

Katherine knelt beside him running her hands over parts of his body. She nodded at Jasper confirming his suspicion. Raising his lip, she pressed on the pink, fleshy gum with her thumb.

Rooster's breath was heavy and slow. A red puddle of blood encircling his nose stood out against the white snow.

"He's bleeding internally, Mel."

Mel knelt and rubbed his thick neck. Hot tears ran down her cold cheeks. His eyes opened and closed between ragged breaths, his wet side rose and fell. She leaned over and kissed the warm skin above his eye. "He can't be fixed, can he?"

Katherine shook her head.

Jasper spoke from behind Mel. "You need me to do it?"

Mel sniffed and stood. She reached for the rifle by his side, checking the chamber for a cartridge, and wiped her eyes on her coat sleeve. She raised the rifle butt and tucked it into her shoulder, closed one eye, and lined up the sights.

"I'm sorry, big guy." Mel pulled the trigger.

Hurling the rifle into the open field behind her, the cold stung Mel's wet cheeks. Mel wiped her eyes again on her sleeves making her way back up the embankment.

She was barely aware of herself climbing into the back of the ambulance beside Jessica.

"I'll meet you at the hospital."

Mel nodded at Katherine's words. Her eyes didn't leave Jessica's pale face.

The ambulance began the slow bumpy ride across the field. Jessica opened her eyes for a few seconds, staring into Mel's eyes, before drifting back into a far-off place. Those were the same innocent eyes that had searched her face for answers when their dad had sat them down in the hospital waiting area to tell them their mom had gone to live with the angels. "But are there horses there for her to ride?" Jessica had asked. Her dad had wept and held both girls to his chest. Mel clung to Jessica's hand and wept now.

Chapter Thirty-Seven

It was snowing again. Mel sat in the corner of Jessica's hospital room watching white specks float on wind gusts out the window. She stretched her neck to both sides. Jessica had come back from surgery a little before noon the next morning. The doctor had said her leg needed pins to insure it healed properly, but she was out of danger. Jessica slept now in a restless sleep. A few times Jessica had whimpered causing Mel to rush to the side of the bed, but she did not wake fully. The doctor had told her not to worry; Jessica would sleep for the next several hours. Mel sipped the cold sludge of hospital coffee from earlier in the morning. She had not left the room since Jessica's return.

Katherine had stayed last night, the roughest, but Mel had insisted she go home this morning. She had called several times throughout the day and was on her way with dinner as Mel watched the flakes settle on the cars in the parking lot below.

A nurse came in to check on Jessica. She was older than the others who had been in and out throughout the day and had just come on her shift for the evening. While she replaced the bag of fluid above Jessica's head, Jessica stirred. Mel walked to the edge of the bed. Jessica squinted her eyes. Mel wasn't sure if this was due to the pain or the strange hospital light above her bed.

"Hey there." Mel took her hand.

It took Jessica a few seconds to focus on Mel's face. One side of her lips went up into a small smile that morphed into a grimace as she breathed in deeply.

The nurse leaned over her. "How you doing, honey?"

Jessica looked at the woman and then at Mel with a scowl. Mel nodded to reassure her.

"We're in Lexington at the university hospital, Jess."

"Why?" her voice scratchy.

"You're all right now. I'm here." Mel smiled and patted the back of Jessica's hand.

"The morphine's going to kick in now, hon. You sleep." The nurse smiled at Mel before leaving the room.

Mel breathed easier. Jessica closed her eyes, but Mel didn't let go of her hand. She rested her forehead on the edge of the crinkly mattress.

This is where Katherine found her.

"Mel, it's me." Katherine rubbed her back between her shoulders.

Startled, Mel's head flew up. She rubbed her eyes. "I must have dozed off."

"How's she doing?"

"She woke up for a minute when the nurse came."

Katherine raised the brown bag. "I brought us dinner."

Mel stood and kissed her. "I'm starved. You didn't know what you were getting yourself into, did you?"

"So far, I love what I've gotten into. You'll know if I change my mind." Katherine pulled the chair Mel had been sitting in over to the small side table.

They ate and talked quietly. Jessica was the talk of every farm call Katherine had made today. Small town at its best. Some wild tales were floating around, but most folks voiced concern for their neighbor. Even the other veterinarians sent well wishes and prayers, hearing that Katherine was coming to the hospital after work.

"I heard a lot about your dad today," Katherine said breaking a biscuit in half and holding the other half out to Mel.

305

"How come?" Mel took the other half of the biscuit.

"I guess things like this remind everyone how fragile life is. Almost everyone I spoke to had a story that included your dad helping them out in some way or another when they were down on their luck."

This lightened Mel's heart, and she knew she wanted this same thing to be said of her in this same community. She was finished running. Here she would build her life and it would include plans to help teens like her.

In severe pain, a pain that would continue for some time, Jessica awoke more often, although still groggy, during the night and the next day. She was banged and bruised but had no internal injuries. Because of her concussion and the hours exposed to the cold temperatures, the doctor, an old friend of their father's, had wanted to keep a closer eye on her for a day or so more. The nurses came in and out and made her eat breakfast. Mel resisted the urge to hammer her with questions when she was awake. She did not want to rush the conversation she was dreading.

That afternoon Jessica sat up in bed looking a little more alive.

"Feel like telling me what happened out there?" Mel asked cautiously.

Jessica stared at her broken leg as if trying to see through a thick fog.

"It had just started to snow. I couldn't resist a ride when I woke up." Jessica smiled weakly and sipped water from a straw. "It was a wonderland out there. A couple of does were grazing back in Clancy's field. We were headed back to the barn. The snow was coming down hard and we cut across the hill by the—"

Jessica stopped abruptly, her mind catching up with the events of that day and her eyes widened. "Rooster?"

Mel couldn't stop the tears. She opened her mouth to speak, but her voice betrayed her.

"He's dead." It wasn't a question. Jessica closed her eyes, laying her head back against the stiff, white pillow.

"He was hurt badly."

"I'm such an idiot." Jessica covered her face with her hands.

Mel rubbed her unbroken leg and let her cry.

Jessica lay still. Tears ran down from the corners of her closed eyes into her hair. Mel thought she'd drifted off to sleep.

"I remember."

Mel leaned in to listen.

"We trotted up that embankment. Just before we reached the top Rooster stumbled. Maybe it was a hole, I don't remember. I fell forward but couldn't catch myself. I couldn't stand up. I couldn't get to him. I pulled myself over and could see him, laying back at the bottom, the way we came. My head was spinning, and everything went dark." Jessica stared at the wall in front of her hospital bed. "How did you find me?"

"Jasper and Katherine found you," Mel said. "Part of me kept hoping I was overreacting. I knew you'd throw a fit with all of us out looking for you."

The corner of Jessica's lip turned upward, and she gripped the white blanket across her lap. "That sounds like something I would do."

"His leg was broken, Jess. Katherine said he was bleeding inside. I didn't know what else to do." Mel brushed away tears. "Jasper and Cody buried him out by Squealer this morning."

"Thank you, Mel."

"I hope I did the right thing."

Nathan stopped by after work insisting that Mel go home, get something to eat, and shower. Jessica echoed this urging. Once out of the parking lot, Mel turned the heat on high and drove with her window down. The crisp air kept her from falling asleep.

By the time she showered and returned, laughter floated out into the hall before she reached the door. Nathan and Katherine sat on either side of the bed, and Nathan was in the middle of a tall tale about his wild days in Scotland.

Nathan noticed Mel by the door. "You smell better."

"Thanks," Mel said.

Jessica ate a larger dinner that evening. Her eyes were brighter. She voiced her opinion about every part of her food, and what they could do with it. Mel knew she was on the mend.

Mel walked Katherine to her car.

"You know, she'll go home soon, and then you'll have a hell of a time keeping her contained."

"She's going to be a bear. I'll try to remember how grateful I am she's alive and not do bodily harm to her myself." Mel smiled. "Listen. I don't know what I would have done without you and Nathan. Thanks."

"You're strong. You would have made it through, but I'm glad I was able to be here for you." Katherine brought Mel's hands up to her lips and kissed them before closing the door.

"Call me when you get home?" Mel leaned through the window and kissed Katherine. She stood in the middle of the parking lot without her coat watching Katherine drive away. The coldness seeped into her skin. The trees on the edge of the parking lot glistened like chandeliers. It reminded her of Boston walks along the Charles River and the journey she'd taken that brought her here.

The doctor released Jessica the next morning with instructions to take it easy, stay away from the barn, and come back the next week. Jessica shot Mel a scowl of betrayal when he mentioned the barn. Mel promised him she would do her best, but she knew what kind of struggle she was in for.

On the way home, Jessica complained about how slow Mel drove, and when Mel tried to convince her to use the front door since it had fewer steps, Jessica flat refused.

"I won't use my own front door like a preacher." Jessica hobbled awkwardly on the crutches avoiding the puddles of melted snow. Someone had shoveled the back steps. Jasper and Rachel had been lifesavers this week, feeding, cleaning stalls, and exercising horses.

The kitchen table and fridge were filled with food. A stack of notes and get-well cards sat on the edge of the table. By the look of things, Mrs. Tomlin wasn't the only one who had been busy in the kitchen. Jasper had mentioned folks stopping by to check on Jessica, but he had failed to mention this.

Sam Houston went wild at the sight of Jessica, circling her feet like a puppy.

"You won't have to eat my cooking for a while." Mel opened the fridge to display stacks of casseroles, lasagnas, and desserts.

"Saints be praised." Jessica opened a bag of cookies on the table. "There are some good folks around here."

After getting Jessica settled on the couch, Mel unloaded the Jeep from the hospital. Jessica wouldn't hear of a bed downstairs. She would sleep on the couch until she was comfortable taking the stairs to her bedroom.

While Jess was sleeping, Mel organized the food left by neighbors. She would send some home with Rachel after work and convince Katherine and Nathan to eat here as often as possible over the next few weeks. She knew she would need all the help she could get keeping Jessica contained, and Nathan was gifted in the art of distraction.

The knock on the back door made Mel jump. Uncle Jerry and Aunt Doris stood on the other side of the screen. "Come in." Mel swung the screen door open.

"We heard about Jess." Uncle Jerry took off his cap and walked in behind Aunt Doris.

"She's sleeping now. Her leg's broken, but the doctor said she should make a full recovery. Please, sit down. Sorry about the mess." Mel scooped up the bags of chips off the table and placed them on the counter by the fridge. "Can I get you some coffee or tea?"

"Coffee would be fine, dear." Aunt Doris nodded her head and took a seat. "We put her on the prayer list at church."

"Thank you." Mel poured three cups of coffee and placed the sugar and cream on the table between them.

"I heard about the fall when I got my hair done." Aunt Doris said. There was an unmistakable hint of rebuke in that statement. Being family and finding out about an accident of this caliber in a public setting was treasonous.

"She was lucky, I think," Mel answered.

"Someone said you put the horse down," Uncle Jerry said.

"I hated to do it, but he was in bad shape when we found him." Mel tried to block out the image of Rooster's head in the crosshairs.

"But you did it yourself?"

Mel bristled. "I can do what needs to be done when I have to."

The next thirty minutes held the bizarre façade of a happy family with an undercurrent of unspoken tension. Aunt Doris talked about the mission work of their church helping the "natives of East Africa," and Uncle Jerry pretended to care about how the farm would manage with Jessica recovering. Mel answered questions when asked, without divulging too many details, wondering what kind of time warp she had slipped into.

Before they walked out the door, Uncle Jerry turned to Mel and opened his mouth to speak. Turning his cap in his hand, he cleared his throat before nodding his head in her direction.

Uncle Jerry threw on his hat and walked out the door. Aunt Doris hugged her and told her to let them know if they needed anything. Mel stood stunned. She couldn't wait for

Jessica to wake up so she could tell her of this strange encounter.

Mel had been right about Jessica. She had hobbled out to the barn by the following Sunday and critiqued every movement Mel made. After a few minutes, Mel had had enough.

"Listen, short of tying you down, I can't keep you in the house, but you're going to have to be okay with the way I do things for a while." Mel pointed at Jessica's leg. "You've got to let it heal properly, Jess. I mean it. Don't be stupid about this."

Mel stood her ground bracing for what was coming. Jessica snarled at her before slinging her crutches against the wall and sitting down on a hay bale. Hearing the shakiness in her own voice, Mel was surprised that her little talk had worked. She was right of course, but she hadn't expected Jessica's compliance.

Jasper worked with Mel to continue the training under Jessica's skeptical eye of guidance. Cody rolled around most evenings now that his girlfriend had left him for a new guy that worked at the feed store. Mel had agreed to help with the training only after Jessica had insisted.

"But the boys know what they're doing," Mel argued. "I don't."

"Yeah, they're fine with the basic stuff, but I need your level head." Jessica pointed at her with one of her crutches. "You know why I train the way I do. The boys have seen one too many westerns and rodeos and don't always take the time to listen and work with the horse. I'll guide you through it."

"This does not seem like a good idea." Mel frowned and shook her head.

"Mel, please. I just got this place back up and running. I need you to help me do this."

So, Mel became a trainer with heels dug in. Jessica barked orders all day long from the office chair they had

311

placed by the round pen. She propped her leg on a stump, Mr. Tomlin had cut to height. By the end of the first week, Mel was exhausted, body and soul, and she carried a bruise on her ass in the perfect shape of a hoof. A bitchy mare had kicked her when she'd bent down to pick up the lunge line she'd dropped.

Jessica had doubled over with laughter. "I saw that coming."

"Why didn't you warn me?" Mel rubbed her backside.

"You've got to keep your head in the game."

Over the next few weeks, Mel got the hang of the training process. Although she knew she would never be a natural at it like Jessica, she surprised herself by learning to read the horses' subtle movements in a way she'd never experienced before.

Rachel worked even harder to keep up with the daily barn chores and maintenance. She even proved herself handy with mechanical issues surprising them both by replacing the fuel pump on the old tractor.

"Dad taught me." Rachel wiped the grease off her hand with a towel. "I was the oldest."

"You miss him?" Mel leaned against the tractor tire.

"Yeah. I miss how we used to be," Rachel answered. "He never minded that I wasn't a girly girl. Called me his little Tomboy. Said he was proud of me for knowing how to do things."

"Our dad was the same, teaching us how to back a trailer, change a tire. He made me pass his test before I could go take my driving test."

Rachel smiled. "We used to be close."

"I'm sorry. Don't give up on him, okay?"

"I won't." Rachel picked up the tools beside the tractor tire. "How did your dad take it?"

"I never got a chance to tell him." Mel crossed her arms.

"I'm sorry. Sometimes I wish I'd never told them. Just let them go right on believing I was straight." Rachel didn't look at Mel. "Maybe it would have been better. They would have been happier."

Mel stood and faced her. "I spent many, many nights wondering what would have happened if my uncle hadn't caught me kissing another girl—wishing I could erase that one moment in time. It brought a lot of sadness into my life and made me miss out on a lot of things. But I've had to learn that my happiness—being who I am—is very important to me. We have to decide for ourselves but having to hide who we are—so that others will be happy—is a difficult way to live."

Rachel turned to face Mel. "Thanks, Mel."

Mel patted her shoulder. "Let's get back to it before Jessica gets after us both with those crutches."

Another surgery was needed, but the doctor was still hopeful of a full recovery. Patience had never been Jessica's strong suit and having to slow down for that recovery to take place tested her limits beyond anything Mel had seen. Nathan stopped by often, and Mel was grateful for his easy-going nature. Jessica was notably less grumpy with him around.

Uncle Jerry stopped by two more times, and the awkward family visits continued. Jessica did not appreciate his visits and barely spoke to him while he was there. Both sisters guessed he was trying to ease his guilty conscience, and neither was quick to help him in that arena.

One evening, Uncle Jerry pulled in just as Katherine was pulling down the drive headed to an emergency on the other side of town. She waved out the window to him as their vehicles passed in the driveway.

Uncle Jerry climbed out of his truck and walked over to Mel still standing at the back edge of the house. "How's Jess doing?"

"She's mending."

"Got a sick horse?" Uncle Jerry asked.

"No. Everyone's healthy, as far as I know," Mel said.

"Wasn't that Dr. Neil that just left?"

"Yep." Mel could tell he was fishing for answers. "She was here for dinner."

Uncle Jerry hiked up his pants' leg and propped his foot on the fender of the flatbed trailer. "It's good of her to stop in and see Jess. They're good folks, her and her brother. I heard she has a knack with the horses."

"She does that." Mel stood tall. "And she's my girlfriend."

"Your what?"

"Dr. Neil is my girlfriend."

Uncle Jerry dropped his foot off the fender. "When are you going to drop this act, Mel? It's gone on long enough, and you ain't a kid no more."

"Why are you here, Uncle Jerry?" Mel snapped.

"Why am I here?" He stumbled over some unintelligible words. "Well, because we're family, and I know your daddy'd want me to check up on you."

"I thought you might be changing."

Uncle Jerry puffed his chest out. "I'm not the one who needs to change. I did what was right."

"No. There's nothing right about what you did. And Dad wouldn't have stood for it, and you know it. That's why you didn't tell him. That's why you lied to him about where I was."

"You just don't learn, do you?" He flailed his hand out to the side." Don't you see? You brought this on this house—our family. No good can come of the way you are."

"Uncle Jerry, I didn't ask to be gay. I just am, and I always have been. And there's nothing wrong with me."

"That's just what you want to believe—that's just what they tell you to believe."

"What is wrong with you?" Mel was furious.

"Dammit, Mel. It's the God-honest truth. You can hate me for saying it, but you are going to burn in hell for the way you're living. I'm just glad your daddy's not here to see this." Spit flew from his mouth as he spoke.

314

Mel stood in front of him perplexed. How did someone become this? She took a deep breath. "I'm glad Daddy's not here to see what you've become."

Uncle Jerry's face flashed red. "Don't you dare talk to me that way. Your daddy didn't have the guts to do what was right when it came to you girls."

"Dad was strong enough to care about your daughter when you turned your back on her," Mel spoke through clenched teeth.

"How did you—how dare—" Uncle Jerry's eyes swelled with fury. "I don't have a daughter."

Uncle Jerry stormed to his truck and swung open the door. Gravel and grass spun as he backed up into the yard and took off down the driveway. His exit was similar to his first visit after Mel's return, but Mel was nothing like that girl now.

Chapter Thirty-Eight

The first warm Saturday of April. Katherine arrived before noon followed shortly by Cody and Jasper. Rachel promised to stop by later with a girl she had started seeing from Nicholasville. Jessica still hobbled around on crutches, but after the last surgery, the doctors said her leg was healing well and spoke hopeful of her ability to ride and train again. Her hard cast would come off next week replaced with a soft cast and a stern warning to take it easy. Keeping her out of trouble at the barn, and even off the horses, had become a full-time job for everyone. Mel had warned her frequently and had demanded that everyone take today off. Jessica said several horses needed worked, but Mel flat refused.

"Hobble on out there and ride them yourself if you want." Mel halfway regretting putting such an idea into her head. "We all need this day, Jess. It's been a hard winter."

Nathan manned the grill and was busy telling those around him that he could have ruled the culinary world if he hadn't taken up teaching. Finn lay attentive under the picnic table piled with food.

Jason's car pulled into the drive, and Emanuel jumped out and made a beeline for Mel. Jason pulled a beautifully carved wooden sign out of the trunk as Emanuel drug Mel over by the hand. It was happening. The board had met many times over the last few months and PRISM had been given the greenlight. Katherine had come up with the name. The first two girls were scheduled to arrive at the end of the month. More would come. Mel knew. She had signed up for classes at the University of Kentucky to begin her master's. She wasn't sure how she would fit everything in, but she was sure of her path.

Katherine walked up behind her. "Surprised?"

"Did you know?" Mel reached for her hand.

"We all did, but Jason swore us to secrecy."

The Jacksons arrive bringing desserts and extra chairs. Their oldest son had been accepted into medical school and would move to Chicago in the fall. Alexandria would be on the advising board for PRISM and had been instrumental in helping Mel get into the graduate program she had wanted.

Jessica sat at the picnic table with Sam Houston resting his head on her cast. Mel handed her a plate of food and a beer. She took a sip and laughed. "You know, you might be on to something with this fancy beer."

"I knew I would convert you." Mel sat down beside her. They clinked the narrow tops of the brown bottles together.

After lunch, Jessica stood up at the end of the picnic table and clanged a fork on a beer bottle. "I know I haven't been the easiest person to be around these last few months."

"Hear, hear." Nathan raised his beer.

The small group erupted in laughter.

"All right, I deserve that." Jessica continued. "But I want each of you to know that it's meant a lot to me that you stuck by me. I won't forget it."

Again, Nathan piped up, "We won't let her, will we, Mel?"

"I'm staying out of this one." Mel leaned back against Katherine's chest and raised her hands in surrender.

"I just wanted to say thank y'all for all that you've been doing around here."

The crunch of gravel turned Mel's head. *Abigail.* She had texted last weekend to say she would be in town. Her mother had had a stroke over the holidays and had been moved to a nursing home in Lexington. Mel had called to invite her over to the cookout. A lanky man wearing a cowboy hat got out of the car with her. Jessica and Mel exchanged surprised looks.

After going over to greet them and introduce them to some of the others, Mel saw Jessica leave the edge of the group and hobble toward the barn. She whispered something to Katherine and placed a kiss on the top of her head before following Jessica.

The barn door was cracked open. Mel waited watching Jessica run one hand slowly along the white blaze of Caesar's nose while steadying herself on the crutches with the other hand. She had bought him off a fellow trainer last month.

"Think he'll work for you?" Mel eased inside between the doors.

Jessica smiled and glanced down at her leg. "We'll have to wait and see."

Mel stood squarely beside her. "You'll be riding again in no time."

"We'll have to wait and see on that too, won't we?"

"You will ride again," Mel said determinedly.

"You don't know that." Jessica shifted her weight and steadied herself on her good leg.

"The doctor said your leg is healing fine. It's just going to take time." Mel paused. "And besides, we've got work to do around here, and I won't allow you to sit around here and do nothing."

Jessica laughed. "Won't allow it, huh?"

"That's what I said." Mel gave a firm nod and walked to the side door of the barn. Three mares with the first babies of the season grazed along the fence. The breeding program would grow slowly; like the new buds on the oak tree above them, these foals were just the beginning of things to come.

Mel walked over to Jessica and put her arm around her. "Let's go have another one of those fancy beers you love so much."

The backyard teemed with friends and family. This was a party their mother would have been proud of. The cool spring breeze drifting through the trees made Mel shiver. Closing her eyes, she listened to the conversations and laughter taking place all around her. She was home.

"A happy ending was imperative. I shouldn't have bothered to write it otherwise."
EM Forster

Let's connect:

CaseyMcKenzieBooks@gmail.com

Facebook: Casey McKenzie
Instagram: awriterandadog

Made in the USA
Middletown, DE
11 October 2022